Praise for *The Discovery of Slowness:*

◆ ◆

"Fluid and suspenseful, a thought-provoking reminder of contemporary society's tendency to speed through everyday life."
—*Providence Journal-Bulletin*

"Elegant, Wordsworthian; it has a phenomenological touch."
—*New Republic*

"Amazing . . . an historical painting, a seafarer's novel, a love story, an outcast's story all in one. This variety appears very harmonious, just as it incidentally, almost secretly, reflects on our right to discover the world at our own, personal pace."
—*Frankfurter Allegemeine Zeitung*

"Nadolny brilliantly sets the narrative pace to the rhythms of the frozen landscape, and to the 'slowness which is bred by hunger.'"
—*London Review of Books*

"Reading this book has a unique effect: it changes one's perception of the world, sharpens one's ear for rhythm and tempo, and sensitizes one for each person's unique inner time. At first glance, it is an historical novel; at closer glance it reveals itself as a plea to respect unalterable human rhythms in a time of rampant development." —*Die Weltwoche*

"This is more than an adventure; it's a meditation on time and perception . . . Not to be rushed, or forgotten." —*Herald*

"In this novel about an heroic anti-hero, the concepts of victory and defeat become unsuitable categories: the name of the game is to insist, gently and stubbornly, on one's own themes, the motifs of one's own life . . . A novel both of power and of cunning, sometimes roguish, gaiety." —*Süddeutsche Zeitung*

"Nadolny's vision is conveyed with restraint and charm . . . He has written a Utopia of character." —*N*

T0273699

The Discovery of Slowness

❖❖❖❖❖❖❖❖❖❖❖❖❖❖❖❖❖❖❖❖❖❖❖❖❖❖❖❖

A NOVEL

by Sten Nadolny

❖❖❖❖❖❖❖❖❖❖❖❖❖❖❖❖❖❖❖❖❖❖❖❖❖❖❖❖

Translated by Ralph Freedman

Foreword by Carl Honoré

PAUL DRY BOOKS

Philadelphia 2005

To my Father
Burkhard Nadolny
(1905–1968)

◆◆◆◆◆◆◆◆◆◆◆◆◆◆◆◆◆◆◆◆◆◆◆◆◆◆◆◆◆◆◆◆◆◆◆◆

First Paul Dry Books Edition, 2005
Paul Dry Books, Inc.
Philadelphia, Pennsylvania
www.pauldrybooks.com

1 3 5 7 9 8 6 4 2
Printed in the United States of America

Library of Congress Cataloging-in-Publication Data
Nadolny, Sten.
[Entdeckung der Langsamkeit. English]
The discovery of slowness : a novel / by Sten Nadolny ; translated by Ralph Freedman ;
foreword by Carl Honoré.– 1st Paul Dry Books ed.
p. cm.
ISBN 1-58988-024-2 (alk. paper)
1. Franklin, John, Sir, 1786-1847–Fiction. 2. British–Arctic regions–Fiction.
3. Discoveries in geography–Fiction. 4. Arctic regions–Fiction. 5. Explorers–Fiction.
I. Freedman, Ralph, 1920- II. Honoré, Carl. III. Title.
PT2674.A313E5813 2005
833'.914–dc22
2005003145

ISBN 1-58988-024-2

Contents

◆ ◆

FOREWORD

◆◆◆

by Carl Honoré

The Discovery of Slowness lingers in the mind long after the final page is turned. One scene in particular stands out in my memory.

At the Battle of Trafalgar, a British naval ship engages a French vessel at close quarters. The men clash in a riot of noise, blood, and panic. A French sniper, hidden in the rigging, eventually pins down the British crew. John Franklin, the Arctic explorer and hero of the novel, watches his shipmates being picked off one by one; a friend dies in his arms. By the time Franklin takes up a rifle to engage the enemy sharpshooter, his shipmates are hysterical, screaming at him to hurry up and fire. He does the opposite: he slows down. The battle rages, bullets ricochet off the wall behind him, but Franklin takes his time. He points the rifle at the rigging and calculates the angles, height, and distance. Then he recalculates them. The tension is excruciating:

> "Shoot, will you!" someone shouted behind him. But John Franklin, who had held a rope in the air for hours, also had the time to take aim. He wanted to fire only if he was completely sure he could hit his target. Once more he assembled it all in his mind: the angles, the estimated height, the scruples he had overcome, the better future. Then he fired. He dropped the rifle, grabbed the second one, aimed it, and fired again, then took the third and padded up the stairs.

vii

When the sharpshooter tumbles to the deck, the message is clear: even in war, when everything speeds up to a blur, slowness can prevail. Franklin refuses to rush his shot. He keeps his head while all around are losing theirs—and he triumphs. His slowness is heroic.

These days, the world needs to rediscover the virtue of slowness. Many of us are stuck in fast-forward. Hurrying through life, with every moment a race against the clock, we teeter on the edge of exhaustion. My own book, *In Praise of Slowness*, challenges the diktat that faster is always better, and chronicles the worldwide movement to put on the brakes. In *The Discovery of Slowness*, Nadolny explores similar terrain through the prism of fiction. The novel tells the story of Sir John Franklin, the legendary explorer who was last seen sailing off in search of a Northwest Passage through the Arctic in 1845. The main building blocks of his biography are all here: early childhood, the naval battles as a teenager, the first ill-fated voyage to the Arctic, the controversial stint as governor of Van Diemen's Land, and finally the Arctic expedition that killed him. During his lifetime, Franklin became a celebrity—people called him "the man who ate his boots," in homage to the desperate measures he took to stay alive during his first foray into the frozen North—and continued to exert a grip on the public mind after his disappearance. Between 1847 and 1859, more than thirty expeditions set off to establish exactly what happened to his two ships and his 129 men in the icy wastelands of the Arctic Archipelago. Countless books have been written on the mystery, some with theories so fanciful they would not look out of place in the pages of a supermarket tabloid, alongside reports of Elvis sightings and stories about Roswell. Even today, Franklinphiles scour the Canadian North for bits of bone, clothing, or other evidence that might unlock the mystery of their hero's demise.

Nadolny is a novelist, however, not a history professor or conspiracy theorist. The meaning of the story interests him even more than do the facts. To give the novel a leitmotif, he endows his hero with a defining trait: *Langsamkeit*, which is German for "slowness," or "calmness." The fictional Franklin is immune to hurry. Everything about him—his speech, movements, thought, vision—is slow, placing him at odds with the culture impatiently gathering steam in nineteenth-century Europe. Thus, the novel works on two levels. It is a fluid, page-turning piece of historical fiction, which artfully evokes battles, voyages of discovery, and the mystique of faraway lands. It is also a dramatic enactment of one man's relentless pursuit of his own destiny. Without ever lecturing, the author delivers a modern meditation on the role of slowness in a roadrunner world.

Three years ago, when I interviewed Sten Nadolny, he suggested that the main struggle of life lies in determining how quickly or how slowly to do each thing. At the time, this struck me as a little overblown, but the deeper I dug, the more it rang true. The struggle to find and live by one's own rhythm defines what it is to be human.

To the fictional Franklin, life is a never-ending "battle against unnecessary acceleration." As a boy, the explorer-in-waiting is already out of step with his peers. His slowness is a cross to bear. He cannot catch a ball or run fast or answer questions at the right moment. He falls prey to the playground bullies, and teachers despair of him. As an adult, he waits too long to kiss a woman, and the moment passes. He kills a Danish soldier because he is too slow to stop strangling him. Fellow sailors poke fun at his sluggish reflexes.

Franklin tries to move with the times, to become, or at least appear, faster. He spreads his fingers out on a table and practices stabbing a knife between them. He memorizes a catalogue of stock phrases so that he can answer questions more quickly. But he never gives up on his own inner tempo. Instead, he dreams of the Arctic, where the days never end and the ice moves at a snail's pace, as "a world in which there was no pressure of time," "where nobody would find him too slow."

After nearly dying in battle, Franklin decides to honor his own pace. Looking around him, he sees a world gone mad. London is "in love with speed," a teeming metropolis where "time was a despot whom everyone had to obey." He understands that quickness has its place but insists that slowness has much to offer, too. He abhors the assumption that "someone was 'better' if he could do the same thing faster."

Gradually, his slowness shows itself to be an asset. At sea, his unwavering concentration makes him a fine watchman. Women tell him they prefer a lover with a slow hand. Others come to see his inability, or unwillingness, to rush as a mark of wisdom, care, and thoroughness. A lieutenant admiringly notes that "because Franklin is so slow, he never loses time."

Nadolny weaves the themes of speed and slowness into the fabric of the novel. During the Arctic expeditions, when cold and hunger slow the men to a crawl, the narrative matches that pace. Franklin seems to reminisce in slow motion. When events happen quickly, we see them through his eyes: moments simply fall out of the narrative, too fast to register. Throughout the novel, time is a haunting presence, sometimes a friend, sometimes a foe, always part of the company.

First published in Germany in 1983, *The Discovery of Slowness* instantly struck a chord with a generation of readers who had grown tired of living too fast. Translated into fifteen languages, it has sold more than a million copies. To many, Nadolny's Franklin has become the embodiment of life lived at a more sensible pace, his stubborn slowness a rebuke to the modern cult of speed and busyness. In Europe, churches, pacifists, environmentalists, management gurus, and even campaigners for lower speed limits on the autobahn hailed *The Discovery of Slowness*.

Americans are famous for their dynamism, restlessness, and impatience, which makes "slowness" a tougher sell here. But the world has accelerated so much that even Americans are now warming to the idea of slowing down. As a work of fiction, *The Discovery of Slowness* turns the search for the right speed into a gripping yarn; it is a manifesto that never preaches. In John Franklin, Sten Nadolny gives us a new kind of hero, a man who makes history by discovering the power and wisdom of his own slowness.

[I]

*John Franklin's
Early Years*

[1]

◆◆◆

THE VILLAGE

John Franklin was ten years old, and he was still so slow that he couldn't catch a ball. He held the rope for others. It reached from the lowest branch of the tree to his upraised hand. He held it as firmly as the tree, and he didn't drop his arm until the end of the game. He was suited to be a rope holder as no other child in Spilsby, or even in all Lincolnshire. The clerk looked over from the Town Hall. His glance seemed approving.

Perhaps there was no one in all of England who could stand still for more than an hour and hold a rope. He stood quietly, like a cross on a grave, towering like a statue. "Like a scarecrow," said Tom Barker.

John couldn't follow the game, so he couldn't be an umpire. He could never see exactly when the ball hit the ground. He didn't know if it was really the ball that one of them had caught just then, or if the player it landed next to had just held out his hands. He watched Tom Barker. How did catching work? When Tom no longer had the ball John knew he had missed the decisive moment once again. Catching—no one could do that better than Tom. He saw it all in a single second and moved faultlessly without the slightest pause.

A blip streaked across John's vision. If he looked up to the hotel chimney, it perched in the uppermost window. If he fixed

3

on the window's crossbars, it slithered down to the hotel sign. That's how it jerked farther and farther down as he lowered his glance, but up it went again with a sneer when he looked at the sky.

Tomorrow they'd go to Horncastle for the horse fair. He had already started to look forward to it. He knew that drive. When the coach left the village, the wall of the churchyard flickered past. Then came the cottages of Ing Ming, domain of the poor. Women were standing outside, without hats, wearing only headscarves. The dogs there were scrawny. One couldn't see the scrawniness on people; they had clothes on.

Sherard would stand in the door and wave. After that came the farm with the rose-covered wall and the chained dog that dragged his own doghouse behind him. Then the long hedgerow with its two ends, the gentle and the sharp one. The gentle end was some distance from the road. It would come up for a long time and take a long time to go. The sharp end, close to the roadside, sliced through the picture like the blade of an ax. That's what was so astonishing: close by everything sparkled and danced—fence posts, flowers, twigs. Farther back there were cows, thatched roofs, and wooded hills, whose coming up and dropping behind had a solemn and quieting rhythm. The most distant mountains, like himself, just stood there and gazed.

He looked forward to the horses less than to the people he knew, even to the host of the Red Lion in Baumber. They would usually make a stop there. Father wanted to see the innkeeper at the bar. Then came something yellow in a tall glass. Poison for father's legs. The innkeeper passed it to him with his dreadful glance. The drink was called Luther and Calvin. John was not afraid of sinister faces if only they stayed put and didn't change their features rapidly in some inexplicable way.

Now John heard someone say the word "sleeping," and he recognized Tom Barker before him. Sleeping? His arm hadn't moved; the rope was taut. What was there for Tom to pick at? The game went on. John had understood nothing. Everything was too fast: the game, the others' talk, the goings-on in the

4

street in front of the Town Hall. It was indeed a restless day. Now Lord Willoughby's hunting party whirled past—red coats, nervous horses, brown-speckled dogs with dancing tails—one big yapping. What did the lord get out of so much commotion?

Moreover, there were at least fifteen chickens in this place, and chickens weren't pleasant. They played gross tricks on the eye. They stood about motionlessly, scratched, then pecked, froze again as though they had never pecked, brazenly pretended they had been standing there for minutes without moving. If he looked first at the chicken, then at the church clock, then again at the chicken, he'd see it standing there as rigid as before—like a warning sign. But meanwhile it had pecked and scratched, jerked its head and twisted its neck, its eyes staring in another direction—all of it a cheat. Also: the confusing arrangement of the eyes! What did a chicken see? When it looked at John with one eye, what did the other one make out? With that it began: chickens lacked the panoramic look that holds everything together, and the speedy, appropriate walk. If one got so close as to catch a chicken in a moment of undisguised change, its mask would drop. There'd be fluttering and shrieking. Chickens happened wherever there were houses. It was a nuisance.

A moment ago Sherard had looked at him with a laugh, but only a quick laugh. He had to try hard to become a good catcher. He was from Ing Ming. Five years old, he was the youngest. "I gotta watch like hawk," Sherard used to say—not "like a hawk" but "like hawk," without the "a," and as he said that his eyes would become very serious and still, like a watchful animal's, to show what he meant. Sherard Philip Lound was little, but he was John Franklin's friend.

Now John considered the clock of St. James. Its face was painted on stone, on the side of the thick tower. It had only one hand, and that had to be pushed forward three times a day. John had overheard a remark that had connected him with this stubborn clockwork. He hadn't understood it, but he had felt ever since that the clock had something to do with him.

Inside the church, Peregrin Bertie, the marble knight, had

been standing for many centuries surveying the congregation, his hand on the hilt of his sword. One of his uncles had been a mariner and had discovered the northernmost part of the earth, so far away that the sun did not set and time did not run out.

They wouldn't allow John up on the tower. But surely one could hold on well to the four small points on top and those many teeth while overlooking the land. John knew his way around the churchyard. The first line on all the tombstones read "In memory of." He knew how to read, but he preferred to steep himself in the spirit of single letters. They were the durable part of writing; they would always come back. He loved them. The tombstones set themselves up during the day, this one straight up, that one aslant to catch a bit of sun for their dead. At night they lay flat and, with great patience, collected the dew in the recesses of their inscriptions. Tombstones could also see. They took in motions that were too gradual for human eyes: the dance of clouds when the wind was still, the shadow of the tower swinging from west to east, heads of flowers turning toward the sun, even the grass growing. The church, in fact, was John Franklin's place. Only there wasn't much to do there besides praying and singing, and especially the singing wasn't for him.

John's arm kept holding the rope. Behind the hotel, a herd of cattle were grazing, covering the length of an ox in the course of a quarter of an hour. That little white thing was the goat; it always grazed along with them, for they say it prevents disquiet and fearfulness in the herd. A seagull swept in from the east and put down on one of the red clay pipes on the hotel chimney. Something was moving on the other side, in front of the pub the White Stag. John turned his head. His aunt Ann Chapell was walking there, accompanied by Matthew the sailor, who held her hand. They'll probably get married soon. He wore a cockade on his hat, like all naval officers on shore. The two nodded in his direction, said something to each other, and stood still. To avoid staring at them, John studied the white stag lying on top of the protruding bay window, the gold crown around its neck.

How did they get it over the antlers? Surely, that again was a question nobody would want to answer. To the left of the stag one could read "Dinners and Teas," and to the right, "Ales, Wines, Spirits." Could it be that Ann and Matthew were talking about him, John Franklin? In any case, their faces seemed worried. On the outside, he still looked all right, didn't he? Perhaps they were saying, "He takes after his mother." Hannah Franklin was the slowest mother far and wide.

He turned to look again at the seagull. Beyond the marshland lay the sandy beach and the sea. His brothers had already seen it. The bay was called The Wash. In the middle of it King John had lost his crown jewels. Possibly one would become king if one found them again. He could hold his breath for a long time when diving. If one owned a lot of things, other people were at once respectful and patient.

Tommy, the orphan boy in the children's book, had simply run away. After the shipwreck he had met up with Hottentots and had stayed alive only because he had a watch on him that ticked. The blacks thought it was a magic animal. He had tamed a lion who went hunting for him, had discovered gold, and had snatched a ship to England. He was rich when he got home, and he helped his sister Goody with her trousseau, for she was getting married just then.

As a rich man, John would study the faces of houses for days and gaze into the river. Evenings he would lie in front of the fireplace from the first blaze to the final crackle, and everyone would find that this was as it should be. John Franklin, King of Spilsby. The cows were grazing, the goat helped to avert misfortune, birds were setting down, tombstones were sucking themselves full of sunlight. Clouds were dancing, peace everywhere. Chickens were prohibited.

"Sleeping Jesus!" John heard someone say. Tom Barker stood in front of him, measuring him through half-closed eyes and showing his teeth. "Leave him alone!" little Sherard shouted at fast-moving Tom. "You know you can't make him mad." But that was just what Tom wanted to find out. John held the rope as taut as he had before and looked helplessly at Tom,

7

who rattled off several sentences so fast that John couldn't understand a word. "Don't understand," said John. Tom pointed at John's ear, and since he was already so close he grabbed it and pulled the lobe. "What d'you want?" asked John. Again many words. Then Tom was gone. John tried to turn around, though somebody held him. "Let go of the rope!" shouted Sherard. "Is he daft!" cried the others. Now the heavy ball hit the hollow in the back of John's knees. He keeled over like a ladder that had been put up too straight, first slowly, then with a bang. Pain spread from hip and elbow. Tom stood there again, smiling indulgently. Without taking his eyes off John, he said something to the others under his breath—again there was the word "sleeping." John got back on his feet, the rope still in his upraised hand. He would change nothing in that. If perhaps by a miracle things went back to where they'd been, what if he had allowed the rope to slip? The children giggled and laughed; they sounded like barnyard fowl. "Give it to him, then he'll wake up." "He won't do nothin'. He just stares." And somewhere, in the midst of it, there was always Tom Barker, watching from beneath lowered eyelids. John had to open his eyes wide to catch everything, for the other boy constantly changed his position. Comfortable this was not, but it would have been cowardly to turn tail. Also, he couldn't run at all, and besides, he didn't have any fear. But he couldn't hit Tom. So there was nothing left but to traipse after him. A girl shouted: "When will he let go of the rope?" Sherard tried to hold on to Tom, but he was too little and too weak. While John thought he was still taking this in, somebody pulled his hair from behind. How did Tom get there? Again, a piece of time had dropped out. He turned, stumbled, and all at once both of them were lying on the ground. Tom's leg was entangled in the rope, which John held tight again. Tom turned and pushed his fist into John's mouth, got free again, and ducked away. John felt a loose tooth in his upper jaw. That wasn't peace. He padded after him like a remote-controlled puppet. He flailed his arms about ineffectually as if he didn't want to hit the enemy, just wipe him away. At one point, Tom actually held out his face to him mockingly, but

8

John's hand stopped dead in midair as though paralyzed, the slap petrified like a monument. "He's bleeding!" "Aw, go on home, John!" The children began to be embarrassed. Sherard, too, mixed in again: "You see, he can't defend himself right!" John kept on going after Tom, fumbling for him, but without conviction. Perhaps they weren't all against him even though they laughed and watched, curious how it would go on. Still, for one single moment John couldn't see why people's faces looked the way they did: teeth bared menacingly, oddly widened nostrils, eyelids clapping open and shut, and each trying to drown out the other. "John's like a clamp!" one of them shouted, perhaps Sherard. "If he grabs a person, he holds him tight!" But no carpenter's clamp can catch anyone who makes himself thin. It became boring.

Tom simply went away, dignified and not too fast, followed by John as far as the rope would reach. Then the others left. Sherard still told him consolingly, "Tom got scared."

His nose was encrusted with blood and it hurt. He held the tooth between thumb and index finger while his tongue still vainly groped for it in the gap inside his mouth. His smock was covered with blood. "Good day, Mr. Walker!" Old Walker had long since passed by when John brought that out.

Now he saw again an interesting blip in his eye. Whenever he wanted to look at it, the blip floated away. But when he glanced elsewhere, it followed him. Moving back and forth like this must be how the eye behaved normally. It leaped from point to point, but by what rules? John shut his right eye and put his finger on the lid and with his left eye explored the High Street of Spilsby. As his eye went roaming, always picking up something new, it landed at last on the father in the window. Who said, "There he comes, the blockhead!" Perhaps he was right: John's shirt was torn, his knee was skinned, his smock bloodied, and there he stood facing the Market Cross, staring and touching his eye. That was bound to offend Father: "To do that to your mother!" John heard, and already the thrashing had begun. "Hurts," John confirmed, for the father had to know whether his efforts were successful. The father thought his

9

youngest had to be properly thrashed so he'd wake up. People who can't fight, yet expect to be fed, will become a burden for the community. One could see that in Sherard's parents, and they weren't even slow. Perhaps he could get work spinning, perhaps field work with a bent back. Father was surely right.

In bed, John sorted out the pains of the day. He loved quietude, but one should also be able to do the hurried things. If he couldn't keep up, everything would go against him. So he had to catch up. John sat up in bed, hands on his knees, letting his tongue examine the wound left by his lost tooth, in order to think better. So he had to study being quick the way other people studied the Bible or deer tracks. Someday he'd be quicker than all of those who were now stronger. I'd really like to be able to race, he thought, to be like the sun, which only seems to wander slowly across the sky, yet whose rays are as quick as the blink of an eye. Early in the morning they reach in one instant the most distant mountains. "Quick as the sun," he said aloud and permitted himself to drop back onto the pillows.

In his dream he saw Peregrin Bertie, that marble Lord of Willoughby. He held Tom Barker tight in his grip, so that he would have to listen to John. Tom didn't get free. His quickness was only enough for a few tiny movements. John watched him for a while and thought again and again what he might say to him.

[2]

◆◆

THE TEN-YEAR-OLD AND
THE SHORE

What was the trouble? Perhaps it was a kind of cold. Humans and animals became stiff when they froze. Or was it like the people from Ing Ming who were hungry? His movements dragged, so some special food was lacking. He had to find it and eat it. John sat up high in the tree beside the Partney Road when he thought this. The sun was shining on Spilsby's chimney pipes, and the clock of St. James, which had just been reset, showed four hours past noon. Large animals, John thought, move more slowly than mice and wasps. Perhaps he was secretly a giant. But it seemed he was as small as the others and he'd do well to move cautiously to keep from squashing anyone to death.

He climbed down and then up again. It was really too slow: his hand reached for the branch and found that it held. He should have had his eye on the next branch long ago. But what did the eye do? It remained fixed on the hand. So it was all a matter of looking. He knew the tree pretty well, but that didn't make it any faster. His eyes refused to be rushed.

Again he sat in the fork of the tree. A quarter past four. He still had time. No one was looking for him—at most Sherard, and he wouldn't find him. The carriage that morning! With rigid stares his brothers and sisters had watched him climb aboard, for they were impatient and didn't enjoy being his brothers and sisters. John knew he looked odd when he did anything in a hurry. Those wide-open eyes, to begin with! For him, the door handle could suddenly turn into a wheel spoke or a horse's tail. Tongue in the corner of his mouth, tense forehead, panting—"He's spelling again," said the others. That's what they called the way he moved. Father himself had thought up that expression.

He made out things too slowly. Blind, it might work better. He had an idea. He climbed down again, lay on his back, and learned the entire tree by heart from below—every branch, every handhold. Then he tied a stocking around his eyes, groped for the lowest branch, and moved his body from memory while counting out loud. The method was good but a little dangerous. He didn't yet know the tree precisely; mistakes happened. He was determined to become fast, so fast that his mouth wouldn't be able to keep up with the counting.

Five hours past noon. He sat, panting and sweating, in the fork of the tree and pushed the stocking up on his forehead. No time to lose; just catch a little breath. Soon he would be the fastest man in the world, but he'd make believe slyly that nothing had changed. For the sake of appearance, he'd still seem sluggish about his hearing; his speech would drag; he'd walk as though he were spelling and lag behind everywhere pitifully. But then there would be a public performance: "No one is faster than John Franklin!" At the horse fair at Horncastle he'd have them put up a tent. They'd all come to have a good laugh at him, the Barkers from Spilsby, the Tennysons from Market Rasen, the sour-faced pharmacist Flinders from Donington, the Cracrofts—in short, all of them from this morning. He'd show first that he could follow the fastest talker, even with completely unfamiliar phrases, and then he'd answer so fast that nobody would be able to understand a word. He'd juggle playing cards and balls until everyone's head swam. Once more John memorized the branches and climbed down. He missed the last foothold and tumbled. He lifted the blindfold: always the right knee.

At noon Father had talked about a dictator in France who had been toppled and lost his head. When Father had drunk a lot of Luther and Calvin, John understood well what he was saying. His walk, too, became different, as if he feared that suddenly the earth might give way or the weather might turn around. What a dictator was, John still had to find out. Once he understood a word, he also wanted to know what it meant. Luther and Calvin—that was beer and gin.

He got up. Now he wanted to practice playing ball. During the next hour he wanted to throw the ball against a wall and catch it again. But an hour later he hadn't caught the ball a single time and instead had drawn a thrashing and made entirely new resolutions. He cowered on the doorstep of the Franklin house and thought it all over strenuously.

He had almost succeeded in catching the ball, for he had invented a helpful device: the fixed look. He didn't, as might be expected, follow the ball with his eyes as it rose and swooped down, but rather kept his eyes on a fixed point on the wall. He knew: he couldn't catch the ball if he followed it but only if he lay in wait for it. A few times the ball would have almost fallen into the trap, but then one mishap followed another. First he heard the words "gap tooth"—that's how he was called since yesterday. Tom and the others were there and just wanted to look on a bit. Then came the smiling game. If one smiled at John, he had to smile back. He couldn't suppress it. Even if meanwhile someone pulled his hair or kicked his shins, he couldn't get rid of the smile fast enough. That's what Tom had fun with, and there was nothing Sherard could do to change it. Then they stole the ball.

Inside the covered passage next to the Franklin house all noise was forbidden. The shouting brought Mother Hannah to the scene, for she was worried about Father's mood. John's enemies noted that she walked and talked just like John. She too couldn't get angry and so let her opponents become insolent. Mother demanded the ball back and they threw it to her but so violently that she couldn't catch it. The boys had grown big; they didn't obey a grown-up when she was slow. Now came

Father Franklin. Whom did he scold? Mother. Whom did he thrash? John. He told an astonished Sherard never to let himself be seen there again. That's how it went.

The fixed look was well suited for reflection. At first John saw only the Market Cross. Then more was added around the center: steps, houses, carriages; he surveyed them all without letting his eye leap or race. At the same time, a vast vision about all misfortune formed inside his head, composing itself like a painting, with steps and houses and the horizon forming the background.

In this place they knew him and were aware of how hard he had to strain. He would rather be among strangers who might possibly be more like himself. There had to be such people—perhaps far, far away. And there he might be able to learn more easily how to be fast. Besides, he very much wanted to see the ocean. Here nothing would become of him. John was determined: still that night! Mother couldn't protect him, nor could he protect her, and he just brought her grief. "Nothing about me is simple," John whispered. "I'll change and then everything will be different." He had to get away, to go east, to the shore where the wind came from. He already began to look forward to it.

Someday he'd come back like Tommy in the book, quick and lissome and clothed in rich garments. He'd enter the church and shout loudly "Stop!" in the middle of the service. All those who had hurt him or his mother would leave the village on their own, and Father would crash down and lose his head.

Toward morning, he sneaked out of the house. He didn't walk through the square past the Market Cross but cut between the stables, heading directly into the fields. They would search for him, so he had to remember to cover his tracks. He passed Ing Ming. He didn't want to wake up Sherard, for he was poor and would want to come along, yet he was too little to be taken on a ship. John reached the stables of Hundleby. It was still damp and cool, and the light was dim. He was eager to know about the strange world beyond, and his plans were well thought out.

In a narrow drainage ditch he waded as far as the stream

Lymn. They'd think he had gone in the direction of Horncastle and not of the sea. He then wandered northward in a wide arc around Spilsby. When the sun came up he groped through a ford across the River Steeping, shoes in hand. Now he was already far east of the village. Possibly he might still meet the shepherd in the hill country, but the man slept into the late morning, true to his view that dawn belonged to the beasts of the forest. The shepherd had time and he thought a great deal, mostly with clenched fists. John liked him, but today it would be better not to run into him. Perhaps he'd mix in. A grown-up would always have different views about running away than a child, even if he was only a shepherd, a slugabed, and a rebel.

Laboriously, John trudged through woods and fields, avoiding every road, crawling through fences and hedgerows. When he had wandered in the dark woods and had gotten out of the forest through the shrubbery, the sun seized him, first with its light, then with its warmth, ever more strongly. Thorns scratched his legs. He was happy as never before because he was now all on his own. Far away, gunshots from a hunting party resounded among the tree trunks. He swung in an arc through the meadowland, for he didn't want to become their target.

John was in search of a place where nobody would find him too slow. Such a place could still be far away, however.

He owned one single shilling, a present from Matthew the sailor. In case of need, he could get a roast with salad for it. For a shilling one could also ride the post for a few miles, if one sat outside on the roof. But up there he wouldn't be able to hold on too well or duck his head in time when they got to low archways. In any case, best of all was the sea and a ship.

Perhaps he could be used as a helmsman, but then the others would have to have confidence in him. A few months ago they had gotten lost on a ramble through the woods. Only he, John, had observed the gradual changes, the position of the sun, the rising of the ground—he knew how to get back. He scratched a drawing on the forest ground, but they didn't even want to look at it. They made hasty decisions that they overturned just as quickly. John couldn't get back on his own, for they wouldn't have let him go. Worried, he slunk behind the little kings of the schoolyard, who owed their standing to their speediness and now didn't know how to go on. If it hadn't been for the Scotsman driving his cattle, they would have had to spend the night outdoors.

Now the sun was at its height. In the distance, a flock of sheep dotted the north side of a hill. The ditches became more and more frequent, the forests thinner. He looked far out into the flatland and discerned windmills, tree-lined avenues, and manor houses. The wind freshened, the swarms of seagulls became larger. With slow deliberation, he vaulted fence after fence. Cows came up to look him over, nodding and swaying.

He lay down behind a hedgerow. Under his closed lids the sun filled his eyes with a red fire. Sherard, he thought, will feel cheated. He opened his eyes to keep from becoming sad.

If he could just stay there and gaze upon the land like a stone, whole centuries long, while grassy plains became forests and swamps turned into villages or tilled land. Nobody would ask him a question. He'd be recognized as human only when he stirred.

Here behind the hedgerow nothing could be heard of the earth's population except the sound of chickens and dogs in the distance, and now and then a gunshot. Perhaps he'd meet a robber in the forest. Then his shilling would be gone.

John got up and walked through the marshy meadows. The sun was already dropping toward the horizon, far behind him above Spilsby. His feet hurt; his tongue was sticky. He circled around a village. The ditches to be waded across or jumped over became ever wider, and John was a poor jumper. At the same time, there were no more hedges. He followed a road, although it led toward a village whose church looked just like St. James. The picture of his parents' home, and of supper, was easily shoved aside. Despite his hunger, he thought with amusement that they'd now sit and wait, they who couldn't wait, collecting remarks for his ears that they now couldn't get rid of.

The village was called Ingoldmells. The sun had set. A girl

16

with a bundle on her head disappeared into a house without noticing him. Then, beyond the village, John saw what he had been looking for.

A leaden-gray, immensely extended plain was lying there, dirty and foggy, like rolled-out bread dough, a bit menacing, the way a faraway star would look when seen up close. John breathed deeply. His feet fell into a stumbling trot, and he ran toward that rolled-out thing as fast as he could. Now he had found the place that was all his own. The sea was his friend. He sensed that, even if at the moment it didn't look so pretty.

It grew dark. John searched for the water. He found only mud and sand and thin rivulets; he had to wait. Stretched out behind a boat shed, he stared at the blackish horizon until he fell asleep. During the night he woke up, wrapped in fog, chilled and hungry. Now the sea had come; he heard it. He walked toward it and, bending over, dipped his face into it a few fingers from the line where the land merged with the sea. But where that line was could not be precisely made out. Sometimes he'd be sitting in the sea, sometimes on land. That was food for thought. Where did that much sand come from? Where did the sea disappear to at low tide? He was happy and his teeth were chattering. Then he went back to the shed and tried to sleep.

In the morning he padded along the shore and watched the spray of the surf. How could he get on a ship? Among the black, smelly, moldy nets, a fisherman was hammering away on the bottom of his upturned boat. John needed to think carefully how to ask his question and to try it out a little first, so the fisherman wouldn't lose patience at once. Far in the distance he saw a ship. The sails were shimmering in the morning sun with many varied reflections. The hull had already dropped below the surface of the sea. The man saw John's glance, half closed his eyes, and examined the ship's sails. "That's a frigate, a man-of-war." A somewhat surprising sentence! Then he went on hammering. John looked at him and asked his question. "Please, how can I get on a ship?"

"In Hull," spoke the fisherman and pointed north with his hammer, "or in Skegness in the south, but only with a lot of luck." With one quick glance he looked John over from top to bottom and, as the gesture of the hammer suspended in midair made clear, with some interest as well. No further words escaped his mouth.

The wind tugged and shoved. John trudged southward. He'd be lucky for sure, so it had to be Skegness! He hardly ever took his eyes off the waves eating incessantly into the land. Now and then he rested on one of the wooden pilings set up at regular intervals to hamper the sea's work on the sand. He looked on as new channels, pools, and holes constantly opened up, soon to be transformed back again into smooth, shining surfaces. Triumphantly the gulls screeched: "Right on!" or "Go to it!" Best thing not to beg at all! Right off on a ship; there'd be food there. Once they had taken him, he'd travel three times around the world before they could send him back home again. The houses of Skegness were already shimmering behind the sand dunes. He was weak but confident. He sat down, and for a while he stared at the fine-ribbed sand and his ears took in the bells of the town.

The hostess at the inn in Skegness saw the way John Franklin moved, looked him in the eye, and said, "He can't move another inch, that one. He's half starved." John found himself seated at a table with a rough cloth and a plate with a slab on it that looked like thick-sliced bread but was made up of small pieces of meat. He was allowed to keep his shilling in his pocket. It tasted cool, sour, and salty and was for the gullet what the bells were for the ears and fine-ribbed sand for the eyes. He ate with deep pleasure, smiling through his meal, unbothered by the greedy flies. The future, too, now appeared rich and beckoning; he could view it all in a single glance, like a meal arranged on a plate. Already he was off to faraway continents. He would explore and learn speed. He had found a woman who had given him food. So a good ship couldn't be far away.

"What's this called?" he asked, pointing his fork at the plate. "That's a jellied dish," said the hostess. "Head cheese, made of pig's head. It'll give you strength."

Now he had his strength, but no ship was to be found. No

further luck in Skegness. Head cheese, yes; frigate, no. But that couldn't deter him. Not far off should be Gibraltar Point, and many ships passed there on the way to The Wash. He'd look around there. Perhaps he could build a raft and get himself out to the shipping lane; they'd see him then and have to take him along. He wandered out of the village and turned south: Gibraltar Point.

After half an hour of walking in the glistening sand, he turned to look back. The town had already become blurred again in the haze. But just in front of it a point moved, clearly recognizable. Someone was coming very fast. John watched this motion with concern. The point became more and more oblong; it hopped up and down. That was no person on foot. Hurriedly, John stumbled to hide behind the wood pilings of one of the breakwaters, crawled flat on his stomach up to the water line, and tried to burrow in the sand. Lying on his back, he scratched the ground with his heels and elbows, hoping that the sea, with a few long, licking waves, would let him sink into the sand with only his nose showing. Now he heard barking dogs coming nearer. He held his breath and stared fixedly at the sky, woodenly, as though he himself were the breakwater. When the hunting dogs yelped in his ear, he gave up. They had him. Now he saw the horses, too.

Thomas had ridden in from River Steeping; Father had come from Skegness with the dogs. Thomas pulled his arm; John didn't know why. Then Father took over. The thrashing came at once, right here under the afternoon sun.

Thirty-six hours after starting out on his escape, John was on his way home, sitting in front of his father on that ever-swaying, jolting horse, and through swollen eyes he gazed at those distant mountains riding back with him to Spilsby as if taunting him, while hedgerows, brooks, and fences that had cost him hours flickered past, never to be seen again.

Now he had no self-confidence left. He no longer wanted to wait till he was grown up! Shut in with bread and water so he'd learn something, he didn't want to learn another thing. Motionless, he constantly stared at the same spot, unseeing. He breathed as if the air were loam. His eyelids closed only once every hour; whatever went on, he let it pass over him. Now he no longer wanted to be quick. On the contrary, he wanted to slow down until he died. Surely it wasn't easy to die of sorrow without any other help, but he'd do it. Outside the passage of time, he would force himself to be late and soon drag himself along until they'd think him dead. The others' day would last only an hour for him, and their hour would be minutes. The sun raced across the sky, splashed into the South Sea, zoomed over China, and rolled over all of Asia like a bowling ball. People in the villages twittered and wriggled for half an hour; that was their day. Then they fell silent and dropped with fatigue, and the moon rowed hastily across the firmament because the sun was already panting up on the other side. He would become slower and slower. The alternations of day and night would finally become just a flickering, and at last, since, after all, they thought him dead, his funeral! John sucked in the air and held his breath.

His illness grew more serious, with violent stomach cramps. His body cast out whatever was inside it. His mind became cloudy. The clock of St. James—he saw it through the window—no longer told John anything. How could he still be identified with a clock? At half past ten it was still ten o'clock. Every evening was again like the evening before. If he died now, everything would be as it had been before his birth. He would have never been.

He was feverish like an oven! They laid mustard plaster on him, poured tea made of mullein and linseed into him. In between he gulped down barley water. The doctor ordered the other children to stay away. They were told to eat currants and bilberries; that was supposed to prevent infections. Every four hours a spoon passed across John's lips with a powder made of Columba root, cascara rind, and dried rhubarb.

Illness wasn't a bad way to regain one's perspective. Visitors came to his bedside: Father, Grandfather, then Aunt Eliza, finally Matthew the sailor. Mother was around all the time, silent and awkward, but never helpless and always peaceful, as though she knew for sure that now everything would be all right after all. They felt superior to her, but they needed her just the same. Father won but always in vain. He constantly assumed a lofty position, especially in his talk, even when he wanted to say something kind: "It won't be long and you'll be at school in Louth. There you'll learn declensions; they'll knock those into your head, and a lot more besides." Protected by his illness, John could study them all with detachment. Grandfather was hard of hearing. He looked at anyone who lisped or mumbled as a provocateur. And anyone who dared to understand what a mumbler was saying was a traitor. "That's how he gets into the habit!" During this lecture, John was allowed to see his pocket watch. On the richly decorated face, the watch bore a Bible quotation starting with "Blessed are they . . ." It was in a crabbed script. Meanwhile, Grandfather told him that when he was a boy he had run away from home to the seashore. He, too, had been caught. The report ended as abruptly as it had begun. Grandfather touched John's forehead and left.

Aunt Eliza described her journey from Theddlethorpe-All-Saints, where she lived, to Spilsby, a trip on which she had seen nothing. Still, her speech droned on like an unraveling kite string. Listening to Aunt Eliza, one could learn that when people talk too fast the content becomes as superfluous as the speed. John closed his eyes. When his aunt finally noticed this she left, exaggeratedly quiet and a little hurt. Matthew came on another day. He spoke sensibly, with pauses. In no way, he maintained, does everything have to go very fast at sea. He only said: "One has to be able to climb ropes on a ship and learn many things by heart." Matthew had especially strong lower teeth; he looked like a well-meaning bulldog. His eyes were sharp and sure. There was no doubt where he was looking and what caught his attention. Matthew wanted to hear a lot of what John had to say and waited patiently until his answers were ready to come out. John, too, had many questions. Evening came.

Knowing about the sea was called navigation. John repeated that word several times after Matthew. It meant stars, instruments, and careful thought. That pleased him. He said: "I'd like to learn how to set sails."

Before Matthew left, he bent over John more closely. "I'm shipping out to Terra Australis now. I'll be gone two years. After that I'll get my own ship." "Terra Australis, Terra Australis," recited John.

"Don't run away again! You can become a sailor. But you're a bit too caught up in thought, so you must become an officer or your life will be hell. Try to make it through school until I come back. I'll still send you some books about navigation. And I'll take you on as a midshipman on my ship."

"Please, say it again," begged John. When he had understood it all exactly he wanted to get better again at once.

"He's much better," the doctor announced proudly. "Against cascara rind no bad blood can win out."

[3]

◆◆

DR. ORME

Buttons done all wrong: start again from the front! Neckerchief tied neatly, breeches closed right? Before breakfast, the outer person was checked by the assistant master. Flunked: no breakfast. For every wrongly done button: a slap on the nose. Hair not combed right: knuckle on the head. The waistcoat collar drawn over the jacket, stockings pulled tight. Innumerable dangers lurked already at the beginning of the day. Shoes with buckles, cuffs, coattails, and the hat, that trap!

Getting dressed was surely good exercise for later. School had its disadvantages, but John was firmly convinced that one could learn something useful for life anyplace in the world, hence also at school. But even if this weren't so, escape was out of the question. One had to wait, if not out of desire then at least from prudence.

No news from Matthew. But why should there be? Two years, he had said, and those weren't over by a long shot.

Learning in class. The room was dark, windows high up; autumnal storms outside. Dr. Orme sat behind his desk as if in an altar niche, with an hourglass in front of him. The grains of sand had to get through the narrow passage to accumulate in the same pile below that they had formed above. The resulting loss of time was called Latin lesson. It was getting chilly, and the fire-place was near the teacher.

The older boys were called moderators. They sat high up against the wall and surveyed all the others. Assistant Master Stopford sat near the door and took down pupils' names.

John was staring closely at the curved lines in Hopkinson's ear when just at that moment a question was directed at him. Still, he got the drift. Careful now! If he answered hastily he'd stutter and choke; that would bother his listeners. On the other hand, Dr. Orme had already made clear during the first week once and for all: "When somebody says something that's correct, he doesn't have to look good." He could live with that.

Reciting, conjugating, declining, using the proper case. When he got that done he had time for Hopkinson's ear curves, or for the wall beyond the window with its wet bricks and its vines tossed by the wind.

Studying during times off in the evenings. Archery allowed in the courtyard. Dice and cards forbidden. Chess permitted; back-gammon prohibited. When he got permission, John went out to his climbing tree; when he didn't, he spent his time reading or practicing. Sometimes he tried to learn speed by using his knife: one hand spread out on the table, with the other he stabbed the triangles between his fingers with his blade. The knife had been swiped from the kitchen. The table suffered noticeably. And now and then he hit one of his fingers. Well, it was only his left hand.

He also wrote letters to Mother and to Matthew. Nobody liked to watch him when he wrote, and he loved writing, especially in fine script. Dipping his goose quill into the ink, wiping it off, then drawing his letters, folding the sheet to seal it—nobody could bear to watch all that.

Turning into somebody else at school, that was hard. Here it was just as it had been in Spilsby: they knew his weakness; nobody believed in his exercises. They were all convinced that he would always stay the same.

* * *

24

Learning how to get along with the other pupils. Aboard ship he'd be involved with many people, and if too many of them didn't like him it could be troublesome.

The other boys were done quickly with everything, and they noticed at once when one of them lagged behind. Names were said only once. If he asked, they spelled them. He could manage following fast spelling even less well than speaking slowly. Bear the others' impatience. Charles Tennyson, Robert Cracroft, Atkinson, and Hopkinson—they all whetted their beaks on John whenever possible. It seemed to him as though they always looked at him through only one eye and with the other communicated among themselves. If he said something they tilted their heads, and that meant, "You're boring, finish up fast." The most difficult was Tom Barker, now as before. If John gave him what he asked for, he acted as though he had asked him for something entirely different. If he spoke to him, he was interrupted at once; if he looked at him, he found a mere grimace. In the dormitory, John and Tom had to bunk next to each other because they were both from Spilsby. They shared a chest between their beds. Each of them knew what the other owned. Perhaps this was good preparation for sea voyages; space was tight there, too, and some people couldn't stand each other.

Nothing could make John miserable; his hope was the size of a giant. Obstacles he couldn't overcome he simply ignored. Most of the time, however, he knew how to manage. He had memorized a hundred expressions. They were lying in readiness and proved most useful, for John's fluency with them encouraged many listeners to wait a little until he got to the point of his answer. "If you wish." "Much obliged." Or, "That stands to reason." "Many thanks for your efforts," one could say all that quickly. He also knew the names of admirals well. Everybody talked a lot about victories, and so he wanted to know and to be ready to supply the admirals' names at once.

He also wanted to learn how to make conversation. He loved to listen anyway and was pleased when bits and pieces he caught fitted together to make sense. He was careful about tricks. Simply saying yes and acting as if he had understood didn't work.

Too often something was expected if he said yes. But if he said no, they'd pounce on him even more. Why no? Reasons! No without a reason was even more quickly exposed than an unfounded yes.

I don't want to make anyone believe anything, he thought. If only others don't try it on me. They must ask me and hold on to wait for my answer. I must get that worked out, that's all.

The tree. The way to it led through the Evangelist Alley and then through a street called Breakneck Lane. Climbing didn't make him faster; he knew that by now. But that didn't make the tree useless. As he moved from branch to branch he found that coherent thought was better there than on even ground. When he had to breathe heavily he perceived the order of things.

From this lookout he could survey the town of Louth: red bricks, white windowsills, and ten times more chimney pipes than in Spilsby. All the houses looked like the school, only shrunken. They also lacked the walled-in courtyard and lawn. The school had three high, sharp-cornered chimneys, as if it contained a forge. There was a lot of hammering.

"Correction Day." There were two of them: rod day and switch day. Could a plant grow in freedom and become a cane? Strange, too, how many names there were when it came to punishment. The head was called a "turnip" or "poet's box"; the backside was called "register"; ears were "spoons"; hands, "paws"—those to be punished were malefactors. John had enough on his hands with current words. This additional vocabulary seemed to him a waste.

Punishment itself he ignored. Mouth closed, his eyes turned to a faraway world—this was how one got over correction days. It was humiliating that the moderators held the delinquent as if he wanted to run away. John ignored them as well. There were also punishments outside the regular order. Being too late for prayers, not having checked out before going to the tree, being caught at a game of dice: then one got it ad hoc. On the school's seal was written: *"Qui parcit virgam, odit filium."*—"He who spares the rod hates the child." Dr. Orme remarked that this was mediocre Latin: *parcere* requires the dative.

Dr. Orme wore silken knee breeches, lived in a house on Breakneck Lane, and, it was said, conducted experiments with clocks and plants—both of which he collected assiduously. An ancestor, they said, had been one of the "eight captains of Portsmouth." Although John never found out what these captains were supposed to have done, the gentle schoolmaster assumed for him something navigational; often John saw in him even a secret ally.

Dr. Orme never shouted or thrashed anyone. Perhaps he was less interested in the children than in his clocks. He left the necessary discipline to his assistant master to enforce and came over to the school only for his lessons.

John wanted to learn better how to behave with people like Stopford; they were not undangerous. On one of his first days at school he said once in response to a question by Stopford: "Sir, I need a little time for the answer." The assistant was irritated. There were crimes by pupils that didn't give even him any pleasure. Demanding more time, that was no discipline.

Thomas Webb and Bob Cracroft kept thick notebooks in which they entered something every day in fine script. On one of the covers was written "Sayings and Thoughts" or "Usual Latin Phrases." That made a good impression. For this reason John started a voluminous copybook with the heading "Noteworthy Phrases and Constructions to Be Remembered," which included quotations from Virgil and Cicero. When he didn't write in it, the notebook was buried in his chest under his linen.

Dinner. After long prayers, only bread, near beer, and cheese. Meat broth twice a week; vegetables, never. Anyone who broke into the orchard and stole fruit got the rod. In Rugby, Atkinson told them, the pupils had imprisoned their rector in the school's jail two years ago. Since then they were given real meat three times a week and were thrashed only once a week. "Is he still in jail?" asked John.

In the navy, too, they had mutinied against admirals!

The dormitory was large and cold. All around them they saw displays of names of former pupils who had accomplished something because they had studied diligently. The windows were barred. The beds stuck out freely into the room. Every sleeper was accessible on both sides. No one could turn to a protective wall to stare at it or cry. One made believe one slept until one slept. The light burned incessantly. Stopford wandered up and down to see where the pupils had their hands. John Franklin's travels under his covers were not noticeable; he withdrew them from sight with his slow, deliberate motions.

Often he learned while falling asleep, repeating what he had been taught, or he talked with Sagals.

He had once dreamed that name. Meanwhile, he imagined a tall man, quiet, clad in white, who looked down from above the dormitory ceiling and was able to listen even to complicated thoughts. One could talk to Sagals, for he would never suddenly disappear. He hardly said anything, only now and then a single word, which, however, made sense even if it was completely outside John's own reflections. Sagals didn't dispense advice, but John believed he could distinctly recognize what he thought by observing his face. At least he could tell whether it was more "yes" or more "no." Sagals could also smile in a friendly, enigmatic way. But the best part was that he had time. Sagals always hovered above John in the dormitory until he had fallen asleep. Matthew, too, would come, soon.

He now understood navigation. He had started with Gowers's *Treatise on Theory and Practice of Navigation.* A miniature ship was attached to the cover. It had adjustable yards—crossbars on its masts—and a movable rudder blade. With them John practiced turning and tacking. The book itself was the ocean; when he closed it he could cover up deep water. He had read Moore's *Practical Navigator* and had tried Euclid. He found arithmetic easy, because nobody pushed him. Sometimes he confused plus and minus and never got rid entirely of the feeling that it may be doubtful whether the difference between such small signs really mattered. Ships drifting off course, wrong compass directions, high-noon readings—all that he could figure out. In the spring he spoke to the bright leaves of his tree more than a hundred times, repeating "Spheric trigonometry, spheric trigonometry." He wanted to pronounce the name of his field of interest without a slip-up.

A new teacher was expected, a young man named Burnaby. Perhaps he taught mathematics.

Navigation: when they used that word in Louth, they thought of the inland canal from the Lud to the mouth of the Humber. So much for Louth. And for all that, the sea was only half a day away. After another talk with Sagals, John resisted the temptation. He wanted to go on waiting for Matthew.

He also wanted to persuade Tom Barker to join the navy with him.

In his notebook John now entered only English sentences for his own use, as well as explanations of his obstinacy and of his sense of time, which he could give easily if needed.

Atkinson and Hopkinson had been to the sea with their parents. No, he had never taken notice of the ships, said Hopkinson. Instead, he talked about bathing machines—cabins on wheels pulled into the sea by a horse so that the bather could allow himself to slip into the water unseen. And the ladies bathed in flannel sacks! Those were the things that interested Hopkinson! Atkinson talked exclusively about a gallows on which the murderer Keal from Muckton had been hanged before being quartered and cast out to be devoured by the birds. "That figures," John answered, politely but a little disappointed. Atkinson and Hopkinson were no ornaments for a seafaring nation.

Andrew Burnaby mostly wore a gentle smile. He said right at the beginning that he was there for everybody, especially for the weaker pupils. So John saw his smile often. It usually seemed a little tense, for anyone who is always present for everybody has little time. He didn't favor physical punishment, but he was ambitious in his use of time. The hours marked by the sand in the hourglass no longer mattered; it was now a question of minutes and seconds. For answers to his questions, he secretly or expressly set an appropriate time limit, and if responses didn't arrive in time they had to be worked up later. John always went over the time limit and then answered one or two earlier questions unexpectedly, out of order, for nothing could keep him from solving a problem, even if it had already become inappropriate. That had to improve! He wrote in his copybook, "There are two points in time: a correct time and a missed time," and underneath, "Sagals, Book I, Chapter 3," so it would look like a regular quotation. He also no longer hid the book under his linen, but put it openly on top. Let Tom read it if he wanted to! Did he anyway, perhaps?

It was raining on Jubilate Sunday, the third Sunday after Easter. John went to the fair with Bob Cracroft. The water dripped from the tents. They splashed about in puddles. John wasn't happy, because he thought of Tom Barker and himself. If there is an ideal human being among us, and not just in Greece, he thought, then he has long, fair limbs, laughs softly, and can be as mean as Tom. Ever since he had started to admire Tom, he looked at himself with displeasure. The way he came on, for example: his legs wide apart, his round eyes, his head askew like a dog's. His movements seemed glued to the air, and he talked like an ax thumping on a chopping block. He didn't find much to laugh at, and when he did he laughed too long. His voice had become hoarse, as though a rooster were crowing inside him. That wouldn't matter at sea. But then there was still something new that kept on happening unexpectedly, a swelling that disappeared only very slowly. Of all things, to be conspicuous in such a spot! "That's normal," Bob had remarked. "Revelations, Chapter 3, Verse 19: 'Those whom I love I reprove and chasten.'" Again proof of the Bible's total unintelligibility. John regarded the bustle of the fair with his glasslike fixed look, as if he were about to catch a ball. Spavens, the one-legged man who had written a book of seafaring memoirs, stood by the fence. "The money has croaked," he announced. "Everything's twice as dear, and my publisher pretends to be deaf."

Not far from him was the booth with the miracle turntable. If it turned fast enough on its own axis, Harlequin and Columbine, who were painted on opposite sides, were united as a couple. It had to do with speed, but John thought that today he didn't have a head for it. He went back to Spavens, who talked slowly, coming up with one word after another the way one tacks up pictures on a wall. "Peace, that's God," he shouted, his nose dripping. "But what does He send? War and want." He pushed out from under his coat the stump of his leg, with its well-turned wooden peg, polished with shoe wax. "He sends us those costly victories to test us even more." With each sentence he stabbed his peg more deeply into the lawn; he had already stomped so violently that he had scooped out a little ditch, and now muddy water spurted at the bystanders' stockings each time he made a jab. Bob Cracroft whispered; "I believe he isn't particularly objective," and then began to talk about himself.

John had come to be well liked as a listener just because he asked when he hadn't understood. Even Tom had said, "If *you* understand something, it must be right." John wondered what he meant by that and answered, "In any case, I understand nothing too soon."

This time John was not a good listener. At the other end of the fair he had noticed the model of a frigate as tall as a man; its hull was black and yellow, and it possessed all the guns, yards, and riggings it was supposed to have. The model was in the navy's recruiting tent. John studied every inch closely and asked at least three questions about each detail. The officer asked to be relieved after an hour and dropped into his bunk.

In the evening, John wrote in his notebook: "Two friends, one fast, the other slow, get through the entire world. Sagals, Book XII." He noted it and placed it on top of Tom's linen.

* * *

31

They sat on the bank of the Lud near the mill. Not a soul was near; only now and then a coach rattled across the bridge. Tom had his foot in the water, one of those extremely beautiful feet. He said: "They fought about you." John's heart beat high up in his throat. Had Tom read his "Noteworthy Phrases"?

"Burnaby said there's good stuff in you. You have insight into authority, and your further education would be worthwhile. By contrast, Dr. Orme thinks you're someone who learns things by rote, who is done no favor with ancient languages. He wants to speak to your father to see about an apprenticeship for you."

Tom had eavesdropped evenings at the open window of the Wheatsheaf Inn. "I didn't hear everything. They didn't say a word about me. Burnaby said—I thought that this would interest you."

"Yes, very much," John said. "Many thanks for trying."

"Burnaby talked about your fine memory. Later he remarked that freedom was only an interim stage. I don't know if that was about you. He shouted in rage, 'The pupils love me.' I believe Dr. Orme was furious, too, but quieter. He said something like 'being God-like' and 'equality' and that Burnaby wasn't mature enough yet. Or that the time wasn't. His voice was rather low."

A coach drove over the bridge out of town. Now John managed to bring out his question. "Have you read in my book?"

"In what book? In your notes? What should I do with them?"

Then John began to speak about Matthew and how he was determined to become a sailor. "Matthew is in love with my aunt. He'll take me along, and you too."

"What for? I'll be a doctor or an apothecary. If you want to drown, do it by yourself." And as though to confirm this, Tom took his beautiful foot out of the Lud's water, in which surely no human being could drown, and put his stocking back on.

Burnaby actually taught mathematics of late, always on Saturdays. It didn't seem to give him any real pleasure that John already knew a lot about it, but his smile remained. When John discovered an error in Burnaby's explanations, the teacher started to talk about education—beseeching, fiery, or a little woebegone, but always smiling. John wanted to try to understand education, for he wanted to make Burnaby very happy. Dr. Orme sat in on Saturdays and listened. Perhaps he knew mathematics better than Burnaby, but a clause in the school's constitution prohibited his teaching anything other than religion, history, and languages.

Now and then he smiled.

John Franklin sat in the school jail. When somebody had turned away impatiently and had not waited for his answer he had simply grabbed him and held him tight without considering sufficiently that the person was Burnaby. I can't let go, John concluded from this, not of any image, any person, or any teacher. Burnaby, however, had concluded from this that John had to be severely punished.

The school jail was the heaviest punishment. Not for John Franklin, who could wait like a spider. If only he could have had something to read! For he had come to love books of all kinds. Paper could wait; that wasn't pressing. He knew Gulliver, Robinson, and Spavens's biography; recently also *Roderick Random*. Just now poor Jack Rattlin would have almost had his leg sawed off. The incompetent ship's doctor Mackshane, probably a secret Catholic, had already put the tourniquet on him when Roderick Random stopped him. With a venomous glance, the quack fled; six weeks later Jack Rattlin reported back for service on two healthy legs. A good argument against all hasty decisions. "There are three points in time: a correct time, a missed time, and a premature time." John wanted to write this in his copy book when he got out again.

It wasn't very comfortable in the school jail. The stones in the dungeon were still wintry. Lying on his back, John spoke to Sagals through the vaulted ceiling—to the spirit who had written all the books in the world, to the creator of all libraries.

Burnaby had shouted: "That's how you all reward me!" Why "you all"? It had been only John in whose grip he had wriggled. And Hopkinson murmuring, full of admiration, "Man, are you strong!"

He wouldn't be able to stay in school. Where could he wait for Matthew? He should have shown up long ago. Better get out as soon as he could! Hide on a barge under a load of grain! Let them think he had drowned in the Lud.

In the port of Hull he could start on a coal-carrying ship, like the great James Cook.

There was nothing doing with Tom. Sherard Lound would have gone along. But he was now hoeing beets in the field.

While John was taking counsel with Sagals, the jail door opened and Dr. Orme entered, his head way down between his shoulders as though he wanted to show that a school jail wasn't really designed for teachers.

"I'm coming to pray with you," said Dr. Orme. He looked at John very carefully, but not in an unfriendly way. His eyelids clapped open and shut as though, under great strain, they were trying to fan air into his brain. "Your books and your notebook were delivered to me," he said. "Who, tell me, is Sagals?"

[4]

◆◆

THE VOYAGE
TO LISBON

Now he was on a ship in the middle of the ocean! "And I'm not too late for this!" he whispered, and smiled at the horizon. He joyfully hit the rail with his fist, again and again, as though he wanted to prescribe a rhythm for the ship in which to pitch its way to Lisbon.

The Channel coast was out of sight; the fog was only a thin strip of mist. The rigging stood up straight or ran crosswise from side to side. At some point it always led to the top, making the viewer bend his head and neck back to follow it. It wasn't the ship that bore the masts but the sails that pulled and lifted the ship, which seemed to hold on only with a thousand lines. What ships had he seen in the Channel, ships with rich riggings and names like *Leviathan* and *Agamemnon*! Since the gravestones of St. James, he had not found so worthy a place for letters as the bow or stern of a ship. In the end, a gigantic ship of the line had emerged from the fog; they had almost been rammed in spite of bells and foghorns.

Before him lay the sea, the good skin, the true surface of the entire planet. John had seen a globe in the library at Louth: the continents were furry and jagged; they locked into each other and spread out to try to cover as much of the globe as they could. In the harbor at Hull he had observed how pyramids of wooden planks were built in the water to prove the land's dominance over the sea. "Dolphins," they called them, to cause even more confusion. The Dutch sailor said: "That's no dolphin, that's a *Duckdalbe*—a breakwater." And since he didn't grin or wink but only spat as usual, it had to be right. John asked him to repeat it and learned the word. He also discovered that the French enjoyed having a long reach and that since the Revolution the concave mirrors of their lighthouses had been made of pure silver. John felt fine. Perhaps all this was already the longed-for freedom.

In Hull, over a dish of jellied meat, he had mused about freedom. One had it if one didn't have to tell others ahead of time what one planned to do. Or if one kept quiet about it.

Half a freedom: if one had to announce one's plans ahead of time. Slavery: if others could foretell what one would do.

All reflections led back to the conclusion that it would be better to come to some understanding with Father rather than simply staying away. One could become a midshipman only through connections. Since Matthew had not returned, only Father remained.

Soon they crossed the third-degree western longitude. The town of Louth was situated at zero; the meridian ran straight through the middle of the market square. Without Dr. Orme— John knew that—he'd still sit there and look not upon the sea but into the defensively poised curves of the ear of Hopkinson who had just been thinking about flannel.

Dr. Orme had changed things at school. They now had a piece of meat twice a week and a new assistant master who kept the moderators in line.

Dr. Orme! John was grateful to him and knew he always would be. Dr. Orme had not maintained that he lived only for him, nor had he talked of love or education, but he had been interested in John's special case, out of curiosity and without a trace of pity. He had tested John's eyes and ears, his comprehension and memory. With Dr. Orme, John felt on safe ground. He wasn't usually concerned about the pupils, but when he did show interest, it was worth something. He never let on what he thought. If an idea occurred to him, he only laughed. He showed his small, slanted teeth and took a breath as though he had just come up from a dive into deep water.

The wind rose and John started to freeze. He went below and stretched out on his bunk.

After a long, rapid talk with Dr. Orme, Father had nodded and said something under his breath that started like this: "The first storm will . . ." John knew what they thought. Dr. Orme believed he wouldn't be able to stand the rolling waves and would end up in the clergy; at least, this was his recommendation. Father hoped he'd be swept overboard. Mother wanted him to succeed in everything but wasn't allowed to say so.

John's look began to penetrate the black plank above his bunk, and soon he was the lost Matthew roaming through Terra Australis in the company of a lion. Later he became John Franklin again and told the people of Spilsby how to make their fields rise up so as to allow the land to sail away. But the wind pushed the land very hard, and along the road fissures opened with a creaking noise; everything burst asunder; everything was shaken up and turned topsy-turvy. John sat up, greatly concerned, and his head hit the black plank. Sweat covered his forehead. Next to his bunk stood a wooden bucket with iron strips around it, built like a small keg but twice as wide on the bottom as on top. John was on a ship in the midst of the Bay of Biscay, in a storm.

Seasickness was out of the question. He was now set to solve a couple of arithmetical problems.

"What's the true time in Greenwich," he whispered, "when . . ." For a moment he imagined those solid piers and imperturbable buildings with their firmly fastened, comfortable benches from which one could watch the ship traffic. He pushed the thought quickly out of his brain. ". . . when at thirty-four degrees, forty minutes eastern longitude . . ." He bent over the side of his bunk and held on to himself with one hand, to the bucket with the other. ". . . the true time is 8:24 P.M.?" Groaning, he tried to figure out the angles in his head. Now whatever was inside him came up. So spheric trigonometry didn't help either. The brain couldn't outsmart the belly, that woeful traveler. A little later John lay as straight as a rod, head and feet propped up, wanting to find out what made him sick.

First was the pitching motion around the imagined transverse axis of the ship, lasting for half a minute, up or down in a very irregular rhythm. That seemed to have most to do with the weakness in his stomach but also with that paralysis in his head, which by and by became as numb as the bucket under him. Whatever fitted together effortlessly on land here became differentiated by the degree of inertia with which it reacted to the ship's movements: the head sooner than the body, the belly sooner than the stomach, and the latter more quickly than its contents. Then there were swayings around the ship's longitudinal axis, a listing and rolling that merged with the up-and-down movements in ever-new combinations. John's brain skidded back and forth like a pat of butter in a frying pan and seemed to melt altogether. With his last strength he tried to discern any regularity, anything to which head, stomach, heart, lungs, and all the rest could cling as a common denominator. "What's the use if I can calculate a ship's position but can't stand its motions?" He sighed and went on figuring, the bucket in front of his eyes. "Answer: 6:05 P.M. and twenty seconds," he whispered. Nothing could keep him from completing a problem.

It seemed to him as if the foreship plunged in too deeply. Perhaps the bow had sprung a leak. The lower the leak's position, the greater the water pressure. Water flowed into a ship at the rate of the square root of its height. So if a ship sank, it sank more and more inevitably from second to second. He'd better go above.

He got through the door after taking careful aim. On deck a fight started between his two poor hands and the rough elements, which, without further ado, put him here, threw him there, and jammed him between the wood and the tackling as it pleased. Each time he found himself again in a new situation, and the heavy seas fed him one huge mouthful of water after another. Now and then he saw people clinging to ropes or beams, looking where to dash for another hold at a precisely chosen moment. That was the only way they could move. It was as if they were trying to trick the storm into thinking they were a fixed part of the ship. They dared to move like humans only behind its back. From the direction of the mainmast he heard a weak bang and furious beating and clattering. Screams, muffled by the storm, reached his eardrums. The main topsail had been up until then; that was over now. The sea appeared white, like boiling milk, and waves rolled in large enough for entire villages to find room in them.

Suddenly he was seized by two fists that didn't belong to the storm. They dispatched him below deck with a speed equivalent to that of free fall. A curse was the only comment. In the bunk room the boatman's bucket had turned over after all, despite its wide bottom. John felt as sick as it smelled. "Still," he said as he keeled over along with the bucket, "it's the right thing for me." He sucked his lungs full of air to keep out any possible dejection. He was a born sailor; he knew that for sure.

"That's the best wind one can have," said the Dutchman. "The Portuguese Norther, always beautiful from aft; we're doing better than six knots." If anyone else had said it, John wouldn't have understood the new word, but the Dutchman knew that his listener understood everything when he was allowed pauses. Besides, they both had a great deal of time on their hands because the sailor had sprained his ankle during the storm.

The weather remained sunny. Off Cape Finisterre they saw a huge mast of a ship drifting by, covered with crabs, already three years on the way if the captain was right.

At night they were approaching a brightly lit beacon. "That's Burlings," John heard. An island with castle and lighthouse. Then he noticed something that reminded him of Dr. Orme's theories.

The beam rotated around the top of the tower like every single revolving light. John saw the beam wandering, but he also perceived that the light would go on being visible on the right side even as the beam was again swinging back to the left, and that it was still on the left side when it turned up again on the right. Present and past—what had Dr. Orme said about that? The light was most fully in the present when, flaring up, it met John's eye directly. Whatever else he saw must have been lit up before and now shone only within his own eye—a light of the past.

Just then the Dutchman came up. "Burlings, Burlings!" he grumbled. "The island is called Berlengas." John still stared at the lighthouse. "I see a trace rather than a point," he explained, "and I see the present only when it flares up." Suddenly he had a sad suspicion: perhaps his eye was lagging behind by one whole cycle? Then the flare-up wouldn't come from the present but from the previous rotation.

John's explanation took a lot of time; it became too long even for the Dutchman. "I see this different," he interjected. "A sailor has to trust his eyes as much as his arms, or . . ." He fell silent. Then he picked up his crutches and hauled his swollen leg gingerly below deck. John stayed above. Berlengas! The first foreign shore outside England. He was doing well again. He put his clenched fist on the plank-sheer, solemnly. Now everything would be different; a little today, all of it tomorrow.

Gwendolyn Traill was thin, with pale arms and a white neck, and so thoroughly wrapped in billowing garments that John couldn't make out anything specific underneath. She wore white stockings; her eyes were blue, her hair reddish. She spoke hurriedly. John noted that she didn't like this herself but felt it was necessary. In this she resembled Tom Barker. She had freckles. John observed the hair on her neck above her lace collar. It was time for him to cohabit with a woman in order to be informed. Later, as a midshipman, he would often be teased for being late, but in this matter he wanted to have a head start. Father Traill was saying something just then; John hoped it was no question. He was talking about a grave. "What kind of grave?" asked John. He wanted to pay attention at mealtimes and make a good impression, because Mr. Traill would write to Father about everything.

Gwendolyn laughed and Father Traill threw her a glance. The grave of Fielding. John answered that he didn't know him and that altogether he didn't know much about Portugal.

All that burring and hissing that came out of people's mouths here was most unpleasant. People in Lisbon talked as if to burn their lips with every word they didn't enunciate at once, and they blew out a lot of air before and after each of them. At the same time, they fanned and waved with their hands. When John got lost and found himself at the aqueduct near the Alcántara, he asked to be shown the way. But instead of pointing in one direction that he could have followed without trouble to the Traills' house, they gesticulated. He found himself in the square in front of the monastery of the Sacred Heart of Jesus. Of course, they were Catholic here; that was to be expected. Not expected, however, was that they would poke fun at the contrast between mighty England and helpless John. After dinner, the Traill parents retired. John was alone with Gwendolyn. She talked about Fielding. Her freckled nostrils flared; her neck reddened: he didn't know Fielding! The great English poet! She got herself properly inflated, as though she would rise at once like a Montgolfier balloon if no one held on to her. John said: "I know great English sailors." Gwendolyn had never heard of James Cook. She laughed; one could always see her teeth, and her dress rustled because she moved around so much. John learned that Fielding had gout. How can I get her to shut up, he wondered, and how do I manage to cohabit with her? He began to prepare a question but was sidetracked because Gwendolyn never paused. He would have loved to listen to her for a long time if only she had kept silent for a single moment. She talked about someone called Tom Jones. Probably another grave. "Let's go there," he said, and seized her arms. But that was wrong thinking again. Since he was already holding her, he should logically not have talked about going and should have kissed her instead. But he didn't know how that worked. All that had to be planned better. He let go of her. Gwendolyn vanished with a few quick words, which were perhaps not meant to be understood. John knew only one thing: he had reflected too long. That was the disturbing effect of the echo Dr. Orme had mentioned; he hung on too long both to the words he heard and to his own words. But a person who always kept on wondering about his own formulations surely couldn't persuade a woman!

In the afternoon he went for a walk with the Traill family through dark alleys alive with the sound of bells. They came upon a hill where they saw houses freely exposed to the light, white like the faces of brand-new clocks, roughly built and without ornaments, and the land around them not green but pale red. Mr. Traill told of a great earthquake many years ago. Gwendolyn walked ahead of them, moving daintily. She got all kinds of things going inside John's body without even looking at him.

But time passed, and the opportunity had slipped by. "It's all right to think things over," Father used to say, "but not for so long that the offer is made to somebody else." A man lagging behind by a full cycle commanded too narrow a present; thin was the line between land and sea. Perhaps he should try to catch the right moments like a ball: if he applied the fixed look in time, these moments would be ready to be grabbed when the opportunity arose and wouldn't escape him. All a matter of practice!

"Soon Lisbon will celebrate the Feast of Saint Mark," Mr. Traill told them. "They'll bring a steer to the holy altar, a Bible between his horns. If he goes wild, the city will be facing hard times; if he holds still, everything will be fine; then he'll be butchered."

Gwendolyn was not completely out of reach. Sometimes she gave him a look. John sensed, beneath all the impatience she imposed on herself, also a kind of patience, perhaps a purely feminine patience he couldn't get at. If he had been unquestionably a sailor and a courageous man, Gwendolyn would have granted him a lot of time. As if to reinforce that thought, a massive three-decker on the Foz da Tejo fired off an interminable salute, which the coastal batteries answered. Gwendolyn and the sea: so far, the two didn't go together. They were like two chairs, and if one sat down between them, one fell on one's behind. So he should become an officer first, and defend England, and then cohabit with a woman! Once Bonaparte had been defeated, there'd still be time. Gwendolyn would wait and show him everything. Before then there'd be no point in attracting attention. In any case, his ship was to leave in two days.

"Well, then," Gwendolyn said unexpectedly after dinner, "let's go to the poet's grave." She was as dogged as John with his mathematics.

Nettles were growing on Fielding's grave, as on the graves of all people who had amounted to something in life. That this was so John knew from the shepherd in Spilsby.

He looked at Gwendolyn, determined to prove that he could do this in all freedom without stammering or his ears turning red. Suddenly he found himself putting his arms around her neck and felt his nose being tickled by a strand of hair. Again, clearly, an entire piece of the act was missing. Gwendolyn's eyes grew anxious, and she pushed her hands between his breast and hers. The situation was somewhat confused. However it was, he felt caught in an opportunity and so decided to ask his much-rehearsed question: "Would you agree to cohabit with me?"

"No!" spoke Gwendolyn, and slipped out of his arms.

So he had been wrong. John was relieved. He had asked his question. The answer was negative; that was all right. He took it to be a hint that now he really had to decide in favor of the sea. Now he wanted ocean and war.

On the way back, Gwendolyn looked suddenly strange, her face flattish, her forehead wide, her nostrils clearly marked. Once again John reflected on why the human face had to look the way it did at all and not completely different.

He had also learned from the shepherd in Spilsby that in this world women wanted something quite different from men.

Seen from the wall of the wharf, Lisbon shone like a new Jerusalem. This harbor—it was truly the world! By contrast, Hull on the Humber was only a threadbare landing place for sloops in need of help. All kinds of ships were here, three-tiered, with golden names on their forecastles. Through such artful slanted windows John would one day scan the horizon as a captain.

43

Their own ship was small. But it floated by itself like all the others and had a captain just like the largest ships. The sailors came on board late, rowed to the ship by natives. Some of them were so drunk that they had to be heaved over the railing by the winch. Father had now and then taken a glass too many, Stopford a few more, but what these sailors did to themselves had to be called by a different name. They fell into their bunks and didn't emerge again until after the anchors had been weighed. Earlier, one of them, who was less drunk than the others, showed John his back: the brown skin was furrowed, crisscrossed by white scars carved out by a belt; they looked like craters and cliffs, so many pieces of skin had been torn off and grown back wrong. The hair on his back, originally of even density, had adjusted itself to the landscape and formed small groves and clearings.

The proprietor of the exhibit said, "This is the navy. For every little shit you get the whip." Could one die of this punishment? "And how!" said the sailor.

John now knew that there was something worse than storms. Moreover, there was alcohol, and one had to keep up with that—it was all part of bravery. They already passed him a glass: "Try it! We call this wind." It was a thin, fluid, sticky sauce, red and poisonous. With strenuous nonchalance John got down two swallows, then listened within himself. He determined that earlier he had been in a somewhat dejected mood. He drained the glass. Now things looked different.

The stories he was hearing about the navy were surely not for the brave!

They traveled more than two hundred nautical miles west, out into the Atlantic, to keep from having to run against the Portuguese Norther. Besides, this allowed them to evade the British men-of-war lurking along the coast, eager to replenish their crews with men from presumably oversupplied commercial ships. A few on board had already been through that; they had been captured like wild animals, had gone through battles, and

44

had escaped again at the first opportunity. They were simply afraid, John thought.

Ten more days and they were again in the English Channel. John was now permitted to eat with the captain, who, besides this honor, gave him grapes and oranges. John also learned from him that every ship had a maximum speed that it could not exceed even with the most favorable wind, even if it were equipped with a thousand sails.

John watched the work on the ship very closely. He let himself be taught how to tie knots. He noted a difference: in training, the name of the game was how fast one could get the knot tied; in real situations, how firmly it held. John watched the sails closely to see which maneuvers actually required speed. In turning, it was clear: the ship's loss of momentum was greater the longer its sails stood against the wind, and so work on the braces had to be fast. There were more such situations. John decided to memorize them in the course of time, like the tree from below.

Now it was up to Father. He had to write to Captain Lawford and see to it that his son would get a place as a volunteer. That he would do this was not very likely. There was still a second possibility: that Matthew would show up after all and take John along.

John was home again. Matthew continued to be lost. Nobody liked to talk about it, and if so, only to dissuade John from going to sea. Just before the end of the summer holidays, the Franklins assembled around the large dining-room table. Father allowed the family to contribute to some decisions. He himself said the most important things, and the others said only as much as was required to keep from looking as though they had said nothing.

"To sea? Once and never again," Grandfather said in a firm voice. Of course, he had to be reminded that he had never gone to sea.

But John needed no support, because something unexpected had happened: Father had changed his mind. Suddenly—as the only one in the family—he was most enthusiastic about a maritime career for John and went over to his side. It also seemed that John didn't have to convince Mother any longer. She looked so encouraging and cheerful; perhaps Father's change of mind had been her work. She didn't have to speak, anyway, not even in a family council. John was too confused for a time to be able to feel pleasure.

Thomas said nothing; he only smiled slyly. And his little sister Isabella wept loudly, why nobody knew. With that the matter was settled.

"If you don't understand an order at sea"—Thomas spoke slowly—"then simply say 'Aye aye, sir' and jump overboard. It would definitely not be wrong." John concluded that he didn't have to think about such remarks.

He wanted to tell the news to Sherard. Sherard would be pleased about it, he knew that, but he couldn't find him. The estate manager said he was working in the fields with his parents and other people from Ing Ming. He didn't want to say where. He didn't want any interruptions during working hours.

It had gotten late. The coach was waiting.

Just one more year of school. For someone like John that was as good as nothing.

[5]

◆◆◆

COPENHAGEN, 1801

"John's eyes and ears," Dr. Orme wrote to the captain, "retain every impression for a peculiarly long time. His apparent slowness of mind and his inertia are nothing but the result of exaggerated care taken by his brain in contemplating every kind of detail. His enormous patience . . ." He crossed out the last phrase.

"John is dependable with figures and knows how to overcome obstacles with unorthodox planning."

The navy, thought Dr. Orme, will be torture for John. But he didn't write that down. After all, the navy was the addressee.

John knows no self-pity, he thought.

But he didn't lower the pen to paper, for to be admired by a teacher rarely helps, and especially not in the navy.

Whether the captain would even read the letter before their departure . . . It was John himself who was determined to go to war. And he was too slow, and only fourteen years old. . . . What could he write? Misfortune sits in its own shoes, he thought. He crumpled up the letter and tossed it into the wastebasket, propped his chin in his hand, and began to mourn.

John Franklin lay awake at night and replayed the fast events of the day at his own slow speed. There were many of them. Six hundred men on such a ship! And everyone had a name and moved about. Then the questions! Questions could come at any time. Question: What's your assignment? Answer: Lower gun deck and sail practice in Mr. Hale's department.

Sir. Never forget to say Sir. Dangerous!

All men aft for ex . . . exe-cu-tion of punishment. That should be pronounceable! Execution of punishment.

All men to the sails!

Receive arms.

Clear ship for battle: a job of grasping the whole picture.

All guns loaded, sir. Move to gun ports! Fasten them!

Lower battery clear for battle! Anticipate everything exactly without question.

Take the man's name, Mr. Franklin! Aye aye, sir—name—write—fast!

The red paint in the quarters below was supposed to prevent spattering . . . the spattering of blood. No, to make it inconspicuous. The sand spread on the floor was supposed to keep people from slipping on blood. All part of combat. Trim sails aft, and so forth, that much was clear. . . .

Best compliments of the captain, sir. Please come below deck.

Sails: great royal, cross royal, head royal. One sail farther down and there was already a hitch. He knew how to calculate the height of the stars at night, their angles of elevation—knowledge he didn't need at all. That kind of thing nobody wanted to know. But: Which line belongs where? Where does the jib boom fit on the martingale, or vice versa? Shrouds and backstays, halyards and sheets, that endless pile of hemp, mysterious as a spider web. He always joined others in lashing things where they also lashed them, but what if they were wrong? He was a midshipman; that meant he was considered an officer. Now then, once more: mainsail, topsail, topgallant. . . .

"Quiet," a voice hissed in the bunk next to him. "What's all that whispering about in the night?"

"Reefing point," John whispered. "Gaff jigger."

"Say that again!" said the other, very quiet.

"Forestay, martingale, martingale guys, martingale stays."

"Oh, I see," growled his neighbor. "But it's enough now."

He could do it with his lips closed; only his tongue moving behind them remained indispensable. For example, he visualized in this way how to get from the bottom of the foremast to the main top by way of the foretop, the foretop mast cap, and the foretop gallant, by climbing up the rat lines and outside along the futtock shrouds, because only that was considered proper seamanship.

Would he be able to notice mistakes? For example, could he discover why the ship lost momentum and stopped moving? And what would he do if part of the running rigging tangled up?

He also noted all the questions that had so far remained unanswered. It was important to ask them at precisely the right moment, and therefore they had to wait. A gig sail was something very special; why? They were moving against the Danes; why not against the French? He also had to recognize those questions that could be asked of him, John Franklin. Question: What's your assignment? Or, question: What's the name of your ship, Midshipman; the name of the captain? When they'd go ashore after the capture of Copenhagen, there'd be lots of admirals running about, perhaps even Nelson himself. H.M.S. *Polyphemus,* sir. Captain Lawford, sir. Sixty-four guns. Everything in order.

He had memorized entire fleets of words and batteries of responses so as to be ready with answers. In speaking as in acting, he had to be prepared for anything that might come up. If he had to get it through his head first—that would take too long. If a question addressed to him became only a signal allowing him to rattle off the requested response without hesitation like a parrot, there would be no reprimand and the answer passed. He had made it! A ship, bounded by the ocean, could be learned. To be sure, he couldn't run very fast. And yet the entire day was filled with running, transmitting orders, running from one deck to the other—all narrow passages! But he had memorized every route; he had even drawn them and had repeated them to himself every night for two whole weeks. Running was all right if nobody came at him unexpectedly. Then, of course, nothing helped, and he had to go on without subtle navigation; the appropriate formula for apologies was well rehearsed. Soon the others learned that it would be better to get out of his way. The officers were hesitant to learn this. "Please imagine it this way!" he had said three days before to the Fifth Lieutenant, who actually listened to him as a result of a hefty rum ration. "Every ship's hull has its own maximum speed, which it can never exceed no matter what the rig or the wind velocity. And so it is also with me."

"Sir. I must be addressed as 'sir,' " answered the lieutenant, not unkindly.

Explanations were usually followed by orders. On the second day, he had made clear to another lieutenant that for his eye all quick movements left a streak in the landscape. "Climb up the foretop, Mr. Franklin! And I want to see a streak in the landscape!"

Meanwhile, things got better. John stretched out contentedly in his bunk. Seamanship could be learned. What his eyes or ears couldn't manage, his head did during the night. Intellectual drill balanced out slowness.

Only the battle remained. That he couldn't imagine. Determined, he fell asleep.

The fleet had already passed through the Sound. They would soon be in Copenhagen. "We'll show 'em," said a tall man with a high forehead. John understood the sound of these words very well, since they had been repeated several times. The same man told him, "Go, cheer the men on!" Something was up with the mainsail; there was a delay. Then the crucial phrase: "What would Nelson think?" He marked both sentences for the night. He also included difficult words, like those Danish landmarks Skagerrak and Kattegat, or words like cable gat and color vat. In response to a carefully phrased question asked after they had received their rum rations, he also found out that the Danes had been busy for weeks strengthening their coast fortifications and equipping their ships for defense. "Or do you think they'll wait till we can join their council session?" John didn't understand this at once. But he had fallen into the habit of automatically acknowledging any answers couched in the form of questions ending on a rising intonation with "Of course not," which instantly satisfied the person who always countered with a question.

They arrived in the afternoon. That night, or early in the morning, they would attack the Danish gun emplacements and ships. Perhaps Nelson might still come to their ship that day. And what would he think? So the day ended hectically, with shouting, gasps, and bruised joints, but without fear or rage. John felt he could keep up, for he always knew what was coming. An answer was yes or no, an order went up or down, a person was sir or not sir, his head banged into running or standing rigging. All that was altogether satisfying. A new difficult word had to be memorized: Trekroner. It was the most powerful coastal battery defending Copenhagen. When it started to fire, the battle had begun.

Nelson didn't come after all. The lower gun deck was clear, fires in the stoves were extinguished, the sand was spread, and all men were at the stations where their duties commanded them to be. One of them, directly at the gun barrel, kept baring his teeth. Another, who pushed the cannonballs into the breech, opened and closed his hand perhaps a hundred times and observed his fingernails carefully each time. Midship somebody started up in terror, shouting, "A sign!" so that all heads turned toward him. He pointed aft, but there was nothing. Nobody said a word.

And while the veteran sailors were feverish or frozen, John experienced one of those moments that belonged to him, for he could ignore the fast events and noises and turn to changes which, in their slowness, were barely perceptible to others. While they were crawling toward morning and the guns of the Trekroner, he enjoyed the movement of the moon and the transformations of the clouds in the night sky almost dead with calm. Unceasingly he gazed through the gun port; his breath deepened; he saw himself as a piece of ocean. Remembrances began to drift by, images that wandered more slowly than he himself. He saw a congregation of ships' masts, standing close together, and behind them the city of London. Always when ships were assembled so closely and quietly, a city belonged to them. Hundreds of riggings hung over the port buildings like a scrawled, elongated cloud. The houses were pushing up to London Bridge as though they were determined to get into the water and be part of it, and were hesitating only at the last moment. Now and then a house really fell off the bridge, always when no one was looking. The houses in London had completely different faces from those in the little village at home. Arrogant, surly, often boastful, sometimes as if they were dead! He had also seen a fire in the docks, and a lady who asked to have all her clothes brought from a shop to be examined through the window of her carriage, because she didn't want to walk through the muck with her shoes. The shopkeeper had customers waiting, but he remained at the carriage door, imperturbable, and answered all questions most courteously. He was so quiet that John regarded him as an ally, although he sensed distinctly: This man is fast. He had a kind of merchant's patience, which was pleasant but not related to his own.

A girl sat in the carriage. White-armed, slender, slightly embarrassed, red-headed English girls were among the eight or ten reasons why it was worthwhile to keep one's eyes open. Thomas had pulled him away in the manner of all older brothers who had to take care of younger ones and were filled with hatred in their impatience. They had bought the three-cornered hat, the blue coat, the buckled shoes, the sea chest, the dagger. A volunteer first class had to outfit himself. As they climbed up the memorial on Fish Street, he counted three hundred and fifty steps. A cold spring; the smell of acrid smoke everywhere. Far in the distance castles could be seen clinging to green parks. He observed an epileptic who banged on something with his forehead, then stared into the distance. There were highwaymen around, he heard, but a gallows stood in Tyborn. As a midshipman, said his older brother, he had to behave like a gentleman. In the market they observed a quarrel. It was about a fish that had perhaps been artificially puffed up, or perhaps not.

Everywhere one could see the masts of ships at least from the topgallant yards upward. The city's thousand chimney pipes were one level lower. It was difficult to conceive that ships could be moved across the sea with the help of the wind, following well-devised plans, even if one knew Moore's *Practical Navigator* by heart. Sailing was something royal, and the ships looked like it. He knew what was needed to make an entire wall of sailcloth stand in the wind at full speed. First one had to build hulls—all the curved, splinted wood, screwed tight, carefully polished, caulked, tarred, painted carefully, even overlaid with copper. A ship's great dignity derived from those many materials and arrangements that were necessary for its construction.

Boom!

That was the Trekroner and the battle!

Act like a gentleman! At the side of the gun, be as little in the way as possible. Running from the gun deck to the quarter-deck and back. Understand orders at once if possible or, if impossible, forcefully request a repetition. "Listen, men!" shouted the officer with the high forehead. "Don't die for your country." Pause. "See to it that the Danes die for theirs." Shrill laughter. Yes, they stirred up the men! Beyond that, the battle seemed to become heavy. The Trekroner and the other guns scored one hit after another. For a man who always reacts a little too late, every support was lost with each one of these jolts. Their own broadsides were worst. Every time they went off, the ship seemed to take a leap. The regular routine went on as they had learned it, only now the purpose was to cause chaos for the enemy, and that got back to them with the kind of suddenness John disliked. From one minute to the next the black gun suddenly bore a repulsively glittering deep scratch, almost a furrow, as if made by an immensely powerful tool that had slipped. The ugly shimmering of this metal wound made a deep impression. A moment later nobody was upright. Who could still get up? Their mechanical tasks were well learned; now partners' work had stopped, for half of them were no longer around. Then all that blood. To see it awash all over was worrisome. In the end, it had to be lost by somebody, for it poured out of people, everywhere.

"Don't just stand there! To the guns!" That was the man who had shouted, "A sign!" Suddenly the gun port had become much wider than before. The missing wood covered several bodies in midship. Whose bodies were they?

On deck, he learned that three of twelve ships had run aground, but not the *Polyphemus*. White smoke billowed out of the side of another ship close by. That image remained fixed in John's eye. On the *Polyphemus*, pieces of splintered wood skidded across the deck as fast as lightning, slicing in circles like mowers' blades. Sadly, John watched ordinarily sedate officers who never had to get out of the way jump aside with most undignified leaps. Of course, they acted correctly, but it remained somehow degrading. He delivered his messages.

Now the companionway looked very different. Obstacles protruded from the wall, detached themselves from above, and swung down at the height of his forehead. Since he could neither get out of the way nor stand still, he received scratches, punctures, and bruises, which certainly made him look like a hero. And at all times he tried to act like a gentleman. One could easily lose an eye; Nelson had only one. What did Nelson think now? He stood on the quarter-deck of the *Elephant*. Nelson would always know everything.

He could hear pumps working. Perhaps they were on fire? Or was the ship taking in water? People were reeling on deck as though they were drunk. The captain sat on top of a cannon, shouting, "Let's all of us die together!" Earlier they had made very different noises. Next to the captain the head of a listener was suddenly missing, and with it the listener himself. John became unhappy. All sudden changes confused him, whether of seating order, deportment, or systems of coordinates. It was hard to stand these constant disappearances of more and more people. Besides, he felt it was a deep humiliation for a head when, in consequence of actions by totally different people, it lost its body just like that. It was a defeat and not really an honor. And a body without a head, what a sad, indeed what a ridiculous sight!

When he got back to the gun deck he was greeted by a sudden sharp brightness and an enormous racket: a ship had exploded nearby. He heard "Hurrah!" and in between, again and again, the name of a ship. In the midst of the hurrahs, however, he heard a penetrating creaking, rasping noise, and then felt a jolt: a Danish ship had come up alongside them. And through the demolished gun port someone jumped aboard.

John caught the image of a light, foreign boot which suddenly pushed its way in and got a foothold. It was a quick, threatening move. Its image remained fixed in John's mind and kept him from a full awareness of further events. His head thought automatically: We'll show 'em! For this was the situation he thought of when he first heard this slogan. Next he saw just that man's open mouth and his, John's, thumbs on his neck. By some chance the man had come to lie under him. Now he had a hold on him—he, John!

When John grabbed a person, there was no escape. Now he saw the pistol emerging at the lower periphery of his vision. The sight paralyzed him immediately. He didn't look at it but rather kept his eye on his strong thumbs as though they could prevail over the pistol, which—it could not be denied—was now pointed at his chest. In his mind, one single concern began to crowd out all others. It grew and grew. It surpassed all boundaries. It exploded. The man could pull the trigger at once and kill him, sending him to death or to perish slowly from gangrene. He was faced with it now: there was no escape. It was about to happen and could not be averted. Suddenly John clearly sensed where his heart was, like anyone who knows that death is inevitable. Why couldn't he knock the pistol out of the man's hand or throw himself to the side? Neither required ingenuity, yet he couldn't do it. He had the man by the throat and thought only that somebody who is being strangled can't fire a gun. But that a man would be particularly inclined to fire if he was in the process of being strangled but hadn't been strangled yet—well, perhaps John wanted to think of that but couldn't because his brain acted as if it were already dead. All that remained alive was the idea that the danger could be averted only by the unremitting, relentless strangulation of that throat. The other man still didn't fire.

He was old for a soldier, certainly over forty. John had never knelt on top of anyone who could be his father. The throat was warm. The skin was soft. John had never touched a person for so long. Now chaos had really set in: the battle inside his body. While he was squeezing the throat, the nerves in his fingers felt horror at its warmth and softness. He sensed how the throat— purred! It vibrated, tender and miserable, a deep, miserable purr. The hands were horrified, yet the head, which dreaded the humiliation of being killed, that traitor-head which thought wrongly, acted as though it had understood nothing.

The pistol dropped to the floor. The legs stopped thrashing. A gunshot wound on the shoulder; bright red blood.

The pistol had not been loaded.

Had the Dane said something? Had he surrendered? John sat and stared at the dead man's throat. He had been afraid of the humiliation of violent death. But squeezing an organism to death belatedly, because fear had not subsided fast enough, meant losing more than one's head. It was a humiliation, a powerlessness which was even more crushing than the other degradation. Now that he had survived, and his head had to admit all his thoughts again, the battle continued inside him: hands, muscles, and nerves rebelled.

"I killed him," John said, trembling. The man with the high forehead looked at him with tired eyes. He remained unimpressed. "I couldn't stop squeezing," said John. "I was too slow for stopping."

"It's done," the forehead answered hoarsely. "The battle is over." John trembled more and more. His trembling turned into shaking; his muscles contracted in different places in his body, forming painful islands, as though in this way they were armoring his inner self or were expelling an alien substance straight through the skin. "The battle is over!" shouted the man who had seen the sign. "We showed 'em!"

* * *

They put out new buoys. The Danes had removed all markings of the waterway so the British ships would run aground. Gradually, the long boat advanced to the edge of an unfathomable depth, very close to the broken, shot-up Trekroner. John sat on the boat's thwart, apathetically, and stared at the shore. Slowness is deadly, he thought. If it is so for others, so much the worse. He wanted to be a piece of coast, a rock on the shore whose actions would always correspond exactly to his true speed. An outcry made him look down: in the clear, shallow water countless slain men lay on the bottom, many of them with blue coats, many with open eyes staring up. Terror? No. Of course, they were lying there.

He himself was part of them; a stopped clock, that's what he was. He belonged to them down there much more than to the crew of the boat. Too bad about all that work. He thought he heard a command but didn't understand it. No one understood a command after all those cannon booms. He wanted to ask for a repetition of the order but thought he had understood it after all. He drew himself up, rose, closed his eyes, and keeled over, very slowly, like a ladder that had been set up too straight. When he was in the water, the question came to him unasked: What will Nelson think? The traitor-head was too slow even here; it didn't want to let go of the question. So the others fished him out again before he could figure out how one drowned.

At night he stared straight up to the ceiling and searched for Sagals. He no longer found him. A god of his childhood only, Sagals had now succumbed, too. A hundred times he rattled off all the sails from the foresail to the cross royal, back and forth. He recited all the rigs from the fore royal stay to the cross royal backstays and all the moving rigging from the jigger boom jib to the fore royal bream. He conjured all the yards from the cross top to the foretop. He cleared the ship for battle with all topmasts, all decks, quarters, ranks—only his own mind had become inextricably enmeshed. His self-confidence was gone.

"I suspect," said Dr. Orme when they saw each other again, "that you're sad about his death." He said it very slowly. John

57

needed to take his time, then his chin began to tremble. When John Franklin wept it took a moment or two. He cried until the urge to weep tickled in his nose and in his fingertips.

"But you love the sea," Dr. Orme resumed. "That shouldn't have anything to do with the war."

John stopped weeping, because he was thinking. While doing so, he studied his right shoe. His eye followed incessantly the shining square of the large buckle: up to the right, down along the side, then farther down to the left, returning to its starting point more than ten times. Then he fastened his glance on Dr. Orme's flat shoes, which had neither tongue nor buckle, but rather left the instep open with a bow in front. Finally he said, "About the war, I was wrong."

"We'll have peace soon," said Dr. Orme. "Then there will be no more battles."

[II]

John Franklin
Masters
His Craft

[6]

◆◆

TO THE CAPE OF
GOOD HOPE

Sherard Philip Lound, ten-year-old volunteer on the *Investigator*, wrote home: "Sheerness, June 2, 1801. Dear Parents!" He licked his lips and wrote without any ink spots—probably Master Wright-Codd, the teacher, would read the letter to them.

"For the ship, it will be the longest voyage it ever made. I'm happy to be part of it, and above all as a Volunteer First Class. The captain refuses all thanks, saying that John Franklin had spoken for me. I'd like to be a captain too someday. I was in London with John. He's become even slower since Copenhagen and broods a great deal. At night he dreams of the dead. John is a good man. For example, he bought me a sea chest just like his own. It's cone-shaped, very deep, and has many compartments. On the bottom it's ringed with a rubbing strip. The handles are loops made of hemp rope. The lid is covered with sailcloth. I'm writing on it." He propped the sheet of paper higher, licked his lips, and dipped his pen into the ink. The page was only half filled.

"I got a shaving kit, too, because John said that someplace in Terra Australis it'll be time. Also, he showed me around the city. People don't say hello there because they don't know me at all. John's aunt Ann (Chapell) is also on board; she's the captain's wife. He's going to take her along to the other side of the earth. She sometimes asks me if I need anything. I'm eager to know how it all comes out and I'm happy. I'll stop writing now because there's lots to do on board."

The ship's captain was none other than Matthew who had come home at last after he had been given up for lost. John Franklin had just turned fifteen.

"He isn't all that well," even Matthew said, and since he was now John's uncle he expressly took his side against the others—Lieutenant Fowler, for example.

A lot of the time John just stood around not knowing what to do, and always where he was in the way. "That fellow's really no great shakes," Fowler remarked. "He's not a bad sort," said Matthew, "only he's a bit hard of hearing just now from the battle." Fowler thought to himself: "That's a month ago by now."

One deck below, Sherard was talking: "B'cause John's incredibly strong. He strangled a Dane to death with his bare hands. But he was my friend even before that!"

When John got a whiff of that talk he suffered even more. True, they meant well, and he didn't want to disappoint them under any circumstances. But he didn't know how to help himself, still less what to do with such praise. At night, when the slain men on the bottom of the sea didn't reappear, he dreamed of a strange figure: symmetrical, smooth without sharp edges, a friendly, well-ordered plane, not quite a square and not quite a circle, with an evenly proportioned drawing inside. Suddenly, however, it would transform itself into something tangled and splintered. It exploded into an ungeometrical grimace and became so nasty and threatening that John awoke bathed in sweat and was afraid of going back to sleep in dread of its return. In the end, he feared the smooth, geometrical figure almost more than the dreadful one it turned into.

The *Investigator*—formerly named the *Xenophone*—was a corvette that had suffered honorable wounds. In the middle of the war against France, the admiralty couldn't spare a better ship for exploration. "As soon as I hear the word exploration," said master gunner Colpits, "I know at once: clear the pumps!" If at least they hadn't changed the ship's name. That provoked fate even more. Mr. Colpits believed in the magical significance of certain days. In Gravesend he had all days of misfortune recorded for the next three years. The woman who read his fortune in the stars had told him: "You must watch out that you don't perish with the ship. If you get away when it runs aground, you'll have a long life." It didn't speak for Mr. Colpits that the crew knew this by heart as early as Sheerness.

When Matthew read out the rules before the start of the voyage, he stuck out his lower jaw so that his teeth showed, and said sharply, "The stars tell us only where the ship is located— nothing else."

Almost the entire crew hailed from Lincolnshire, as if Matthew had collected on one single ship those few among the farmers' sons of the county who weren't afraid of the sea. The twin brothers Kirkeby came from the city of Lincoln and were fa- mous for their muscles. With their own hands—the oxen had collapsed—they had pulled a fully laden cart over the Steep Hill up to the church. The two of them looked very much alike; one could tell them apart only by the phrases they used. Stanley's comment was usually "That's just what the doctor ordered." Olof said only "Beastly good!"—about the weather, the to- bacco, the work, the captain's wife: "Beastly good!"

Then there was Mockridge, the cross-eyed helmsman with the clay pipe. He had one talking eye and one listening eye. If John looked into the long-range, listening eye, he often understood Mockridge's words before they were out. Most of the time, though, it was safer to look into the short-range, talking eye.

Mr. Fowler and Mr. Samuel Flinders were lieutenants and arrogant like so many of their kind. The crew called them "luffs" because they liked to make wind. Seventy-four men, three cats, and thirty sheep made up the ship's population. After two days John knew them all—even the sheep, and especially the scientists: one astronomer, one botanist, and two painters. Each of them had his own servant. Nathaniel Bell was also a midshipman, and not yet twelve years old. He suffered badly from homesickness immediately on the pier in Sheerness, although his three older brothers were with him and coaxed him. Even the familiar smell exuded by the sheep didn't help: it merely increased his suffering.

Sheep dung, according to Mr. Colpits, could be extremely useful. "For caulking small leaks, the best thing you can get," he announced lugubriously. "Alas, we must expect bigger ones."

The *Investigator* was a warship, so there had to be ten marines and a drummer on board. They were commanded by a corporal, and he, in turn, by a sergeant. In the harbor, they had already drilled diligently and marched up and down on deck until they got in the cargo officer's way. Mr. Hillier let them know that he needed the space for more important work; loading and storing of provisions was a job to John's liking. Where should they stow two spare oars? Where to put fifty boxes of soil for plant specimens? Was it true that zwieback and pickled meat would last one and a half years, and the rum for two years? John calculated. The books in the cabin—if one included the *Encyclopaedia Britannica*—contained enough material for a solid year. Where to put the presents for the natives: five hundred axes and hatchets, one hundred hammers, ten kegs of nails, five hundred pocket knives, three hundred pairs of scissors, innumerable pieces of colored and transparent glass, ear and finger rings, glass beads, colorful ribbons, sewing needles, and ninety medallions with the King's picture on them. Every item was noted carefully on double-entry lists, and Mr. Hillier knew in his sleep where each could be found. Matthew replaced some of the big guns with light carronades, and even those he stowed where they were least in the way. When Mr. Colpits's face showed that he was going to make a remark about that, Matthew got ahead of him: "We're researchers. We're getting a pass from the French government."

The first annoyance! For a time no one could talk to Matthew, and everyone stayed out of his way: scientists, midshipmen, and cats, even the cook.

In Sheerness two high officers of the Admiralty inspected the ship. Most of Matthew's requests had been granted: brand-new sails had been hauled up the rigging, looking like thick sausages; new ropes of good Baltic flax were put in where the old ropes had turned brittle. The bow shone with copper up to the hawse-holes, for they had to count on drift ice. But then the great gentlemen noticed women's washing on a line. A woman on board? On such a long voyage? "Impossible!" they said, and Ann, against whom no one in the crew bore the slightest ill will, had to leave the ship. Women were usually tolerated quite well on ships that didn't actually go into battle. You heroes of administration! You weren't willing to allow cheerful, healthy, comforting Ann to remain with her Matthew! The captain was white with rage. "Never again," he muttered in a peculiarly low voice. "I'll never again follow just any lousy instruction from above. I won't even read that stuff!"

They put out to sea. The next annoyance already awaited them. Before Dover, Matthew sent the pilot away and relied on sea charts. A few miles farther on, in Dungeness, the ship ran aground on a sandbank. They trimmed the sails and lowered the boats into the water. The current helped. Shortly they got free. But now the *Investigator* had to go to Portsmouth into dry dock before starting its long voyage. They had to check whether the ship had been damaged below the water line. Matthew dropped a quiet remark—though distinctly audible to all—about the Admiralty and its maps.

Mr. Colpits, however, was glad. He viewed the sandbank as the one mishap that had been prophesied and believed that now he wouldn't perish. Mockridge thought of other things. "Portsmouth," he mused. "I know a lot of girls there." The eye geared to distances had already focused firmly on girls. Stanley Kirkeby agreed and declared that this was just what the doctor ordered. His brother Olof was silent. He always judged only after the fact. Every "beastly good" presupposed a present test. Also, it wasn't sure yet whether the crew would even be allowed ashore.

*   *   *

John Franklin wanted to be like every man. He therefore listened closely when the others talked about women. "I like 'em with bigger hips," said the gun master. Boatswain Douglas wagged his head: "Depends, depends." The gardener had a different opinion. Obviously, they all visualized precisely what their recollections offered. John was especially interested in how one went about this practically. He approached Mockridge and put some carefully thought-out questions to him about when and how. Here, too, the answer was mostly "Depends," but John remained obstinate. "Does the man undress the woman first?" he asked. Mockridge mused for an unusually long time. "It gives me pleasure that way," he said. "But you're the suitor. Things are done the way you want them." The way Mockridge did them was surely the way it's done. John was still concerned about the many buttons. "Where things are buttoned, tied, and laced you have to find out for yourself. And don't forget: pay cruder compliments only to older women! Are you scared?" John was indeed scared, and for that reason, completely against his instincts, he started to tell how before Copenhagen he had after all . . . with his bare hands . . . a soldier. He was immediately ashamed. Mockridge looked at John gently with his listening eye geared to distance and turned his sharp, talking eye on the bowl of his own pipe. "Once you lie with a woman, you'll be able to forget Copenhagen."

On land, John wanted to gaze at all the women, trying to memorize their clothes. But there was so much to see that he almost lost sight of his objective. The city was brimming with scores of sailors; so many young men in one place didn't exist anywhere else in the world, and he was part of it. He also wore a uniform, and if he just stood there he was one of them. He didn't know how to dance, though, and there was much dancing.

He couldn't see enough of the town hall. It was a narrow building in the middle of the main street with vehicles crowding around it. Then there was the semaphore tower in the harbor, where many arms were waving to receive and confirm orders from the Admiralty in London. For the first time, John sat in a seamen's pub. The innkeeper asked for his order and he read off one of the names written above the bar: Lydia. They all laughed, because that was the name of a ship out of Portsmouth. Those names were inscribed as solemnly as were the drinks.

Fortified by a Luther and Calvin, he again turned his attention to women. Their dresses varied greatly. Common to them all were the respectable, menacingly protruding bows of their bodices. What standing or moving rigging was hidden underneath was not easy to make out. It would all come out upon sampling. Mockridge took him to a house on Keppel Row and said: "Mary Rose is all right. You'll have fun. She's a sweet fat girl, always gay. When she laughs she wrinkles her nose." John waited outside in front of a low building while Mockridge negotiated something inside. The windows of the house were blind or curtained off. If one wanted to see anything one had to go in. Then Mockridge appeared and took him indoors.

John discovered that Mary Rose wasn't fat. Nor did she wrinkle her nose. She had a bony face; her forehead was high, as though it had been put together from many arched lines. Something about her reminded him of a ship. She was a man-of-war of the female sex. First off, she pushed up a window to let in some light; then she examined John carefully. "Did you fall into a bush?" she asked, pointing at his head and hands. "That was no bush. I was in the battle of Copenhagen," John answered, subdued, and stopped.

"And you have your four shillings?" John nodded. Since she fell silent, he saw his task clearly before him. "I will now undress you," he said intrepidly. She looked amused under those multiple arches of her eyelids, eyebrows, skull bones, and the little bays where her hair began. "That's what you think!" she said, smiling. Her gentle mouth could say mocking phrases in a very friendly way. In any case, so far this was nothing to run away from.

Half an hour later John was still there. "I'm interested in everything I don't know yet," he said.

"Why don't you grab this—do you like it?"

"Yes, but things aren't functioning right with me," John ascertained with some disenchantment.

"Not so important! There are enough big guns around here."

At this very moment the door opened, and a large fat man stood there with a questioning face. Obviously he wanted to come in.

"Out with you!" Mary Rose shouted. The fat man went away.

"That was Jack. He's a big gun, for example—in feeding himself and in guzzling." Mary Rose was in a good humor. "Once when his ship had run aground they threw him overboard and the keel became free at once." She leaned back and laughed heartily, her eyes closed. John could now view her knee and thigh and imagined how it went on from there. He picked up his trousers from the chair, checked what was up or down. Then he rummaged until he brought out the four shillings. "Yes, you'll have to pay," said Mary Rose, "or else you'll think you had no fun at all." She took hold of his head. John's lips felt her eyebrows; he sensed the tiny hairs. Gentle and peaceful was this feeling. No need to strain or to plan anything, for it was her hands that moved his head back and forth. "You're a serious lad," she said, "and that's a good thing. When you get older you'll be a gentleman. Let me see you again—it'll work next time. I know that." John rummaged in his pocket once more. "Here," he began, "I've got a brass chain link." He gave it to her as a present. She took it and said nothing. When he left, she said in a rough voice: "Trip up old Jack when you go out, will you. If he breaks his neck I'll have the night off."

When John got back to the ship, for once both of Mockridge's eyes seemed to focus on him at the same angle. "How was it?" John reflected for a moment, then made a decision and stuck to it. "I'm in love," he said. "Only I was a bit discouraged at first because of the buttons." That was no lie, really. For a long time the pleasant scent of her skin lingered on in his mind. And he continued to hope that the slowness of women had something to do with his own.

* * *

No damage to the ship below the water line. Now Matthew also had his pass for the *Investigator* and, despite the mishaps at Dungeness, the blessing of the naval authorities. Another researcher, Dr. Brown, and the long-awaited master sail-maker Thistle had also come on board; the crew was complete. Matthew ordered to weigh anchor.

Four days later they came upon the Channel fleet—not a pleasant sight. There they were lying again, those hunks with their high decks crammed to the top with gunpowder and iron, better suited for shooting than for sailing, waiting in ambush for the French.

"Never again," John said with relief. They were heading for waters outside Europe where their only concern would be observations and good maps. The beautiful strange world—he would now really have to see it, or he could no longer believe in it. The sea itself had to lure him out of his doldrums. He was no longer a child. When Sherard said once, just as in the old days, "I watch like hawk," a strange feeling came over him as though he had to weep for something lost.

But now he was on the way.

Whoever goes to sea cannot be desperate for long. There was too much work for that. Matthew put his crew of farm boys through the paces until their eyes fell shut while they were still standing. John learned not only all the maneuvers and battle positions but also every block, every fitting, every seam. He knew where ropes and chains squeezed each other, how to fit each eye into its place, how to splice whippings, how to latch the topmasts to the mainmasts. He knew the commands for all sailing maneuvers from memory, and there were many of them. His only worry was the tomcat Trim, a beauty of a gray tiger who didn't feel the slightest pity. The animal sat at table in the midshipmen's mess where, he discovered, his paw could easily knock a piece of roast off the slowest midshipman's fork—to be devoured later, in some safe place. The trick succeeded much too often. John's table companions now anticipated it, choking with laughter. Unhappily, John noticed that this made Trim more and more popular. It was, however, one of those worries over which one could forget bigger ones.

The awful figure at night appeared more and more rarely. In his dreams John was now busy setting sails. He heard his own voice yelling: "Sheet forward! To the topsail lines! Pull tight! Hoist topsails! Secure topsail lines!" And the ship reliably did exactly what it was supposed to do.

At the outset of their navigation lessons Matthew said he didn't believe that anyone in the world could do anything without knowing the stars by name and position. Then he explained the firmament and the sextant. John already knew how to find his way, but now he held the precious instrument in his hand for the first time. Mirror and calibration marks on the segmental scale were precise to one-sixtieth of an inch. A ruler with the Oriental girl's name of Alhidade turned in the center. John learned first of all never to drop a sextant on the floor, and next, how to operate it. "Either precise figures or prayers. There's no third way," said Matthew. When he peered through the diopter to establish their bearings, he himself came to look like a precision instrument: his left eye closed, surrounded by small sixtieth-of-an-inch wrinkles, nose turned, upper lip pursed as though in an expression of deepest contempt for all imprecision. His chin pulled back as far as this was possible for Matthew. There stood a man who knew exactly what to look at before he acted. John and Sherard agreed that they loved Matthew best when he took bearings.

Then there were the chronometers, which Matthew lovingly called the guardians of time. Only by fixing Greenwich mean time precisely could one calculate which longitude had been reached, either west or east. These time guardians had been built individually by craftsmen working by hand over a long period of time, and they bore proud names: Earnshaw's Nos. 520 and 543; Kendall's No. 55, Arnold's No. 176. Each had its own face—black ornaments on shining white—and each in its own way was a little fast or slow. Only synchronization guaranteed precision. Each individual quirk was brought to light through constant comparisons. Clocks were creatures. The greatest miracle about them was that the driving power of the spring was perfectly balanced by the mysterious braking power of the anchor. If a time guardian was slow by only one minute, the error in calculating one's position amounted to fifteen nautical miles. The compass, Walker No. 1, was also a respectable figure. It tended to be so sensitive that it overreacted, especially in the proximity of cannons.

John loved to look at land and sea maps. He gazed at them until he believed he understood each line as well as the causes for the earth's shape in this region. He calculated the coastlines by dividing them by the distance between Ingoldmells and Skegness—a very useful measure. "When you get down to it, a map is something impossible," said Matthew, "because it transforms something elevated into something flat."

John liked best watching them measure speed. When for the first time he was allowed to take the measurement himself, and feelingly let the log line unravel, he was completely happy at last. After letting it run for eighty feet, the log was set correctly; the beginning knot zoomed forward and Sherard turned the glass around. Sand and measuring tape ran for twenty-eight seconds; then John stopped it and took the reading. "Three and a half knots. It isn't great." He measured again.

John would have even taken log line and hourglass into the bunk with him at night if he had been able to measure how quickly a man slept or how far he could travel in his dreams.

Matthew had his quirks. Day after day he had the hammocks aired, the walls washed with vinegar, and the decks scrubbed with the "holy stone." The thundering noise of those scrubbing blocks woke any late sleepers in the morning.

They were given sauerkraut and beer; large quantities of lemon juice were also made available. In that way, Matthew wanted to prevent scurvy. "No one will die on my ship," he said in a menacing tone. "Except at worst Nathaniel Bell, of homesickness."

"Or we'll all die, but not of any disease," murmured Colpits in a circle of petty officers. He was again convinced that the prophesied beaching still lay in the future. There was a third possibility: the ship took in two inches of water per hour. The carpenter crawled about in the ship's bilge for hours on end, emerging again on deck with a white face and asking to see Matthew privately. Rumors started at once.

"I bet one of the planks is made of mountain ash," one of them surmised. "That'll send us to the fish for sure." "Don't talk nonsense," shouted Mockridge. "Look at the deck planks of juniper wood. They'll compensate for any weakness."

There was much talk while they were pumping, and no reason will help against an old story, above all when it seems to be confirmed. After three days their faces became even longer. "Now she takes in four inches per hour," the First Lieutenant said. "Soon we'll need no cats. The rats will drown on their own."

Madeira! John was on land again. The ground was so firm that he tottered incredulously. The war was coming closer and closer. The soldiers of the 85th Regiment had just been landed, and they were chasing away all the rabbits and lizards in the city of Funchal with their incessant trench digging. Funchal was to be defended against a French attack. However, this attack threatened only because of their fortifying. England had occupied Portuguese Madeira in all friendship. As always when John had his own ideas about something that were perhaps not shared by others, he felt a rising concern. But, he thought, I'm not well enough informed.

In Funchal, the *Investigator*'s seams were caulked. They spent nights on land—the officers and petty officers in a hotel. John learned how many fleas and bedbugs can gather in one single place at the same time: it was something for science.

The vats were refilled with water, and Matthew bought beef. He explained to his midshipmen how one can tell the meat of an old cow from that of a young one by its bluish color. Madeira wine was too expensive for him. A barrel for forty-two pounds sterling—that was piracy by other means! Those prices might be paid by tubercular English lords and ladies who rode in ox carts and read novels.

The scientists tried to climb Pico Ruivo, a high mountain on the edge of an ancient, expansive volcanic crater. They never reached the peak because of blisters on their feet. On their way back their boat filled with water, and they lost their collection of insects. "What a shame! Nowhere in the world are there more interesting bugs than in Madeira," sighed Dr. Brown.

When under a gentle southern breeze the ship left the island again, only Franklin and Taylor were on the quarter-deck; the others were eating. Taylor saw a red dust cloud sweeping over the water from the northeast. Neither of them at first drew any conclusions. John thought, Desert. He imagined how the wind lifted the red sand of the Sahara, how it chased the sand beyond the shore and over the dark sea, perhaps as far as South America. Something seemed odd to John. "Stop!" he said, and a few minutes later, "But the cloud has . . ." A little later all sails stood back; a violent squall raced from the northeast and slammed into the weak south wind, plucking the tackling of the *Investigator*. One of the spars came down, slapping on the deck, and a huge chunk of elm crushed one of the cats—but not Trim the tomcat. Still, the whole thing passed without severe damage. They all feasted on a giant turtle they had fished out and drank some Malmsey to the dead cat.

John pondered. He had seen it coming, and yet he had stood around not knowing what to do. What was needed in action was unreflective knowledge instilled by practice—the blindness. Instead of shouting, "Stop, the cloud . . ." he should have shouted, "The wind is turning!" A good six minutes would have remained for them to protect the spars by dropping and bracing them. They might even have been able to strike the topgallant sails. John became convinced that he had to practice the unforeseen. One of these days he wanted to save a ship by acting quickly and correctly.

Sherard asked him set questions: "There's a storm and there

isn't enough space on the lee side for jibing." Or: "Man over-board on a course close to the wind." Each time, John took exactly five seconds to visualize the whole thing well in his inner eye. Then came the answer: "Call out 'Man Overboard!' Toss the man a daytime life buoy but not on top of him—makes no difference with nighttime life buoys, since it's dark anyway. Heave to. Lower boat to water on lee side. One person always keeps an eye on the man." "Good," said Sherard. "Now you see flames on the foredeck." Five seconds. Take a breath. Then: "Change course to leeward at once. Batten down hatches! Un-load guns! Ammunition overboard! Shut powder chamber! Throw bolts! Hoist boats on yards and lower to water level! . . ." Matthew had been standing behind him for some time. "Not bad," he commented. "But perhaps you're starting a little late to put out the fire." John understood slowly, then turned red. In a small voice he mumbled: "To the buckets . . . !"

No land for weeks. By now it had become so warm that people didn't run around in jackets even at night. John easily enjoyed the calm of the sea, a calm quite apart from the strength of the wind. The crew worked better and more steadily. Even gun master Colpits became friendlier, although he could use his ammunition only for peaceful ends. When Stanley Kirkeby wounded his arm and developed a fever, he had to imbibe a mixture of gunpowder and vinegar. He got back on his feet fast!

In his dream John saw a new figure. At night the ocean suffused by moonlight became an image of itself. It reared up to a curled cloud of water circling around itself like a spiral growing larger and larger at the top, like a luxuriating plant, like a flickering and burning bush of water or a vortex created not by wind and current but by its own power. The sea gave itself its own body, being able to nod, to strike attitudes, to point the way. This gigantic figure grew effortlessly in his dream, emerg-ing from the deceptively eternal expanse of the horizon; it was like a truth that would make everything different. A crater opened up toward heaven, a mouth or a gorge. Perhaps the whole thing was a leviathan, perhaps a dance of millions of tiny creatures. John often dreamed this dream. Sometimes far-ranging reflections followed him after awakening. Mary Rose in Portsmouth occurred to him, and the fact that what mattered to women was not an outer but a hidden, inner moment. Another time he mused about the trek of the children of Israel through the Red Sea and fancied that not God but the sea itself had arranged their rescue.

When he was lying in his hammock in the morning, pondering, having been awakened sometime before by the thuds of the "holy stones," he experienced moments of intoxicating clarity. He sensed that something new was beginning, still very slowly. Even his back sensed what the sea looked like that day. It would not be long before he would be a sailor through and through.

[7]

◆◆◆

TERRA AUSTRALIS

The *Investigator* soon leaked again despite repairs, and more than ever. "Now she takes as much as five inches per hour, that old souse!" said the boatswain's mate. "If we don't get some caulking done again at the Cape, we might as well make ourselves at home in the lifeboats. One storm and we'll need no doctor!" But this was one of the few pessimistic sentences that were spoken. Mr. Colpits had gone over to meaningful silences, and the rest of the crew thought, We'll make it as far as the Cape.

The summer kept advancing, and it grew warmer and warmer. The season for shorts seemed to have stood still. Now it was October, which here was the beginning of summer. By its incessant heat, the perpetual summer changed people. Nothing on board was unimportant: everyone received a hearing. All this gave John the feeling that he was no longer as slow as he had been only a few months ago. Moreover, Trim couldn't shame him anymore. John gave the tomcat a little morsel before he could use his claws to get it.

Matthew was irked because he couldn't find an island named Saxemberg. A certain Lindeman was supposed to have sighted it a good hundred years ago—he had given precise coordinates. But though three men had looked out for it day and night, no Saxemberg was seen. Perhaps Lindeman had been mad, or his chronometer had belonged to the devil. Or the island was too flat and so had remained below the horizon. Possibly they had sailed past it by a mere fifteen nautical miles. "If it isn't found by anyone, it belongs to me," Sherard said. "I'll build a house on it that no one can take away from me."

At the Cape of Good Hope, a squadron of British warships lying at anchor helped out with carpenters and materials. Fresh caulk was squeezed into the bruised seams of the *Investigator.* Nathaniel Bell, more homesick than ever, was sent back on one of the frigates. To take his place, another midshipman came aboard, Denis Lacy, a fellow who talked a great deal about himself because he decided that the others had to know whom they dealt with. For the present, John could keep out of his way.

Since the astronomer had to be taken into Cape Town because of violent attacks of gout, Lieutenant Fowler and John had to set up an observatory. As their telescopes scanned the sky, they noticed that the road from Simonstown to Companies Garden led directly past their station. Whoever moved on it—gentlemen on their morning ride, slaves with firewood, sailors from ships in False Bay—they all stopped and asked if there was something interesting to see. Good thing Sherard was along! He made a fence out of posts and ropes, drawing all questioners to himself, and told them, with innocent eyes, such sensational news about the sighted heavenly bodies that the gentlemen resumed their rides and the slaves took up their burdens again.

After three weeks they resumed their voyage. The last European warships disappeared from view. "I think I always want to be where human bodies aren't at stake or, if so, where they're treated with respect," John told Matthew.

The other knew what he meant. "Where we're going, a war ⁻an be stifled as long as it's small."

The *Investigator* sailed directly eastward at six knots. In about thirty days they would reach Terra Australis at a point already known—Cape Leeuwin. John imagined the natives. "Are they all naked?" Sherard asked. John nodded absent mindedly. He thought what a wondrous person a white man must be for the natives because he came from so far away. They would always listen to a white man at length, even if they didn't understand a word. Also, John was curious to see whether there were actually fish and crabs that climbed trees in order to spy for the nearest body of water. Mockridge had told that story, and one could usually rely on him. Of course, he did not yet know his way about Terra Australis.

John's new tormentor turned out to be this Lacy.

Whenever Denis Lacy watched John Franklin he became impatient. "I can't watch that," he said, and smiled apologetically. He was the fastest, and he showed it to everyone, not just to John. From his greater speed he deduced the right to take out of other people's hands whatever they were doing. "Let me do that!" He had scrutinized every action that took time and divided it into smaller time segments. The longer a person talked, the more often Denis interrupted him to assure him he had understood. In between, he leaped up because he had to do something—straighten a mug that might otherwise fall off the table, scare Trim, who might be about to sharpen his claws on a uniform jacket that was lying about, or peer out the window to see if by chance land might be in sight. Also, he seemed to be in love with his own legs, and he liked to skip playfully back and forth or race down the companionways in a manner that made them sound like a drum roll. He clambered swiftly along the yards without looking for a foothold on the ropes and got as far as the spar without using his hands. Everyone was waiting for him to leap from the top of one mast to another. When he actually stopped to lean against something, he secretly admired his muscular legs. He didn't intend to be mean to his more deliberate fellows. At one point he even promised to do better. "Still," said the geologist, "he's a pain in the neck!" Compared with Denis Lacy, everyone felt like a turtle.

"Land in sight!"

The drum roll called the whole crew on deck. Matthew pretended to be grim, but his eyes sparkled with satisfaction. After a thirty-day voyage he had made it to Cape Leeuwin precisely by the mile. "From now on we'll explore unknown shores. The man in the lookout is vital. Reefs might be anywhere."

Matthew lowered his voice. "We'll also meet natives. I promise here before the mast that anyone who starts a quarrel with them won't get away with fewer than thirty-six lashes. We're explorers, not conquerors. Besides, the guns are below deck."

The gun master raised his eyes to the heavens and moved his chin back and forth as though something were rubbing his neck. Matthew went on: "One can also start quarrels by getting involved with their women. Don't let me catch anyone! Besides, Mr. Bell will now examine everyone for venereal disease. Orders from above. But that doesn't mean by a long shot that you may do what I forbade you to do. Anyone who steals nails or other means of payment will pull guard till he drops. Nobody will shoot without an order. Any questions?"

No questions. Bell could start his medical examination.

Matthew didn't introduce the Australians with much fervor, but he had sailed too long with Captain Bligh and had also heard too much about Cook's and de Marion's bad experiences to be careless.

Judging by the expression of the examining surgeon, John and Sherard concluded that they probably didn't suffer from a venereal disease. They were very glad about that.

First shore visit on Cape Leeuwin. The lieutenants remained on board and cleared a carronade to cover any flight of the boats back to the ship. At first Matthew started a search for a bottle that Captain Vancouver was supposed to have left here about ten years ago. "Was anything in it?" asked Sherard. They discovered an abandoned hut and a garden grown wild, a devastation. A copper sign hung in the fork of a tree. "August 1800. Christopher Dixson. Ship *Elligood.*" While they stuffed themselves with oysters, which grew profusely by the thousands along the cliffs, Matthew remarked, "This place seems to be a bit overcrowded. In ten years' time we're already the third ship. Never heard of Mr. Dixson."

In the gentle ruffled water of the bay, the *Investigator* lay like a completely strange ship, full of majesty. From a distance her planks looked watertight. The young painter William Westall was making a drawing of ship and bay, and, chewing, the captain looked over his shoulder. "But one can't see that she's got two anchors. I'd prefer to see both chains in the picture." That was Matthew! He wanted to be sure that all the work they'd been through could be seen.

When they started their land exploration, they suddenly heard loud clapping that sounded like applause. But it was only two black swans taking off from a pond. And there were no crabs climbing trees.

Then they saw the first native, an old man. He approached with uncertain steps, took not the slightest notice of the white men, but conducted a long conversation with invisible friends in the forest. When Mr. Thistle shot a bird, the old man didn't seem the least bit startled. He was surprised only briefly and continued his exchange. A little later ten brown men, naked like the old man, came toward them carrying long staffs. Matthew told his men to stand still, and he held out to the Australians a white handkerchief with the hunted bird on it. But perhaps just this kind of bird was a bad omen. The men turned unfriendly and began to wave them back toward the ship with fanning arm motions. They also didn't take the handkerchief. When they saw the *Investigator* lying there, they pointed at it again and again and said things in imperious tones. They couldn't be misunderstood. "It means, 'Go home,' " surmised Mr. Thistle. Matthew thought it possible they might want to visit the ship and made inviting gestures, whereupon the brown men signified that he should bring the ship to them. So dealing with the natives became somewhat troublesome. A missionary would have produced a cross and intoned prayers, and that might possibly have been better than a handkerchief and the wrong kind of dead bird. Women were nowhere to be seen. They were surely kept hidden. John thought of Mr. Dixson of the *Elligood*. One couldn't possibly know how he had behaved. The Australian men peered from under their thick brows with serious expressions, like masters of the house being introduced to somewhat dubious visitors. Their beards and hair stood on end, perhaps also a sign of suspicion, just as with Trim the tomcat. "They look as much alike as animals," Olof Kirkeby said to his twin brother after examining them closely.

The Australians at first talked a little among themselves, then more and more, and finally some of them began to laugh. Soon all of them did except for one; they talked and laughed. Matthew supposed that they had gained some confidence after all. Mr. Thistle opined that their present manner was their normal behavior, which had given way to fearful astonishment only briefly when they saw the white men. Sherard said, "They laugh because we're wearing clothes." John stared at them for the longest time before he said anything. His answer came when they all thought the question had been disposed of—so late, as usual, that only Matthew and Sherard were listening. "They know by now that we don't understand their language. That's why they deliberately talk nonsense and laugh about it." Matthew was taken aback and slapped his thigh. "Right!" he shouted, and said the whole thing once again, a little faster for the others. Now they all looked very closely: he was right! Then they all looked at John. Sherard spoke into the silence. "John's clever. I've known him for ten years."

Meanwhile, Mr. Westall had finished drawing his view of the bay. Every hill, every tree was drawn accurately; so was the ship with its anchor ropes, and the open sea. In the foreground stood a gigantic tree that didn't exist anywhere. Its branches framed everything, and in its shade a young native couple, beautiful to look at, were leaning against it, gazing at the ship with admiration. "I'll paint the girl more exactly once we've seen some women," remarked Mr. Westall. John sensed rising doubt but didn't know yet how to define it.

Something was wrong with the whole situation. John felt as though he should shout "Stop!" immediately, but he didn't know what to stop. Something was out of the ordinary about his own people. What was there in them that had been altered by the natives' presence? John now observed the Englishmen as closely as he had watched the Australians before.

The Kirkebys remained silent. They gaped incessantly at the savages and appeared dumb. But others walked over to the natives far too closely, gesticulating far too rapidly. Perhaps they wanted to soothe them, perhaps even only show them that they had new thoughts about the situation, but that did not moderate their obtrusiveness. They wanted to disconcert them, as they all had wanted to disconcert John before they knew him well. The sailors who put their heads together and laughed about the natives were especially embarrassing. "Greater respect, gentlemen!" said Matthew in a dangerously quiet voice. "No more jokes; not even good ones, Mr. Taylor!"

Suddenly John knew how it was: they all believed that the natives had not been taught sufficiently whom they were dealing with. The white men believed they were not given proper respect. They expected the error to be corrected.

When the Englishmen were back in the boats, John was too preoccupied with himself to continue watching the others closely. Then he heard Matthew's voice saying sharply, "I won't wait for long, Mr. Lacy!" It concerned a rifle that Denis had wanted to fire out of sheer high spirits.

John noticed that Matthew moved more quietly than usual, more sluggishly than anyone else at this stopover. Among the Australians there was also a man who behaved that way. He, too, sat quietly, laughed rarely, and noticed everything—his eyeballs were constantly in motion.

Then there was a shot. The brown men fell silent. Nobody had been hit. One of the marines had pulled the trigger of his weapon by mistake.

But why did this happen just as they were leaving? And why did it happen to a man who had been expertly trained in the use of a rifle?

After a few more days they met an entire tribe along another section of the coast. Now it included also women and children, who, however, were soon brought to safety. John could tell the Australians well apart, for he looked at them long enough. Not even Dr. Brown could do this equally well, though he was, after all, a scientist, who measured the natives from head to toe. He entered in his log: "King George Sound and environs. A. Men. Average samples—20; Height—5′7″. Thigh: 1′5″. Shinbone: 1′4″."

"What'll we do with those figures? Are we getting them clothes?" asked Sherard. "No, that's ethnography," answered the scientist. John had to write down the names of the body parts they had measured: *kaat*—head; *kobul*—belly; *maat*—leg; *waleka*—behind; *bbeb*—nipple. It was a barter: nails and rings in exchange for weights and words.

When Matthew discovered the words for fire and arm—and therefore the Australian name for rifle—he ordered drum rolls at the shore, causing both white men and natives to assemble, full of curiosity. He lifted a rifle high up in the air and shouted several times in Australian, "Fire! Arm!" Then he fired at a bailing scoop that he had ordered placed on a rock and hit it so well that it was swept into the water. He had the rifle loaded again and the bailing scoop put back in place. Now John had to fire. He didn't understand immediately—this was because he disagreed and didn't want to do it. For the first time in a long while he moved even more slowly than usual, but he couldn't help moving. He couldn't oppose Matthew.

It was a tin bailing scoop that made a lot of noise, and John was extremely slow. Matthew wanted to show the natives that even slow-moving Englishmen could produce sudden changes with a firearm. John had a steady hand and knew how to aim. He hit the tin. He didn't get applause, because Matthew had forbidden it. It was to appear like an everyday thing. The results were odd. The Australians laughed, perhaps in embarrassment. They never used the word "firearm"; they had a different word for a rifle. That birds and bailing scoops keeled over when hit they had seen for themselves. Perhaps they didn't know yet that it would be exactly the same for people. Anyway, the whites had now arrived at the view that their superiority would be acknowledged by the savages, and so they again had more respect for their captain.

Since he now had some time, John sat in the top of a tree for a long while observing both Englishmen and natives. He decided that the Australians, too, were now practicing ethnography. Each time a boat came over from the *Investigator* they eyed and touched the smooth-shaven whites in order to assure each other that even in the case of these newly arrived specimens, they weren't dealing with women.

During their entire trip along the coast, what John Franklin liked best was sitting in the top of the foremast. He could see and hear reefs in time, for he never did or thought about two things simultaneously. It took a little while until he would sound off about surf he had sighted, but it didn't matter if it was only a few seconds. It was only important that someone not become absent-minded out of boredom or even start dreaming. "It literally smells of sandbanks," said Matthew. "Have soundings taken, Mr. Fowler, and send Franklin to the foremast—nobody else!"

John himself knew how good he was in the lookout. He was contented to take his place. He thought, I'll be a captain who never goes under. A whole crew will stay afloat with me, whether seventy men or seven hundred. The different tinctures of the water, the scenery of the shore in the background, the endlessly straight horizon—his eyes could never feast long enough on them all. The navigation charts in front of him showed almost nothing but dotted lines or completely uncharted areas in the region of Terra Australis; at most he noted the words "Presumed coastline." John's fantasy added, Presumed city-to-be, Presumed harbor. Every mountain he saw would someday have a name; roads would surround it. Continuously he spied for what Matthew called "the crucial bay"—a bay that would perhaps lead to a wide passage across the Terra Australis. He, John Franklin, wanted to be the first person to see that passage, even if he had to pull guard on the foremast two or three times in succession. Matthew had said that, too.

The captain had the power to name everything. Every island, every cape, every inlet was therefore given one of the dear old names from Lincolnshire: Spilsby Island, Donington Point, and one fine day there was a Franklin Harbour in Spencer Gulf. John and Sherard at once imagined a city of Franklin that would grow there. Sherard sketched the outlines of the place and already knew now what would make the city rich: cattle and sheep breeding, slaughterhouses and wool mills. Sherard's special ship went to the South Pole every six months to pick up ice for the Lound Cold Store. "I freeze the meat and thaw it again when a famine breaks out." Sherard's favorite story was the Feeding of the Five Thousand, and he would supply technical explanations. John agreed. He also remembered the jellied pig's head. The entire world could be as beautiful as life on a ship if only everyone did something that benefited others, too.

"But one's got to be rich," Sherard assured him. "If you're not rich you can't help anyone. I'll bring my parents over. They'll learn to read and will go strolling all day long."

John sat in the foremast and petted Trim the tomcat. Lying adventurously aslant, Trim stretched to meet John's hand, hardly like the beast who had clawed him to get tidbits of roast. Born navigators couldn't be separated forever. For John, along with the rest of the crew, believed firmly that Trim had the brains of a sailor. A story was told about him that he could coil the end of a rope, even shorten a topsail. Also, he always looked at least half a mile beyond the horizon. Watching him carefully, one might even believe this. Spying through the slits of his pupils, he seemed to see a lot more than Matthew's bulldog eye, John's bird's eyes, or Mockridge's refined, complicated viewing gear. If Trim looked anywhere with interest, something was up. And it was so now.

Trim looked far into the distance, as though the sea would reveal itself there and the great vortex would appear on the horizon. John followed his gaze but saw nothing. Whatever he could ascertain made a calm, regular impression. The picture was almost too symmetrical: the ship's bow below him, the coast on the port side, and, stretching out far on the right, a calm ocean with gentle, distant cloud banks. But still there was something! A white rise above the sea perhaps twelve nautical miles ahead—the tip was barely recognizable even through the telescope, possibly a rock. John sang out what he saw. "Could also be an iceberg!" he called below. For a good quarter of an hour longer he stared motionlessly. Why did the object come up so fast when they were doing only three knots? "A ship!" shouted John, and stared through the telescope, open-mouthed. At once the deck below was crawling with people. A ship? Here? Matthew came aloft and convinced himself. Yes, it was a ship with square sails. Royal and topgallants were already quite visible; it certainly wasn't a craft manned by natives. "Clear ship for battle!" Matthew shouted, and collapsed the telescope. On deck there began a fearful scurrying back and forth, a slaving away like dogs with those damned guns, which had to be heaved into place and cleared of rust with iron scrapers. From above, it looked as though the smooth, well-rounded ship had suddenly burst into a thousand splinters with all the activity. Pulleys crowed, iron screeched, gun mounts thundered. Soon there would be real splinters. That surely was what John had seen in his dreams since the start of the voyage. Now death came and made it all true. Vacantly, John stared at the point on the horizon: with that point commenced all misfortune. Trim had long since gone below again and had crawled into Matthew's cabin, which the cats considered a safe place.

The drum roll began. Mr. Colpits was flushed red with all the responsibility, and he roared as loud as he could. He had just two hours' time if the wind held. Numbly, John heard the familiar music: Extinguish the fires; spread the sand, bring up the ammunition. It had again come to that.

An hour later he knew even more. The strange ship had two sails below the bowsprit, which John had heard about in stories: they were called the spritsail and the counter-spritsail, and they were used only on French warships. Soon he also saw also the French flag waving. On the *Investigator*, Taylor hoisted the Union Jack. The largest sails were furled into bulging balls of sailcloth to keep them from being shot to tatters—the French were known to aim for the tackling. The fuses were burning. Next to the helmsman already stood his replacement. But we have a pass, thought John. He tried to imagine Matthew's thoughts. They won't ask for a pass, he thought; they'll do away with our discoveries by sinking us. They'll name the land after their revolution; there'll be no Franklin Harbour! The relief man came up the mast. John made room for the sailor, then climbed down. Matthew fired up the crew: "We won't tolerate this! If they try anything we'll teach 'em a lesson!" Of course, it was rather obvious that the enemy ship was better armed than their own. Besides, they hardly needed to shoot at the *Investigator*. The ship already took in eight inches of water per hour on its own account.

John now knew precisely what he had felt at Copenhagen: fear, panic! This time he didn't want to be fearful, although he felt strongly urged that way. He wanted to do the most reasonable thing after precise observation and logical deliberation. Still half an hour—at most. Now they passed out the rum. Everything was prepared for a catastrophe. Whether they would survive it was another question.

John listened. Quite distinctly, he heard an order. Where it had come from was unclear, but it seemed to be a good order. John acted as fast as he could.

Sherard stood at one of the port-side guns and looked over to the French with awe. The beast had at least thirty guns. He turned to John, but he had disappeared. Yet—there he came from the back holding a folded white flag in his right hand. Sherard was confused. Taylor was the signal ensign. Somebody shouted: "Hey, Mr. Franklin, what the hell . . ." But John didn't turn. He seemed not to have heard. Leisurely, he tied up the flag and hoisted it—hand over hand—to the top. At that very moment, an explosion: a shell burst in front of the *Investigator*'s bow. In the other ship the guns had long since been readied; it looked depressing. Through all this noise, Sherard heard how the Second Lieutenant said something coldly to John Franklin's face. Taylor came up and hurried to get the white cloth down again. That, however, entailed some difficulties. Any knots John Franklin pulled tight no Taylor could untie.

Then from the quarter-deck sounded Matthew's voice: "Leave the rag up there, Mr. Taylor. What d'you think I'm giving orders for?"

Someone called from the foredeck: "Look at that!" On the French warship's mast rose a British flag high up and joined the Tricolor.

For one moment there was a deep silence. Something was still unclear to Sherard. Why John and not Taylor, why then had Taylor . . . But he couldn't think further. General jubilation broke out.

Le Géographe was a research ship equipped with a British pass. Both ships now lay alongside each other; there was hardly any doubt left of their peaceful intentions.

"*Fraternité!*" shouted the French. "Nice to meet you!" roared Mockridge over to the other deck. Someone started a song, clearly in a wrong key; then followed a thunderous song in an amazingly correct tone pattern. The French weren't at a loss for songs, either. The officers on both ships had trouble making themselves heard even to those standing next to them. Trim appeared on the quarter-deck, testing, blinking his eyes at the scene, then lifting his hind paw languorously and beginning to wash himself. Matthew ordered his boat readied. "The captain is leaving the ship, gentlemen!" The midshipmen hurried to the main shrouds and raised their hats. The boatswain blew his regulation whistle. The ritual came off just as it did at home in Spithead, and perhaps that was all to the good in a situation in which one still didn't know how long the peace would last. The *Investigator* was still clear for battle and had turned its broadside to the other ship. But perhaps this was done only to keep the gun master quiet.

"What was that awhile ago?" Sherard asked his friend, but he didn't know himself. Mockridge only remarked: "Mr. Franklin has good eyes. He can see many orders without hearing them— and even through thick walls."

The ships remained together for the night and half the next day. The captains talked exhaustively, the crews waved at each other. War in Europe, peace south of Terra Australis. For the first time since the beginning of history, two European ships of different nations met in this part of the world—and they did each other no harm. Mr. Westall said: "This was for the honor of mankind." John was silent, but Sherard was under the impression that he was secure and lighthearted as never before. He even seemed to understand more swiftly what was said to him. John surely must be in league with a great good power, and above all with Matthew. And he's my friend, too, thought Sherard.

Meanwhile, Trim slept on a tarpaulin and Mr. Colpits complained: "First all that slaving, then an eternity with the fuse in hand, and finally, like that cat up there, it's all gone to the dogs."

[8]

◆◆◆

THE LONG VOYAGE
HOME

I n the captain's cabin of the East India ship *Earl Camden*
stood Lieutenant Fowler of the Royal Navy and Captain
Dance of the East India Company.

"You'll have a great deal to tell me, Mr. Fowler," said
Dance. "But you must first get back to England. Whom do you
still have with you of the old *Investigator?*"

"The painter Westall will be on the *Earl Camden.* . . ."

"I know his older brother. He paints good pictures on Biblical
themes. I know one of them: *Esau Demands Isaac's Blessing.* All
right. Go on."

"John Franklin. Midshipman. Eighteen years old, more than
three years at sea."

"Good man?"

"No complaints, sir. The first impression he makes is, to tell
the truth, . . ."

"Well?"

"He's not exactly the quickest kind."

"Lead in his arse? Snail's pace?"

"Perhaps. But of a special kind. No complaints. Without him,
we may not have survived."

"How's that?"

"When the *Investigator* had to be finally scrapped, we left
Sydney and continued our voyage on the *Porpoise* and the *Cato.*

90

But two weeks later we ran aground on a reef. We saved ourselves in a single boat and reached a small sandbank with few provisions. The mainland was a good two hundred miles away."

"Most regrettable."

"When the captain took off in the boat for Sydney to get help, the first of the crew began to give up hope. The sandbank was no more than just a few feet above water level. Provisions were scarce. No one counted on the captain's possibly getting through. We waited for fifty-three days."

"And Franklin?"

"He never gave up hope. He's probably incapable of doing that. He seemed to get things organized to last for years. We elected him to the Sandbank Council."

"What does that mean?"

"We were close to mutiny. Franklin convinced the most desperate among them that there was time and that a slow mutiny was better than a quick one. The Sandbank Council was the government of all for all."

"Sounds very French. But perhaps appropriate for sandbanks. Now what special things did this Franklin accomplish?"

"Right from the start he began building a scaffold on which to store the provisions high above ground. When we were done with that after three days, a storm came and flooded the sandbank but not the scaffolding. Because Franklin is so slow, he never loses time."

"Good. I'll take a look at him. And you, Mr. Fowler? Could you perhaps train our gun crews? Peace is over again. We have to count on French capers."

"You'll let yourself be drawn into combat, sir?"

"Possibly. My squadron will consist of sixteen ships, and none of them unarmed. Well, then?"

Formally, Fowler was a passenger. But he gladly took this opportunity to get in a few licks at Napoleon Bonaparte. He agreed.

Since the *Earl Camden* was not due to leave for a few more days, John Franklin sat idly next to the painter William Westall in the harbor of Whampoa watching what was being loaded. Ships with a draft of more than eight feet were not permitted upstream to Canton. They were waiting for their cargo here in Whampoa: copper, tea, nutmeg, cinnamon, cotton, and more. Just now the port officer asked for a sample from a bag of spices. John had heard that a lot of opium was shipped here, too—many thousands of cases a year. People who smoked opium saw colorful images and didn't think of how things might be improved. But in this bag there was only agar-agar—sea algae pressed into the shape of rods to be used to jell the juice of English pig's heads to make head cheese.

John also knew now what homesickness meant.

In the warm spring sun, the wall they sat on smelled exactly like the gravestones at St. James's in Spilsby.

"I've been painting the wrong pictures. This won't do anymore! One has to paint differently," Westall said in a low voice, with a furrowed forehead. "All I've done is describe everything in exact detail—forms of the earth, plant growth, human figures, exactly as in nature—to be recognized."

"But that's good, isn't it?" John remarked.

"No, it's deceptive. We don't see the world as a botanist who is at the same time an architect, a physician, a geologist, and a ship's captain. Recognizing isn't at all like seeing; the two often don't even agree, and it's sometimes a less effective way of determining what is. A painter shouldn't know; he should only see."

"But then what does he paint?" John asked after extensive reflection. "He already knows a lot."

Westall replied: "His impression! What is strange, or at least what is strange within the familiar."

John Franklin, always looking on with a friendly and faintly surprised expression, was an ideal listener for relentless thinkers. Therefore he heard many phrases no one else wanted to hear. And he remained curious even when he hadn't understood. Thoughts strange to him filled him with respect. Naturally, he had become cautious. Ideas could go too far. Boatswain Douglas had announced shortly before his death that in infinity all parallel lines came together at a right angle. He had maintained this entirely without teeth and then died immediately—scurvy. John also recalled Burnaby, how he had talked about equality, smiling with wide-open eyes, yet at the same time often so confused. Caution could do no harm.

"From now on I'll ask all possible questions," said Westall. "Anyone who refuses to ask questions will do nothing right one day, not to mention painting." He started on it at once: "For example, we think we know what's permanent in this world and what's changeable. We know nothing! Only at our best moments do we have an inkling, a presentiment. And good pictures contain that presentiment."

John nodded and looked at the gigantic city built on water, a compound of junks and landing platforms. He listened within himself to see whether he had understood Westall's statement. Thousands of people moved and traded before his eyes—hungry as well as rich people. Everything John saw served trade: mat sails, parasols, walls with undulating ramparts, raftlike barges unloading, and the long poles used to punt them toward the larger ships. For days he had watched business life around him: grass mats being exchanged for copper coins, silk for gold, pieces of lacquered wood, or fragile things made of glass. What was truly significant was not immediately apparent. It's an element that is always present, an element not perceived the way a painter sees things but known by logical reflection: without patience no trade could be trade. Without patience, merchants were just robbers. Patience functioned like the escapement in a clockwork.

"I'd certainly like to know what's permanent," John told Westall, who had expected no answer and so had long since gone on talking. John felt related to the unchangeable, but it was difficult to grasp.

By now he had come to know so many different places; still, he had found no greater certainty among them. In fact, it was always questionable why the unchanging did not change. Why did the ostrich have feathers yet didn't fly? Why did the turtle wear a heavy armor, yet not a single fish did? Why did stallions grow no horns but roebucks did? "There's simply no certainty," insisted Westall.

Almost more disquieting was the dissimilarity among human races, especially since opposites clashed in each one of them. Australian people supported themselves on canes and gazed slowly, but they could also grab fish out of a stream with their bare hands as quick as lightning. The Chinese held their bodies upright with effortless tension; they appeared so proud. Yet if one spoke to them they made many bows one after the other. The French were solemn and enthusiastic and wanted to change everything, yet they used an infinite amount of time preparing and consuming their meals. They loathed English cooking even when they were on the point of starving. John had seen this himself in Sydney. As for the Portuguese, they always figured on the next earthquake and built their houses accordingly. But their churches were constantly rebuilt in the greatest splendor in just the places where they had collapsed. And the English! They were full of love for their country, yet liked to travel as far away from it as possible. Westall nodded.

"Nothing can be predicted. Nobody can give a reason why something happened in this way and not in another. Stronger than all predictions are coincidence and contradiction."

John admired the painter. He was only five years older than John yet had the strength to take up the challenge of things and to ask whether they really were as they appeared. For him, John, this wasn't the point at all. People who asked a lot of questions had to do it fast. Everyone tries to shake a questioner as quickly as possible. Moreover, John knew very well that one could not always agree with the answers. After an out-of-place answer one also had a sense of disquiet.

He would have liked to hear more about coincidences, especially about accidental death.

Denis Lacy was stretched out again before his inner eye. He had crashed down upon the deck from the topgallant, fifty feet up. Why did the quickest plunge down and not the slowest? Why did it happen after they had won through, and the remaining crew was on its way to Canton? John again saw the dreadful picture with precision. The entire city on the water could not cover it over. He saw the pool of blood Denis lay in with his smashed skull: bone splinters stuck through the cloth of his shirt like long spokes; his chest still heaved and sank; foam oozed out of his mouth and nose, then his heart stopped beating. To get away from this image, John recalled Stanley Kirkeby, how his backside was bitten by a seal on Kangaroo Island, quite painfully, to be sure. But even here, why did something like this happen, why didn't it fail to happen? Or the cargo officer being pitifully stung by a red jellyfish when he fell from the boat. The rash could be seen for weeks, and it had been the only jellyfish far and wide! Or the master sail-maker Thistle and Midshipman Taylor—eaten by sharks when their boat capsized in the surf—why only they, why not Mr. Colpits, for whom this would have been at least no surprise? But he was the sort who didn't get lost! On the contrary! He now sat in Sydney, administering a warehouse on order of the governor, and ate regularly and well.

"One should work out tables on how people live and die," said John. "A kind of geometry." He already knew how to do it. With constant measurements for all imaginable speeds. He involuntarily thought of the "time guardians" and of Matthew who was now on his way to England with those invaluable sea charts, with the mail, and with Trim the tomcat. He'd see Matthew again in Spilsby. Sherard, on the other hand, had stayed in Terra Australis in order to settle and perhaps build a harbor. Nothing could keep him from it.

Mockridge was dead. Three men had drowned when the *Cato* had been smashed on the cliff, only three, and one of them had to be Mockridge! One could accept that people were different and that one liked some and not others. But that chance did as it pleased in these things, that was bitter! John pulled himself together and returned to his conversation with Westall. "That stuff about precision and presentiment—I still have to think about it," he said. "I can't paint pictures. I want to become a captain. For that reason, I'd rather know as much as possible."

* * *

"And now let's hear what you've been through, Mr. Franklin," said Captain Dance. "Please give me a comprehensive report." John had expected that. Dance wanted to form a picture of him. As far as the voyage itself was concerned, he had undoubtedly heard it all from Lieutenant Fowler. John was prepared. He had considered what would be pertinent in his summary.

Every report had its external aspect, which hung together logically and was easy to grasp, and an internal one, which would light up only inside the speaker's head. What he had to suppress was that inner aspect, which would only have caused irksome stuttering and all kinds of mistakes in delivery. John therefore had to allow time for it without allowing it to affect the outer aspect. Only a few months ago he would have been inclined to repeat the last word of each passage for the sake of these inner pictures, before he would go on with his story. Now he knew how to make pauses. Cold-bloodedly, he risked that the other person might interrupt him and be offended if John didn't let himself be stopped.

He began with a well-rehearsed sentence. It contained the names of the ship and captain, the size of the crew, the number of guns aboard, the time and date of departure from Sheerness. From then on: key words, dates, positions, everything in as regular a sequence as possible. The information fixed in this way appeared generally valid as properly reported. Up to the encounter of the *Investigator* and the *Géographe*—Captain Nicholas Baudin, thirty-six guns—Dance had accepted his pauses patiently. At that point, however, he said: "Faster, Mr. Franklin. What's there to think about? You were there, weren't you?" For that, too, John was prepared.

"When I tell something, sir, I use my own rhythm."

Dance swung around and stared at him with astonishment. "I've heard something like this only once. From a Scottish church elder. Go on!"

John reported on their two-year voyage around Terra Australis—or Australia, as Matthew would call it for the sake of simplicity. He spoke of Port Jackson, of their stay at Kupang on

Timor, of the dreadful outbreak of just that disease which Matthew had sought to conquer. Numbers of losses. The ship almost sinking, kept above water only by the backbreaking pumping of the few healthy men left. What had happened, the dying, the pumping, the dread of falling ill—all that John packed into his pauses. Dance heard only numbers, geographical terms, and pauses. Port Jackson for the second time. The governor declared the ship no longer seaworthy, a wreck. For the voyage home via Singapore the crew was distributed among the ships *Porpoise, Cato,* and *Bridgewater.* Those who wanted to remain in the colony in order to settle there would receive permission. Long pause for Sherard Lound. A quarrel had not been in question—Sherard simply had his own dreams. "This pause is becoming too long," Dance reminded him sternly. He feared the young man would be even more halting when they got to the first shipwreck: *Porpoise* and *Cato* at the same time in the middle of the night. No help at all from the *Bridgewater,* sailing in the immediate vicinity. Captain Palmer! East India man like Dance himself. He knew him from the early days. A miserable whist player; now, too, a sailor who neglected his duty. Ugh! Dance noticed, with amazement, that he had raced ahead of John's report and had therefore not been able to follow him. While he had exercised himself about Palmer, the midshipman had clearly overtaken him, and despite a long pause for the shipwreck, the noise of bursting planks, the screams of the helpless, the bleeding cuts from coral, and the dead Mockridge, Franklin was already on the sandbank with the provisions they had managed to save. Hunger and waiting. An officer shoots two men to death in self-defense. Fowler hadn't reported that at all. Franklin didn't say a word about the mutiny. He talked around it. The proposal to build rafts from the remaining wood and to paddle west was discarded. He talked more extensively about Flinders, their captain: "He sailed a good nine hundred miles in an open boat back to Port Jackson in order to return with three ships and save his crew. Matthew Flinders—an extraordinary navigator!" The midshipman concluded with a single sentence: "The people on the sandbank went on to Canton in the *Rolla;* only the captain"—here a small pause for Trim—"went directly to England on the schooner *Cumberland.*"

"Let's hope he gets there," said Dance. "We're at war again."

John understood and was fearful. "But he's got a pass," he said.

"Only for the *Investigator.*" The captain's finger drew as many lines on the table of his cabin as there are furrows on a forehead. Then he came to the point: "You're our passenger, Mr. Franklin, but I hear you're a competent signal man. . . . Are you listening, Mr. Franklin?"

John was troubled. He thought of Matthew. Painfully, he turned back to Dance: "Aye aye, sir."

"The *Earl Camden* is the flagship for a squadron of East India men. I'm the commodore. And herewith you're signal ensign."

Commodore Nathaniel Dance was sixty years old, tall, haggard, with a large nose and tangled gray hair. His words, if he didn't explicate Bible passages or talk about intellectual matters, were deliberate and clearly understandable. Each movement emerged from the previous one without strain. His eyes could sparkle mischievously, as happens often with good-natured people. He acted as though he were impatient, yet he listened nonetheless. Sometimes he said something rude, like, "Thank you. I'm beginning to be bored."

He quarreled with the painter Westall even at table. He believed that art must be beautiful. But it can be so only with the help of precise details. Creation is more beautiful than anything man can imagine. Westall responded cleverly that man was the crown of creation and the spirit within him the highest. What is beautiful is not the physical construction of things but what eye and mind made of it. Part of that were premonitions, fear and hope. After table, Westall grumbled: "The painter Nathaniel Dance is his uncle. For that reason this tar thinks he knows a lot about painting."

The next day the quarrel started up again. The commodore seemed to like nothing better than to throw the artist into confusion. "Painting fear or the arbitrariness of eyesight? Why not just blindness? I have sixty years of fear and arbitrariness behind me! No, Mr. Westall; man must rise above his weakness through God's mercy. Your brother knows that. Think of *Esau Demands Isaac's Blessing*—now that's a picture! Art must be edifying!"

The *Earl Camden* left Whampoa at the head of a squadron of fifteen heavily loaded East India ships. The ships' armaments were weak and they weren't as solidly built as warships; above all, they were more weakly manned. No marines on board. The tackle was made of untarred manila hemp and seemed easy to handle. But after a few days John noticed that this was so not just because of the hemp but also because of the crew. The dark-skinned lascars were superbly trained, quick-witted, and hard working. A few sailors' wives were on board, too, dark-skinned as well as white. No one thought anything of it. An India boat was not a floating combat station. The hull was painted with black and yellow stripes to deceive pirates, but inside it was a peaceful ship. Working day and night, John soon taught himself to remember the entire squadron precisely. He knew the lascars by name, just as he knew the officers. Again and again he wondered what made a good captain and whether this would be true of Dance.

Who in this world should rule over all others?

It would, in any case, be true of people like Matthew. There were reasons for this. For example, after the shipwreck he stayed on the sandbank as long as necessary to fix one star in a clear sky and so establish his position. He had to wait three full days and for the storm to pass. John knew many people who would have left long before. They would never have reached Port Jackson, not to mention a return. Perhaps Matthew was slow, too, before he had made it to captain? If Mockridge had been correct, Matthew had become a midshipman only because the housekeeper of a battleship commander had interceded for him. And if Matthew hadn't had friends in the Admiralty, above all a man named Banks, he would have been relieved of his command when his wife was discovered on the *Investigator,* or at the latest when they ran aground in the Channel.

Whether a man could sail around a continent in a rotting ship with a deathly sick crew and still make reliable maps—that sort of thing was not decided beforehand by admirals on shore. If a man was slow he could accomplish a great deal, but he had to have good friends.

Anything the commodore wanted to tell his flotilla passed through John's hands, and whatever came back his eyes read first. Meanwhile, he knew cold all the flags and their combinations. When he looked he could do so with automatic "blindness"—it was possible to do that with flags. Sometimes Old Man Dance watched him. His glance seemed approving. He said nothing.

John had made a list of his own aims: To reach every port by means of his nautical skill. To prevent mishaps—for example, to avoid drifting toward shore in a storm. Never to have to be ashamed, like Captain Palmer of the *Bridgewater.* And not to be guilty of producing bad results, not to cause the death of others. The list was not all that long.

The squadron passed through the South China Sea and was approaching the Anamba Islands. "I hope nothing happens," Westall said all of a sudden, and didn't take the trouble to elaborate.

"Sails in sight!"

Their fears were confirmed: French warships. "They've been lying in wait for us," muttered Lieutenant Fowler. "If I were in command here I'd use every shred of the cloth and draw out our formation in three directions." "It would be our only chance," remarked another. "Those fellows have seventy-four guns apiece; they'll put us in their pipes and smoke us. We ought to have been ahead of the wind long ago." And one of the younger men said, "The old man is too slow."

Who should rule in this world? Which third man among three should tell the other two what to do? Who saw most? Who was a good captain?

Just then Nathaniel Dance clambered up the mainmast to survey the situation from the proper height. But who checked whether an aging commander still had the sure eye or whether he had lost it? Now he was finally at the top, painstakingly adjusted the sights of his telescope, peered into the distance, and blew his nose. Then he climbed down again, not a bit faster than before. He didn't have to call the officers together. They and the crew were already standing there.

"Gentlemen," said the old man as, unabashed, he swung his left leg back and forth: it had gone to sleep in the lookout. "There are five Frenchmen out there; they're up to something. But they didn't calculate correctly. Mr. Sturman, please be so good as to make the ship ready for combat. Mr. Franklin?"

"Sir?" That had become automatic. When John heard his surname, he supplemented it at once with "Sir" without further thought. So his answer was no slower in coming than that of all the others.

"Set the signal: squadron clear for combat. Close ranks on line. Heave to!"

Uncertain cheers sounded. At bottom they were all very depressed. At first the flags John raised brought only queries in return. The entire flotilla was stunned with disbelief. Finally something like a battle line developed after all. But then an astounding event occurred. The warships heaved to also. Their hulls could not yet be recognized from the top. "Ours can't be either," Fowler said, on the gun deck, giggling. "They won't dare do a thing before tomorrow."

The sun set behind the island of Pulau Aur, whose tip could just be made out. The wide-bellied merchantmen were lying there in their grim black-and-yellow garments, as though they were heavily armed ships of the line. They were sheep in wolves' clothing. The French wouldn't allow themselves to be bluffed for long! During the night everyone expected the command to set sail, but it didn't come. Dance actually wanted to remain where he was. Nobody slept. A few said hoarsely, "Why not fight? We'll show 'em!" Some felt an inkling of courage rising to the surface of their consciousness, but those whom it didn't seize hoped at least that the French would pull out on their own to escape from an assumed superior English force.

There were no signals to be set in the dark. John had time to occupy himself with his doubts. Decisiveness and self-confidence were not easy to come by today. He could not rely on the fact that he always did the right thing. There had been that white flag on the *Investigator* long ago. Quite distinctly he had heard an order that had perhaps never been given. If so, he would have had to face a possible court-martial under any other captain.

On the other hand, Nelson! He had simply ignored the order of the highest admiral to retreat before Copenhagen—no court-martial! But even Nelson had been protected by his success after the fact. Only those could maintain certainty who were themselves of great permanence—like the stars, the mountains, and the sea. And they in turn possessed no words with which to tell what they had come to know from their long existence. On this score, John discovered, there was more freedom than one could wish. One could, of course, do the right thing, but it was always possible that all the others thought it wrong. They could even be right.

Day broke. The sails on the horizon were still there and did not stir. The French continued to heave to, lying motionlessly in the wind. The commodore let his ships sail on in the old direction to force the enemy into a decision. It didn't take long for the French sails to multiply and grow tall. Now John was very busy. Dance changed course again and sent the fleet directly toward the enemy.

To his annoyance, John noticed that he was trembling. And because he noticed it, his fear worsened. That the battle of Copenhagen would repeat itself he considered not probable, but that was of little help. He therefore tried to imagine that all this would be over sometime. Pulau Aur lay to the west. He thought how after the battle the survivors would flee to this island, English as well as French. Would they share their food and make decisions together? Or would they kill each other?

Even this thought already contained his fear. He resolved to think of completely different things that were useful and kind. He ticked them off. "Food, water, tools, bandages, ammunition . . ." Things that had to go into the lifeboats in case of shipwreck. If he couldn't conquer his fear, at least he could get rid of that miserable trembling.

Why didn't Dance flee during the night? That risk would have been smaller. He couldn't possibly dare take a chance on being boarded.

John felt weak, but he observed, decoded, reported, confirmed everything correctly. When signals came, they set his mind into motion outside himself. If none came, he continued his list: "Telescope, sextant, compass, chronometer, paper, plumbline, fishing rod, kettle, needle . . ." The list was long enough for his fear. Among the few things not to be saved from a sinking ship under any circumstances was the "holy stone."

The trembling actually got worse.

"Spars, sailcloth, twine, flags . . ."

The warships came on fast.

"Signals," John murmured. "Dear God, if possible, just signals this time."

On the *Earl Camden* one of the first French shells hit the helmsman. Dance looked toward the waiting replacement and pointed his chin in his direction. With this gesture he bent his head slightly so that his forehead pointed to the helm and his chin to the man. He could also have said: "You! Take over!" But the place at the helm was awash with blood, so he preferred to talk with his chin and forehead. Then he pulled out his watch and studied it carefully, as if the precise moment in time were the most important aspect of James Medlicott's death.

John's trembling became more violent. He wondered how he could hide it. No one could hold on to his own face, his own body. He bent down, grabbed the dead man by his back and knees, and lifted him up the way one would lift women and children. Mockridge had once told of an accident involving a nine-year-old boy in Newcastle who, in his fatigue, had plunged one evening into a running machine. The story had frightened John very much. He had often imagined how he would have carried the wounded child away if he had been there.

"But the man is dead!" one of the lascars shouted. John gave no answer. He carried the corpse carefully, bumped into no obstacle. Of course, what he did was nonsense. But he finished it now, especially since it covered up his trembling. The guns roared; the ship jerked and buckled. John laid down the dead man alongside the wounded and walked away as fast as he could. The surgeon would determine that there was nothing that could be done. John climbed up again. He firmly believed that it was not cowardice that had made him do this. Rather, it was a kind of disapproval. Yes, that's what it had been. But it had not been unworthy. John's breath became quieter, his fear abated. Above, the French boarding attack would come soon. John refused to acknowledge it, exactly as he did everything else in that situation. There was nothing but defiance within him. He said, "I cannot condone this. I will not fight."

He wanted to see, to wait like a mountain, dead or alive. For war, all of them were too slow, not just John Franklin.

John climbed the last stair to the deck in deep calm. There was hardly a more resolute person on this ship; that much was sure.

But the test did not materialize.

Everything turned out differently.

After three-quarters of an hour John had to send another signal: general pursuit of the enemy for up to two hours. The French had enough and decamped. They were chased by six-teen British merchantmen with a well-stocked cargo of Japanese copper, saltpeter, agar-agar, and tea in their bellies. Five men-of-war, bristling with guns and ammunition and with a battalion of marines standing ready with fixed bayonets, had taken a powder.

At one point, John noticed that all around him everyone was laughing like mad because at that moment the world could not have been crazier and brighter and because someone on the foredeck had shouted, "I think they didn't want to get us!" John also perceived that he had long since joined their laughter, that it didn't end his defiance but rather, on the contrary, his defiance actually expressed itself in this laughter.

From the quarter-deck the commodore shouted: "Mr. Westall! Have you made a few sketches?" The painter replied: "Unfortunately not, sir. I was a bit surprised by the way this exercise went off." Now the word "exercise" made the rounds, and the laughter continued.

Nathaniel Dance had put all his cards on this victory. Now he was a hero. They all were heroes.

The commodore invited his officers and captains to the flagship to celebrate the "Victory of Pulau Aur." He raised his glass: "We were successful only because God looked upon us with favor and because we didn't act precipitously. Scrutinize three times; act once. Young people don't always grasp this. Being slow and faultless is better than being quick and final. Isn't that so, Mr. Franklin?"

Now they all looked at John, probably because they expected him to say joyfully "Aye aye, sir," as he was supposed to. But he only looked at the commodore and trembled slightly. That was really unusual! They were all astonished. But he was just busy preparing a sentence he wanted to say. To avoid trying their patience, he began his introduction: "Sir, I disapprove . . ." and considered some more how he should go on. Everyone was suddenly very still. So he might as well attack the most important sentence at once: "The war, sir, is too slow for us all."

Amid the rising raucous laughter, he feverishly compared once more what he had said with what he had wanted to say. But that no longer helped, especially since Fowler slapped him on the shoulder, shaking up everything all over again.

Only the commodore had perhaps understood, or had wanted to understand. "Neither too slow nor too fast," he said seriously. "My times are in thy hand. Deliver me from the hand of mine enemies and from them that persecute me." Then he added: "Now even Mr. Franklin is talking in sentences rather than in pauses. We'll still get a lot out of him. Today's a good day."

Although none of those present could make head or tail out of that, they all laughed as though responding to a successful joke, for that was the way to behave toward a victorious elderly gentleman.

Soon everyone on the *Earl Camden* knew that John had meant it differently. He went to Dance and all the others and corrected his sentence. To Westall he said: "I wished I were always courageous right on the spot, but whatever I do must also be correct. Everything I do comes hard, even courage."

Westall winked: "But you give a good picture of it."

Ceylon lay behind them. They passed Cape Comarin. John looked out to sea while the painter sketched him. Westall's tongue licked his lower lip incessantly, for he couldn't draw in any other way. John started to talk again.

"Mr. Westall, I must tell you something, too. I find precision still better than presentiment."

Westall measured the distance between John's eyes with his raised thumb and the beginning of his ears with the side of his left hand. "This picture will be exact," he said.

John was very content. He was quiet and sat without moving. If Mr. Westall was going to paint him in the good old way, then he had to take care not to disturb the picture by stirring.

In the roadstead in Bombay they saw the monsoon coming up. William Westall left the ship. He said: "I want to stay here and paint India. I'll start with the monsoon. My brother's most beautiful picture is called *Cassandra Prophesies the Destruction of Troy*. My picture will be called *The Coming of the Monsoon*. And it will express the same thing—only better." John didn't understand a word, and he was sad, because this dear, crazy man was now gone, too.

Portsmouth! Fortifications and docks looked as they always had. The entire city appeared as though he had seen it only yesterday. No one here was moved even to set down his glass upon hearing that one John Franklin had come back after three years. Portsmouth bubbled with young men and women, with noise, toil, and initiative. The city was preoccupied with itself. If old people lived here, it was only because of this spirit, not in spite of it. Nobody raised roses here; nobody preached or listened to a sermon. One lived fast because life could end so fast. They worked hard in the docks, even at night, by the light of oil lamps. It was a hungry, fast city, and in that it always remained the same.

John found out that an unsuspecting Matthew had been caught by the French in Mauritius and had been arrested as an alleged spy. He had assumed that the peace was still in effect and had therefore anchored in French Mauritius although his pass had been valid only for the late *Investigator.* One hoped they would allow him to keep those sea charts that had cost him so much effort, and would send him home soon.

Mary Rose was still there.

She lived as before on Keppel Row, only two houses farther down. On top of the fire hung the big water kettle in a small, well-built rack; with it she could brew tea without taking the water off the fire. Altogether, she seemed to be well.

She said: "You talk faster than you did three years ago."

"I've got my own rhythm now," replied John, "but I'm also more disapproving than I used to be; that speeds things up."

Mary's face had more wrinkles around those arched lines. John looked at her breathing body. In her armpits, fine, delicate little hairs shimmered in the light. That down had the strongest effect; it did much for John. Big things were set in motion. "I feel like a sine curve; everything is constantly rising." Soon he forgot geometry and realized instead that much can be made good in this world and that two human beings are enough to make it work. He saw a sun filling up the sky, which paradoxically was at the same time the sea and warmed him from below instead of from above. Perhaps the present is like that when once in a while it doesn't run away, thought John.

He heard Mary's voice: "With you it's different," she said.

"Most of them are too fast. When it gets to the point, it's already over."

"That's exactly what I've been thinking for some time," John answered, and he was happy because Mary made him feel well understood. He observed her shoulder blade, how the white skin was stretched taut over the arched bone. Most delicate was the skin on her collarbones—that did it to him again, promising a new present and a new sun from below.

Mary showed John that there is a language of touching and feeling. One could speak in it and answer in it. Any confusion was out of bounds. He learned a great deal that evening. Toward the end, he wanted to stay with Mary for good. She said: "You're crazy."

They talked deep into the night. It was hard to talk John out of anything. If other suitors were waiting outside, they had long since gone away, disgruntled.

"I'm so glad that I can now do everything with my body," John murmured. Mary Rose was touched. "From now on you needn't travel around the world for three years for something like that."

In front of the White Hart Inn stood old Ayscough, eighty years old, sixty-five of them spent as a soldier in Europe and America. Every day he was there when the post coach came, closely inspecting everyone who got off and asking where they were from.

He recognized young Franklin by the way he moved. He held the midshipman's hand with a steady grip, for he wanted to be the first to hear everything. "Well," he said at last. *"You already have a ship again,* and a *big one.* You'll soon be in combat again to defend England."

Then John went off in the direction of his parents' house. The sun was climbing through the fruit trees. He had yearned to be away from here for as long as he could remember. But while his hopes had been directed toward faraway distances, he had actually looked at these chimneys, at the Market Cross, and at the tree in front of the Town Hall. Perhaps homesickness was only the desire to recapture that early hope. He wanted to think about that and put down his luggage next to the Market Cross.

Yet now he had a present hope, a fresh hope. And it was better founded than the earlier one. How, then, did this homesickness come about?

Perhaps he had loved all these things here at a time he couldn't remember. But now the strange distances were here. It seemed to him that even the spring air on the wall in Whampoa had smelled more intimate than these steps leading up to the Market Cross. Still, there remained a suggestion of love.

"Yes, homecoming," sounded the voice of old Ayscough, who had followed him. "When it happens, all one can do is sit down." Midshipman Franklin got up, brushed the dust off his trousers. He wondered whether love of one's country was more of a duty or rather something one was born into. This, of course, was not the sort of thing one could ask an old soldier.

The house in the narrow passage now belonged to a strange fat man who always said "ha—hm" as a greeting, an explanation, a farewell.

His parents lived in a smaller house. Mother's eyes sparkled gaily, and she called out John's name. It was quiet, for Father said little. He seemed sad, and John felt pity. Was there no money anymore? Father used to have means. John preferred not to ask. He had heard, after all, that the good times were over. About Thomas, Father said only brusquely that he now commanded a volunteer regiment. They would punish Napoleon if he allowed himself to be seen in these parts.

Grandfather had meanwhile become stone deaf. To anyone who talked at length he gave a long look saying: "You don't have to shout! I don't understand you anyway. Anything important I notice on my own. Nobody needs to tell me."

Walking toward Ann's house, John tried to recall Mary's face. But he couldn't get it together, and this made him wonder. Did one forget the outside of a person if one loved her? Perhaps one did, just for that reason.

Ann Flinders née Chapell had become a bit more rotund. She

was pleased to see John. She had heard about Matthew's misfortune some time ago. "First the admirals, then the French—and he hasn't done anybody any harm!" She was sad, but she did not cry. She wanted to hear all about the voyage. At last she said only, "The French will have to atone for all that."

Then he visited Sherard's parents, the Lounds.

Since getting Sherard's letter from Sheerness, they had heard nothing more from him. The letter Matthew had taken along had surely been confiscated. And he hadn't written a line from Port Jackson. John thought of the part of the world where his friend had decided to establish himself—beyond the blue mountains, where all rivers flowed toward the west and where convicts from Botany Bay were making their way if they were able to break out.

"He's in a green land where there's lots of fine weather," said John, "but the postal service is poor there."

Conditions in Ing Ming had worsened. More people, less food. The Lounds still owned their cow, but the common meadow had become much too small for the cattle of the poor. "The big folks simply shift the fences. And the meadow has been grazed over so much that not a single blade of grass dares to peek out." Father Lound was a thresher. One and a half shillings per day during harvest time. His wife might have spun flax, if the spinning wheel had not long since joined the tea kettle at the pawnbroker's. He was the man who always said "ha—hm" to everything.

"Our younger ones are still all at home," said Father Lound. "The wages are much higher in the marshlands. Or we can also go to the spinning mill. There the children can earn, too, even in the winter. Perhaps things will be better after we win the war."

They showed him Sherard's last letter. He read about himself: "At night he dreams of the dead."

The village seemed deserted. Tom Barker had become an apothecary apprentice in London. Others were serving in the army; many had gone away. In the church stood Peregrin Bertie, Lord of Willoughby, surveying an assembly of empty pews.

The shepherd was still around, the slugabed and rebel. He stood at the bar of the White Hart Inn and didn't allow anything to pass unscathed. "Getting around in the world? For that I don't need a ship," he said. "The earth turns of its own, you know."

John took this in patiently. "But you turn along with it," he answered. "So you'll always stay where you are."

The shepherd giggled. "Well, just lift your feet."

Then they talked about the common meadow. "Do you know what a miracle it is? A meadow that grows smaller and smaller the more mouths feed on it."

"I don't believe in miracles," remarked John. "That's for children."

The shepherd drank up and became rebellious again. "Wrong! In economics, surprise begins only when you start thinking. But you've become a hero, haven't you! Do you at least send some money home?"

[9]

◆◆

TRAFALGAR

D r. Orme looked at John thunderstruck without saying a word. Then he got up and was very pleased. "John!" he exclaimed, and his eyelashes seemed to fan air toward his brain. "I've been waiting for you! But I hardly had any hope."

John himself wondered about the sober way in which he now regarded his old teacher. I mean something to him, he thought. That suits me; I think I like him, too.

They sat down at the garden table behind the house on Breakneck Lane. A pause ensued, for they didn't quite know how to start. Dr. Orme told "a little story to loosen up." He was simply always a teacher.

"Achilles, the fastest runner in the world, was so slow that he couldn't overtake a tortoise." He waited until John had fully grasped the madness of this assertion. "Achilles gave the tortoise a head start. They started at the same time. Then he ran to where the tortoise had been, but it had already reached a new point. When he ran to the next point the tortoise had crawled on again. And so it went, innumerable times. The distance between them lessened, but he never caught up with the tortoise." John squeezed his eyes shut and considered this. Tortoise? he thought, and looked at the ground. He observed Dr. Orme's shoes. Achilles? That was something made up. The teacher had to laugh. One of his small, crooked incisors was now missing.

"Let's go in," he said. "Meanwhile, I've made some progress with my investigations of nature." Inside he unlocked the door to a small room.

Now John grabbed his arm: "The story of that race—only the tortoise could have told it!"

Inside the little room stood a small, carefully constructed apparatus, a disc that rotated around a perpendicular axle when one turned a crank. On each side, front and back, a picture had been painted—a man on the left side of the front, a woman on the right side of the back. When the crank was turned, they appeared alternately. "I know this from a fair," John said, "on Jubilate Sunday six years ago."

"The wheelwright built the crank for me," explained Dr. Orme, "and the watchmaker did the counter. When you turn the crank rapidly, Harlequin and Columbine are united and become a couple." He looked in a little notebook and read out to him: " 'My own eyes are deceived already after 710 rotations. For the deacon Sexton Reed, this occurred after 780; 630 for Sir Joseph, the High Sheriff; 440 for my laziest Latin pupil; and for my quick housekeeper, 830 rotations.' " John saw a little hourglass attached to the lever of the counter. "In how much time?" "Within sixty seconds. Please sit down. I'll turn the disc faster and faster, until you can see the little couple clearly. Then I'll hold the speed and reverse the hourglass, and with that I'll switch on the counter."

Carefully the teacher began to crank. He looked at John eagerly. The mechanism began to burr, the tone became lighter and lighter. "Now," said John. The tiny cogs began to turn. With each turn the cog counting single units activated the cog counting tens by means of a nodule, and that cog similarly activated the cog counting hundreds. When the last grains of sand had dropped, Dr. Orme reversed the hourglass again, and the counter stood still. Solemnly he said: "Three hundred and thirty! You're the slowest." John was pleased. His uniqueness was assured.

"This indicates a very important difference among people," said Dr. Orme. "This discovery will bring great benefits."

In the afternoon Dr. Orme went across to the school building to teach. John didn't come along. He was afraid he might have to tell the pupils about his adventures. What moved him personally they wouldn't have understood, and he didn't want to tell anyone simply what he knew they wanted to hear. He preferred to go to his old tree. But even the tree had become a stranger to him. Now he no longer needed a tree; he had ships' masts. He stopped and stood beneath it, looked up one more time, and went on. He wandered through the town and pondered man's speeds. If it was true that some people were slow by nature, this should remain so. It was probably not given to them to be like others.

He sat down happily at Dr. Orme's supper table. The world should stay as it was! Now there should have been head cheese! But how could the quick housekeeper divine that?

John wanted to ask Dr. Orme whether there would be no more wars in the future. So far it didn't look like it. But perhaps there might be eternal peace after the victory over Napoleon? John kept on postponing the question; he didn't know why.

Dr. Orme mentioned other gadgets that he planned to have built. "I can't tell you anything more specific yet. It's got to be thought through some more." In passing, he reported on an Irish bishop, the Bishop of Cloyne, who had established a theory of perception: "He thought of the whole world, with all its people, things, and motions, as an appearance only. It was therefore a story which God told to minds by means of artificial sense impressions—perhaps only to one mind, that of the Bishop of Cloyne. In the end there was only his mind, his eyes and nerves, and the images God sent him."

"Why should He do that?" asked John.

"The meaning of creation is not known to man," answered the teacher. "Besides, a good story doesn't need a purpose."

"If He can create illusions of everything," John mused, "why is He so stingy with miracles?"

That question was more than Dr. Orme could answer. He told

John what interested him in this problem: If the Bishop was right, with what sort of apparatus did God infuse the human mind with such pictures? "Of course, this is only a working hypothesis," he said. "God's ways are inscrutable."

An uneasiness still kept John from asking about peace. He loved Dr. Orme as a person who didn't fall back on God when he had to explain something. John wanted it to stay that way.

Dr. Orme himself brought up the subject. Mankind will learn, he suggested. It learns a little more slowly than He had assumed. "That's because the most competent among them will always try to change that small part of the world which they know. One of these days they'll discover the world instead of improving it, and not forget what they already discovered."

Lengthy phrases about the world were not to John's liking, but he found it quite in order when clever people like Dr. Orme or Westall came to formulate them in conversation.

He hoped Dr. Orme would write this down.

"Something occurs to me about forgetting," said John. "I fell in love with a woman and slept with her, but even now her face escapes me completely."

There followed a brief interruption, because Dr. Orme had inadvertently placed his cup on the edge of the saucer.

No time left for Mary Rose. John was ordered to report to the *Bellerophon,* lying in the Thames estuary far away from Portsmouth. On the boat to Sheerness he talked to a lieutenant wearing the insignia of a commander—a haggard man with dark eyes and a long pointed nose. It looked as if a second nose had been planted on top of the normal one as a kind of extension. The lieutenant's name was Lapenotière and he talked extraordinarily fast. He commanded the schooner *Pickle,* one of the smallest ships in the navy, mostly deployed in spy missions along the French coast. The crew of the *Pickle* reconnoitered fortifications and caught boats on patrol. The commander was famous for his skill in interrogating prisoners. "As a Frenchman, you have a great deal to offer," said another officer.

"I'm English," Lapenotière countered aggressively. "I fight for the good passions of man against the bad passions."

"What are the good passions?" the other officer asked.

"Faith and love."

"And the bad ones?" asked John.

"The same freedom for everyone, megalomania of logic, and—Bonaparte."

"That's true, by the deuce! God bless you!" shouted the officer, leaping up and bumping his head against the deck plank.

John found this excessive. He disapproved.

The French should stay out of England. That was all.

Judging by the crew, the *Bellerophon* was an Irish, not an English, vessel. With its seventy-four guns it had produced noise and death in many battles—a celebrated ship. Why so many of its sailors were Irish nobody knew. Among seamen the ship was known as the "ruffian" or "brute." In the year 1786 she had been recalcitrant enough to launch herself on her own before the official date, her emergency baptism being conferred with half a bottle of port. The *Bellerophon* was exactly John's age to the year. Matthew, too, had served on it as a midshipman. Its figurehead was a devil baring his teeth. Surely it was again a Greek, like that one-eyed figure on the prow of the *Polyphemus*, which had also been without arms.

This was truly a different ship from the *Investigator*! Thick wood everywhere, heavy tackling, wide passages, countless men, soldiers in red coats, and even some in blue who had to do with field guns. Blue as well as red soldiers drilled on deck daily, those poor fellows. Pitying them, as well as feeling sôme contempt, the crew watched as they marched in cadence, responding rhythmically to commands like "Load and Lock Safety!" and "Right Turn!" and "About Turn!" Only the Australian natives had really been able to find pleasure in drums and marching. In the end, they had drilled along with the English, using their canes and soon making a dance out of those many turns and abrupt movements. John resolved to observe mankind. If mankind had learned anything, it should have something to show for it.

There was hardly anyone in the crew and among the common soldiers who had not been pressed into service with alcohol and beating. A few women were on board who were there voluntarily, or forced by their men. They lived below deck, wore trousers, and looked like any other sailor. Nobody talked about it, and something one didn't talk about didn't exist. On an Irish vessel that was disguised as an English ship, this could surprise no one.

Where were they going? To Brest, they said. Harbor blockade —an interminable job. Everyone was in a bad mood, not to speak of those who had been pressed into service. The midshipmen's mess was located way down on the orlop deck, below the water line. On the table were cigars, grog, cake, cheese, pipes, knives and forks, a flute, hymnbooks, teacups, the remains of a pork roast, and a slate. All around it: boredom and scuffles out of boredom; also the sayings of nineteen-year-old Bant, who thought he knew everything: "Women around thirty are the best!" He used to proclaim such things. He came from a village near Davenport where they were surely happy that he had decided to join the navy. "Those of around thirty know their stuff. They've got everything twenty-year-olds have, too, but you don't waste your time. Those of around forty are better still." Walford, the oldest member of the mess, blew smoke into the air. "Shut your mouth!" And after a while: "Somebody has told you this tale; probably a seventy-year-old." Bant became furious, but before he could say or do anything he was rapped across the fingers with the flute, so that he sat paralyzed with pain. So fast was Walford! Besides, the older man was always right. That was one of the principles they were to defend against Napoleon.

John's misery began with the others' boredom. If one hadn't learned to be cruel, one at least had to know how to be insolent. During the early weeks hardly anyone respected John. But he didn't lose his self-confidence. He knew the situation would change. One person now and then asked for his advice: Simmonds, the youngest, who had come directly from home.

Sometimes John thought of the future. What would a man like himself do when the war was over? A midshipman without a ship didn't even get half pay. Settle in Australia with Sherard? But where should he look for him? John was one of the older men by now. Simmonds was fourteen; Henry Walker, sixteen years old.

Cruising before Brest throughout the entire autumn and winter. A person like John could bear that. He learned the new signal codes and read all the books he could lay his hands on.

The war would be over sometime. He would try to join the East India Company.

He felt pity for Simmonds. When in the evening Walford rammed his fork solemnly into the table, as was the custom, the younger men had to leave the mess and go to their bunks. They were told they were still growing and so needed more sleep, but that was only a pretext. The true purpose was to humiliate them. If Simmonds overslept his watch—it happened easily, because he slept on the lower deck with the gun master—Bant would look him up and push his hammock from below until he fell out. The little fellow was covered with bruises and scratches, as John had once been. He also attracted teasing in other ways. He still had to learn the simplest things. He didn't even know how to put a rope end on a hawser. That was partly his doing; he lacked seriousness. Instead of learning, he told of his dog in Berkshire. He was a friendly, easygoing fellow, always agreeable and self-confident. But he'd look for a windlass to brace the main yard near the foresail mast. John stopped him: "You've simply got to think. It can only be at the mizzen." He also explained more complex things. In the course of time, John learned that even the older men knew less than he did. He had never forgotten a thing; his head was like a well-stocked barn. At first this annoyed them. But he wouldn't be kept from passing on his knowledge, for he considered it his duty to do so if others lacked it. After six months they all knew him well enough. As he had anticipated, he was now respected. He was consulted on important matters and was given time to respond. One can't accomplish more, he thought. Only one error remained: the war.

Winter was over. Finally away from Brest. A new captain took command. John Cooke, a bald-headed, slender man with a cleft chin. He looked almost as noble as Burnaby and smiled a lot. Cooke was Nelson's man through and through and knew something about firing men up. Nelson was still far away chasing part of the French fleet. But Cooke had already transformed the ship, as though the admiral were standing next to him on the poop deck. He made speeches about death, glory, and duty, and combined all this with great friendliness. He listened closely to everyone without reacting explicitly. Perhaps he only made believe he was listening, but they all felt he acknowledged their presence in a higher sense. It seemed as if an era of freedom and goodness were about to dawn: Bant no longer sulked; Walford became helpful and encouraging; all of them were striving to improve. The captain's words alone had accomplished this! Only John listened in vain for his inner voice. "I don't notice anything yet." He had especially strong doubts about the word "glory." Glory: one wanted to be on the better side, but there was no certainty who in a battle was on the better side. In general, nothing could be reliably proved by death. John composed his own speech in his mind. His tongue moved behind closed lips. He was soon clear about glory. At the word "honor," however, his tongue stopped and stood still and his thoughts went back and forth. There was such a thing as honor. What precisely it was he still had to explore.

The *Bellerophon* sailed to Cartagena, in Spain. The figurehead was painted afresh. Nelson himself came on board, too. A delicate, decisive gentleman who also knew how to smile. When he stood before the crew of the *Bellerophon*, he spoke in a whisper, almost beseeching. He appeared like a man filled with love— love of glory, and love for his own kind. And so soon there was no one who didn't want to be of Nelson's kind.

"I won't be infected by this," said John. This man Nelson

seemed to be utterly certain that they would all do what he loved them for, and they did so. He loved madmen, and so it seemed tempting to go mad for England. Suddenly the seamen pressed into service and the abused soldiers were all determined to become heroes. They now believed they were among the greatest of the earth. They had only to show it. Honor committed everyone to do what he had already been praised for. Honor was a kind of proof to be furnished after the fact.

"What's the resistance in human flesh and ribs to the thrust of a saber? How strong is the wall of the heart?" These were the things fourteen-year-old Simmonds wanted to know. "You just have to want to do it. Then it's child's play," sixteen-year-old Walker assured him. They all felt very powerful and longed for the intensity of death and horror in order to see whether they could get through it, whether calmly or with an excess of spirit. Everyone who hadn't yet had the experience wanted to know it. And new people were coming along all the time. John felt old. He watched young Simmonds closely because he would have liked to find out how quickly his patriotic zeal increased, whether it was stronger in the evenings than in the mornings, and whether it came from an inner or an outer compulsion.

The French and Spanish ships were still lying under the protection of the batteries of Cádiz. The *Bellerophon* sailed there; the entire fleet converged in that place. One evening, John said in the mess: "With three hundred rotations per minute, I'm not well suited for combat." They didn't like to hear that.

"I don't believe you're a Quaker, Franklin," said Walford. "But you lack passion." What a Quaker was John knew very well, for he knew everything on a ship: Quakers were dummies used to fill a gun port when guns were being repaired or taken ashore. A dummy he didn't want to be! He now doubled his efforts at work. He was also signal ensign again. He was in perfect command of all regulations, of all errors and their corrections. He wanted to be so good that nobody would miss his passion.

He heard a lieutenant say: "The noblest idea of mankind is self-sacrifice. We don't go into battle to kill but to risk our lives for England." Those would have been precious sentences for his notebook of phrases, if John had still owned one. While he was talking, the lieutenant's eyes went straight through his audience. His face showed a kind of fearful contentment, as if he were thinking: So far, so good; so far everything is clear, so far I haven't made a mistake.

There was much talk of courage. If the words were at all effective, men would implement them by showing this courage in battle. Many also wanted to be promoted, because they believed that then they would no longer be tormented when the time of heroism had passed. And they also figured that in a crew of a thousand men usually no more than two or three hundred would fall and that there were always survivors, even in burning and sinking ships.

The British fleet now lay southwest of Cádiz; morning dawned. Breakfast; rum ration; ship cleared for battle. Bant put down his cup: "A glorious time! And we're allowed to be with Nelson!" So he now talked this way, too! But though he looked fervent, like a dog before the hunt, his words did not sound genuine. He simply came from Davenport. Simmonds was different. He really felt greatness; he thought he could sense the truth. "Now I want to know it for sure!" he said. John believed him.

John Cooke delivered his final oration. "We are on the way to immortality," he said, smiling. "Give even more of yourselves than usual, just a little more and you'll be three times as good as the French."

How did he figure that?

A first-aid station was set up in the midshipmen's mess. In his eagerness Simmonds could no longer walk normally; he could only run as if it were a matter of life or death. Perhaps frivolousness transformed itself into strength and courage. John noticed something similar in the crew. Only here and there heroism seemed to grate a little, as if it hadn't been greased enough. On the foredeck, John heard the phrase "The dead see it differently."

He memorized it, so he could say it fast, and then fired it at Walford. John was still confident that there would be no battle.

But now the lookout shouted: "Foreign ships!" It didn't take long before the sea was white with sails as far as one could see. John stayed very calm, but it seemed to him for a moment as if he smelled snow in the air. His nose was cold. An irregular column of floating fortresses moving northward took up one-third of the eastern horizon. They had left port, then had turned around, and were now trying to get back to Cádiz.

The cold had to be inside him. John stood on the poop deck with the Third Lieutenant. That's where he should be. But he felt sick. "Signal from flagship, sir." "What's the order?" John noticed he was trembling again after all. It was none of the signals he had learned. It started with "253"—that meant "England." Surely an unclear signal would follow. John didn't understand it; he had to keep his stomach under control. The usual fixed look didn't bring the expected clarity. John barely breathed; he was on the defensive. He would never be like Nelson. He would never belong to that league of men who were prepared to believe in each other in everything, even courage, until victory. Just don't puke on the deck, he thought, for that would be like spitting on the Crown. He wanted that in no case.

A sparse wind blew from the northwest. "Quick into battle!" they all said. "Only quick!" They had no more time; they now needed glory, if only to get it over with. The heroic mood could not be sustained forever. The worst that could happen now was that the battle would not take place. Twenty-seven British warships were swaying toward the enemy in an uncertain breeze, carried by the ongoing swell; thousands of men looking forward—bones, muscles, fat and nerves, skin, veins, sweat and brains, all committed to blind fury—they had already pledged their blood. From afar it looked imposing and threatening. From close by, the volunteer wanted to become a midshipman, the mate a quartermaster, the Fifth to become a Fourth Lieutenant. John marveled again at how strange people looked. But wasn't this battle necessary? Nothing in it was mad. "To defend England," he said aloud, but that didn't make it any better.

What did the hills around Spilsby care whether the French were in the land? It was less fear that paralyzed him than deep irresolution. What to do? He didn't want to return to the state of defiance that had overcome him on the *Earl Camden.* To carry the dead and to view the world like a mountain? It was the trembling after all. Another possibility was to see things like the Bishop of Cloyne: he, John Franklin, was the human spirit, and someone created everything for him as an illusion in order to see whether he flinched when it became uncomfortable. That's what he wanted to try: nothing really existed; the only certainty was that everything was appearance.

Still, he felt useless and isolated. Even the ships now looked quite alien to him. But he was a sailor on a man-of-war; he couldn't change his profession in the midst of battle. With clenched teeth he hoisted the unclear signal up the top. He breathed as deeply as possible and worked methodically. His eyes fixed in front of him, he followed the middle line of the ship and viewed all movements as though they took place only along the outer edges. It helped a little, and calm returned. But just then Rotherham, the First Lieutenant, looked at him sharply.

"Franklin, you're actually trembling!"

"Sir?"

"You're trembling!"

"Aye aye, sir." He, too, now probably thought he was a Quaker. Why, if they all believed in each other's courage, did they make an exception of him?

The captain went below and announced Nelson's signal. The men grinned, and cheered. They now wanted to hear the big words; they couldn't get enough of them. With chalk left over from their navigation lessons they wrote on their gun barrels: BELLEROPHON—DEATH OR GLORY. Outside, a French two-decker was approaching. The first shot sounded from across the water.

Someone started up a rhythmic chant and they all joined in. The entire ship roared like a giant with a rattling voice: "NO FEAR OF THAT!" again and again, menacing, imprecating, "NO FEAR OF THAT!" John felt as if the menace were directed at him.

The lower sails were guyed high; they rose like curtains. The forward guns began to fire. With what happened now John was well acquainted—smoke, splinters, and two kinds of screams: the communal and the individual kind. And that cursed trembling! John stood on the quarter-deck only four steps from John Cooke, who wore epaulettes on his shoulders. Dear Lord, he could take them off by unbuttoning them! They made him into the best target!

A dying man lay on the floor, whispering; "NO FEAR OF THAT!" He was Overton, the sail master. John carried him and an Irish boatswain down to the table into which Walford had rammed his fork every evening for the entire year. What the surgeon held in his hand was hardly better.

"I'm going back to the others, Mr. Overton; I can't leave them alone." No answer. He seemed to prefer to die before the operation.

Breathe calmly! Quarter-deck. Midship. The glance fixed on everything and nothing: the larger view. The French had shot the sails to rags, and the enemy ship now lay with its port side directly along the starboard side of the *Bellerophon,* shooting like mad anything that came out of its guns. Then the boarding attack. Two hundred men stormed, roaring toward them from the French forward deck, thin blades flashing in the light. For seconds the waves made the two ships drift apart, and the assault troops fell into the gap. They stumbled and vanished, clinging to one another like grape clusters with surprised eyes even in falling. Only a bare twenty reached the foredeck of the *Bellerophon,* and they were killed at once. John looked in another direction. The ship was now under fire from three sides.

John Cooke keeled over. "We'll take you below, sir."

"No, let me rest for a few minutes!" answered the captain.

"There!" shouted Simmonds. "Over there in the mizzen!"

Inside the tangle of tackling on the other ship John saw the barrel of a rifle. He recognized a three-cornered hat and beneath it a narrow ruddy forehead, an eye at the gun sight. He decided to ignore this and lifted up the black sailor who had just been hit. As John and Simmonds were climbing into the companionway he bent over a second time. "It's again the one in the mizzen!" Simmonds shouted. "I know the sound by now." One could actually distinguish individual shots. The rifle fire had become sparse. "If we don't shoot him, he'll kill us all!" One single man, then, threatened them all with a rifle and a wide-open sharp eye hidden among the tangled ropes. Anyone who tried to kill him would himself be the next victim.

The black sailor had stopped breathing; his heart stood still. They let him lie there and turned around. "Let me run ahead, I'm faster!" said Simmonds. He raced up the stairs but leapt suddenly, trampling back and forth like a frightened animal, missed the top step, and fell back toward John.

There was a hole in the middle of Simmonds's neck.

The Frenchman must have the companionway constantly in his sight. Perhaps there were two up there—one to load, the other to fire. John bore Simmonds below in his arms. "Too much honor," whispered the little fellow. All of a sudden he says such things! Simmonds wasn't old enough to crack jokes —or was he now after all? For a moment John thought of the Irish bishop and his theory. It had let him down badly.

The wounded man's throat rattled; a long-drawn-out, plaintive sound came out of his gorge. In front of them a bullet had broken the railing. John had to use Simmonds's body to push back the splinters like a trap door. But I can't carry you all below, he thought. I won't carry another one; I'll stay above. In the first-aid station Simmonds still seemed to be alive. Cooke was already dead. John felt a pounding, oppressive rage. He tried to get a clear mind again by recapitulating the colors of the last four signals: "Four, twenty-one, nineteen, twenty-five." It was good to try the simplest way at every opportunity.

Dr. Orme had advised listening to one's own inner voice, not to that of others. But what about that fear? John stood around for a while with his arms hanging down. I look stupid, he thought; I even look like a coward. The others laugh at me, and they're right! This couldn't go on; he couldn't be a spectator any longer. Simmonds groaned and died. John tried to glance past him with his fixed look but he didn't succeed.

He had to do it! He had to go above! To stay out of it had

been a dream. Gone was the irresolution induced by his mind. But now his body rebelled. His legs became lame; his tongue stuck; chin and hands trembled even more than before. John followed the mind's command; he wanted to see how far he got. He loaded the first rifle on the lower deck. He threw up doing it and soiled the weapon. He had to wipe it off; then he climbed back to the middle deck. There he found a second rifle already loaded. A moaning marine loaded the third one for him and passed it to him directly at the top stair. John had three rifles now. He knew he couldn't fire as long as he trembled with fear and rage. He couldn't be at odds with himself. He had to subdue his rage, allow his fear to subside, and suppress his disgust with his conscious will, and to stop all of this took time. What good would it do if he heaped all the guilt on himself and missed the target? He raised the first rifle outside his cover high above his head, pointing it toward the mizzen of the French ship without letting his hands be seen. Angles and distances had to be estimated from memory. Behind his right hand a light-colored cavity suddenly opened up in the wood of the companionway. He had also heard the shot and the ringing of the ricocheting projectile. Following that, he could determine the angle even more precisely. He corrected his direction.

"Shoot, will you!" someone shouted behind him. But John Franklin, who had held a rope in the air for hours, also had the time to take aim. He wanted to fire only if he was completely sure he could hit his target. Once more he assembled it all in his mind: the angles, the estimated height, the scruples he had overcome, the better future. Then he fired. He dropped the rifle, grabbed the second one, aimed it, and fired again, then took the third and padded up the stairs. Was the sharpshooter still there? The tangled tackling was now even denser; the torn French topgallant concealed the exact position. Without cover, John fired once more at the mizzen. Nothing stirred there.

Only Lieutenant Rotherham was standing on the quarterdeck. Walford had gone to the enemy deck with a boarding party.

Then he saw how the wind under the ragged topgallant on the

other side wafted the three-cornered hat out to sea. Under the mizzen, one foot suddenly appeared dangling. It was only a tiny movement, a foot slipping a few inches lower because it no longer sought a hold. "There, see!" cried one of the Irish sailors.

The enemy sharpshooter had tumbled down, head first. It was as though the head had wanted to go down first and the body were following reluctantly, seeking footholds again and again on spars and topmasts until it had to get down into the sea.

"It's got him!" exclaimed the boatswain.

"No, I did," said John.

On the poop and quarter-decks of the *Bellerophon* alone eighty men lay dead or mortally wounded. The survivors were too exhausted to cheer. On both ships there reigned silence. It stank.

Simmonds was dead. He knew it now.

"On that point you may be right," crowed Walford. "The dead see it differently." He alone seemed to want to regain his composure by making speeches. There was too much to do. Signals had to be deciphered. Admiral Nelson had been shot. Collingwood was now commander in chief. Walford went to the French ship *L'Aigle* with the Fifth Lieutenant and a prize detail, and Henry Walker to the Spanish ship *Monarca,* a ship manned mostly by Irishmen.

A storm came up and raged more violently than the one John had gone through in the Gulf of Biscay when he was fourteen, and it sank more ships than the guns had done. Above all, the prizes were lost. The sea had its say. There were leaks to caulk, and they had to pump until they collapsed. All night long they struggled to keep clear of the threatening shore.

Early in the morning, the storm abated. John went to the orlop deck and sat down someplace among the wounded, apathetically. He was too tired to think or to weep, even to sleep. He let the images come and go, faces of men to whom he had become accustomed in vain. Muckridge, Simmonds, Cooke, Overton, the black sailor—the French sharpshooter got in between and then, suddenly, Nelson. What a waste that was! "None of it for the honor of mankind." And what he himself had done he still had to ponder. One of the women saw him sitting there. She must have thought he was about to weep, and said: "Hey hey!" John lifted his fist from his forehead and answered: "I can't recall them all anymore. They all went too fast."

"One gets used to that," said the woman, "and to worse things that you don't even know yet. Here's something to drink." With their stolid domesticity, the women lent the war an air of matter-of-factness it didn't deserve. This woman was of the pale kind, with freckles. She had belonged to the paymaster, who was dead now. Hours later John no longer knew whether he had kissed her or had slept with her or whether it had all been merely a fantasy, a vision as suggested by the Bishop of Cloyne. No sun, in any event; no present tense.

He still worked reliably. "I can be awake for thirty-six hours and still work," he said in order to hold on to something, since the victory over the French gave him little. But he did remark that the number of hours that had elapsed was no indication of the amount of time that had passed. Besides, he didn't know whether shooting someone could be considered work. In the distance he observed a signal from the *Euryalus,* Collingwood's new flagship. The schooner *Pickle* was ordered to London to bring victory tidings. For a moment John imagined the commander Lapenotière, the man with the long nose, as he appeared in London and, for all his eloquence, had to say only four words to make everyone leap to his feet: "Victory at Cape Trafalgar!"

The *Bellerophon* was anchored at the Spithead before Portsmouth. Southsea castle turned toward them brightly with its banners. To the right one could discern with a good telescope the hulls of ships that had been outfitted as prisons—moldy, worn-out men-of-war that were now to receive the French prisoners of war. Those gigantic old truncated hulls were painted gray and stripped of their masts, each now equipped with its own pointed roof and several chimneys. They looked like plump houses standing in the water. What is a ship without a mast?

The streets of Portsmouth were still teeming with throngs drunk with victory—or did it only seem so? Perhaps it was just the alcohol. After all, it was Sunday, and the dockworkers did not have to go to the shipyards. On top of the semaphore tower, John noted, the signal flags were being waved busily. Evidently another message to the Admiralty was being produced to be relayed from hill to hill all the way to London. Surely it was still another confirmation of victory—the sort of things admirals liked to hear.

John headed for Keppel Row as quickly as possible, and among the many low houses he immediately found the right one.

An old woman he did not know peered out of Mary's door. "What Mary? There's no Mary here."

John said: "Mary Rose. She lived here."

He had recalled her face again long ago. And the house was the right one.

"Mary Rose? But she's gone under." The door slammed shut. Inside, John heard laughter. He pounded until the door was opened once more. "Well, then, nobody here's called Mary," said the old woman. "Or are you thinking of the old woman next door—what's she called still . . . ?"

"No, young," said John, "with high arches above her eyes."

"She's dead, isn't she, Sarah?"

"Nonsense, Mother. She's moved away. She was crazy."

"Such arches above the eyes belonged only to one person," said John.

"Well, then you'll find her." With that the old woman went inside again. The younger woman hesitated another moment. Then she added: "I'd let it go if I were you. I believe the woman you're looking for was taken away. She is, I think, in a work-house someplace. She probably couldn't pay anymore."

Workhouse—that was the poorhouse. There was one on Warblington Street. John went there and asked to speak with Mary Rose. The porter was regretful. They didn't have anyone by that name. In the rear an old man screamed again and again: "Help! Rats! Rats!" The porter said only, "Try in Portsea. Elm Road."

Half an hour later John reached that place. Another poorhouse, surrounded by a thick wall. There were no windows, only holes through which those miserable inmates peered and begged from passers-by. Innumerable old hands, twisted by gout, stuck out of these holes; between them, two children's arms. The matron was very friendly. "Mary Rose? That's the one who killed her child. We no longer have her here. She'll be in the White House on High Street. Is anything wrong, Mr. Officer?"

John turned back to the city. If this place was a poorhouse, what would a prison be like?

The guard at the White House shrugged his shoulders. "Not here in any case. Perhaps on one of those prison hulks about to be deported to Australia. Or try the new prison. Penny Street."

John marched there. Darkness had fallen. On Penny Street he found out that nothing could be done until morning.

Since he had definitely decided to sleep in a bed that night, he rented a room in an expensive hotel, The Blue Posts—nothing else was available. He didn't much feel like seeing the *Bellerophon* and his mates. First he had to find Mary Rose again, even if he had to take her off the hulk.

The next day dawned. Determined, John pushed his way into the prison's workroom accompanied by an official. He saw a few spent, worn people who pulled tow out of tar-stained ropes, their fingers bleeding. Another official arrived. Yes, there was a Mary Rose in the place, but she was dangerous and uncontrollable. She'd often scream for hours. Why did he want to see her? "To convey greetings," John said, "from her family."

"Family," the official echoed doubtfully. "Well, then, perhaps this will quiet her down a bit." He went to get her.

The woman wore chains, hands tied behind her back. She was not Mary Rose at all, at least not the one John was looking for. Rather, she was a somewhat plump young woman with a sickly pallor and a completely vacant gaze. John asked her where the other Mary Rose was, the one from Keppel Row. She suddenly gave off a laugh. When she laughed she was almost pretty to look at, because she wrinkled her nose.

"The other Mary Rose. That was me, of course," she said.

Then she started to scream and was taken away.

John drifted about the city and reflected. At noon he lingered for a long time near a soup kitchen for the needy and asked about Mary's arched eyebrows. Some of them said again: "She's gone under." For there had been a ship by that name.

Otherwise they knew either no one or too many women by that name. Specially constructed eyebrows they did not recall, or they had not looked that closely anyway. How could they! Not look? They wasted everything good, starting with their dull eyes. But perhaps they thought of themselves as wasted. He noticed that misery repelled him.

For three days John remained in the city. He visited the worst dives, which mostly bore proud names like the Heroes; he had even been to the notorious Ship Tigre on Capstan Square. Nothing! He asked three unemployed dockworkers, but they had other worries. A scoundrel named Brunel had set up a new machine on which ten unskilled workers could produce as many tackle blocks per day as one hundred and ten skilled men. They were looking for gunpowder to blow the thing up. John advised against it and walked on. He asked about a hundred sailors, around thirty streetwalkers, two doctors, a town hall scribe. He inquired even at the Methodist Sunday School. In the pub Fortune of War an old man showed him his wilted arm in place of an answer; one could see on it the tattoo of a beautiful naked woman, once drawn with brimming breasts and full flowing hair, but now somewhat damaged by the wrinkled skin. Above the tattoo John read "Mary Rose," and below, "Love."

Finally he found a whore who said: "I knew one who looked like that. But her name wasn't Mary Rose. She got married a little while ago—to a tradesman or hatter from Sussex. What she's called now I don't know."

The soles on John's shoes had worn thin. He felt every stone. At one point during the day he sat on top of a cart at an intersection and didn't know how to go on. He stared in front of him and said: "So that's how it is."

The *Bellerophon* soon sailed away. His sea chest remained on board. One didn't necessarily have to be where one's sea chest was. The man who had hoisted the great unclear signal on the *Victory,* an able seaman named Roome, had deserted at the first opportunity after the battle. But John didn't want to do that under any circumstances. He couldn't imagine what he would do. They had refused to release him to serve with the East India Company. So what was left for him? Moreover, his mates were now all he had. At least he knew them. He found it harder than ever to address anyone, to acknowledge that he knew no way out. He got up to walk to the pier.

"To defend England," he said, and smiled that thin smile which he disliked in other people.

The last person he asked about Mary Rose was a little boy. He didn't know her either, but he made John stay and wanted to know about animals on the other side of the earth. John sat down and told him of a giant monitor, a lizard named Salvator. He had observed the monitor in Timor. But he was now amazed that quite against his will he managed to say so many bitter things about this strange beast.

"The lizard Salvator doesn't flee. But it also doesn't like to fight; that's against its nature. He's smart like a human and enjoys friends. But he barely moves—most of the time he just sits—and so he finds few friends. He grows older than all the other animals; all his friends die before he does."

"What does he do, then?" the boy asked impatiently.

"He's modest and good-natured. Only chickens upset him. He gobbles them up whenever he can. At close range, he sometimes doesn't see very well what's ahead of him."

"Better tell me what he looks like."

"He has high shields above his eyes, and nostrils the shape of eggs, and there are yellow dots on his black skin. His tail is long and jagged. His tongue is thin. With it he examines everything very carefully."

The boy said: "I don't think I like this one so well. He's certainly poisonous."

"No, poisonous he's not," John answered sadly. "But people think he is. Therefore, he has to suffer so much. The Singhalese torture him with rocks and fire."

"If he's that slow it's his own fault," the boy decided.

John got up. "Slow? He's only slow apparently. The fastest runner in the world can't catch up with him, and he can see many miles in the distance, to the other side of the horizon."

With that he went, and that was his farewell to Portsmouth.

He was infinitely tired. He didn't believe he would go under; still, it seemed to him that in an as yet undetermined way, everything was over even if it went on. He couldn't cry like a child anymore, especially since he no longer believed that weeping could change anything in the world. But instead, a lasting sorrow nested deep inside him—a sorrow that shunned the light and was universal. It spread out yet remained concealed. It bore the name of Mary Rose within, but it held out its hand to the rest of the world. John did not want to go under: he again decided to endure. He carefully avoided his tendency to disapprove. For that he was praised and made a lieutenant. That was no mean feat.

For ten whole years he relegated the most important decision, the decision concerning his life, to his sea chest. That time became almost too long.

[10]

◆◆

END OF
THE WAR

In the mud, beside the broken gun mount, someone woke up. He raised his head, moved his fingers, then turned his hands in their wrists, his arms in his shoulders. Gingerly he began to touch all over his body. In the middle of his forehead he found a bleeding hole, another one in the back of his head. His ribs and one shoulder, too, throbbed fiercely with pain. He couldn't move his legs.

For a while he just sat there, staring at his boots, watching them lie so incredibly still. Then he pulled himself up on the wreckage of the gun mount, just a little, and tried to look around.

A short distance away a dead Englishman was lying in the trampled-down swamp, an American a few steps farther on, then again an Englishman, all their faces contorted by exertion and rage, the American with his saber still in his fist raised high above his head, strained.

At first the lame man attempted to clamber up the small embankment so somebody could see him. But the thin, grassy shrubs broke off too easily; they gave no support. He took a breath and looked at the sky. Above round little puffs—possibly still the remnants of gun smoke—appeared sharply edged gray patches of clouds. The sun remained hidden.

All around him he heard the moans of the few who were still

alive. Nobody answered his call. The soil was powdery on top of the knoll, trampled loose by the boots of the attacking English who were now lying there and of the Americans in their counterattack.

The noise of battle could still be heard a few miles off. The lame man began to scoop out holes with his hands to pull himself up the slope. He soon noticed that there was no point in holding on to corpses. They gave way and slithered down altogether, taking the climber with them. It was cold and seemed to grow colder. Mid-January; then, too, the loss of blood. Something was on fire nearby; now and then his breathing was throttled by a fat, sooty cloud.

Far away, a man was walking, tall and slightly bent. For one long moment it seemed he was dressed in white. His movements were clumsy and groping. He stumbled again and again over debris and dead bodies, even trod painfully upon a wounded man's chest.

Now his voice could be heard. "Blind!" he shouted. "I'm blind! Does anybody hear me?"

"Come here!" shouted the lame man.

It took a long time for the blind man to come close. His mouth was smiling, but the top half of his face looked red, as if paint had been slapped on it. He said: "Can you lead me out of here?"

"I can't move very well. My legs. But at least I can see."

"Then I'll carry you. Just give me directions."

"Too much honor," said the lame man. The blind man heaved him on his back.

"Two points to port. More. Now straighten. Steady as she goes. Right!"

This new form of locomotion had to be practiced. As a first step they fell off the slope the lame man had spent an hour climbing. There they lay.

"I didn't see that peg."

The blind man's mouth smiled even though it pointed in the wrong direction. "The blind carrying the lame—what do you expect?"

* * *

135

That's what war on land is made of: arduous lying and crawling on damp ground, constant getting down and getting up again in various positions, none of which allowed a wider perspective. It was a situation without any freedom. Sailors in a land war—what misery! On that the lame man and the blind man agreed. They had had enough. There had been that explosion in the ammunition wagon. Or the way the American schooner on the Mississippi had sneaked up on the British camp and shot it up, and how the *Carolina* itself was then blasted into the sky. "I saw a burning glove flying in the air. I'm afraid it was the hand itself." They had helped to dig the canal between the Bayou Calatan and the Mississippi, had commanded the open boats with which they tried to attack the American gun ships. They had rowed thirty-six miles against the current by night only to arrive by daylight—a fine target for the marksmen on the other side. Why had he gotten through all that without a scratch, and what for? Today they had moved on New Orleans. The battle was lost. Anyone who might still be alive wouldn't be for long.

It didn't matter which one of these two had endured worse particular horrors. To find a way into the open land was the name of the game, even if it was the desert itself. There was still more life there than here. To find some rest meant remaining in one place, anywhere, and never returning. Neither to help nor to be helped—just to get away from here as best as one could!

The lame man gazed over the top of the blind man's head into the swaying, bouncing landscape and began to talk about himself. "I'm twenty-nine years old. Ten years of that I spent in war service. Netherlands, Brazil, West Indies. I've done everything wrong. At the same time, I knew better. But it'll be different. There's still time."

They were now on a passable road. The blind man marched along and said nothing. He didn't even give his name. But he seemed to want to listen.

"As early as Trafalgar I lost sight of myself, and then more and more. Yet all I wanted was to get rid of that trembling. I didn't want to appear cowardly or stupid anymore, never again! That was wrong."

No answer.

"A head can mislead the person who belongs to it. It can be a traitor head and so spoil everything for a long time. But I believe one can survive even long-term mistakes.—More to starboard. Always stem against the turn or you'll go in circles."

The blind man kept silent, corrected his course, and strode on.

"I now speak of seeing; forgive me. But it all hangs together because of that. There are two kinds: an eye for details, which discovers new things, and a fixed look that follows only a ready-made plan and speeds it up for the moment. If you don't understand me, I can't say it any other way. Even these sentences gave me a lot of trouble."

The blind man didn't say a word, but he seemed to think.

"In battle only the fixed look is possible—nothing else. It assaults, and it's set like a trap for three or four possibilities. It works only when one must harm others in order to save oneself. If it becomes a habit, one's rhythm gets lost, one's own style of walking is gone."

For some time now the lame man had been leaning against a tree stump while the blind man rested.

"I've become addicted, addicted to war. Did you say anything, blind man? Did you say 'slave'?"

The blind man crouched down and remained silent. The lame one continued: "I'm getting confused. I see a column rising from the sea, a tower of water. I see black before me. We loved Nelson. He forced us out of our ordinary pace and increased our rate of fire. We would have never won—"

"Where are we?" he heard the blind man ask.

"At home at the shore," he heard himself reply. "Behind Skegness on the German Sea. Gibraltar Point." He closed his eyes and slid to the ground.

He still heard the blind man saying something, but he could no longer make it out.

* * *

137

"He's much better now," said the surgeon of the *Bedford*. He was satisfied. "I've never seen anything this crazy. A hole in front and a hole in back. Yet the bullet didn't pass through his head, only under the skin along the skull, clear all around. It's something for science." "You were presumed dead, Mr. Franklin."

The wounded man opened his mouth. Whether he had understood was hard to determine. But that didn't matter to the doctor.

"They were about to bury you. We're only puzzled by one thing: how you got to the shore in the first place—and so far away from the landing dock . . . ?"

John Franklin whispered something: "A blind man . . ."

"What did you say?"

"You haven't found a blind man?"

"I don't understand you, sir."

"A man dressed in white who was blind?"

The surgeon was startled and looked worried. "There was no body near you, not even a dead one. It's been a few days, of course. Perhaps you have only—"

"Then I'm not paralyzed, either?"

"Paralyzed? You moved your legs in your fever as if you wanted to cross an entire continent. We had to tie you down."

"What ship are we on?"

"Your own."

Franklin was silent.

"The *Bedford*, Mr. Franklin. You're Second Lieutenant here. You are Mr. Franklin!"

The wounded man turned to him with large eyes.

"I know who I am. Only the name was a little strange to me."

Then he fell asleep again. The doctor went above to report to the captain.

Peace. Only the medal for bravery still remained as a reminder of the failed attack on New Orleans. And daily work . . . for that was now more arduous. So many were missing.

The battle, they said, had been superfluous. Unfortunately,

the news of a long-since-concluded peace had arrived too late. But what did "too late" mean? They hadn't waited for it long enough. That's what it meant.

The ship was now on its way to England. During the first weeks they still talked about their defeat. Five and a half thousand British against four thousand Americans. But in blindly running against them, the British lost two thousand men at the start, while the Americans, thanks to their secure fortifications, lost only thirteen, and those only because they broke out and wanted to become heroes.

What Franklin had to say about this was amply expressed by his silence. To talk about the senselessness of a battle was to attribute sense to war itself. Then, too, he was still very weak. "A few hidden deserters and some contraband," one of them said, "were not worth a war with the Americans." That person could actually imagine aims that might have been worth it.

"We shouldn't have set Washington and Baltimore on fire. The Americans are relatives, after all." War was good, only not against relatives.

"If only Pakenham, that raving mad general, hadn't been there!"

"If the Americans hadn't been such good shots! How did they come by that, actually?"

"They shouldn't have been given their independence."

Franklin groaned and turned to the wall.

"He's still weak," he heard them say.

Three weeks later he was on duty again. Only now he was what he had been even more distinctly. He breathed differently; his body was at rest; his mind was no longer out to cover up, to betray, or to impose its will.

"He's become different," they said, and watched him closely. And John himself thought, I'm not afraid anymore. Can I be affected at all? That question almost called up a new fear.

The captain was a Scotsman named Walker, a warrior through and through, emaciated, nervous, but always in a grimly happy mood when events began to tumble over one another. He and Pasley, the first officer, were models of brevity and precision. They lived on quickness the way others live on tea, rum, tobacco, or good words. Their manner toward John was outwardly correct yet merciless. In vain he had tried his best. In any event, he had learned a great deal at this price. When they spoke to him it was always either a message or an order. It never contained the slightest commentary. When asked to repeat, they kept the original wording to prevent confusion. But though they already saved much time with their brevity, they also tried to save more with their quick tongues. John had been their most favorite victim. They set traps for him every day with their rapid sentences and incomplete messages— big and small traps. The least of them had been to let him do things that had long since been taken care of. "But I told you that, Mr. Franklin." And they harassed him with their impatience when he asked them to repeat what they had just said.

But that was over now. All at once John was strong enough to bear the impatience of others, and with that the game was at an end. He moved at his own pace. He gave orders the way a carpenter drives nails, each straight and deep until it held. He paused where he wanted to, and not where others interrupted him. He renounced the fixed look and the snarl even when things got tight.

It was not a comfortable voyage home. Many times breezes turned into storms, and just before they got to the Azores the shout went up: "Fire in the stern!" Each time, John Franklin was the officer on watch.

He had long since realized that there were better officers than he, for he knew his profession intimately. He lacked the capacity for fast action, and without quick, alert friends, he got into difficulties. But suddenly he had these friends.

"Check if the watch is complete, Mr. Warren. You can do that faster." John was satisfied that Midshipman Warren did what he was told at the required speed. He depended on others and carefully selected whom to rely on for what occasion.

"Things aren't any easier for him than before," Captain

Walker said through his teeth, "but suddenly he has pulled himself together. He knows what he can and what he can't do. That's half the job."

"But he's lucky, too," remarked Pasley. Then they ceased to make comments for several weeks. And looked for other victims.

Peace lay ahead, but it also meant poverty. For unemployed officers there was only half pay, not to speak of now nonexistent prize money. For petty officers and crews there wasn't a penny. And in England there was want.

"We don't have a chance," grumbled the paymaster.

A pause; a thoughtful silence. "Then we should take it," joked another.

"We ourselves are the chance." The listeners turned their heads: Franklin. Not that they had understood him. But if anybody considered carefully what he said, it was Franklin. So they still thought about it for a little while. He always had the courage to look stupid long enough to be smart—one could well copy that! In other respects, too, he had a tough skull. No bullet could get through it. God surely still had plans for Franklin. They helped him where they could.

John felt that after his conversation with the blind man, who may not even have really existed, he had greater strength than ever before. Besides, the scar on his forehead earned him a new, inexplicable respect, and that made him even stronger than he actually was.

The last will be the first, he told himself, and saying that he also recalled Walker and Pasley—after all, he was no saint.

The time had really come for him to have his own command.

Peace. Even the second one! After the first peace Napoleon had been imprisoned on Elba. But he had broken out and made himself master of France once more. War again, and then the great defeat. This peace seemed to be final now—all of London was blazing with flags.

For the officers there were balls and elegant dinners. Speeches in honor of . . . , cheers, champagne and beer.

John stood on the side, somewhat detached. At the same time, he had nothing against this jubilation for peace. But it seemed to him that he was not well suited for general enthusiasms, and now less so than ever. He wasn't very happy about it. I have to manage, he thought, even out of some sense of duty, not to be completely out of step with the nation.

John talked about the *Investigator* and about Sherard with another officer. "How's that?" asked the other. "Sherard Lound? Are you sure his name wasn't Gérard? I heard about a Gérard Lound." John asked about details.

This Gérard was supposed to have been Second Lieutenant on the *Lydia* on its voyage to the Central American coast. He had a somewhat dubious reputation. Also, there was to have been something between him and Lady Barbara Wellesley on the voyage around Cape Horn. Yes, yes! The captain himself had intervened, by the way—and the teller of the tale looked around—rather to the displeasure of the lady. Lound had disappeared without a trace after a skirmish in the year 1812, and there is a rumor that the captain himself . . .

John was not interested in these stories about love triangles, and he believed firmly that it was all a mix-up of names. Sherard Philip Lound built on Australian land and lived in wealth and pleasure; John did not want to doubt it.

Hugh Willoughby, a relative of that sculptured Lord Peregrin Bertie, had discovered islands hundreds of years ago on which the sun produced no days or hours. John had never forgotten that. Now it obtained a new meaning for him. John Franklin, lieutenant of the Royal Navy, currently unemployed and at half pay like thousands of lieutenants, was the only one who knew precisely what he wanted. In society he kept his dream to himself. But in his own mind he said again and again: "Nobody has been at the North Pole yet!" Since the sun did not set there in the summer he was sure of two things: there would be open water and time without hours and days.

142

In London, John stayed at the Norfolk Hotel, where he had seen Matthew Flinders for the last time. He even managed to rent the same room; that was important to him.

Over there on that bed the Captain had sat five years ago, pale and red-eyed from his imprisonment and all that worry. The French had changed the map of Australia without further ado: Spencer Gulf and the Gulf of St. Vincent they had named after Bonaparte and Joséphine de Beauharnais, and the only man who would have never allowed this, Captain Nicholas Baudin, had perished in a storm. Add to all this his treatment as a spy, years of arrest in damp quarters, illness—poor Matthew!

Trim the tomcat, his only friend on Mauritius, had landed in the cooking pot of hungry natives. They sent the fur back to Matthew. Meanwhile, the maps were corrected again; one could even find Franklin Harbour once more. Only Trim Bay, an inlet in the extreme north of Port Philip, was not entered. If ever a settlement were to be built there, it had to be called Trim City. John would work for that if he ever gained influence.

If Matthew were still alive, John thought, he'd want to go to the North Pole, too. Just to see what was there.

Dr. Brown—Robert Brown of the *Investigator*—was now a well-known natural scientist. John needed his help for the North Pole project and looked for him.

It was toward noon. There seemed to be no one in the Royal Society whom he could ask. They all sat in the lecture hall listening to a disquisition about astronomy by a man named Babbage. John found himself a chair and concentrated. He knew so much about stars that he could follow even a fast speech.

Two women entered and sat down in the row behind him. John's neighbor turned around and said in an undertone, "Since when do women have any business in science? They should stay at home and make puddings." The women heard it. The younger one leaned forward and said, "But the pudding is already done, or we wouldn't be here." Then they both had to burst out laughing and infected others who had overheard the exchange. Dr. Babbage asked the audience with some heat what was so funny about Galileo's discoveries; he pretended to want to laugh, too. But everyone quickly saw that he didn't really, for he took the stars too seriously.

After the lecture, John went up to the younger of the two women and asked her what she found especially interesting about astronomy. She looked at him quizzically and replied that she adored Charles Babbage. She didn't mean this seriously. John found this out with a few well-aimed questions, and she finally admitted it. There was a twittering sound to her voice, and she enjoyed questions that she could answer unseriously at first. Now and then she laughed and hopped on one foot. A crazy young woman she was.

"Our man of the Sandbank Council!" Dr. Brown called out. "Do you still remember the Great Reef? What a giant you've become. A man whom no one can stop, am I right?" John pondered for a long time how to respond to this. He didn't care for such talk, but he needed Dr. Brown.

"I can be stopped," he replied. "My mind is open to arguments." Dr. Brown laughed and exclaimed: "Good answer!" They had become strangers to each other after all those years.

But then they talked about Matthew Flinders and came closer again. Dr. Brown had not forgotten the brave captain and had many words of love and respect for him. "But one thing is a shame: he had invented a method whereby one can adjust a wrong declination of a compass by inserting a small metal rod, and he has never written it up."

"I know all about it," said John.

"What? Write a report, Mr. Franklin, with all calculations and drawings. I'll submit it to the Royal Society and to the Admiralty. The invention shall bear Flinders's name."

"I'll do it," answered John. Then he began to talk about the North Pole. Dr. Brown raised his eyebrows, but he listened closely. In the end he promised to use his influence for John. A voyage to the North Pole, or some other voyage of discovery, good! He would speak with Sir Joseph and with Barrow. There was no money at present, but perhaps . . . "I'll write you in any case what I've found out, Mr. Franklin, one way or the other."

A written report was even harder than an oral one. For days John had labored over it. Now he wanted to see something of London. He looked up Eleanor Porden, the lady with the pudding, and asked her whether she would drive him around a little in her carriage. She laughed and agreed at once.

Her father was an important architect, and rich. He had built castles and rotundas for the king. She was his only daughter.

"Let's go to the Waterloo Panorama," she proposed. "It's supposed to be very true to nature." John recalled she had hinted that she was writing poetry. Rather not bring that up, he thought. But as soon as they were in the carriage they got to the subject. "Wait a minute! I'll read you a poem!" John hardly needed to wait; she read three poems at once. The rhymes seemed to have been done properly. To be sure, some phrases like "Well now!" and "Woe" appeared a little too often.

"I'm having a hard time with love poems," John said with some formality. "Perhaps after so many years in the war I'm not as well attuned to love." The poet fell silent, taken aback, and after a few seconds said: "Well now . . ." Since she was now quite still, John decided to recite the only poem he could recall:

> He little knew at what expense
> He was to buy experience.

It was, he explained, from "Johnny Newcome," but for him it was always a poem about voyages of discovery.

She was still silent.

He simply loved short poems, he said, subdued.

Eleanor pulled herself together. They were now close to the Panorama. In the domelike tent John looked absent-mindedly at the many tin warriors and their little horses. The fallen soldiers, especially those of the lower ranks, were always a little smaller than the live ones. Their color was paler, too; they seemed to blend with the earth. John explained to Eleanor the advantages and disadvantages of the fixed look by using the Panorama landscape as a model. Then they went on a little tour through town.

"Odd," Eleanor remarked. "When you walk through a crowd you don't get out of anybody's way. All you do is apologize—that's the only thing that distinguishes you from a bear." Her voice twittered. John mused about that. She watches me, he thought. Possibly she regards me favorably as a person. He began to prearrange his sentences in his mind to answer her.

John experienced the city as rather bewildering. If only people would go about their business and stay their course in a clear and orderly fashion! But there were constantly unexpected turns and arbitrary collisions. Everyone under twenty and male was sparring with someone of the same kind. Either the assailant or the victim could be counted on to get under John's feet. And then the coachmen! Worried, John stared at these thoughtless creatures with their round hats, watched how they passed each other in the most unmanageable places, hub to hub, racing as fast as they could. All of London seemed to be in love with speed. Good thing there were pedestrian walks now—elevated paved strips along the roadways. But if one ran into four drunken soldiers on these pavements, one would be pushed over the edge and so be doubly endangered. If one stood still to gain a larger perspective, somebody would at once jostle one from behind and step on one's heels. Throughout all this unpleasantness, Eleanor continued their conversation, unperturbed.

"Would you like to meet my father, Mr. Franklin?"

"I can't support a wife," John answered. He had stumbled into a fence and had to pluck a sleeve from the wrought-iron tip. "I'm on half pay and I don't want other people's money except for an expedition. We should write to each other, though. I regard you well, too."

Miss Porden could look out of the corner of her eyes in such a slantwise fashion, one had to be prepared for everything. "Mr. Franklin," she said, "that was too fast for me."

* * *

John looked for work in vain. Hungry sailors and melancholy officers were sitting around everywhere in the harbor towns. Most of the ships had been scrapped or were still kept around for a few years as prison hulks, like the old *Bellerophon.*

The official at the maritime bureau assumed a pained expression when John told him he wanted to go on voyages of discovery or none at all.

"But everything's been discovered," said the man. "We just have to watch over it."

"I can wait," John said brightly.

He had confidence in the future. Hadn't he been lying on a battlefield with paralyzed legs a bare year ago? He got away then—how no one could say—and he wasn't dead or mad or even lame. He didn't know how that had come about, but it gave him courage. Now his chances were also slight. Might not something inexplicable happen to him again?

He delivered his account of Matthew's compass correction and decided to go to Lincolnshire. He told Dr. Brown and a few others how they could reach him there. Then he said his farewells.

The post coach stood ready in front of the Saracen Head in Snowhill. It was five o'clock in the afternoon.

"Spilsby?" asked the coachman. "That must be a slow place." John found his judgment about the insolence of coachmen confirmed. But then he learned that the remark had not been directed at him. Every place was called slow if posts rarely went there.

John rode outside to save money. He noted with pleasure that he was no longer afraid of falling off. So fifteen years at sea had not been in vain.

John viewed the moonlit night from the roof of the coach. He observed many sturdy church towers with notched crowns growing smaller and smaller in the distance as they passed from hill to hill, and farms bunching up together fearfully.

One could see the plight of the villages two miles off, first by the badly patched roofs, then by the broken windows. Crop failures during this and the previous year—there was no money.

All at once he saw why the night was so unnaturally bright: a fire was burning. Somewhere toward the east, in the direction of Ely, it burned in at least three places. What was happening in this land? John was a sailor. He didn't count on grasping everything at once. But one could feel ill at ease in the country after so many years.

He already knew from letters what to expect at home: new faces, lack of money, and worried reports. In 1807, Thomas, the eldest, had taken his life, because the family fortune had run through his fingers in financial speculations. Six years ago Grandfather had died; Mother in the year following. Father now lived in a farmhouse outside the village, cared for by one of his daughters.

The horizon was dark again. John admitted to himself that he felt cold.

They reached Boston in the early forenoon. Here John heard some news. There were "Luddites" about now. These were unemployed men who painted their faces black at night and smashed the mechanical looms to pieces. And in Horncastle there was now supposed to be a navigable canal to Sleaford and even a library.

From Stickford on, the road became steadily worse. John rode inside for the final stretch. His heart was beating. He got off in Keal and, carrying his luggage, walked toward Old Bolingbroke, where his father lived. If he was still alive.

Some distance away he saw a figure standing on the side of the road, swaying, leaning on a cane. The man seemed to correct each movement after it was made. He was more preoccupied with that procedure than with anything else that went on around him. That's the way Father looked now.

He recognized John only by his voice, for he could see almost nothing. "I'm tired," he complained. Time, strength, everything dissolves of its own accord, not to speak of money. John asked whether he should support or lead him. He then held out his arm to his father in the way one would proffer it to a lady.

Elaborately, the father apologized for his slowness. John studied his father's hand, which had so many bumps, stains, and veins; he passed his fingers over it. The old man was a little surprised.

John talked of the cool weather and of his journey. He named Huntington; he named Peterborough. Father liked to hear the familiar names and was grateful when the words came out clearly, one by one. Just before they got to the door he turned to John and peered closely at his face. "Now you're here," he said. "How does it go on?"

[III]

Franklin's Domain

[11]

◆◆◆

HIS OWN MIND AND
THE IDEAS OF OTHERS

I n front of the White Hart Inn in Spilsby a coach arrived, and John asked about letters.

No letter from Dr. Brown; no work! Only Eleanor Porden had written a long letter, for she loved to write. John postponed reading it until a better day.

A great deal had changed in Spilsby. And old Ayscough no longer waited for coaches and travelers. John found his gravestone near the tower of St. James. The shepherd had been convicted as an arsonist a few months before and had been sent to Botany Bay. He had set fire to three large barns on the estate. Why had he done that? A pity for him.

And Tom Barker, walking through the forest, had been robbed and killed by a highwayman. He had probably defended himself. But what sort of a person enjoys killing an apothecary?

The Lound family no longer lived in Ing Ming. At night, so the story goes, they had taken off across the village border. Their destination had been Sheffield, the coal city, where the steam pumps were nodding. There was said to be work there now. Nobody had heard anything of Sherard.

John went back to Bolingbroke and thought grimly: I can wait.

For a fee of one pound, ten shillings and sixpence he joined the First Reading Society of Horncastle. It was a great deal of money, but there were almost eight hundred books that could be borrowed, and John wanted to make use of his waiting time. With Cook's travel guides, he climbed on the post coach to Louth. He wanted to talk with Dr. Orme at length about the North Pole.

But Dr. Orme was dead. During the previous year, in good health, he had suddenly collapsed. In the church John found a tablet enumerating all his academic and ecclesiastical titles. There were so many—only first letters could be chiseled into the slab.

For some time now his successor had lived on Breakneck Lane. He handed John a parcel wrapped in thin leather and tied and sealed many times with the address: "John Franklin, Lieutenant, Royal Navy, for his eyes only." The schoolmaster surmised: "It'll be a Bible." He invited John to sit down and look at it, but he declined. He preferred to go back to the cemetery, for he wanted to be by himself when he read Dr. Orme's message.

The parcel contained two manuscripts. One of them read:

The Origin of the Individual
through Speed
OR:
Observations for Distinct Time Senses
which GOD
Planted within each Individual
as Represented in an Outstanding Example

The other manuscript bore the title

Treatise Concerning Useful Arrangements
Appropriate for Creating Images of Movements
for the Sluggish Eye
Useful for Edification and
Instruction and
For the Prophesy of the Word
Of THE LORD.

154

The accompanying letter read only: "Dear John: Please read these two notebooks. I would like your opinion. Regards," signature—that was all. There was nothing in it to weep about. It sounded so sprightly and brief—the letter writer had not counted on death. John inspected the writings immediately, as if Dr. Orme were waiting for a quick answer.

The first manuscript described him, John, without naming him, referring to "Pupil F." He felt a little uneasy and didn't know why. He immediately turned to the second treatise, especially since it contained colorful sketches. It also seemed to him that in these "Useful Arrangements" the sentences were much shorter than in the "Origin of the Individual."

John hid the manuscripts from his sister and others in the house. He didn't want anyone to study Dr. Orme's thoughts before he knew them himself.

He went down to the river to read them. There was a castle ruin in Bolingbroke where a king had been born a long time ago. John spent the entire day sitting at the base wall of the collapsed porter's lodge. Cows and a goat were grazing by the river. Now and then gadflies buzzed him; John let them bite him and read on.

The most important of the useful arrangements Dr. Orme was writing about was called the "picture rotor." That was an apparatus into which a big book was clamped. With the help of a powerful mechanism, the pages were turned in sequence at lightning speed. A picture was drawn on every page, each only slightly different from its predecessor. And so if all the pages passed by the eye within a few seconds, the illusion of a single, moving picture was created. Dr. Orme held that this deception of the senses took place not only in slow people but in everyone. He had to know this; undoubtedly he had tried it out on his quick housekeeper. John decided to speak to her about it. But where was the equipment? Sold? Taken apart or stored in an attic on Breakneck Lane? This new idea caught John's imagination. He'd go to Louth again tomorrow. Dr. Orme had also suggested a further way to make this idea useful. With a magic lantern he wanted to transfer the picture produced by the book optically and to project it on the wall of a darkened room. In this way, a number of people could watch an entire story in moving pictures while being comfortably seated. They would comprehend how one event emerged from another even without words and could participate in an event without getting into danger or making mistakes.

John's mind was completely captivated by Dr. Orme's inventive spirit, especially since some of the problems had not yet been solved.

For example, a veritably stupendous number of pages was needed to tell longer stories in this pictorial way. Several artists would probably have to draw the images for such a picture rotor, taking many months. Moreover, the larger number of pages required for this purpose involved a technical difficulty: one had to be able to clamp several volumes into the machine so that the next one would start without delay when the preceding one ended. A third obstacle was the optical transmission. Dr. Orme doubted whether there were sources of light strong enough for proper illumination.

As to the light, John did not foresee a problem. Modern lighthouses could beam their rays for miles ahead with silver concave mirrors—something that could also be used in an indoor hall. The real obstacle seemed to him to be the artists. He couldn't imagine a William Westall drawing the same landscape a thousand times, each with only a very slight variation. He would paint each picture with different sentiments and moods. Clearly, the artists were the weakest point.

Dr. Orme had proposed representing sublime moments in English history, if possible, nothing warlike, but rather portraits of a peaceful and orderly national life "as in a moving panorama." He thought of pictures of reconciliation and communal prayer, of the happy homecoming of a ship, of instances of nobility and of a gentle spirit encouraging imitation. Divine miracles, on the other hand, were to be excluded. The Feeding of the Five Thousand or the Healing of the Lepers would not be suitable topics, for to show them would mean imitating God.

It had grown dark. John mused about the Feeding of the Five Thousand, packed up his notebooks, and wandered back. He almost got lost, so deeply did he brood over what he had read. Now he would have liked to talk this over with Sherard Lound.

Just before falling asleep, he started up once more.

"Printing machines!" he murmured. "Special printing machines that print the same thing a thousand times and still can take care of the changes." But where would he find the money? With that he fell asleep.

In Louth, neither the housekeeper nor the schoolmaster knew anything about Dr. Orme's experiments. There was also no more equipment. What had been found in the way of metal and wooden parts, cranks and screws, had been sold to sundry craftsmen. And in the writings he had left behind, nothing had surfaced that would point toward the picture rotor. Deep in thought, John rode home again. An idea he couldn't realize for lack of money was a poor pastime. Besides, under certain circumstances something like this could keep him away from the North Pole, and that was out of the question.

But he didn't want to be idle during this waiting time. Something respectable had to be found, if at all possible something that also brought in money.

The villagers and squires now treated him with respect, largely because of his tall stature and the scar on his forehead. If he asked anyone to repeat what had been said he was no longer mocked and left standing but first heard an apology, then the repetition.

For a grown man the country was actually pleasant.

However, John wanted to make one more attempt. A possible patron for the picture rotor among the members of the Reading Society was the apothecary Beesley, a tenderhearted herb collector, well-to-do and of a passionate nature. He was devoted to English history, and he listened carefully to John's report about the invention.

"A good idea! I'm curious if it works." But something seemed to disturb him. "Tell me, Mr. Franklin, how did Dr. Orme get to pictures of history? The spirit of past times can't be caught in pictures."

John feared that Mr. Beesley was right.

"History, seriously pursued, belongs in the realm of uncertainty. A picture is a certainty."

Assertions setting up contraries always sounded right at first blush, at least to John's ears. But he didn't want to give in without a fight. Therefore, he spoke urgently of the betterment of mankind by good example. "To improve mankind!" answered the other. "Only three things can do that: the study of the past, a healthy way of life in nature, and medicine in the case of illness. Everything else does not improve anyone. It's only politics and diversion."

It became clear to John that he could not impress the apothecary. Should he tell him about the North Pole? But he could predict the kind of answer he would get. He therefore spoke only very little about himself. Beesley was pleased and paternal.

"In the study of history, slowness is an advantage. The scholar decelerates the fast-moving events of past days until his mind can fathom them. Then, however, he can demonstrate to the rashest king how he should have acted in battle."

John was perplexed. The apothecary was not joking, he hoped. Altogether there was something impenetrable and removed about him.

Soon all that changed. He suddenly became so eager that John was prepared to think of him again as an honest man.

"Not three miles from here! Englishmen against Englishmen! And even today their bones come to light in the fields of Winceby when they are ploughed. Flowers grow there that are different from anywhere else. That's what I mean, Mr. Franklin, this feeling! To know what can happen on a spot of earth in the course of centuries. It expands one's perspective, one's entire person."

John knew what moved the apothecary and he respected it.

"Breadth of the horizon," Beesley explained, "is the highest aim that can be reached by man."

John tried to think of this from the angle of spheric trigonometry, but Beesley had long since passed this by.

"I'm working on a history of Lincolnshire with particular reference to the nobility," he continued. "There are genealogies to pursue, chronicles to read, records of ownership to examine, and to imagine oneself in the skin of persons in high places. Will you help?"

When he was talking, Beesley's chin was hopping up and down like a mouse in a trap: it interfered with listening. John hesitated.

"History is intercourse with greatness and duration. It allows us to rise above time."

"But I'm a sailor," John demurred.

"And where is your ship?"

John considered. There were so few activities in which slowness was a virtue. Rising above time—that was tempting. But he couldn't earn any money with it.

John was noticing at last that he was unemployed and felt useless. Never had he imagined that he of all people would be bored. But this waiting was different from any waiting in the past. He used to have an occupation, an objective—and now it didn't go any further! Again and again he wrote to London, but except for meaningless promises there was no reply.

Unused skills were no skills. Perhaps one could never rekindle them again?

Reading increased the thirst for action instead of dampening it. He had learned how to join mind and body on a ship; he had become a good officer and was strong as never before or would ever be again. Should nothing come up for him now? Half pay—that was not only something cut in half but really only nothing, without coherence. It was threatening, especially at night, when he lay awake like a live, sad picture rotor.

* * *

Flora Reed, a preacher's widow, was known to be a radical. She owned Robert Owen's tract *New View of Society* and quoted from it in arguments with Beesley the apothecary.

John sat with Mrs. Reed in the Fighting Cocks Inn in Horncastle all afternoon. She was pleasant and respectful. He had trouble only with what she said.

She could not be won over to the moving pictures because she found, as she put it: "Hunger and want can be grasped without artificial means. Simple truth is sufficient for all who can hear and read. Whoever can't do that, Mr. Franklin, won't be made any wiser by your gadget." Something about that was not quite logical.

Now she had near beer and cake brought in. John was glad of the interruption, for listening was strenuous. Mrs. Reed's voice was soft, and even when she became agitated its volume did not increase, only her lisp. Her hair was smooth and black. Her eyes flashed when they recognized danger.

"The wide horizon? Did Mr. Beesley say that? I take it he came to history from collecting herbs. Mr. Franklin, the horizon lies right here in front of us, not behind us! It's always where it doesn't go any farther, isn't that right?" As a navigator, John had objections, but he didn't want to hurt Mrs. Reed's feelings. She had also gone on. "Think of the corn laws! France has a good harvest in its barns; it could help with the overflow. No one should have to go hungry."

She looked at him amiably but very directly. John wondered if she liked to look him in the eye or if her fixed look accounted only for her desire to watch over the coherence of her arguments. If only she had spoken a little more loudly! ". . . and why are the borders closed? Because the landed gentry make money on scarcity, and the landed gentry alone make up Parliament!"

"Mrs. Reed. Since Trafalgar I'm a bit hard of hearing. The cannons!"

"Then I'll come closer," said she, without raising her voice. "Now to the poor: they set the barns on fire and so even increase the scarcity. Blindness here, greed there, that's the horizon. Did you want to say something?"

160

"No, just go on." It occurred to John that he would much rather read about all this someplace; this was too fast for him. But Flora Reed pleased him. How long had the preacher been dead, he wondered.

". . . salt tax, bread tax, newspaper tax, window tax. But all this money still flows again indirectly into—"

"Just a moment, Mrs. Reed, I—"

"Yes indeed, Mr. Franklin! For naked want prevails every-where. Look around yourself! Poachers, thieves, smugglers everywhere, and why? Because they have no other—"

"I believe I'd much rather see that somewhere—"

"When the landowners' conscience pricks them! Only then, and not a minute sooner!"

"Yes, I think that, too," John nodded. "But I was too long at sea. Many things I don't know very well . . ."

While he spoke, Mrs. Reed had shoved a piece of cake into her mouth, and she watched John with friendly eyes until she could continue. Smiling, she said: "No picture apparatus, Mr. Franklin, no history! One newspaper that prints the truth, a league against poverty and for the suffrage of the poor—we must accomplish something like that!"

John experienced this decisiveness as most agreeable. When Flora seized his hand, he couldn't doubt her words. There was something leonine about her, and she looked graceful in her silence. But even then she fixed him so firmly with her bright eyes that he too had to return her gaze firmly.

"Do you know what I like about you, Mr. Franklin? With most people everything moves fast until they understand, but when they get to the point it's already over. You're different. Join us in our fight; it's your human duty!"

The truth, he thought. That's what decided him. In a newspaper dedicated to the truth it didn't matter whether the editor was a little slow. Of course, he couldn't earn anything with that either. . . . "Good," he said.

During the war he had suffered because in an acute emergency he could not help with any presence of mind. How often did he get there too late! He had exposed himself to a hail of bullets in order to prove that he might be slow but was no coward. Now he discovered through Flora Reed that, fast or slow, one could do one's human duty only by acting in support of the right side. It suited him well. He saw Flora more and more often. He borrowed Owen's tract and learned that poverty caused all other sufferings, war included, and that no man could be good if hunger left him no choice. Everybody wants to own something, but when few own so much and many nothing at all, hate had to be the result. Hence, there had to be equality and education for equality. That was a general law, for that's what Flora, Robert Owen, and all of them who had thought about this were saying. In Flora's mind the world's misery hung together like a net, and one could rely on its coherence. Nothing simply existed for itself. Each single instance was grounded in the whole and came into existence only because of the whole. Therein lay the reason for its persistent survival.

There was a rule to explain any change or disappearance. Now John had something with which to ennoble his waiting time. For wasn't it true that each person was given life so he would do something for his kind? And if this was true, then logic required that one start with the most urgent and life-saving tasks. Everything else one could leave to those whose insights had not yet matured. If he had to wait, he wanted to do something to save mankind; that seemed to him as it should be. For too long he had looked fixedly past the misfortunes of others so as to protect himself. No. Since he had to wait in any case, he wanted at least to become truly good.

John began to think again about the construction of the picture rotor after all. If misery could be grasped as soon as it was evident to the eye, an apparatus that could show something like this without any words would be useful!

Just as John tried to imagine the advantages of universal suffrage, it occurred to him that the rotation could be replaced by a stack of uniform picture plates. As quick as lightning, the plates would fall one by one into a metal frame, each visible for only a fraction of a second. Everything depended on a mechanism for moving the stacks at a uniform speed. John made a drawing. The apparatus had a capstan bar and a pawl rim strongly resembling the windlass of the *Bellerophon.*

John wrote down what he had figured out, copied Dr. Orme's explanations and drawings, and sent everything to Dr. Brown in London. He didn't want the invention to remain unknown.

One and a half years passed, and he still had not read Dr. Orme's paper about Pupil F. Some sure instinct held him back. And it had been Dr. Orme himself who had recommended that he listen to his inner voice.

He knew almost all the travel books and, in addition, the writings of Spence, Ogilvie, Hall, and Thompson. He had learned in the Fighting Cocks Inn how to observe the coherence of one's arguments. With Beesley the apothecary he had wandered all over the herbaceous battlefield of Winceby. He now had his own opinion about titled families. "The gentry is noble. That's fine. The gentry, however, is also often stupid, and that's disappointing."

At home he planted and harvested, even replaced the roofing, walked with his father, and renewed acquaintances.

With Flora Reed he had spent first one night and then several. He had again recalled the tender language he had known since that evening in Portsmouth, now realizing that one could speak it with any other woman, even if one didn't love her. The preacher had been remiss in this; the language of the Bible had seemed to him sufficient. Perhaps he had even died of it: duty toward one's fellow man is not enough to give pleasure to others, not to speak of oneself.

One and a half years! He helped with Flora's meetings of farm laborers, ladled out soup, checked drafts of leaflets, and set and printed them at night. He watched as renewed acquaintances turned hostile, he listened to angry speeches, and he suppressed his own anger. He tried to live on his half pay, even cared for chickens. He learned first to understand and then to fear the rage of the poor, both the communal and the lonely rage. A house was set on fire, the home of the rich farmer Hardy. On flat rocks nearby one could read in red letters: BREAD OR BLOOD! and DOWN WITH THE THRESHING MACHINE! Those were the times!

Doubts, nothing but doubts! There was no such thing at sea.

He loved Flora Reed only halfheartedly; he knew that. It was enough to cohabit with her. The idea of her was durable; it gave him peace of mind. But now she began to change. Could the idea bear that? How much was duty toward mankind worth if it became a straitjacket? Or was it he, John, who changed? Everything here on land was only half a loaf, himself included.

John resurfaced from the network of rules governing duty toward mankind. They formed an element in which he could move only by holding his breath. To catch some air he had to get out, even if he was able to hold his breath for a long time.

He began to annoy Flora. He said things like, "Man must be able to rise above time."

"What's wrong with the sun and the present?" she mocked. Now she wore that thin smile that John didn't like even on himself. John and Flora had looked for an escape hatch in love and found that it was no way out.

John became more and more heretical. "Has it been proved, then, that misery can always be grasped directly?" Or, "Why is there only one misery? I maintain that there are many kinds, and they have nothing to do with one another." Sometimes he made Flora so sad that she didn't much want to answer. Then he was sad, too.

The compulsion to be constantly occupied with what is important to mankind necessarily affected more and more thoughts and actions. John sensed that someday, simply out of duty toward equality, he would have to discover that he was interchangeable with others. But from his time in the navy he knew full well what it was like when one's unique self became insignificant. There remained only the escape into quickness. Someone was "better" if he could do the same thing faster. And this choice was not open to him.

He had wanted to talk about this with Flora for a long time. But she didn't know the navy.

Something had to happen.

He left the house early one morning. He took the road to Enderby, then turned east, reached Hundleby and Spilsby, and then headed toward the sea, this time without crawling through hedgerows. In Ashby, a pale boy was painting a fence. An old man greeted him in Scremby; he let his pipe go out in astonishment: only poor and fat people would walk that far across the land.

From the direction of Gunby Hall he heard gunshots from a hunting party. The landed gentry went on fox hunts, shot pheasants, and thought up ever more severe laws against poaching. John perceived the rural scene very differently now and disapproved of a great deal. For example, just for stealing a small piece of meat, twelve-year-olds were sent to Van Diemen's Land, where no one knew them. He spent the night in Ingoldmells and then a whole day sitting on the dyke watching the ocean's work on the sand as though he were seeing it for the first time. And he imagined he heard through the roar of the surf a babble of voices as on ships at sea. He heard commands, singing, jokes, curses. Booms creaked and tackling blocks twittered. "Let's go!" was the word. "Make fast," was the word, "to the top halyards! Pull in hard! Raise the topsail!"

He needed the movements of the sea, and sailing was more important to him than breathing.

So he dreamed and thought. He also saw new images: river bends, boats, wild animals, dangerous moments. Now icebergs appeared, ice floes crunching under the keel, then a wide, glistening passage opening up. The ice belt vanished and the polar summer arrived and with it a world in which there was no pressure of time. That was his home—not Lincolnshire, not England. The entire rest of the world could only be a vestibule leading to this home—an entry to pass through.

He walked back to Ingoldmells and took the post to Bolingbroke. Through the window he saw hedgerows and country roads jerking past and thought: Their movements are deceptions. They are really caught here, while only I and the distant mountains are actually traveling.

Then he remembered Lieutenant Pasley, who now had his own ship. And Walker, who commanded a warship with twenty-four guns. He was not envious of the guns but he was of the sea.

He had to become a captain! To find the Pole! He'd worry again about the land after that.

English history was for Beesley, the world's misery was Flora's domain, and the invention of gadgets belonged to Dr. Orme and his successors but not to John. And what Dr. Orme had written about Pupil F he wanted to read only after he had reached 82 degrees northern latitude.

His decision was firm: he wanted to try the whalers. He sat across from Flora, irresolutely caressing her knees, and began a well-rehearsed declaration about one's duty toward mankind: "If I want to light my neighbor's stove, what good does it do if I know where the stove is located and march up to it vigorously? The torch has to burn properly, that's what matters. What good does it do if my motions are correct but they come too soon?"

"Skip it," remarked Flora. "You're not great at examples. I'm not that neighbor." She looked at him as steadily as she had done the first time, but her eyes were dark.

John felt he was as obtuse at that moment as his predecessor, the preacher. Perhaps it was Flora's doing? "It could be that this whole thing about the polar sea is nonsense and I'll come back soon . . ." John realized he was lying.

She was silent. This silence! She had become a tyrant.

"Perhaps you'll see me again soon. I'll come back and will be an editor." His lying became more and more oppressive.

"And will the torch burn then?"

"Possibly. But no. That's nonsense. I don't know any of this."

Flora blew her nose. "You're no editor. God bless you!" She kissed him.

Then he went. Heavens, he was glad to be rid of her! In his pleasure he did not even feel pity.

When he went home to say good-bye to Father and Sister, a strange carriage was standing in front of the door. From it emerged a gentleman named Roget—Peter Mark Roget. He brought greetings from Dr. Brown in London.

"By the way, I read that paper about the picture rotor. Too bad the author is dead. I'm very much interested in optic phenomena. You should see my kaleidoscope sometime. I hope we'll have a chance to talk soon."

"No," answered John. "I've made my decision. The world is full of important ideas, but I'll follow my own mind."

Mr. Roget's features suddenly took on a searching look. "You'll stay in England?"

"No, I'll go back to sea. I'll even reach the North Pole one of these days, but I couldn't succeed in that if I stayed in England."

"Then I can assume in any event that we'll soon have a conversation." Roget began to enjoy himself visibly. "The President of the Royal Society has sent me to you—Sir Joseph Banks, who's at present in his county seat in Revesby. Would you perhaps wish to accompany me to him?"

John was silent, perplexed, and began to suspect something.

"He knows you. He read what you wrote about Flinders's compass. And Sir John Barrow, the first secretary of the Admiralty . . ."

"What's the meaning of this?" John asked hoarsely.

Mr. Roget hesitated. "Actually, Sir Joseph wanted to tell you himself. You—will take over a ship in Deptford and go to the North Pole."

[12]

♦♦♦

VOYAGE INTO
THE ICE

*T*he expedition. Everyone in Deptford knew what that meant. It consisted of the copper-plated brigs *Dorothea* and *Trent,* which were being loaded with everything needed at the North Pole.

"Above all, leather jackets and fur coats!" the furriers hoped.

"Suspense novels," said a bookseller. "It's very dull there."

"Audacious men," surmised the ladies of London society, and let themselves be driven there by coach to sightsee.

Everybody insisted on knowing the precise orders received by the expedition. One person wanted to hear about it directly from the Admiralty, the other from Captain Buchan, commander of the enterprise. Some cited Lieutenant Franklin, captain of the *Trent.* Others doubted it: "Franklin? He never says anything."

"A slow captain. That sort of thing won't wash," Midshipman George Back announced. "How will it be when we're on the high seas?"

Andrew Reid looked at his friend with admiration and contradicted him only to continue the conversation. "But the chickens disappeared from board fast enough, George."

"That'll prove to have been a mistake. Chickens are fresh

meat. But that's not the least of it. Whenever he speaks there's first of all a pause. How can anyone like that give orders?"

They were fresh out of maritime school and knew exactly what had to be done. Back already had a nickname for Franklin: "Cap'n Handicap."

The first night on board John had a fever and shivered. In his half sleep he heard countless voices conveying incomprehensible messages, demanding decisions, and criticizing something he had supposedly ordered. He tossed back and forth, ground his teeth in his dreams, and sweated through his blanket. In the morning his neck muscles were aching and he padded out of his cabin with a crick in his neck.

Fear it was, nothing but fear, yet hard to conquer. Close-mouthed, he went through the entire ship, returned salutes, accepted reports, and tried to transform himself from a member of the Horncastle Reading Society into a captain. He knew this from before: fear of not being able to understand everything, of no longer being able to do things very well yet of not being able to defend himself if he was simply passed over. Fear that no one could adjust to his pace and that in trying to adjust to the pace of others he would fail miserably!

The *Trent* held only 250 tons, but at the moment it seemed to him more gigantic and incomprehensible than his very first ship, that merchantman on the voyage to Lisbon eighteen years ago. This kind of fear was familiar. So far it had been dispelled by his habit of wanting to see everything through to the end, with or without luck. But now another fear was added: if he were to fall deathly ill now, or go under, or be replaced, he would have waited and struggled in vain for years!

The strength, calm, and self-confidence he had found on the *Bedford* after the Battle of New Orleans seemed to have gone into hiding—in any case, this state could not be recalled on command. He also lacked a mystique: a scar whose history nobody knew didn't help anymore.

A good antidote to fear was—learning. To begin with, John learned the instructions of the Admiralty.

The North Pole was not the primary destination of their voyage but only one of several way stations, of interest to the Crown only insofar as it might be located in an open sea through which one could sail to the Pacific. A whaler had reported that the ice fields in the extreme north tended to loosen. Secretary Barrow had hoped for this information. He announced immediately that he and a man named Franklin had always believed in an open polar sea. The expedition, at first mildly ridiculed, now seemed extremely important to everyone.

The *Dorothea* and the *Trent* were to sail through the opening between Spitsbergen and Greenland, then cross over the North Pole to the Bering Strait, and call on the port of Petropavlovsk on the Kamchatka peninsula, where Cook had landed in his day. From there, duplicates of logbooks, travel notes, and maps were to be sent to England by land, while the ships would continue to the Sandwich Islands to spend the winter, returning to England the following spring, preferably once again across the North Pole.

A second expedition was to find a way to the Pacific along the rim of the North American continent. But it was believed that this route was more problematical.

How these politicians and merchants were interested! John put his papers down on the cabin table and spun them around with his fingers. Excitement pulsed in his throat. From the North Pole on, everything would be new; one just had to get there.

He also learned his ship by heart, memorizing whatever figures he could lay his hands on. He checked the calculations of anything that had to be calculated: weight of the load in relation to total weight, trimming, sail area; lateral plane, draft. He already hit upon the first detail: the *Trent's* draft seemed to increase more rapidly than could be accounted for by the daily increase of the load. He figured once more precisely, then called in Lieutenant Beechey, his first officer. Beginning immediately, he wanted a report from every watch as to how deep the ship lay in the water and how high the water level was in the bilge.

Did the lieutenant notice John's insecurity and disquiet? But Beechey was tactful. When their eyes met, he turned away blinking. When listening, he seemed to examine the condition of the deck planks; when talking, he would scan the horizon with his eyes narrow slits, his lashes white. His face betrayed nothing more than a kind of ill-tempered guardedness, and he never spoke one word too many.

So John's calculations were correct! The *Trent* had a leak. It did not seem to be big, but the trouble was it couldn't be found. The water flowed into the hold, but where it came from could not be determined. They kept on looking. The pumps, then, already sounded in port! But John felt strangely relieved: a leak, that was at least a real worry.

The overall commander of the expedition apparently believed that John was a protégé of the Secretary of the Admiralty. David Buchan, a red-faced, impatient man, never wanted to listen for any length of time and above all didn't want to postpone their departure because of a leak.

"Are you serious? You have a leak but can't find it? Are we supposed to wait till the polar summer is over again? Let your men pump for a few weeks; they'll notice soon enough where the water comes from."

Buchan's rudeness only made John calmer. Now he had a concrete adversary; that helped and was comforting. "Sir, of course I'll go to the polar sea even with a leak!"

That sounded so self-assured and cutting that Buchan became a little insecure: "If the topic isn't exhausted by the time we get to the Shetlands we'll take the *Trent* out of the water and look at it from the outside."

April 25, 1818, was the day of departure. The pier was bright with faces. Eleanor Porden turned up to wish an astonished John lots of good luck, slipping him a lengthy poem at the end of which the North Pole itself, speaking directly, declared itself conquered. John knew now: she really liked him. She even admired the long ice saws and the equipment with which seawater was supposed to be desalinated. She was enthusiastic about

171

research, mesmerism, and electric appearances, and she implored John to observe whether a particularly high degree of magnetism was in the air in the polar region and how this affected sympathies among people. When saying good-bye she fell twittering on his neck. With the best of will John could do no other than to reach around her waist. If only he wouldn't always hold on to everything so long! He sensed that he ran the danger of being conspicuous to her and to others, and so he hurriedly withdrew into important calculations about the expedition's course. Then they cast off. Daffodils were blooming. Even as a thin line in the distance, the shore was aglow with yellow.

The water poured in more voluminously every day, and there were not enough men. For a full crew the *Trent* lacked exactly one-sixth of its regular complement. Every man spent half his watch on the pumps.

In Lerwick, despite all his efforts John found neither the leak nor any volunteers to reinforce the crew. The people of the Shetlands lived off seafaring and whaling, and they knew well what it meant when a ship, reeling in shallow water, is looked over inch by inch. When they were told that only the copper plates were being fastened more securely, they laughed, embarrassed. Nobody wanted to be hired on a leaking ship. John began earnestly to fear that this invisible hole in the hull would cheat him of the North Pole.

Buchan thought of replacing the missing sailors by pressing men into service. But since this was now illegal he said to John: "I'll leave it to you, Mr. Franklin."

When John was alone with his first officer, Beechey scanned the horizon with his gray eyes and remarked, "The crew will stick it out. It's a good crew. Three or four forced men who don't share their mood are worse than none at all."

"Thank you," John mumbled, perplexed.

The good thing about Beechey was that he spoke his mind when it was needed.

* * *

Seaman Spink, from Grimsby, knew how to tell more stories than three village oaks taken together, and he had indeed gotten around more. At the age of twelve he had been pressed into service for a while. He had sailed with the little ship *Pickle* under Lapenotière, was taken prisoner by the French, had broken out, and, in the company of a man named Hewson, had fled across Europe to Trieste. He told of an Alsatian cobbler whose boots lengthened one's steps so that with them one could march almost twice as fast as a Frenchman could run. He told of the peasant women in the Black Forest who could hide two or three escapees from Bonaparte under their wide Sunday skirts. And in Bavaria they had rowed across the stormy Chiemsee in a boat with only one oar. Then, in a fishing village on the eastern shore, they had consumed a tender roast with a wondrous dumpling that allowed them to march on for a fortnight without a pause or a morsel of food, as true as his name was Spink.

They all rushed on deck: a narwhal had been sighted. His horn stuck out distinctly. That was a bad sign. There was only one thing worse: when the ship's bell would start ringing of its own. But that never happened, or it could never be told because soon thereafter the ship would sink with mouse and man.

It was not mentioned again. After all, in the open polar sea beyond the ice barrier, completely different creatures of gigantic dimensions awaited them. The Admiralty even figured that after the pack ice had melted, these creatures might penetrate southward to the Atlantic trade routes and devour a ship or two. Even if nobody in the *Trent*'s crew was superstitious, nobody could be entirely without fear.

There was not a soul on board who was rebellious or lazy. John had prepared himself for the fact that sooner or later he would have to order his first punishment, but so far that sort of thing was not in sight. For some time now every commanding officer had to keep a Logbook of Punishments. John opened his book every evening and wrote in it, "No infractions of rules today."

He could not make head or tail of George Back, or rather, as far as Back was concerned, he did not know his own mind. There remained a shyness, an awkwardness, a guardedness. This could not be explained in official terms alone. John put it out of his mind. It was better not to understand Back at all than to misunderstand him. Back might possibly save his life someday! Instincts were good but only when expressed clearly.

A slight guardedness remained.

He now had the courage to request that statements be repeated, that impatience not be allowed, that his own pace be imposed on others for the good of all: "I'm slow. Please adjust accordingly." Back got to hear this in a most amiable way, and his reports became useful. Man Overboard, Fire in the Ship? No reason to swallow entire syllables. It was important only that the captain understood where, what, and when. Confusion was more dangerous than any emergency, and the captain's confusion was the most dangerous kind. They all learned that.

Endurance. John needed no sleep. He practiced phrases and words as he had as a ship's boy. The way orders should begin: for example, Mr. Beechey, please be so good and let . . . ; Mr. Back, would you be so kind as to . . . Kirby, see to it at once that . . .

He again thought about the fixed look. It was and remained dangerous. But when this look was not part of war service and was used only rarely, it no longer determined a slave's speed but rather represented the power to act instantly exercised by a good commander who usually relied more on the study of details and on dreaming. Slowness became honorable; speed became the servant. The large overview was not a good view, for it overlooked too much. Presence of mind, raised to a law, created neither a present moment nor a specific point of view. John opted for absent-mindedness and was sure of himself. He thought of devising a system by which one could live and lead ships as well.

Perhaps a new era would begin with him, John Franklin? 74 degrees, 25 minutes. They had reached the latitude of Bear Island.

* * *

Beyond 75 degrees northern latitude it began to snow. John sniffed outside his cabin door and looked at the quarter-deck covered with white powder. It had smelled exactly like this when he had seen snow for the first time. He looked around furtively, then dared to go outside and began to do an ungainly bear dance in order to see whether his feet left imprints. He felt so young that he had to think about it: Perhaps it was real! How do I know, then, he wondered, that I'm over thirty just like the others? If I'm slow like a clock, then it takes longer, too, until I've run down. So perhaps I'm only twenty. Abruptly he ended his bear dance, because Midshipman Back stared at him from the main yard, seriously, almost as though admonishing him. John wanted to ignore him but couldn't help looking at his own foot prints through Back's eyes and calling to mind his own movements. He had to laugh, and he looked at Back again.

The other laughed back with white teeth. A handsome fellow. "The snow is wonderful, sir!"

No, it wasn't possible to detect irony in that statement. Yet . . . ! He put captain's wrinkles into his face, turned away brusquely, retiring into his cabin, slightly irritated.

He recalled polar magnetism. But how could one measure that?

Now it became seriously cold. The tackling iced over; ropes in use froze so stiff they couldn't be distinguished from fixed lines. The men on watch had not only to pump but also to beat the lines with sticks to keep them moveable. All maneuvers with sails turned into adventures, and the cold got worse. Everybody coughed, heartbreakingly. John, on the other hand, was delirious with joy.

Since there continued to be no infractions of rules, he studied the snow and entered the shapes of snowflakes in his Logbook of Punishments. "In principle, snow is hexagonal," he wrote. After all, research was the purpose of the trip. Amused, he thought of the admirals' faces when, after a long detour through

Mother Russia, the Logbook of Punishments of the *Trent* would finally reach them.

For the first time the ships sailed through drift ice. The ice floes clinked and scraped along the sides of the hull.

Nobody wanted to sleep. No one was used to thinking of the phenomenon of night being so bright. The low sun shone upon the white sails, the ice sparkled as if it were made of diamond caps and emerald grottoes; a frozen city grew and unfolded in wild figures. Nautical language was almost superfluous: they sailed from the "church" to the "fortress," then, bearing past the "cave," to the "bridge." Ice shimmered below the surface of the water, reflecting light. The sea was cloaked in creamy white; seals swam in it as in luminous milk. The crew hung on the rigging and stared at the sparkling hunks of ice that kept pushing behind the ship's keel as though wanting to catch up with it. The sun sank toward midnight, red and alien: the largest banana in the world. It didn't even actually sink—it only went into hiding for a short time, took a bath, and reappeared to dry itself.

Beechey said: "All this is well and good, but how do we persuade the next watch to get some sleep?"

It was an evening sky of infinite duration, shadows becoming gigantically long, and when swaths of mist rose, they turned at once into reddish clouds, changing colors up to the northern horizon.

John looked out on the ice, studied its forms, and tried to understand what they meant. It was true, then, that with its own power the sea could surpass itself. Here was the proof. Here he discovered the meaning of his dreams.

Hour after hour he drew shapes of icebergs in his Logbook of Punishments. He added colors: "Green on the left, red on the right, the reverse ten minutes later." He tried to invent names for what he saw, but that didn't work very well. Rather, the sights were like music that would have to be transcribed in a score. The fine-ribbed sea lapped playfully around the ice figures and bore them along in a rhythm, while they themselves seemed to make up a harmony as of musical sounds, although they were also in a sense splintered and split. Yet their effect was to create a feeling of calm and timelessness. Nothing like this could be ugly! Here it was peaceful. Far behind them, somewhere in the south, men worried about the misery of man. In London, time was a despot whom everyone had to obey.

Above 81 degrees latitude the ice floes turned into platforms, and those into islands. At one point, under the most favorable transverse wind, the *Trent* simply stood still and didn't budge. "Why don't we go on?" Reid called from below, and a few minutes later the second mate, Kirby, came on deck: "Why aren't we moving?"

Waiting made the crew restless. Yet in this case there was nothing, but absolutely nothing, to be said against waiting. Perhaps the two ships locked into the ice field might actually drift with it in the right direction. But then came the signal from the *Dorothea*. Buchan ordered: "Chop ice! Haul ship!"

Ten men tried to open up the ice ahead of the bow with axes and spades, ten more strained to pull a rope two ship lengths ahead. A few hours later they were so exhausted that at the end of the watch they were giggling to keep from crying. And yet the whole effort was mounted only to satisfy their and Buchan's impatience. They tried even the most senseless actions if that gave them the feeling they were in motion.

But what if the ice field was drifting south instead of north? Even then it would have been an open question whether Buchan would notice it. He liked to navigate "by instinct."

John ordered music to give the hauling crew at least some cheer. Seaman Gilbert led the way, fiddling. He was just the right man for the job. His musical skills could indeed produce a limited range of distinct tones, yet they were not good enough to make anyone stop and listen.

Oddly, the closer John came to their objective, the more strongly he sensed that he no longer needed it. The complete silence, the absolute timelessness—what, seriously, should he do with them? He was a captain and had a ship; he no longer wanted to be a strip of shore, a coastal rock that looked on for millennia without guilt. Clock time was as essential as weights and measures, because goods and labor had to be distributed justly in this world. The hourglass had to be turned around, the ship's bell had to strike every half hour so Kirby didn't have to pump longer than Spink and Back didn't have to freeze longer than Reid. That wouldn't be any different at the Pole, and John was content with it because he was content now with everything, except perhaps with Buchan's overall command.

He was ineluctably drawn to the Pole, but not because he wanted to start all over again from then on. After all, it had already begun! The goal had been important only for the sake of finding the path to it. He had now taken that path, and the Pole reverted to being a mere geographical concept. He longed only to remain en route—just as he was now, on a voyage of discovery—for the rest of his life. Franklin's System of Life and Travel!

Buchan had taken their bearings in relation to the stars and had made his calculations. So had Franklin. Buchan arrived at 81 degrees 31 minutes; Franklin, 80 degrees 37 minutes. Flustered, Buchan calculated once more and met John by a few minutes, just to save face. Evidently the ice was drifting southward more quickly than they could chop their way open to the north.

Then two gigantic ice fields slunk toward each other and took the *Dorothea* in the middle, squeezing her until the timber of the frame cracked and the ship was even slightly lifted. A short while later the same thing happened to the *Trent,* only less severely. Now they sat tight, as though riveted in place. An iceberg approached more and more closely from aft as if to mock them.

"I'd like to know how the iceberg does it," said Spink. "Perhaps someone's pulling him from below." He pointed down to the sea and meant it as a joke, but they all remembered the narwhal and remained silent.

At all events, it was still as never before; the ship didn't move an inch. Suddenly Gilfillan, the ship's doctor, stormed out of his cabin, shouting: "I think some liquid is running under my bed!"

Franklin went down with the carpenter and asked to be shown the place. Below Gilfillan's bunk was the room where they kept liquid spirits. "Nothing's allowed to run there," the commander concluded. They listened inside the chamber where rum was stocked: yes, something's running there! The supply master checked their inventory. Nothing was missing.

Thus they found the leak. A worker at the shipyards had taken out a rotten bolt and had simply smeared some tar over the gap rather than putting in a new bolt and securing it. The tar didn't stop the water, but it prevented the gap from being seen from the outside. When the *Trent* had been made waterproof again some liquid of a sort still ran down a few gullets. Hours later they got back on their feet and realized that the ship floated again in the open sea.

The ice did as it pleased.

They saw storm petrels fishing and flying so closely along the valleys between mountains of waves that the space seemed as tight as that of a cannonball inside its barrel. Young codfish, shimmering like golden crystals, were lying on the deck planks in the low light, spread out like a treasure lifted from the sea. They saw bears, white masses of fur, irresistibly lured by the burning fish oil, padding nearer and nearer over snow hills and across ponds. Nothing could stop them.

One day a herd of walruses tried to overturn the boat with their tusks and round skulls—a furious mass attack. When shortly afterward the men stood on the ice floe, the animals tried to tip the other end of the ice with their weight, inviting them to a sliding party that would have ended on their tusks. The sailors fired their muskets, but not until the heavy leading bull was killed did the herd finally swim away.

The next outing on foot was even more dangerous, because a heavy fog came up and each man had to hold on to the other by his jacket. They wanted to walk back to the ship by following their own tracks. John Franklin checked the direction with his compass. But it became apparent all of a sudden that the tracks were strangely fresh and, in addition, became more and more numerous. According to both compass and clock time they should have been back on the ship long ago.

They had lost their way and had wandered in circles.

John ordered the men to build an emergency shelter out of ice plates. Reid made no bones of the fact that he would have preferred to go on simply at a right angle to where they had been walking.

"We'll stay warm that way, and we've got to arrive somewhere."

"I take my time before I make mistakes," Franklin countered amiably. He ordered them all to wrap themselves up as warmly as possible and sit around the oil lamp. The muskets were carefully loaded in case a polar bear might drop by.

John crouched and reflected. Whatever the others put forward—proposals, theories, questions—he only nodded and thought some more.

Even when Reid whispered to Back, "You're quite right about the 'handicap,'" John pushed all questions aside. He now needed only time.

A while later Reid asked, "Should we simply wait here, sir?" But John still wasn't ready. There was no reason to end his reflections prematurely, even if death was at the door. Finally he got up.

"Mr. Back. Fire a musket every three minutes, thirty times all told. After that, fire every ten minutes for three hours; after that, once an hour for two days. Please repeat."

"Won't we be dead by then, sir?"

"Possibly. But until then we fire. Please confirm."

Back repeated his instructions, stuttering. Just as nobody counted any more on getting an explanation, John said: "The entire ice field is turning around. It's the only solution. That's why we are walking in circles even when according to the compass we are always marching in the same direction. If there had been a wind we would have noticed it at once."

Four hours later they heard a faint shot in the fog, and then again and again answers to their own shots. An hour after that they heard voices calling out; men with ropes became visible at last; and, behind them, barely a hundred feet away, they saw the towering stern of the *Trent*.

"You're a lucky dog, sir!" Back remarked, relieved and insolent but without a trace of condescension. Rather the contrary! Reid pulled a face. To him Back said, "If we had listened to you we would now be somewhere else; we'd probably be icicles!" Reid was silent. He suddenly gave himself a jolt and stomped violently on a snowflake. John wondered. How could one stomp on a snowflake? Or was there still something else?

In the bright light of day, and from the main mast, one could observe the entire labyrinth. Even if they had gone in the "right" direction they would have missed the ship by a wide distance from where they had been. Had they gone in the opposite direction they would have reached a point where nobody would have looked for them. It would have been a death trap of the first order, and John wasn't caught in it.

It's easier for me now, he reflected, and there are no more problems with Back. The kings of the schoolyard are beginning to listen to me. He had hardly thought of this when suddenly he knew: Back reminded him of Tom Barker, his schoolmate of twenty years ago.

They had not even reached 82 degrees latitude, and already Buchan wanted to turn back. "We ought to find a protected harbor and repair everything."

"We ought . . ." John noted the unaccustomed words. He felt challenged to contradict.

"The polar summer will be over before we'd be done with that. Those damages aren't really that great. Let's have one last try!"

"Do you want to play daredevil?"

"Sir, so far we've discovered nothing and proved nothing."

"I'll tell you something!" Buchan replied. "I believe that what you want to prove is something personal. I've watched you. You want to prove that you're no coward. Perhaps cowardice is your problem."

John decided that he didn't have to think about such remarks. "Only a single try, sir. We haven't much time left, but the open polar sea can't be very far."

"Oh, to hell with you! And what if there's a storm?"

"By then we'll surely be in a proper channel and will be protected. We have to try farther west."

Buchan wavered. The summer was nearing its end. That was a fact.

"I'll decide."

For five days they sailed northwest past a wall of pack ice— first the *Trent,* and the *Dorothea* a quarter mile behind. John looked through the telescope. "They're sailing too close to the pack ice. When the wind stops, they'll drift to the lee shore with the tide." Beechey nodded: "They're bored! they want to watch the seals. And yet the weather outlook isn't very good." John ordered to reduce the sail area to a minimum. Only as a precaution.

"And do you know what's best of all!" exclaimed Gilbert. "We'll arrive at the Sandwich Islands six weeks from now. The reporters are already waiting."

"And the girls," Kirby added. God knows, he always talked about girls. No charitable storm blew that word out of his mouth.

The storm broke suddenly, as though it had been lying in wait in the wings. A calm, silvery sky kept on smiling above racing thunderclouds. Consequently, the violent squall appeared as a particularly vicious attack.

Excitement. Change course: "Hard on the wind. Away from the ice." Will we make it? Hasty prayers. Several voices screamed suddenly: "Man Overboard!" Gilfillan, the doctor, had been swept into the sea by a single blow. But now what? Two basic rules checkmated each other: never drift toward a shore in a storm, and keep your eye on the man when a man's overboard. John decided that here he could judge only blindly. He had given such cases some thought. He kept his eye on the man. Lower boat into water on leeside! Heave to! A dreadful loss of time and distance from shore. One man pointed toward the ice shore; the *Dorothea* already lay helplessly by the wall, rolling and thumping among blocks of ice. She couldn't get away. She would be ground to pieces! In just a few hours she would be nothing but wooden parts that would turn into fuzz. Amen. In the face of this storm, she couldn't escape.

Gilfillan's body was saved, but was he still alive? Hanging on the line, Spink had thrown himself on top of him and had brought him in, ever laughing. Each person got his strength from something. Spink had to laugh even while risking his life. Gilfillan breathed again. Done. What next?

Get over to the *Dorothea* by boat? Sheer suicide. No, let's get out of here while the going's good, they screamed! But John Franklin knew his own principles! "Never be ashamed like Captain Palmer!" That was fifteen years ago. And the *Bridgewater* had soon disappeared without a trace, not a single survivor. The sea's justice is horrible, and it had to be taken into account.

Questions came—more and more urgently. Franklin thought about them and gave no reply. The swift, raging seas were not simply heavy; they contained ice fragments as big as launches that pushed the ship abeam of the storm. Soon it was clear: it would be a miracle if the *Trent* got across. And John didn't believe in miracles; that was something for children.

The critical moment had arrived; even Beechey became nervous: with their slow captain the whole ship would be wrecked. But why did Franklin stay so calm? What did he actually believe? Why did he stare at the shore; what did he look for with his telescope?

"There!" John shouted. "We've got to get there, Mr. Beechey!"

What did he mean? Into the pack ice? Voluntarily?

"Precisely that!" John grabbed Beechey by the shoulders and held him. "Logic!" he roared against the storm. "Logic! In pack ice we're secure. The only solution!"

And an inlet actually opened up, a fiord barely wider than the ship. The captain had seen it; he still had that much calm in him. But now they had to get in. That just couldn't be done. Two ship lengths before the inlet, a huge ice block smashed the rudder, and just as they reached their goal a heavy breaker turned the *Trent* abeam of the sea. At once the starboard side of the ship crashed into the massive pack ice. All the men tumbled down; no one could hold on to anything. It was as if someone had pulled a rug out from under them. In addition, a terrible sound, the signal for the dead: the ship's bell started to strike. John clawed his way upright again and pointed up the foremast, shouting, "Shake the reef!"

They all looked at him as if they were seeing the first signs of insanity. The next heavy wave came thundering toward them and again smashed the ship into the wall like an egg into a frying pan. The masts bent like plant stalks. And someone was supposed to go aloft and—what did he say?—"Shake the reefs"? The ship's bell rang like crazy. Of course it did! Everything was finished! It wouldn't stop till they were all dead. The men clutched at whatever was handy; no one stirred anymore. The next big wave, the same play. The ship was lost.

John Franklin seemed stranger and stranger. Now he grabbed his left shoulder with his right hand, held it tight and pulled at it with all his might. Did he want to demote himself in rank, or even tear himself in two? At any rate, he had gone mad; here was the proof! Gilbert cursed, Kirby prayed; they all prayed. Would Kirby ever speak of girls again?

Franklin had torn the sleeve out of his uniform jacket, crawled up to the ship's bell, and between two strikes of the storm warning said to the first officer, "Mr. Beechey, please be so good and have the reefs taken out of the foresail." Then he wound the uniform cloth around the bell's clapper, tied a knot, and pulled it so tight that it might have choked an elephant. "Now we have some quiet!" he said contentedly, as though he had gagged the storm, too.

And all at once they felt again something like safety. The bravest among them dared to go aloft to the top of the foremast and shake the reefs. They saw from above what John already knew: the bow of the *Trent* had struck a short way into the inlet; with full rig on the foremast, without the reef, they might succeed in sneaking the ship all the way in, if they could make it swerve away from the ice wall between two breakers. Others removed cloth still remaining on the main mast; no one lost a hold, and as the sea retreated before making another terrible run, the *Trent* turned obediently, even without a rudder, and slipped away from the storm. The wind drove it into the ice mountains, still threw several bits of debris into its splintering stern, and tore the sails into rags. With a loud crunch the bow wedged itself between the glasslike walls and went on crunching. Finally the ship lay still. One could hardly sense the motion of the sea, not a breath of wind. Where did the wind go?

Now previously prepared fenders were brought out, thick stuffed walrus skins to protect the ship from further friction and jolts.

The cook, a man with a wooden leg, limped out of the galley and appeared on deck, quite pale. "Have we landed? Do we have to leave?"

How could they help the *Dorothea?* First of all, they had to get over the glass walls! The first man leapt across from the topgallant span to the ice: Spink, of course, laughing loudly. He tossed a lanyard to the ice wall; now people, equipment, loose tackling, and above all the entire anchor line of the *Trent* could be heaved over. John Franklin had a plan again; there was no doubt of that. No one thought to ask any questions. Only Beechey, who had to stay on the ship, said briefly: "Good luck, sir! I bet you'll get them all out of that wreck." "Oh, no," answered John, "we'll get the ship to safety. An inlet like ours is just a hundred paces ahead of its bow."

Back had listened in. "How do you know?"

" 'Sir.' I'm addressed as 'sir,' " answered John, with pointed slowness. "I've seen the inlet."

For half an hour they fought their way across the crevasses opening in the ice plateau until they reached the cliff above the

Dorothea. Deep down she still hurled herself against the ice wall long since surrounded by the debris of her own yards and spars and one of her boats. How many might not already have succumbed?

In a great hurry they lowered the end of the anchor line down to the *Dorothea* and a short time later hacked an abutment into the ice around the majestic summit on the other side of the fiord. Thank God Buchan grasped the situation at once! The anchor lines were spliced together, wound around the foot of the foremast, and pulled through the grooves they had carved into the abutment at the other end. The storm let up slightly, but the swells were as dreadful as ever.

Twenty-five men stood in the holes they had chopped into the ice and tugged the rope with all their might. The ship hardly moved from the spot. Or at best, by inches! John divided them into two shifts and took his watch from his pocket. Each group labored for ten minutes; then it was the other's turn. Any man who let go of the line dropped to the ground as if unconscious; some of them vomited. Presumably the ship became heavier and heavier as the water poured in. John took all necessary steps to get the survivors out of the wreck, and the exhausted crew thought they might as well start now.

"Two hours by now!" Kirby panted, his face pale. "We've got to give up."

"He has no sense of time!" Reid panted back. If he had had enough breath, he would have said more. An hour later he could barely form even this first sentence in his mind. Talking was impossible for them all. During this time, John pulled the line, too, although this was usually not acceptable for an officer. But the bare arm was freezing!

All at once the ship gave way and came along! Length by length, it crept forward beneath the cliff. Now Buchan had the foresails cleared and unfurled as the *Dorothea* lay before the gap. Laboriously, the half-wrecked ship slouched into the inlet, more like a saturated sponge than one of His Majesty's ships.

Saved! A single boat lost, but two ships saved and all men well.

Back went over to John Franklin and said, "Sir, I apologize. We owe you our lives."

John looked at him, and after all the exertion he couldn't get the captain's wrinkles out of his face quickly enough. Why did Back apologize? For Tom Barker, he thought. Odd idea. As a captain, he didn't always have to ask when he didn't understand a sentence. He could pick what he had to know, and Back's motives weren't part of it. Back became insecure and wanted to turn away. But in place of any response John simply put his arm around Back's shoulders and embraced him.

Meanwhile, Beechey had secured the *Trent* with only five men and had caulked the first leaks. John embraced him, too.

The sail maker tried to untie the sleeve of John's jacket from the ship's bell to sew it on again. But he had surely imagined that untying the sleeve would be an easier task. It took him almost a quarter of an hour. What changes a storm could bring! Suddenly Reid no longer spoke to Back or, when he did, his remarks were cool and ironic. Sometimes he withdrew, and when he returned he looked as if he had been crying. Spink seemed to understand him. He told the young man a story—to him quite alone. It had to do with the adventures of the Patagonians, those giant people down at the southern end of South America who could grab several steers at once by their horns and for whom there existed equality in love. There were no preferences among them; love there was as universal as air is for breathing. But just that seemed to be the point that made Reid sad. With that he really got tears in his eyes. He had been saved, as well as his ship, and his companions—and he wept because he had convinced himself that a certain person loved someone else.

"Perhaps somebody will understand those midshipmen," said Beechey.

"Give him a lot of work to do," answered Franklin. "He must not weep but learn his profession."

On taking their bearings they discovered that they had passed 82 degrees latitude. John got out Dr. Orme's treatise on Pupil F. Now he was not a pupil anymore. He could read it.

*   *   *

He even felt suspense. "The creation of the individual through speed"—he had always feared that the essay would tell him how things would go on in the future. Now he even hoped so, for it couldn't be anything bad anymore.

Dr. Orme used difficult phrases like "differences among people insofar as, measured by individual appearances, they are distinguished by the completeness of their vision . . ." These differences Dr. Orme did not find in the mechanical properties of eye or ear, as one might think, but in the orientation of the brain: "Pupil F is slow because he has to look at everything that comes into view for a very long time. The image held by the eye remains in place to be thoroughly explored; succeeding images glide past unexamined. Pupil F sacrifices completeness for detail. For the latter the entire head is required, and it takes some time before there is room for the next unit. Therefore, a slow person cannot follow fast developments—"

But I have blindness and the fixed look, thought John; why didn't he mention those?

"—but he can grasp unique appearances and slow developments better."

After that, Dr. Orme wrote about the "ominous acceleration of the present time": he proposed measuring everyone's speed with instruments and deciding on that basis what each person is suited to do. There should be "synoptic" and "individuated" professions. Many senseless exertions and sufferings would be unnecessary if their speed were measured early on. In schools, separate sections could be organized for quick and slow children.

"One should let the quick live quickly and the slow slowly, each by his distinct temporal measure. The quick can be put into synoptic professions, which are exposed to the accelerations of the age: they will be able to bear up well and perform their best service as coachmen or members of Parliament. Slow people, on the other hand, should learn professions requiring detailed application, such as craftsmanship, the medical arts, or painting. From their withdrawn position they can follow gradual change and judge carefully the labor of the quick and of the governing."

Flora Reed would have become quiet with rage, John thought. Of equality, not a trace. But he had that thought too soon, for only a few lines farther on Dr. Orme moved to the matter of universal suffrage. Every four years, the population of England, perhaps even only the slow—also the women!— should select the best among the quick who had proven themselves as a new government. "The slow," argued Dr. Orme, "know how to judge aptly after four years what has changed and how they have been treated."

John reflected for a very long time, then pushed the treatise aside. "No," he said proudly and sadly at the same time, "he's made something up."

If his teacher could have known what John could do now and what he had done, he would have written a different essay. If a slow person, against all predictions, had managed to survive in a fast profession, that was better than anything else.

He turned to Franklin's System. His first points were already inscribed in the Logbook of Punishments:

"I am the captain and I never leave any doubt about that, above all not in myself. All others must adjust to my speed, because it is the slowest. Only when respect is created on this point can there be safety and alertness. I am a friend to myself. I take seriously what I think and sense. The time I require for this is never wasted. I allow the same for others. Impatience and fear must be ignored if possible; panic is strictly forbidden. In shipwrecks, the first things that must be saved are: MAPS, OBSERVATIONS AND REPORTS, PICTURES.

Almost every day brought new sentences to be added. The last one read: "The slower work is more important. It is the first officer who makes all normal, quick decisions."

They were sailing back to England on painfully repaired ships and were glad to get back at all. Work on the pumps was even harder than it had been on the way out.

Perhaps the open sea at the Pole was a fairy tale. But John did not believe this had as yet been proved.

London received them with great joy. Actually, it was widely believed that they had come directly from the Sandwich Islands.

Buchan and Franklin delivered their first report to Sir John Barrow at the Admiralty. Buchan praised John Franklin highly, and he hardly knew where to look.

"And now, Mr. Buchan," Barrow asked, "you'll probably want to get back to the ice soon?"

"Not exactly," Buchan replied. "To cruise in this region for half an eternity one must love the company of men more than I do."

"And you, Mr. Franklin?"

John, thinking about Buchan's last remark, was a little startled, because Barrow's question had now obtained a secondary meaning for which he needed more time. Confused, he only got out, "Oh, of course I will."

"Good," Barrow responded with an amused drawl. "Then I'll probably have a new command for you."

That same afternoon, John Franklin appeared at Eleanor Porden's and proposed marriage—in well-prepared sentences. She felt both pressed and flattered, changed the topic for the moment, and asked about polar magnetism. "Actually," she said, "I had expected news only of that."

What John could offer on the subject of polar magnetism didn't seem satisfactory, even to himself. He therefore came back to his proposal. Suddenly Eleanor looked at him, appearing very grown-up, and said, "I believe you want to prove something." But she declined for the time being—"for reasons of slowness," as she put it.

John thought it over and concluded that this pleased him quite well. In the evening he found himself with a not inexpensive harbor whore. Before he could prove his most important point, she first wanted to know everything about Kamchatka and her colleagues there.

"Sure you were there!" she urged again and again. "Sure you were there. You just won't tell! Stubborn, like all officers!"

[13]

◆◆

RIVER JOURNEY
TO THE ARCTIC COAST

This time John Franklin was the sole commander of the expedition, although not as the captain of a ship, for it was to be a land journey. With him were the physician Dr. Richardson, the midshipmen Back and Hood, as well as Seaman Hepburn. Bearers, guides, hunters, and food supplies were to be provided in Canada by the royal fur-trading companies.

On Exaudi Sunday, the sixth Sunday after Easter, 1819, they left the dock at Gravesend on the *Prince of Wales*, a small ship owned by the Hudson's Bay Company. John was prepared for everything he could think of. He had even practiced marching, measuring the average length of his steps by pacing between two London mileposts. Moreover, he had equipped his compass with a retractable ring for his thumb, enabling him to take the bearings of a landmark above the line of his outstretched arm and the upper rim of the compass. Knife, drill, awl, and whistle for emergency signals had been supplied to everyone, also wire for fastening snowshoes and, upon the advice of a postilion, stockings, undershirts, and ankle-length drawers made of lamb's wool, which itched fiercely.

John was glad that one person would be along whom he knew: George Back. He had volunteered, announcing that he would go for Franklin through thick and thin. Talk like that embarrassed John, but it was good to have a quick man to rely on. He decided to make Back his unofficial first officer, to whom he could delegate the "normal" fast decisions. Of course, he'd still have to prove himself. There would be others. John observed them closely, because he wanted to apply the system he had developed on the *Trent* to everyone in his party.

"The captain of the *Blossom* could have remained a happy man, and the *Blossom* a happy ship, if they had not made him its captain—for he was no captain." Dr. Richardson paused and sucked on his too tightly stuffed pipe until the meager glow turned into a reddish hue illuminating his scrawny face. Thick puffs of smoke seemed to darken the weak evening light coming in through the mess window. Yes, the *Blossom*! Dr. Richardson had been on its unfortunate voyage as the ship's doctor, and he told of it all in great detail. Franklin, of course, asked himself why.

"A weak captain can be influenced by everyone who calls him strong. He listens to flattery and malicious insinuations, for truth is his enemy in any case."

There had been an insidious cargo officer on board the *Blossom*, Cattleway by name, who liked to spy on people and then spread his ill-gotten knowledge. If he didn't find anything he could use, he simply made up lies. The captain, however, believed him. Two lieutenants were put in irons because of supposed disloyalty. When they were later prosecuted in a court-martial, the court condemned not the officers but the captain himself, and the slanderous seaman was sent in irons to Van Diemen's Land. John thought of that island south of Australia that Matthew had circled and explored. Not a bad punishment, he thought, to work under an open sky and to help cultivate new land. For that's how he imagined what happened to the convicts.

"And why was this captain weak?" asked Richardson, quickly answering himself: "He lacked the blessings of faith. He who does not let the Lord guide him cannot guide a ship." Again he busied himself lighting his pipe, perhaps so as not to watch John while the story took its effect. And it was doing that! He wants me to say something about it, thought John; but he was cautious. If this man Richardson was so devout, he would not be easy to deal with. He derived authority from God—that was dangerous to Franklin's System. There are too many interpretations of God's will. Generally, John found religion useful when it was a matter of maintaining understanding and order. Passionate visionaries and witnesses, on the other hand, made him uncomfortable. He therefore replied only: "Guiding a ship, that's navigation. That's all I know."

The expedition was to reach the northernmost edge of the continent and then push eastward along the unexplored shore up to Repulse Bay, where a Captain Parry would be waiting for them with his ship. If the project proved successful, the Northwest Passage for which Europe had been looking for two centuries would be found! And for that there would be a fat purse of twenty thousand pounds! The "crucial bay," then, was the bay that opened to a canal: John had never wavered from this dream since his return from Australia. In addition, the Admiralty expected careful descriptions of all Indian and Eskimo tribes they encountered. Friendly attitudes were desired; barter of alcohol against furs permitted; no firearms. It was important to see that the natives became accustomed to helping any stranded passenger ship by supplying them with food if necessary—it would do them no harm.

"It'll do them harm in any event," Back suggested casually. "Let's just hope they don't find out while we depend on them."

The briefest sentence of all was spoken by Hepburn, a Scotsman from near Edinburgh. "It'll happen," he said. Hepburn had been going to sea since childhood. After the shipwreck of his China clipper he was fished out by a warship and pressed into the navy. Four times he tried to desert, but he had volunteered for this expedition. Only he knew why.

In the dock at Stromness, in the Orkneys, they encountered the brig *Harmonie,* belonging to the Herrnhuter Brotherhood.

Franklin, Back, and Richardson were rowed over for a visit. They met a few recently wedded Eskimo couples—Christians, of course—and a Lutheran missionary who was busy teaching them how to improve their prayers even further. He understood only German and Innuit. Without an interpreter nothing could be done.

Innuit, that's what the Eskimos called themselves. It meant simply "humans." They appeared modest, clean, and obliging, and Richardson suggested that the blessings of religion were already apparent. One could see it in their eyes.

Back smiled. But he did this often enough, for he was pleased with himself and wanted to please others, above all Franklin. John sensed this. But if Back could do something to contribute to an atmosphere of confidence and trust, it would be welcome. Morale was high.

After a collision with an iceberg, which smashed the rudder, the *Prince of Wales* finally anchored at York Factory on the western shore of Hudson's Bay.

On land, new names and faces had to be impressed upon their memory: Frenchmen, Indians, officials of the fur-trading company, as well as a major of the Royal Engineers named By, who was explaining the feasibility of digging canals from the bay to the Great Lakes. He also told of the *Frontenac,* a steamboat that cruised around Lake Superior emitting black smoke. Technology was winning everywhere, and By was its man.

"If you don't find the Northwest Passage, gentlemen, then I'll simply build a canal with a hundred shiploads of explosives." That's the kind of fellow he was, that By! John didn't like him much, and answered only, "It'll be difficult to find captains and crews for such ships."

They started almost at once, after only a few days, for it was September and Franklin wanted to get as far as possible before winter. They paddled against the current with a few Indians and French-Canadian trappers up rivers and lakes to Lake Winnipeg, then on the Saskatchewan River to the trading post called Cumberland House. Women were along, too.

The trappers, who spoke only French, called themselves voyageurs. They weren't friendly to anyone, except possibly their dogs. François Samandré owned two women, whom for the duration of the trip he loaned to colleagues for money. Two other voyageurs had only one woman between them, undoubtedly beaten twice as often as the others. Drunkenness brought these sullen fellows into an incredible rage about everything: themselves, the women, the boats, even the dogs. One morning John assembled the crew and told them he would send away any ruffian who beat people up. When in one case he actually did so, things got a little better.

Their diet consisted mostly of pemmican—a mixture of fat and minced dried meat blended with sugar and berries—an odd paste, but it gave strength. It was sewn into steer hides in packages weighing eighty pounds each.

All those loads, all that hauling! Often the boats had to be portaged to get around waterfalls, up hills without paths or footholds. The battle against the current alone made their shoulders ache; dampness and cold made it worse. The doctor couldn't do much about this with his pious talk. But he had taken some good ointments along, too.

Back was efficient but much too impatient. True, they didn't progress very fast, but they had to adjust to that. The voyageurs rested after each full hour and smoked a pipe. If they needed that—well and good. They measured the length of the river segments by the number of pipes smoked: they had to smoke, or else their standard of measurement wouldn't work.

When for once they had the current with them at last, on the Echimamish River, the Indians suddenly didn't want to go on. Their souls had not kept up with them; they had to wait.

John understood Back's urgency, but in private he admonished him to respect local custom. Besides, Back couldn't stand boredom and didn't want to be boring himself—he was an entertainer and always sought out the telling point, even if it hurt—but he didn't understand that on such a long journey, it was justice that mattered more.

John began to find the other midshipman, Robert Hood,

much more pleasant. Hood, like Back, had received instruction in drawing and painting and was (supposed) to capture in sketches anything that might be of importance. But what was of importance? Hood was a dreamy, quiet man. He didn't concern himself with the actual goal of the expedition but rather with anything that stirred his imagination: reflections of light in the shallow water of a river bend, the cleft nose of a voyageur, the figure created by a flight of birds. Back made fun of him, and Hood's good-naturedness only spurred him on. John realized that Hood was not the quick man he could make into his first officer, but he was most like himself and John therefore believed in him the most.

By the end of October they reached Cumberland House. Here they had to stay, for the smaller rivers were already frozen over solid. The local company manager or governor assigned them an unfinished building that they could complete and equip for the winter. Hood built the fireplace; he knew how to do that. "He's a fire maker," said the Cree Indians, who valued him highest among the Europeans, whom otherwise they didn't think much of. Rifle bullets had decimated their once powerful tribe, and alcohol had the remainder by the scruff of the neck.

"The power of the whites will grow and grow," one of the Crees told Robert Hood. "No one will be able to stop them. They will perish only when they have destroyed everything. For then the warriors of the Great Rainbow will chase them away and put everything back the way it was."

"I destroy nothing," Hood replied quietly. "I don't want to leave traces behind. At most a few pictures."

They sat around the fireplace every night: the leather-faced doctor reading his Bible; heavy, sleepy Hepburn; and slim Hood, who whenever he thought of something blinked his eyes and opened his mouth without saying anything.

It became obvious that no one liked George Back. The beautiful young man who always wanted to say the unexpected soon had everyone against him, though he was never openly discussed. Just for that reason he edged closer and closer to John. He kept him informed, admired him, wanted to be admired in turn. It was like an offer: he wanted to get something back for his admiration. But since he could exchange only actions for Franklin's admiration, he became more and more nervous. Great deeds could not be accomplished in a winter camp.

While they were walking to a tea given by the local business manager, Back said to him above the crunching snow under their feet: "Sir, I simply love you. If that's a problem, it's still no catastrophe." He said it so—facetiously. John sensed with annoyance that his ears were turning red while he was searching for an answer that would end the conversation in one blow. But that would have led nowhere. John knew his own head. If he reacted too quickly, the situation would shift in directions he could not manage. Calm and caution, then!

The steps continued with their crunching noise. Their breath formed clouds of mist. They had nearly reached the business manager's blockhouse. "A catastrophe, I daresay, it is not," said John. "But I'd like to see something good come of it. You exaggerate too much, Mr. Back. Must you?" He slowed his steps because they were approaching their host's door too quickly. He recalled a motto he had learned from the shepherd in Spilsby: "Between overstatement and understatement lies one hundred percent." Alas, the shepherd hadn't adhered to it himself.

They arrived at Mr. Williams's with red ears. Indian tea, ship zwieback, and corned beef, but no good news about provisions for the expedition. On the way home, John considered whether part of the crew might not still travel ahead to Fort Chipewyan that winter to procure supplies at the fur-trading posts there.

Back agreed enthusiastically. "The two of us, sir!" But when the day of their departure drew near, John decided that in addition to Back he wanted Hepburn to go with him. Back's hunger could not be stilled with justice and reason, but anything else would be out of the question for a commander. Fate must take its course.

The three men left Cumberland House on January 15, 1820,

on snowshoes and with two voyageurs and two dog sleds, guided by Indians, piled so high with food that there was barely room for the sextant. Some tracks had to be dug in the deep snow ahead of time to keep the dogs from jumping around and bothering each other.

For weeks they journeyed through endless forests with gigantic trees, their tops rustling in the wind. It would have been beautiful had it not been for the snowshoes, which felt like punishment for every wrong one might have ever done. They clung to the boots like enormous ducks' feet of wood and webbing, and their weight in pounds turned into hundredweights as they became encrusted with snow and ice. The human being is designed wrongly for snowshoes; there should be a much greater distance between the ankles! After only a few miles the pain remained steady, for the edge of the duck's foot always hit the same spot. "Go slower!" John admonished. "You'll conserve energy!"

Back was strong, well rested, and fast. Too fast! Perhaps he just wanted to endure more hardships than John—a rather questionable source of energy, but effective.

Back rushed ahead. Back waited impatiently! Back seized the initiative! And his smile seemed to John to become ever more predatory.

"Why so fast?" John asked. "It's a very long way."

"That's why," replied Back insolently, and grinned. Hepburn was visibly annoyed, but his rank was lower and he had to keep himself in check. Back made him feel he was in the way, though actually it was John who was purposely slowing down their pace.

The voyageurs looked thoughtfully down their noses and were silent. They could have kept up with Back, but for them this trip was work for pay, pure and simple, and so extra efforts should not certainly become routine. Besides, they could tell the difference between a commander and a midshipman.

When they made a rest stop, though Back was far ahead, Hepburn said casually to his superior, "He wants to show us." With that he put ointment on his sore ankles as if nothing had been said, and John Franklin fidgeted with compass and sextant for the longest time before replying. "Strength can also be something other than mere speed," he said as he took bearings through the diopter.

It was John Franklin who made these stops, and he did so even when he didn't need them for himself. It was not that the navigator needed the pause, but rather that the pause needed the navigator. This Back was a giant of ambition, but when there were delays he was a dwarf about time.

They arrived in Fort Chipewyan at the end of March. John saw the representatives of the fur-trading companies immediately to inquire about the promised supplies. It was exactly as he had feared: much amiability, many empty words, supplies nowhere in sight. When he became more stubborn, the amiability cooled and the derision became more pronounced. "Everything in my power"—this was how Governor Simpson described his support for the expedition. But, alas, this was not very much—in a brutal and degrading way, as good as nothing. The Hudson's Bay Company referred them to the North-West Company, and the latter back to Hudson's Bay: they had obviously been fighting for years. Neither wanted to trade at a disadvantage by contributing more to the expedition than the other. Orders sent by the government in London were mere paper here: it was a big country. Moreover, the fur traders and officials didn't think much of naval officers with wanderlust. For them Franklin and his men were only naive would-be heroes. Going on a pilgrimage on foot or in a birchbark canoe? "They'll never reach the polar sea," one of them said within Back's earshot. "And if they do, the first Eskimo attack will wipe them out. Why give them supplies if we're so low ourselves?"

And John was told a joke, ostensibly crude yet kindly, though also suggesting something else. "You were at Trafalgar. You'll make it. If not with your head, then with your character."

Back became more and more incensed. He couldn't stand watching how Franklin began by politely accepting these declarations by the local powers before asking anew. He noticed that they laughed about Franklin, and perhaps he feared that some of that derision might be directed at him. When they were alone, he delivered a raging speech to the officials in charge as he would have done it if he had been John Franklin. The phrase "We know what game is being played here" occurred several times. That, too, John had to listen to. He tried to calm Back: "You must be able to join games you might lose. That they make fun of us is irrelevant. I never knew anything different. And it never stays that way." "You're too goodhearted!" Back exclaimed. "You put up with too much!"

John nodded and thought some more. Then he said, "I'm more than ten years older than you. I learned to look stupid for a long time—until I'm smart. Or until the others look even more stupid than I do. Do you believe me?"

It was difficult to comfort Back. John sensed that here, too, he was concerned with something different from what he said.

So Hepburn seemed preferable as a man to talk to, a man who kept faith and didn't grouse about it. One didn't have to deal with him one way or another except if one wanted to. If he didn't exchange a word with Hepburn for days, it was all right, too.

A commander was like a physician: he liked the healthy person better, but most of his time he had to spend with the sick— the sicker, the more time.

In June, Dr. Richardson and Hood followed in canoes. After endless sessions with the officials, John brought them around, wearing them down by attrition, with a tactical mix of extreme politeness, constant repetition of the same arguments, and a complete abandonment of any sense of time. He never hinted that anyone might not truly want to support the expedition, refusing even to expose their hypocrisy with accusations: he knew he could play this game longer than the others. Perhaps Back learned a little. Obstinately, John continued to treat that scoundrel Simpson as a friend and patron and became such a nuisance that suddenly provisions for several weeks and a dozen voyageurs became available after all. Further supplies of double that amount were to be sent later to Fort Providence. John got it in writing. He assured Simpson with a vigorous handshake, and without batting an eye, that his noble and humane attitude would be praised in England.

Now their route led northward down the Slave River; they were on their way to the coast. The distance from Fort Chipewyan to Fort Providence at the Great Slave Lake amounted to only ninety pipes. They took two days to cross the lake, often completely out of sight of the shore. A violent windstorm forced them to seek shelter on an island—a foretaste of the canoe trip that was in store for them on the arctic sea. The base at Fort Providence, on the northern shore of a bay whose extreme end formed the estuary of the Yellow Knife River, belonged to the North-West Company. They allowed Franklin to take one of their officials along with them. Friedrich Wentzel was a German who knew several Indian dialects. Unless they succeeded in securing Indian support, they would have to call off the expedition, for the supplies were insufficient by themselves and had to be supplemented with continual hunting. In this part of the world, only the Indians were skilled enough to hunt extra game for others as well. Wentzel promised to arrange a meeting with the chief of the Copper Indians, who were indebted to the North-West Company and so might be persuaded to lend his warriors as escorts if certain promises were made.

John Franklin noted sadly that he was becoming more and more nervous and irritable the closer they approached their meeting with the Indians. Everything depended on them, and he knew next to nothing about them! He had two interpreters along for the Athabascan language: Pierre St. Germain and Jean-Baptiste Adam. Wentzel seemed to possess enormous knowledge, but his way of talking was wearisomely encyclopedic, like a collector with a box of note cards. "The Tsantsa-Hut-Dinneh are more warlike but also more dependable than the Thlin-Cha-Dinneh, who live farther north and are commonly known as the Dog Rib Nation. Athabaskic is one of the most difficult Indian dialects of the Kenai language, upon which I would not like to elaborate at this point." Writing of this sort made John even more restless.

The chief of the tribe was called Akaitcho, which roughly means Big Foot. He was reputed to be a prudent man, and that was welcome: fifty years ago the Copper Indians had gone with a fur trader named Hearne to the polar sea who had not been able to prevent a gruesome massacre among the Eskimos there.

John saw the Indians approach across the lake in a long line of canoes. Behind him, a tent had been erected at the fort. The flag was waving, and next to him the uniformed officers and Hepburn were lined up in formation. Upon John's command they had put on their decorations. He wore none himself. His instinct for dignity told him that as the highest chief, he should be able to do without them.

Akaitcho climbed out of the first canoe and strode slowly up to the Englishmen without looking right or left, so that John had to take him most seriously. This was no man who would let his warriors fall upon Eskimos and chop off their hands and feet. Whoever walked this way kept his word.

In contrast to his warriors, the chief wore no feather head-dress; he was dressed in mocassins, long blue trousers, and a wide shirt with crossed shoulder straps hanging loose over his trousers, belt, and powder horn; a beaver cloak hung from his shoulders to the ground.

No word was spoken. He sat motionlessly and smoked the offered pipe and sipped so little of an offered glass of rum that the level of the liquid hardly dropped before he passed it on to his companions.

Then he began to speak, and St. Germain interpreted.

He was pleased to see such great chiefs of the whites in their midst. He was prepared to accompany them to the north with his tribe, although he had already had one complaint about his first disappointment: he had been told that the whites had a very strong magic medicine, and that a great medicine man was with them who could call the dead back to life. So he had already looked forward to seeing his deceased relatives once more and to be able to speak with them. A few days ago he was told by Mr. Wentzel that this was not possible, and he now felt as though his friends and brothers and sisters had died for the second time. But he was prepared to forget this and to hear what the white chiefs were planning.

John had prepared his response as thoroughly as Akaitcho. He took care to speak even more slowly.

"I am pleased to see the great chief about whom I have heard so many good words." St. Germain began to translate. It seemed to John as though the interpreter required at least four times more time for the Indian than for the English text. It struck him that Akaitcho bowed slightly several times. Odd how many Indian words could be made of a dozen English words.

"I was sent by the greatest chief of the inhabited earth, for all of the world's people, white, red, black, and yellow, are his children who love and venerate him. He is full of goodness, but he has also the power to compel people. That is never necessary, for all of them know his goodness and wisdom."

This time St. Germain required only at most one quarter of John's speaking time. John, who had a feeling for how much time things had to take, remained silent and thought this over.

"Mr. Wentzel. Did he translate correctly?"

"Beg pardon, sir," said the German, "but Athabaskic is indeed extremely—"

"Mr. Hepburn," said John, "would you please fetch Parkinson's chronometer for me, the one with the second hand." He stipulated to St. Germain that the translation must be neither longer nor shorter than the time he, Franklin, required for the original. Hepburn monitored this, and lo and behold, it worked!

Akaitcho sat motionless as before, but his eyes betrayed that he had great fun with this incident.

John continued. The supreme white chief wishes to let his Indian children obtain even more beautiful things than before. For that reason, he wishes to discover a place on the arctic sea where the largest canoes in the world can land. Also, the supreme chief wishes to find out more about the land and about the Indians and Eskimos. It was very painful to him to hear that these two did not always live in harmony, for the Eskimos are his children, too. Finally, John revealed to the Indian that they had few provisions. These he would distribute gladly, but after that they would all have to depend on how industriously the Indians applied themselves to hunting. He would give them ammunition for that purpose.

Akaitcho understood that John took the reconciliation with the Eskimos very seriously. He admitted that there had been wars, but now his tribe was filled with longing for peace. Unfortunately, he added, the Eskimos were perfidious and unreliable.

When in the afternoon John thought back on this scene, he was pleased with his success not only for the expedition but also for how he had achieved it. He took it as proof that peace can happen when one approaches the adversary not fast but slowly. This was a point in favor of Franklin's System and of the honor of mankind. John took a sip of rum on that.

It also occurred to him that Akaitcho had recognized him at once as the highest-ranking person and had sat down opposite him although he had not seated himself in the center. He asked St. Germain about this. "The chief was of the opinion that you have several lives, sir: because of the scar on your forehead and, if you excuse me, because of your—'wealth of time.' And whoever is immortal must be the chief. So stupid are the Indians!"

John looked darkly at the interpreter: "How do you know that the chief is wrong?"

On August 2, they climbed into the canoes, more than two dozen men and a further dozen Indian women and children.

John Franklin now knew the names of the voyageurs from memory: Peltier, Crédit, and Vaillant were the big men; Perrault, Samandré, and Beauparlant were little. John's mind resisted Benoît's name the longest; that was because Benoît had such a melancholy look. John had a talk with him. He was not French-Canadian but from France, from a little village named St. Yrieix-La-Perche, near Limoges, and after ten years he still suffered from attacks of homesickness. In this way, John managed to retain a simple name in combination with a complicated one.

Jean-Baptiste and Solomon Bélanger were brothers who didn't like each other. A third Bélanger had been a sailor who had been killed in the Battle of Trafalgar. "Sharpshooter?" John asked, biting into a zwieback but keeping it quietly in his mouth to be able to hear the answer. "No, gunner," answered Solomon. John resumed his chewing.

Vincenzo Fontano hailed from Venice. The only Indian among the voyageurs was Michel Teroaoteh, an Iroquois of the tribe of the Mohawks.

Among the Copper Indians, next to Akaitcho, Keskarrah, the scout with a bulbous nose was most conspicuously memorable. He had an unbelievably beautiful nineteen-year-old daughter who remained in the mind of every man in the expedition without any effort. Of all people, deep-thinking Dr. Richardson was the first to direct his fascinated eye to her knees, murmuring something like "divine creature" and trying quite openly to impress the line of her thighs upon his mind. With the explorer's privilege he named the maiden by what he saw: Green Stockings. Midshipman Hood, too, riveted all his sense of detail on Green Stockings. He now saw only her, and she seemed to him different with every move she made: the bold nose, the black hair, the proud curve from chin to ear. Hood filled his sketchbook with these drawings. To rivers and mountains he was hopelessly lost.

For days they paddled up the Yellow Knife River. The Indians did not hunt enough, and since, in violation of their agreement, half the tribe stayed with the chief and used up many of their supplies, John began to worry. When Akaitcho insisted that the ammunition he had been given had been lost when a canoe capsized, John realized that it would make little sense to become angry. His system provided that one must believe what each person says. He rationed what was still on hand and allowed only as much powder and lead to be distributed as was needed for each individual hunting expedition. At the end of the day, the hunters had to turn in either the game or the bullets. Akaitcho didn't like this, but John presented these new rules to him so calmly in a very slow, deliberate speech that he could not feel offended.

One could gain strength from the beautiful landscape. It even helped against fatigue and foot blisters. At least the eye was searching for nourishment when hunting and fishing by net brought poor results. Two partridges and eight gudgeons—that was bad. Three dozen hard-working people ate a lot. The voyageurs bore the main burden in carrying boats around waterfalls and rapids, and they were therefore the first to find the landscape picturesque no longer. Rivers were beautiful when they flowed broadly and smoothly. Forests were delightful when they revealed reindeer tracks.

As food continued to be scarce, an open rebellion broke out. John listened to the voyageurs for half an hour without saying a word, then declared that he knew full well that he was demanding superhuman efforts from them. Any man who didn't think he was up to it was free to return home without any danger that anybody would be angry with him. "This isn't an expedition like any other," John said, and wrinkled his forehead because it had suddenly occurred to him that Nelson's address on the *Bellerophon* had begun with the same words. In any case, it worked: the voyageurs, despite roughness and alcohol, were still something like Frenchmen. If he had dressed them down, they would have left, but this way it became a matter of honor. They went back to work.

Akaitcho complained that the expedition was making too little progress because of the burden of gifts they were carrying for the no-good Eskimos. He warned of a possible early start of winter: even now a thin cover of ice was visible on dead arms of the river in the morning, and it was only mid-August.

Hood was so much in love with Green Stockings that he had a hard time even managing his hours of guard duty. All day long he thought only of ways to get closer to her and at least touch her little finger. "If it goes on this way," Back remarked sarcastically, "he'll expire with love. He's going to simmer away before our eyes; it's got to be put out in time."

Back's behavior changed from day to day, and always for the worse. He started to shout at the voyageurs. He talked about Franklin behind his back—Hepburn had hinted at something like that. He believed the Indians were undependable, thievish, and mendacious, and declared this more and more openly. Worst of all, he talked in an unbearably obscene way about Green Stockings' visible and invisible features and how he was going to demonstrate to Hood how to make use of them.

When John asked him to respect Hood's feelings for the good of the expedition, Back looked at him insolently. "Respect feelings? What kind of advice is that coming from you of all people, sir? Many thanks!"

Just what I feared, John thought. First he loves me, then he hates me. He knows no boundary between acceptable and unacceptable feelings; this is sad and dangerous. But he knows how to draw! Green Stockings modeled for a portrait, and he painted such a good picture of her that Keskarrah became worried. "It's too beautiful. When the Great White Chief sees this, he will demand her for himself!"

About Wentzel, Back said, "Now that's a real German! Everywhere in the world you see them standing around brooding about why they can't move like anyone else. And most of the time they try to prove that the reason is their intelligence, and then they start to teach the rest of mankind."

John had long ceased to react to each of Back's remarks—his secret first choice was now Hepburn. But this time he replied, "It's the problem of slowness, Mr. Back! And Wentzel really knows a thing or two."

At a lake the Indians called Winter Lake the travelers remained for a few days, built a blockhouse as a base for a possible return trip, and provided themselves with game to salt and even convert into pemmican for the long haul up the Coppermine River.

Night frost became more severe. One morning Akaitcho announced that he opposed continuing northward in this season. "The white chiefs may do so, and some of my young warriors may accompany them so they won't have to die alone. But as soon as they climb into their canoes, my people will mourn them all as dead." Cautiously, John pointed out the discrepancy between these words and other words the chief had spoken in Fort Providence. Akaitcho replied with dignity: "I eat my words. Those were words spoken for summer or autumn, but soon it will be winter."

Back fumed about the "savages" and their false promises. Even Dr. Richardson started to talk again about how Christian culture would do these primitives a world of good. John would have still liked to reach the Coppermine River and perhaps even the sea. He thought it over for a whole night before he said anything. In the morning he knew that Akaitcho was right when he feared a catastrophe in an area so poor in game and wood. Indians had frozen and starved to death before up there— Wentzel told of the death of entire camps. John announced to the chief that he was grateful for his kind and wise counsel. They would spend the winter here. Akaitcho bowed contentedly, as if he had not expected anything else, but he was very glad that John had given in and became downright talkative in his pleasure. John discovered that he was held in great esteem by the Indians because they believed he spoke often with the spirits of the dead: they had observed him when, in thinking about something, he laughed apparently without reason and moved his lips.

The blockhouse was named Fort Enterprise. It would remain their home for at least eight months; that much was sure. And the officers knew at last why the Indians had called the lake Winter Lake as early as four days before.

Back began to woo Green Stockings in an intentionally crude and insolent way. Apparently he wanted to prove something again. Meanwhile, Hood had reached the point of holding her hand now and then, and gazing into her eyes; he did not let himself be pushed to adopt a faster pace, even by Back. John suspected that there had been words between Hood and Back, but if so, it was without success. Back didn't stop touching Green Stockings to point out for which details of her person his compliments were intended. Sometimes he made her laugh, but John was almost sure that she rather detested Back.

One evening, Hepburn reported that Messrs Back and Hood had agreed on a duel the following dawn. This was no laughing matter. John didn't doubt that Hood was serious, and Back was sufficiently vain to push the matter to the limit. John ordered Hepburn to use the 12:00-to-6:00 A.M. watch to stuff the primers of the gentlemen's guns with pemmican. Then he spoke with each of them individually—they promised to be reasonable. Hepburn nevertheless did as he was told, and successfully. The next day at least one partridge owed him its life.

John Franklin had the excellent idea to send Back together with Wentzel to Fort Providence to look for the expected delivery of supplies. Sullenly they departed. All at once peace reigned in Fort Enterprise.

The Indians hunted. The women sewed winter clothes. During the time he did not attend to Green Stockings, Hood built an excellent stove, far more economical with wood than an open fireplace.

Hood loved this Indian girl more and more intensely. His eyes filled with tears of pleasure when he saw her again after only a few hours of separation, and sometimes no one saw hide nor hair of them for days. Akaitcho and Franklin exchanged not a single word about it—they held this situation to be too unusual to drown it in obvious protests—but they talked of many other things: the compass, the stars, the signals with which whites in one big canoe communicated with those in another, Indian feasts and legends. John wrote down one or another of these. The voyageurs cut down trees and built a second hut. It became cold frighteningly fast. Akaitcho had been right.

Weeks passed. Now and then John sat in front of the hut, bundled in heavy clothing, looking at the autumn storm sweeping swarms of the last leaves off the branches. John picked out a specific leaf and waited for it to fall. Often this allowed him many hours of aimless and unhurried contemplation. A warrior brought letters from Fort Providence. Back and Wentzel had not found the supplies and had now gone on to Musk Ox Island, where they were supposed to be waiting. There was also a letter from Eleanor: "To Lieutenant Franklin, Commander of the Land Expedition to the Arctic Ocean, c/o Hudson's Bay or Elsewhere." Graceful good Eleanor! John saw her before him, talking constantly to everyone about everything. For her the world was language, and therefore, in her view, there had to be a great deal of talk. Still, Eleanor was always pleasant and without malice; perhaps she was the woman to whom he would best like to be married after all. She could bear years of her husband's absence well, for she had the Royal Society and her literary circle. Of course, there were also other women—Jane Griffin, for example, Eleanor's friend, equally curious and well read but with longer legs—and she didn't write poetry. When John noticed that his mind wanted to dwell on the legs, he quickly put Jane Griffin out of his head. Need came easily to a man here in the wilderness, and it was not easy to help oneself; the bedstead of reeds and furs made noise at the slightest movement. Everyone except Hood suffered greatly. There remained only stalking game by oneself in the forest. But God and the Indians saw everything. Once, when Hepburn returned from a hunt without spoils and pretended not to have seen any game, old Keskarrah with the bulbous nose said to St. Germain with a stolid expression: "There was game enough, but perhaps what the white man had in his hand wasn't a rifle." Since tact was not his strength, St. Germain passed this on to Hepburn, who was at first annoyed, then finally had to laugh himself.

John took up Eleanor's letter again. She asked him to check whether the pantheism of the Indians could be compared to that of the Earl of Shaftesbury. A paragraph on Shaftesbury's teachings followed. Then she again returned to the theory of the melting polar ice: the increasingly dry weather of the last few years spoke for it. Between London Bridge and Black Friars

Bridge, John read, the Thames had dried out completely during the last winter. It was possible to cross it on foot and find hosts of odd things sailors had thrown overboard in the course of centuries for fear of customs inspectors. They included even a silver christening font of very Catholic appearance. Near the end of the letter she wrote: "A fortnight ago there was a ball at the Thomsons! Oh, if only you had been there, dear Lieutenant." Eleanor loved to dance quadrilles, and always "con amore." John loved best not to dance at all.

In the evenings John talked more and more often with Richardson. The doctor was pious but not a bad fellow. He wanted to know the truth. If he was told the truth he could be tolerant. While he firmly believed that the doubter John would have to be converted someday, he tried it also with questions, and with listening, and that was not a bad route to choose with John, if one had the patience. On Monday evening Richardson asked, "Aren't you afraid of nothingness?" And John was thoughtfully silent until Tuesday. Then the doctor asked, "If there is such a thing as love, doesn't there have to be a pinnacle, a sum total of love?" But this time John answered yesterday's question: "I'm not afraid because I can only imagine nothingness as rather quiet." He remained silent about love for the present. On Wednesday evening they talked for a very long while, this time about eternal life. As Richardson spoke of the prospect of seeing lost people again, John became so much interested in this subject that he entirely forgot his answer to the question about love. Looking at Hood, love seemed to him to end up more in a kind of sickness than in God.

"Some people are engaged in going, others in coming. Whatever comes fast, goes fast. It's the way things look through a carriage window: nothing and nobody is preserved. More I don't know."

"But for that we have eternal life."

"I don't long for eternal life," answered John. "But I lack the years between twenty and thirty. If there had been no war, perhaps I would have already discovered a lot by now." He said this without bitterness, because the discoveries might still take place.

As he looked at the shaggy tree and mused, old names and faces occurred to him again, one after the other. Dr. Richardson learned a little about Mary Rose, Sherard Lound, Westall, Simmons, Dr. Orme. "You'll see them again," Dr. Richardson consoled him, "as sure as parallel lines meet in infinity." John contradicted: "Only if one follows them in the right direction, for parallel lines must, of course, lose themselves on the other side." At some point he also explained Franklin's System to the doctor. "Well and good," answered the other, "but it isn't sufficient to draw strength from slowness. It's only a method, and God is much more than a method. You, too, will need Him, perhaps even on this journey."

John remembered the verse inscribed on the old church bell at St. James in Spilsby that was broken last year. Not wanting to leave the doctor without a reply, he recited it:

> The glass doth run
> The globe doth go
> Wake up from sin—
> Why sleep you so.

Why it had entered his head he didn't know, but when he had told it to the doctor, they both went to sleep at last.

After four months, Back and Wentzel returned. They had achieved nothing and blamed each other for it. None of the promised supplies had reached Fort Providence, and on Musk Ox Island in the Great Slave Lake they found only a few sacks of flour and sugar, as well as several opened bottles of liquor. They did, however, find the promised Eskimo interpreters there.

Back had tried in his way to get supplies in Fort Providence. Wentzel, he said, had let him down. "He shows greater understanding for the supposedly dire straits of the fur traders than for ours. He didn't stand up for us." Wentzel retorted, "Mr.

Back shouted at the gentlemen in charge. You don't get any-where that way."

If the Indians exerted themselves and worked hard at hunt-ing, perhaps enough food could be gathered for the journey after all.

Snow melted more and more. The lake burst and sang. It was May.

Hood went on loving Green Stockings, who was pregnant. By whom? In addition to Hood's view, there was also another.

The Eskimo interpreters were flat-nosed, woolly-haired fel-lows with wiry bodies. Their names were Tattanoeack and Hoeutoerock, meaning something like belly and ear. Since no one could pronounce their names, John called them Augustus and Junius. They were not very resourceful hunters, but were excellent anglers. It seemed as though they could almost smell fish through the thickest ice.

By June 14, rivers and lakes were navigable enough to allow John to decide that they should start. Maps and notes were locked in a small side room of the blockhouse. Hepburn nailed a drawing on the door showing a menacing fist raised with a blue shimmering dagger. Since here in the north everyone is entitled to use a hut—whether Indian or white—the maps had to be protected in some way. Akaitcho agreed that the drawing would be more helpful than a lock.

It was the first warm day, and it quickly became so hot that they sweated. Swarms of mosquitoes, sand flies, and horseflies enveloped them, so that they felt as though they were walking in the shade. Nobody could say where these insects had come from so quickly and how they knew that they could tap humans for blood. Hepburn, slapping his own face without catching any of the tormentors, asked furiously; "What do they do when no expedition comes through here?"

Since the heavily laden canoes still had to be dragged on skids over snow and ice, the expedition got no farther than five miles on the first day. At night it was so cold that nobody could sleep.

Shaken by frost, Hepburn shouted into the dark: "The beasts won't survive this!" In that he was mistaken, however.

Green Stockings did not come along. She stayed behind with the tribe. One of Akaitcho's warriors stayed behind, too—for her. Everyone except Hood knew this. Even John.

Hood talked of returning at the end of the journey to live with Green Stockings in Fort Providence, or wherever. They all nodded and remained silent. Even Back kept his mouth shut.

John Franklin was admired by the Indians for not killing a single fly. When one of them stung him while he was fixing the sextant he gently blew it off the back of his hand, saying, "There's enough room in the world for both of us." Akaitcho asked Wentzel, "Why does he do it?" and Wentzel asked John. The answer: "I can neither eat it nor conquer it." "That's right," Back whispered behind John's back. "He'd never catch a mosquito."

Wentzel heard this remark and passed it on to John. Conversely, John was equally sure that Back would pass on to him everything that Wentzel secretly told him as well, and that both of them would never understand how little this interested him.

Nothing escaped Akaitcho—not John's disappointment over the fur-trading companies and Back's foolishness or the tensions within the group. One day he said, "Wolves are different. They love each other, touch each other's noses, and feed each other." Adam translated.

John became slightly unsure. He could hardly answer Akaitcho without talking more or less about his companions. So at first he merely bowed his head and kept silent. By evening he had an answer: "I've thought a great deal about the wolves. They have the advantage of not being able to talk about each other."

Now Akaitcho bowed.

After four weeks they had almost reached the mouth of the Coppermine River. From here on they might at any time meet up with the Eskimos getting copper from the river bank. Akaitcho thought it best to wander south with his tribe. He was probably unsure just how his warriors would deal with the Eskimos. "They say about us that we're half man and half dog. They themselves drink raw blood, and eat maggots and dried mice. We'd better turn back. From now on you'll have to feed yourselves."

It was agreed that Wentzel would go with them and stock Fort Enterprise with food and ammunition in case the expedition failed and they didn't reach Parry's ship.

Hood wanted to know from Akaitcho where the tribe would be next spring. With an inscrutable face Akaitcho explained that they would be in the region south of the Great Bear Lake. Keskarrah held out his hand and said, "When you're starving, drink a lot or you'll die."

Here it was again, the good wrinkled elephant hide of the sea! Soon East India men would glide through here in long columns, as well as ships bound for Australia, San Francisco, Panama, or the Sandwich Islands. But actually—of what interest were passenger ships to John! He had to laugh. He was in fine spirits.

It was quiet here on the hill. From the moss-covered knoll the men peered beyond the estuary of the Coppermine River to the sea. In the distance, two flat, snow-covered islands were marked off against a pale pink sky—or was it ice this soon? The air felt like a void. Of insects not a trace. Except for the rustling of their clothes and the cracking of their ankles, they heard not a sound.

Before John's eyes lay unknown land, quiet and limitless like his father's garden decades ago. And the sea was indestructible. A thousand fleets had not left a trace. The sea looked different every day and remained the same, till all eternity. As long as there was the sea, the world was not wretched.

John's reveries were suddenly interrupted, for the voyageurs came up to him and declared, with great determination, their unwillingness to go on the ocean in their fragile canoes. Back told them it was not at all dangerous. Hood thought it might be beautiful. Richardson knew with certainty that a hand above us protects us all. Hepburn grumbled, "Are you men or aren't you?"

John heard it all with only half an ear. Since he respected the voyageurs, they waited only for what he had to say. He looked far away while arranging his sentences. Then he turned and looked at Solomon Bélanger, and said, "This isn't just a walk. But greater dangers lie behind us than lie ahead." He looked again at the sea, then spoke into the silence as though he spoke to himself: "Else what we started can't be continued. It's part of our expedition."

Solomon Bélanger decided that it would just have to be done. Back made a face. The rest of the British admired John openly. They got ready to move on.

Back seemed to be unable to get rid of something—a desire for mockery, a malice, a rage. But no one was waiting to hear his opinion, no one like himself. Therefore, he finally said to Hood as if to apologize, "I don't like these addresses. He acts like a saint whom everyone must support, like a kind of Nelson."

[14]

♦ ♦

HUNGER AND
DYING

A field full of bones and skulls, split by the blades of Indian battle axes—that was the spot at Bloody Falls where fifty years before Samuel Hearne had been unable to prevent the bloodshed.

John Franklin knew he needed Eskimos. He feared they would not have forgotten the long-ago disaster. Where people did not keep records about themselves, the past was not harmless. The slain men on the bottom of Copenhagen harbor came back to him often even now. "Behave like gentlemen!" "No fear of that!" How little help these phrases offered once one was a commander.

It was quite possible to instill confidence in two or three natives approaching slowly. It got bad only if an entire tribe or no one at all showed up.

The bay was empty; not even birds could be seen. John held a list of names in his hand intended for mountains, rivers, capes, and bays: Flinders, Barrow, Banks, names of British companions, and of Berens, governor of Hudson's Bay Company. Oh, names! If they starved or were killed here, none of the names would stick to these rocks. But now they at least helped him to overcome his unease. He had walked all over the field of bones as he had walked all over the battlefield of Winceby with the apothecary. He had wanted to make clear what the crux of their meeting with the Eskimos would be. But for Back these old bones were obviously only proof that the Eskimos could be managed if they became troublesome.

Suddenly Hepburn's eyes were riveted on the sea. "Good heavens! It's starting!" On the periphery of his field of vision John noticed only that the bay had somehow darkened. He turned.

About one hundred kayaks and a few larger boats were coming their way. They approached almost soundlessly, the way game is stalked on a hunt. The whites rushed to their rifles. John shouted: "Load and put on safety! But not one shot, not even a warning shot, or a shot by accident! We'd be lost!"

Clearly the Eskimos had followed each of their moves, for the boats made a ninety-degree turn, synchronized like a school of fish, and steered toward a point on the shore a hundred yards away from the British.

"I'll go alone with Augustus," John said calmly. "If anything happens to me, Dr. Richardson will be in command."

"And if you're taken hostage so they can get to us and murder us all?" asked Back.

"We've got to have their spirits on our side," answered John. "Oh well! Do what I say."

Augustus was instructed to keep two steps behind John. They walked as slowly as Akaitcho had walked at Fort Providence. Perhaps even more slowly. From Akaitcho and Matthew Flinders, John had learned what it took to be a chief.

Meanwhile, the Eskimos, who had landed, were standing about like a thick-furred pack, motionlessly scenting, all staring in the same direction. Many of their faces were tattooed; their hair was black. John thought it would be difficult to tell them apart. Now he stopped and gripped Augustus's arm firmly. He counted silently to twenty, then said: "Start your speech."

Augustus knew what he had to say. John had made sure he had memorized the sentences. He had also checked, with Junius's help, whether they meant what he wanted to say: peaceful intentions, presents, bartering food for "good things"; had they seen a big ship coming from the direction dawn comes from? And, again and again, peace.

When Augustus finished, the Eskimos threw their arms up in the air and clapped their hands high above their heads like an enthusiastic opera audience. What in hell did hand clapping mean in this part of the world? Perhaps not applause at all. Loudly and rhythmically they all shouted in unison, "TEYMA! TEYMA!"

John hoped this didn't mean revenge. He thought of DEATH OR GLORY and BREAD OR BLOOD. He couldn't ask Augustus because he was surrounded by hand-clapping Eskimos; nor did he want to run after him. Everything, he knew, depended on his own show of dignity. So he remained standing, accepting the ever-swelling chorus of Teyma cheerfully and proudly as an act of homage, hoping intensely that it didn't mean more than "Good day."

"Teyma" meant "Peace"!

The presents were distributed: two kettles and several knives. Now the bartering began. The Eskimos offered bows and arrows, spears and wooden sunglasses, wanting anything they caught sight of in the way of equipment and metal objects. Soon they began to take what they needed. With the friendliest smiles in the world they nudged forward and were everywhere, stealing Back's pistol and Hepburn's coat. Back wanted to retrieve his pistol, but they shouted loudly "Teyma!" and didn't give it up.

John sat like a mountain and didn't stir. He knew that he was the last person who could protect himself from these nimble fingers. He therefore asked Hepburn to join him. Just then an Eskimo tried to pull a button off his uniform jacket. John only looked at him with concentration. Hepburn rapped him across the fingers and pointed at Hood, who was offering buttons for barter. For a while this worked.

The situation was confused and could be managed only by waiting. John sensed that the fate of the expedition would be sealed if he were to rise, show agitation, and shout commands. Besides, the Eskimos knew very well what rifles and pistols could do. When one of the whites came near his weapon, several Eskimos clung to him, shouting "Teyma! Teyma!" in unison and clapping him, gently and in cadence, on the left side of his chest.

Hood found himself a rope and tied the box of nautical instruments so tightly to his thigh that nobody could steal it without dragging him along as well. Then he pulled out his sketchbook and began to draw one of the women. He devoted a great deal of effort to the tattoos on her face, the bones of her forehead, her eyes. Eskimos clustered behind him, looking over his shoulder, telling the model in loud voices which part of her body was being worked on. The woman readily held out everything she believed required special precision: teeth, tongue, right and left ear, feet. The outcome was an odd picture: the details did not produce the accustomed whole, but it pleased the Eskimos very much. They stood bowing their heads right and left to take in all the subtleties. Almost all of them came to watch. When he had finished the sketch, Hood gave it to his model as a gift, kissing her hand. For a moment she stood stock still with pleasure; then she did a handspring.

But now came the sorcerer. Laden with the head and furry coat of a bear, he circled several times around the whites on all fours, growling and groaning. Augustus explained that this might indicate misfortune: the sorcerer believed drawing and painting were dangerous. Suddenly all the Eskimos ran away. They rushed to their boats and paddled away in great haste, leaving behind many of the objects they had acquired with so much cunning and skill—including even some of the things they had obtained through barter. The woman left her picture behind but grabbed the protractor, that drawing instrument Hood used to commit his readings of landscapes to paper. At the last moment, she changed her mind, returned the protractor, and grabbed her picture after all. She leaped into the last boat—an open boat in which only women were sitting. Within a few minutes the bay was as empty as it had been in the morning.

"We're saved," said Dr. Richardson, "but it was a failure just the same. We'll never get anything to eat out of those people!" Augustus confirmed this: "They don't want to have anything to do with us. They're Innuit from the western shore. In the summer they live in huts of driftwood, in the winter in igloos made of ice, but always on land. They've met whites off and on and had bad experiences with them. They wanted to kill us, but too many powerful spirits were on our side. The Spirit of the Bear wanted to eat us, but the Great Woman Who Lives under the Sea would not allow anything to happen to us."

"Then let's go out to the sea," John countered. "She can protect us even better there."

On August 21, they pitched their tents at Point Turnagain. Their problems had increased. The lengthy, drawn-out Bathurst Inlet had not proved to be the long-sought water connection with Hudson's Bay. It was simply another bay that came to an end: five days in and five days out again along the opposite side, and August was half over. Following this disappointment, they paddled eastward along the shore until they finally had to give up hope of reaching Parry's ship before the onset of winter. They had marched on foot to the next large point of the Kent Peninsula and had named it Point Turnagain for the present— their renewed and now final return.

They were hungry.

Not even fishing brought in enough food, to say nothing of hunting. If only there had been time to learn from the Eskimos what they needed to know about fishing grounds and seal territories. Augustus and Junius were not at home here. Or if only they had better rifles with a longer range: there was no cover to hide behind in this bare country when stalking game—if game was sighted at all.

This was not how they had imagined the Arctic coast. They had expected not this dead silence but seals and walruses on ice floes and rocks and polar bears swaying over hills, cliffs full of auks and other large birds, a fiery sea of red flowers—music for the eye.

John had intended to name the place for Wilberforce, the fighter against slavery. But now that they were turning back here, this was out of the question. The philanthropist deserved better than a point that marked an end of the line.

The voyageurs were pleased about life for the first time in a long while—they were getting back on land. On the other hand, the Eskimo interpreters were disturbed: deep in the land, the Woman Who Lives under the Sea would not be able to protect them.

"The captain of the *Blossom* could have remained a happy man, and the *Blossom* a happy ship, if they had not . . . Did I tell you this story before? God knows, hunger makes me soft-headed." Richardson fell silent.

Lacunae opened up in their memory, and there was no strength left for reflections or meaningful conversations. The only thing that had become stronger was their capacity for unbridled fantasy. Delicious pemmican was waiting for them in Fort Enterprise, with well-aged halves of reindeer carcasses, rum and tobacco, tea and zwieback. And Hood was talking about Green Stockings. The child must be born by now.

Onward! On to the southwest until they reached the fort! Hunger displaced all other worries: the voyageurs didn't bat an eye when in crossing Coronation Gulf in the open sea their boats were surprised by a heavy storm coming up from behind; they fought all day to keep the light canoes from capsizing, and toward evening the storm chased them toward a rocky shore at breakneck speed. The sailors thought the end was near; the voyageurs, on the other hand, saw land—finally land, tent sites, and rich meals. John sat stoically in the boat, entering each of the islands in his logbook as they passed by on the right and left, while Hood bent over his sketchbook and drew the outlines showing how the rocks were formed right under the foam of the sea. "Maps, observations, reports, and pictures," John had said. "Once we start to think only in terms of meat and firewood, we won't get very far." It was a similar situation in the storm. So they held out, each in his own way, until they reached a sheltering bay that no rational mind could have expected or hardly an eye could have seen. They landed in fog and darkness and collapsed just where they stood.

In his dream, John saw images of storm and rescue and of a newly built, perfectly functioning picture rotor that projected them on a wall. He tried to impress the construction graphically on his memory, but in the morning he could no longer put it together. Still, he felt renewed vigor: whenever machines appeared in his dreams, his sleep was especially sound.

A few days later, at the estuary of a river John named after Hood, they jettisoned their superfluous baggage—above all, the remaining presents—and piled it on a small knoll, built a stone pyramid over it, and placed a British flag on top. At least they wanted the Eskimos to meet their successors in a friendlier way.

Then they paddled up the Hood River until a gigantic waterfall forced them to a halt. Between rock needles rising up like walls, the torrents of water plunged down in cascades—a lonely, treeless place of solemn beauty. It was a good place for the name of the liberator of the slaves, and the appropriate counterpart to Hearne's Bloody Fall. Contentedly John entered the name "Wilberforce" in his map.

It had turned cold, and game or footprints were nowhere to be discovered. The pemmican was at an end. Junius pointed at the rocks: a slimy lichen grew on the wall face that was edible. It tasted awful, but it was better than nothing. At night everyone lay awake in the tent. They observed that the lichen caused vomiting and diarrhea. Hood suffered the most. He kept nothing inside him.

On the next day, August 28, again only two fish and one partridge; also two sacks of rock lichens. The voyageurs called them *tripes de roche*—"rock tripe." John had the large canoe rebuilt to make two smaller ones, which were easier to carry and sufficient for crossing rivers. Then two more miles of walking, very arduous. Thus ended the day. It was snowing.

* * *

None of the Englishmen was a good hunter. John was not quick enough, Back not sufficiently patient, Hood was a bad shot, and the doctor was nearsighted. At most, Hepburn had some luck now and then. It was a fact that without Crédit, Vaillant, Solomon Bélanger, Michel Teroaoteh, and the interpreters they would have starved to death. But recently the better a voyageur was as a hunter, the more he tended to ignore orders. For days and nights they stayed away from the camp, refused to account for used or retained ammunition, and secretly consumed some of the game they had shot by themselves. Only Solomon Bélanger continued to remain honest.

"Now we're following a new system," said Back, as if parenthetically. "They have rifles and ammunition; we have only sextant and compass. And that keeps no one from stealing."

"The system is working," John replied. "Everyone knows that nobody can get through alive without us navigators. And when we do, he wants to return as an honorable man."

When Perrault insisted he had taken only a certain amount of powder and lead, Back agreed, all evidence to the contrary. He was impenetrable again—what game was he playing? Did he want to curry favor with the voyageurs? When he knew he couldn't win, did he think surrender was preferable to open defeat? Did he want to survive a bloody rebellion by offering himself as a false witness?

John clenched his teeth and wanted to put the thought out of his mind. His system prescribed that nothing like this must be considered possible unless it became a fact. But however ashamed he was, he held on to this suspicion as a form of security.

September 1. Hood was truly ill. The *tripes de roche* had been a disaster for him, and as a result, he declined more rapidly than the others, not only because his resistance was lower but also because he suffered more from hunger.

The cold grew worse. The heavy snowflakes had seemed pretty, but now they were only dry white dust creeping into their clothes. At night it took more than an hour before the stiffly frozen blankets became warm enough to allow anything like sleep. They stuffed their boots under their bodies so they would not have to thaw them out in the morning. To do that would require a fire and therefore a search for wood.

Hunger induced a kind of slowness that was not seeing but blind. They were, of course, still moving ahead; they tried to look cheerful and confident, but they made errors about the most obvious things. They crossed rivers in a canoe without taking anything along. They gaped at the approaching edge of a waterfall without springing into action. Their condition was reminiscent of that advanced state of drunkenness when gaiety tips over into misery. Not a single animal for food! Even rock lichens weren't easy to find anymore; they had to be dug out of the snow first. They found the remainder of a wolves' meal—half-rotted reindeer bones, which they prepared by holding them over a fire until they had turned black. "That's no help," Junius said. "We've got to make soup out of it." John suggested they try that, but the others wanted to have something between their teeth. Soup! What did an Eskimo know about English and French stomachs! John gave in! He thought the moral lesson was more important than the experiment with the soup. Junius's feelings were hurt. He disappeared for good with fifty pounds of ammunition.

Morality was also on the way out. When one got down to it, it had already been abandoned many miles before. It didn't help much that in many ways weakness seemed similar.

Step by step, constantly trudging across a trackless snow cover interrupted only by rivers and lakes.

Now and then it seemed strange to John that his feet were moving, strange, too, how without his doing his right heel always hit his left ankle—never the other way round, constantly, without fail. Weakness taught everybody how crooked one's frame was. Postures became more and more bent. Odd—wasn't man born with a straight back? Their beards were iced over completely; they couldn't be unfrozen without a fire. And they weighed some! Such a frozen beard would be enough by itself to make a man bend forward. Their thoughts became dimmer and dimmer, and they feared tackling anything firmly. Now and again one of the voyageurs flew into a petty, childish rage about nothing—Perrault screamed that he didn't want to walk behind Samandré anymore because the creases in the dumb seat of his trousers moved back and forth so idiotically. Then they trotted on again for hours without a word. Suddenly they thought that they might be moving away from the fort instead of toward it! Perhaps their fate had been long since decided.

Why did George Back have so much strength? Was it just that someone so vain and so fickle could hold out for so long? Beautiful people often have strengths at their disposal that cannot be easily gauged. Bent on saving their beauty above all else, that gave them their sense of purpose.

For supper, *tripes de roche,* just a handful for each after hours of searching. Gray, wrinkled faces.

September 14. Sighted a few reindeer but bagged none. Michel's fingers, trembling with excitement, had gotten on the trigger by accident and a shot had gone off too soon; the whole thing was lost. Michel wept in despair; Crédit joined him.

Hood had fallen far behind. He arrived at the tents a few hours later, aided by Richardson. They had just harvested a few *tripes de roche,* the stuff that didn't agree with his stomach. "I frolicked about a little." He smiled. Then his knees gave way and he collapsed. He was not unconscious—Hood was too curious about what went on around him for that—but he couldn't draw well anymore. His eyes and brain were occupied with all kinds of things, only not with his own suffering.

Perrault rummaged in his bag and pulled out a few morsels of meat for Hood, saying he had saved it during the last few days. He gave Hood his last handful of meat. All nineteen of them wept, even Back and Hepburn. What did it matter where Perrault had actually gotten the meat? There it was once more, the honor of mankind—for only a brief moment, it is true, but clearly apparent.

"And I think Junius will come back, too," said Augustus. "He'll bring much meat."

"Yes, meat!" They embraced each other as if drunk with hope. They'll be home soon. A mere stroll!

Thus ended September 14, a good day.

September 23. Peltier, who had complained for days about the weight of the canoe, threw it on the ground in a fit of rage, shattering some of the wooden crossbars. He had to pick it up again and keep on carrying it, because with a little luck it could still be repaired.

When the snowstorm set in, Peltier turned the canoe so that the wind could blow it out of his hands. Now they had to leave it behind for good. Peltier showed frighteningly little shame in pointing to his triumph. Jean-Baptiste Bélanger carried the other canoe—for how long? John appealed to his conscience: "We're on the right track, but without a canoe we're lost."

Soon John discovered that they were not on the right track. In these parts magnetism was unreliable; jeering, the compass needle twirled around the dial as if on a merry-go-round. A bad moment: the half-starved commander had to tell his half-starved crew that they had to change course. This required courage, which by now had come to involve an enormous effort.

"The hour of truth," Back mumbled, and looked into space. "He's blown it!" hissed Vaillant.

"If you knew as much about navigation as I, you wouldn't be afraid. It's a bit difficult here, but it all works according to logic and science." They believed him only because they had to. They had all grown too weak to believe in anything. They were now all afraid that they would die.

Hood's courage was important. The midshipman looked like a corpse, but his confidence put anybody who felt the remotest self-pity to shame. Somehow, they all knew that when Hood died, the end would not be far off.

When, at a lake shore, John ordered that the ice be cracked for fishing, all the nets were found to be missing. The voyageurs had thought them too heavy; they were lying buried in the snow miles away. Two hours later, Jean-Baptiste Bélanger stumbled like a bad actor who had been told to stumble. The place, however, was well chosen. They were just crossing a steep slope. Their last boat was smashed.

In the evening they chewed on a partly decomposed reindeer skin that they had scraped out of the snow. Here there were not even *tripes de roche,* or firewood. If I found Trim the tomcat, thought John, I would shoot him at once and consume him. He was alarmed at the thought but too sick to prohibit it entirely; it therefore took an even more tormenting path: cat flesh, the most delicious meat in the world! John tried to direct his fantasies on another track: head cheese made of pig's head. But the traitor-brain didn't go along: it made the head cheese taste like *tripes de roche* and Trim's poor body like filet of veal.

On September 25 several voyageurs ate the top leather of their reserve boots, and the next day they tried their soles. Hood, too, tasted it. He didn't get down much. He looked at John, shrugged his shoulders with a great effort, and whispered, "Pretty tough. When I buy boots in London next time . . ."

Hood still managed well during the day, but at night he became delirious, raving about Green Stockings and his child. He had two Indian women now, a big one and a little one. Then again he imagined he was at home in Berkshire cutting thistles and nettles on a sunny morning. "Unbearable to listen to!" was Hepburn's comment.

On September 26, they came upon a great river.

John shoved his heavy tongue in place and murmured: "This is the Coppermine River. We must get across, then we're almost there." They believed him only after more than an hour, but they no longer had a boat. "Build a raft," mumbled John. After three days, something resembling a raft was finished. But how could they keep it from drifting with the current as they crossed? Richardson, who called himself a good swimmer, tried to get across with a rope in order to set up what he called a "ferry station." He prayed awhile, then undressed to his underwear and started to swim. But he froze stiff almost at once. They pulled him lifeless out of the water with the rope and undressed him completely to rub his body with snow. Horrified, they stared at his naked body, eighteen fearful pairs of eyes in emaciated faces. Solomon Bélanger was the first to speak: *"Mon Dieu! Que nous sommes maigres!"* he moaned. Benoît, the man from St.-Yrieix-La-Perche, suffering a new attack of homesickness, sobbed loudly, and soon all of them were in tears. When weeping broke out now, it became infectious at once. Perhaps we've all become children again, not more than three years old, thought John, wiping away his tears. Desperately they rubbed Richardson's body. He came to, but they kept on rubbing, as if with their last strength they wanted to restore his original figure, to put more on his ribs than snow and tears.

A snowstorm. The first raft got away and disappeared in the rapids. Only with the second raft did they get across the river on October 4. No time to lose! "Only forty miles to Fort Enterprise!" But how much time does forty miles take if one can't go on? How much can be asked of a man's will? Actually, the will was supposed to command, "Go on! Go on! Don't die!" But again and again he ran off course, made common cause with the stupid body, and self-importantly considered reasons for immediate surrender—sinking down, sleeping, and dying. The will was a sturdy but vain fellow, swayed with unpredictable ease. Suddenly he would announce, full of energy and noble defiance, "All this is too much to ask of a man. Now is the time for courage to take a break." As soon as the tired, sick body heard this, he followed gravity and lay down. Good thing this didn't happen to all of them at the same time!

John had not yet collapsed, but he knew he had strength only because he was the commander. My system does not protect me from the vagaries of fate, he thought. Sometimes I'm the right man for a situation, sometimes the wrong one, and one can die of that. We should have cooked that soup! We would have had . . . If I don't watch out, then . . .

Suddenly he saw the town of Louth before him, surrounded by its peaceful cow pastures, hills and forests in the distance. He even saw barges laden with freight passing through the canal. Then he was in the town, watching people walking on both sides of the street, cheerfully waving, respecting and understanding each other. On the other side of town, a gigantic mountain—but that was he himself! Only he and the other mountains were truly traveling. He alone was the commander. He held the rope for others. . . .

When he came to again, Augustus sat beside him whistling a tune.

"Why are you whistling?"

"Whistling drives death away!" the interpreter replied.

John got up. "That's how it is, then? I thought that I was a mountain and that my feet could walk on without me. Where are the others? Has Dr. Orme shown up yet?"

Augustus looked at him in alarm. John turned around vigorously and marched on. He now realized that what he feared most was happening: he found himself in a sea of madness, was capsizing, and would sink then and there, like a badly navigated ship. Fear made him walk faster and faster. It seemed to him as though the first heralds of madness were already reaching out their hands to seize him so that he might believe in the devil, be pursued by the dead—who, being even slower than he, would have to catch up with him. There were not only badly navigated ships; there were also unfortunate ones.

Back's the one who drives me crazy, he thought. Whether my suspicions are justified or not, he drives me mad. I must send him away.

A sextant, a compass, a sketch with the locations of Fort Enterprise, Fort Providence, and most of the important lakes and rivers—that was what Back received from John. The ammunition was divided: Back received a good fifth. After all, he had only four men with him, and they were the strongest: St. Germain, Solomon Bélanger, Beauparlant, and Augustus. Moreover, he'd be in Fort Enterprise, where the supplies were waiting, long before the others. Let him help himself! Even if there were fewer provisions than expected, even if Back and his men used up too much, it was still far better than a mutiny of the quick against the slow.

So the system was preserved: John Franklin remained the commander, and they could all keep on being men of honor.

Back marched off; Franklin stayed behind. They had to wait in any event for Samandré, Vaillant, and Crédit, whose condition had meanwhile become worse than Hood's. Half an hour later, Samandré dragged himself into camp and told them that the other two had stayed behind in the snow; he had been unable to persuade them to get up. Richardson retraced Samandré's footsteps. He found the two men in an open field, half frozen and no longer able to talk. Since he was too weak to carry either one of them, he returned to the others.

Franklin had sprained his ankle and was limping. Who had enough energy? They tried to persuade Benoît and Peltier, who were still the strongest, to bring in the two lost men, but in vain. On the contrary, the two voyageurs urged John to send them after Back and to leave it up to everyone to see how they could get away. John grabbed Benoît by the shoulders and shook him as hard as he could. "You don't know the way! Do you understand? You don't know the way!"

"We'll follow Mr. Back's footsteps."

"A little snow or rain and you won't see them anymore. Then it'll be over for you!"

Benoît saw the point with difficulty. But he didn't want to pick up the freezing men: "Then it will be all over for me, too!"

For a few moments John fought with himself. Finally he said; "Let's go on. We'll leave them behind."

It was a defeat. He had not been able to save these two men. What kind of a commander was he? Now at least he had to keep the rest from dying of despair or blindness. But his foot got more and more swollen and became cruelly painful. He began to sense how this journey would end for him.

After a few more miles Hood collapsed, unconscious. Since he couldn't be carried, somebody had to stay with him. Richardson wanted to be the one: He knew John would send food from the fort to keep them both from dying. "No," John replied. "I am the captain! Also, I'm slower than you. I'll stay with Hood. You go on with the others. Here are the compass and sextant."

He made this decision because he couldn't go on, and only for that reason! He couldn't keep up with the others, and therefore, as matters stood, he couldn't lead them.

They pitched one of the tents and bedded Hood down inside. Then the doctor assembled the rest of the crew around him. John impressed on them: "You must stay together! Anyone who walks ahead is gone, for he'll lose his way and drag the others in his tracks with him into disaster. Stay together!"

Hepburn stepped forward. "I'll stay with you and Hood."

Richardson took off. John and Hepburn went looking for firewood, *tripes de roche,* and deer tracks. They felt no more hunger, only weakness. It was no longer a matter of well-being but, with a great deal of luck, of surviving.

Hepburn shot a partridge, which they fried. They fed it to Hood and he seemed to recover a little. For themselves they found a small quantity of *tripes de roche.*

Two days later, Michel, the Iroquois, suddenly turned up. He had asked Richardson's permission to return to the tent along with Perrault and Jean-Baptiste Bélanger. Unfortunately, he had lost those two in the dark and hadn't been able to find their footprints. That surprised John, because it had neither rained nor snowed, and the wind had died down completely.

Fontano was probably also dead, Michel went on. He had been hit when crossing a lake and had broken his leg. They had had to leave him behind, but he hadn't discovered him on his way back.

Michel had been lucky and had found a dead wolf, probably killed by a blow of a reindeer's horn. He still had some of the wolf meat; they devoured it greedily and praised the Indian highly. He asked for an ax to get more. When he was gone, John worried about this and began to calculate.

Where does Michel get so much ammunition? It's improbable that Richardson left it for him; and why does he have two pistols? When Michel got back and served them more wolf meat,

John asked about the pistols. Michel replied that Peltier had given him one as a present.

They went on eating greedily and felt as though strength were already returning to their miserable skeletons. But John's mind worked strenuously: he was trying to remember something. At one point he left the tent and stood outside to allow inner pictures to pass by his eyes unimpeded. When he returned he said, "I simply don't pay enough attention to details! I could have sworn this was Bélanger's pistol."

The others stared at him, horrified.

"Do you think I did him in?" asked Michel in an imprecating voice. "That isn't true." Suddenly his hand was on one of the pistols.

"No, no," said Hepburn, "nobody thinks that. Why would you think so?" The Indian became calm again. But none of them wanted to eat any more wolf meat.

For days Michel didn't allow the British to talk to each other alone. When they talked in his presence, they had to use a slave language: saying innocuous things that he understood and at the same time communicating something he didn't understand. "Did perhaps more wolves get killed in this way?" No one dared to utter the names Perrault and Fontano. Or, "If a reindeer no longer fears the wolf, it'll certainly kill more of them."

Still, Michel suspected dimly what they guessed and feared. He refused to go hunting and became more and more tyrannical, ordering who had to sleep where. But the British realized without speaking to each other: if Michel had known the way and had been able to read a compass, he would have long since killed them, or, worse still, made them part of his food supply.

"Why don't you hunt, Michel?"

But he refused. "There's no game here. We should start for the Winter Lake at once. We can always come back for Mr. Hood later."

John thought it over. "Good. But we must first collect food and firewood for him, because he can't move." He was only looking for a chance to speak to Hepburn. Michel agreed. They left the tent and went off in different directions. As John was chopping wood—as loudly as possible in order to signal to Hepburn where he was—he heard a shot from the direction of the tent. He got there at the same time as Hepburn to find Hood lying dead beside the fire. The shot had pierced his skull. Michel stood next to him. "Mr. Hood was cleaning my rifle. That's when it must have happened."

They buried Hood with difficulty, covering him with a little snow. Now John and Hepburn did not need any lengthy communication to understand: Why had Michel left his weapon behind if he was going hunting? How could a half-conscious Hood have even thought of cleaning it? Above all, the back of Hood's head showed traces of powder burns: the bullet had entered his head from the back and had left it through the front. And for some time now their pistols had been within reach.

Now that Hood was dead, the journey could be resumed. They took down the tent and John fixed the course. By evening they had managed only two miles, because of his sprained foot. Their meal was furnished by Hood's coat of buffalo leather. Michel didn't let them out of his sight for a moment.

Again and again Michel asked, "How many miles still? In which direction is the fort?" "It's still far," said John. But after three days Michel thought he could recognize with certainty a rock that was only a day's march from Fort Enterprise. John shook his head. "Impossible," he said. The next morning the Indian crept out of the tent early and took his weapons with him. He wanted to try to gather some *tripes de roche.* He had never offered to do that since they had formed the rear guard.

"I'm glad," answered John, and Hepburn added, "You're a good man and a friend."

They waited until the steps outside had moved away. "He only wants to load his rifle. He's got nothing in it anymore!" said Hepburn. "When he comes back, we must be quick." John loaded his pistol carefully, as though he were doing it for the first time in his life. Hepburn said: "We've eaten the meat. We're his accomplices if we don't kill him at once!"

"For the first time you're talking nonsense, Hepburn," answered John. "He wants to kill us, that's the reason—more reasons we don't need; more are bad for us!" But Hepburn still seemed to fear that John wouldn't pull the trigger. "I'll do it for you, sir—it's easier for me."

John stretched his arm toward the tent flap, holding it at the height of his shoulder while hiding his hand behind a piece of luggage, so that Michel could not see it when he entered. With the slightest turn of the body the pistol could be aimed at his head as soon as he appeared. John remained in this posture, rigid and tense.

"No," he replied. "I'll do it myself. Ten years of war—what do you think I did all that time? Only one always kills the wrong men."

"The wrong men?" Hepburn did not understand. "And your arm, sir?"

"I can hold up my arm for hours," said John. "I could already do that when I was ten. He'll sneak up and listen. We've got to talk loudly about harmless things or he'll shoot us from the outside through the wall of the tent, because he realizes we're about to do something."

"It'll be a fine day today, sir!" said Hepburn. "I think the weather's on our side, too." He added in a low voice: "I hear him."

John cleared his throat. "Then let's get up slowly, Hepburn. I'll fetch firewood . . ."

At this very moment Michel appeared in the tent entrance, his rifle at his hip, ready to fire. He was aiming at John. Hepburn drew his pistol fast. Michel turned the barrel of his rifle toward him. The picture of this scene remained fixed in John's eyes. The next thing he became aware of was that Hepburn had seized his hand and held it for a long time. They did not say a word for minutes. Hepburn spoke first: "You shot him through the forehead, sir. He suffered nothing; he didn't even know it." John answered: "This journey was one week too long." The next day they saw the fort lying at the lake shore.

*　　*　　*

235

In the blockhouse they found four living skeletons who could barely rise: Dr. Richardson, Adam, Peltier, and Samandré. No supplies, not a bite of food! They had scraped off the top of a reindeer blanket that had been discarded half a year ago with their knives and had consumed the shoes they had worn to get there. "Where are the others?" asked John. The doctor tried to answer. John admonished him not to speak in a voice that sounded like the grave. Richardson rose, clawing his way up the center beam with spidery fingers, stared at John with bulging eyes, and said in a rattling voice: "You should hear yourself just once, Mr. Franklin!"

Richardson had found nothing but a note from Back: "No food and no Indians here. Going farther south to find people. Beauparlant dead, Augustus missing. Back." Wentzel had apparently been there and had taken the maps, but he had not kept his promise: he had not seen to the supplies.

Hepburn dragged himself outside and tried to shoot something. He was lucky and came back with two partridges. Greedily the six men devoured the raw meat—barely more than a morsel for each. That was October 29.

Their journey was not yet at an end.

Peltier and Samandré lay dying. Adam could no longer get up or even crawl. His abdomen was swollen. He was in great pain.

The doctor sat by the tiny fire Hepburn had lit and read aloud from the Bible. It seemed oddly alien and crazy: in the midst of the Arctic, a man sat and read in a broken, barely understandable voice crochety sentences from an ancient book of the Orient that likewise could be barely understood. Still, it was a comfort to them all. He might have just as well snapped his fingers and hoped for rescue from that—if he believed in it himself, it was also a comfort for the others.

In confidence, John told Richardson what had happened. They looked at each other for a long time with their bulging eyeballs, bent forward, coughing slightly, looking like two miserable old drunks in London's Gin Lane.

"I would have done it, too, Mr. Franklin," the doctor finally muttered. "But now, pray. Do pray!"

They discussed the situation. Gradually they began to lose their minds. Yet each of them considered his own capacity for clear thought greater than that of the other. Therefore, they all talked to each other in a calming, endlessly patient, and simple way, constantly repeating everything because they forgot what had just been said.

It all depended on Back.

During the night of November 1 Samandré died, and when Peltier noticed this he lost all hope and died three hours later. The others were now too weak to carry the bodies out of the hut.

Hepburn and John, who could still move about on their hands and knees, tried to find *tripes de roche* and firewood, but they fainted constantly and returned with slim pickings. They had long since begun to burn every piece of wood that could be spared: inner doors, shelves, floor boards, the wardrobe.

Now Adam lay close to death. He had not spoken for days, had not even tried to find a more comfortable position.

"He'll come," said John.

"Who?" whispered Richardson.

"Back. George Back. Midshipman George Back. Don't you understand me, Doctor?"

He broke off, because he realized that Richardson had been speaking, or rather hissing, for some time. Now he repeated it: ". . . is good. All will turn out for the best."

"Who?" asked John.

With a movement of his head, Richardson pointed at the ceiling.

"The Almighty."

"Don't know," whispered John. "You know, of course, I . . ." They were lying wrapped in the remnants of their field blankets. The fire went out. They were waiting for death. It stank.

On November 7, Akaitcho, chief of the Copper Indians, arrived with twenty warriors at Fort Enterprise in the deepest snow. Although near starvation, a walking skeleton, Midshipman Back had made his way to the tents of his tribe with great tenacity and begged the chief for help. Despite the severe frost and nearly insurmountable snows, Akaitcho had fought his way from the Great Slave Lake to the Winter Lake in only five days. He found Franklin, Dr. Richardson, Hepburn, and Adam still alive.

At first the Indians refused to enter the hut because corpses were lying there. They said whoever does not bury the dead is dead himself and needed no help.

Franklin alone could still grasp the situation. It took him an hour and a half to drag the two corpses through the door and cover them outside with a little snow. Then he collapsed and lost consciousness.

The survivors were given pemmican and drink. The doctor forbade them to eat too much too hastily, but he was unable to stick to his own prescription. Terrible stomach pains set in; only Franklin was spared them because after his great exertion he had become so weak that he had to be fed, and that was done more cautiously. The Indians stayed with the rescued men for ten days, until they could start the journey to Fort Providence together.

Eleven men were dead. In addition to the four British, only Benoît, Solomon Bélanger, St. Germain, Adam, and Augustus remained alive, the latter having reappeared after all. But John knew he could not have kept anyone else from dying, perhaps not even himself. Back and the Indians were the rescuers of the survivors.

"After such a journey," Richardson speculated, "the rest of life will go by quickly toward its end." John Franklin now had another worry. He thought it possible that he would never be given an Arctic or any other command again. He had neither found the Northwest Passage nor reached Parry's ship by land. They had not even been able to establish relations with the Eskimos. For long nights John pondered what the errors had been that had led to the deaths of so many people. It had been wrong to rely on Wentzel, but that couldn't have been all of it. Should they have turned back immediately after their first failure in making contact with the Eskimos? No. One might have had better luck with other tribes. Should he have threatened any person with instant death who lost or destroyed supplies—anyone who stole or embezzled something? No. His system, "Faith for Confidence," would have been compromised even more rapidly, and for any other system their physical power would have been inadequate. Should he have brought along better hunters from England, people who also knew more about survival in this cold desert? But who would that have been?

He said to Richardson, "The system was right, only we should have learned more things better in time. I'm the one who made the mistakes. One can be lucky in spite of them, but I wasn't. The system works. I want to show better next time how well it works."

"It's quite similar to my system," answered Richardson with a thoughtful nod. He meant it without mockery, lovingly. "In any case, I won't again have the idea of comparing you with the captain of the *Blossom.*"

John Franklin thought some more. "The admirals won't discern the slightest success. They'll believe that I'm the wrong man. And they'd be right." He was silent. "But when one looks at it all from a different angle, then I am the right man—and they couldn't get a better one. I'll just have to help the admirals to see it in that way."

Franklin took heart again. In any case, he had remained sure of himself, even during the worst moments. Neither fear nor despair had crippled him. He was stronger than ever before in his life.

Northwest Passage, open polar sea, North Pole. With or without the Admiralty, he would reach these three objectives on his future voyages. But in no case will anyone under his command ever starve again. That was as certain as the Crown of England.

[15]

◆◆◆

FAME AND HONOR

The clock faces in London were white these days. And many clocks now had second hands; only ships' chronometers had used them before. Clocks and people had become more precise. John would have welcomed this if the result had been greater calm and deliberation, but instead he observed everywhere only time pressure and haste.

Or was it that nobody wanted to sacrifice time to him, to John, anymore? No, it had to be a general fashion. Reaching for one's watch chain had become a more frequent move than reaching for one's hat. One hardly heard curses anymore; the exclamation "No time!" had taken their place.

John felt estranged. Added to this was the fact that he had too much time on his hands himself: a new command was not in sight.

He had been received with scorn and blame. Dr. Brown was monosyllabic; Sir John Barrow, blustering and ungracious. Davies Gilbert, the new head of the Royal Society after the death of Sir Joseph, was icily friendly. Only Peter Mark Roget now and then sought out John in his home to chat about optics, electricity, slowness, and fresh ideas for the construction of the picture rotor. He avoided the topic of magnetism, presumably because of the magnetic North Pole. So much tact was

almost unbearable! Most of the time John sat ruminating behind his window at 60, Frith Street in Soho, thinking about the
possible course of the Northwest Passage and how he could
make it all good again and go on with his life in the necessary
consistent order. In the house opposite, an old woman polished her window several times a day, sometimes even at
night. It was as though before she died she wanted to accomplish one single thing no one could find fault with.

Often it helped him to walk the streets—to go on deck, as
John called it. He wandered through London and set himself
objectives in order to forget, however briefly, snow, ice, hunger,
and dead voyageurs. He looked at the new houses: they had
fewer windows now because of the window tax. He studied iron
bridges: the carriages made a racket when they drove over them
and that was annoying. Then he took up women's clothes: bodices had moved farther down, to the middle of the body, and
seemed more tightly laced; skirts and sleeves were puffed up, as
though in the future, women would claim more space for themselves than ever before.

John was also abroad at night, because he often had trouble
falling asleep. A few times he got involved with wild women who
wanted to make him buy them gin by the bottle. Robbers didn't
dare come near him. His body had become as heavy and strong
as it had been before the journey.

One early Sunday morning he watched two gentlemen duel-
ing with pistols in Hyde Park. They were miserable shots, perhaps intentionally so: after a slight wound, they let it be. In the
afternoon he observed how three drunken oarsmen couldn't
manage the current under London Bridge. The boat crashed
against the pier; all of them drowned. Suddenly people had time
to gawk! Time pressure was nothing but fashion; here was the
proof.

In a street stall, for the fee of a penny, he could read newspapers standing up: the Greeks were rebelling against the Turks;
China had prohibited the opium trade. The first steamship in
the navy. That was a laugh! All they had to do was to shoot at
one of those paddle wheels and the thing would go in circles

and offer the best target. Then, too, parliamentary reform! Many words for it, many against. It was all a matter of timing: Push through reform quickly before it's too late! Choke off reform quickly before it's too late!

Twice he went to the Griffins' house, but beautiful Jane was, so they said, on educational tours somewhere in Europe most of the year.

What to do? Where to turn?

He also sat in coffee houses. There he could get pen, ink, and paper whenever anything important occurred to him. Actually, nothing occurred to John, but he ordered writing materials just the same, stared at the white sheet of paper, and thought, If I have something important in mind, I'll just write it down. Well, perhaps it also worked the other way round: If I have something to write on, perhaps something important will come to me. And so it happened: suddenly the Idea appeared. It seemed fool-hardy to John, but that spoke more for the Idea than against it, especially since the project was in some respects similar to a long journey. The Idea: writing! John conceived of writing a book to justify himself, a fat book in which he would seek to convert all skeptics and convince them of his system. And since he knew what a footloose fellow the human will was, he commit-ted himself in writing then and there. He wrote on the white sheet: "NARRATIVE OF A JOURNEY TO THE SHORES OF THE POLAR SEA—not under 100,000 words." That rescued the plan at the last minute, for the head had already begun to whisper its objec-tions. For example, John Franklin, if there is anything you can-not do, it's writing books!

The first words were surely the hardest:

"On Sunday, May 23rd, 1819, all of our people embarked . . ." "Our people?" But they went on board themselves, not just some other people who belonged to them. So he'd better say, "traveling party." No, "the men under my command." But that was also wrong, since the phrase didn't include him, and he had installed himself on the *Prince of Wales* at the same time. "I and the men" pleased him as little as "the men and I." "We embarked in full number" was inaccurate; the "entire party including my own person" discouraged reading. "On Sunday, May 23rd, 1819, our entire party led by me embarked . . ."—Well, now what?

The head said, Throw it away, John Franklin, you'll lose your mind over this! The will quacked in a monotone, Keep going! And John himself said, "Almost a dozen words already as good as set."

The old woman polished her window, and John wrote his book, day after day. Soon he had written more than fifty thousand words and had reached the first encounter with Akaitcho and the Copper Indians. Writing was as arduous as a sea voyage; it generated the energies and hopes it needed while also providing enough for the rest of one's life. Whoever had to write a book could not be desperate forever. And despair over proper formulations could be conquered with sufficient industry. In the beginning, John especially had to fight repetitions. All his life he had refused to use several words for the same thing. He therefore had to distinguish between basic and superfluous words and keep his stock as limited as possible. Now, however, it happened that the same words occurred ten times on one page; for example, the phrase "to be found in," as in an enumeration of Arctic plants. John would even wake up in the middle of the night with a start, searching for repetitions as one would search for some obstinate vermin preying on one's sleep.

Still another thing disturbed him at first: the more zealously he described the actual episodes, the more they seemed to retreat. The mere act of formulating it in language turned what he knew by experience into something even he himself saw only as a picture. The air of familiarity was gone; in its place he had retrieved the lure of strangeness. At some point John began to think of this as an advantage rather than a disadvantage, although in the light of his aim to describe something familiar it was actually a disappointment.

"The chief came up the hill and with a measured and dignified step, looking neither to the right nor to the left—" John let this passage stand, although he knew it conveyed but little of the feelings he had at the time he viewed this scene, of the unclear, uneasy situation and the strange hope the chief had instilled in him from the first moment. Still, it was a useful sentence, because it allowed, and indeed compelled, everyone to project his own feelings into it.

So finally something good came of the disappointments of writing: a new work that John could accomplish, because in it he wanted to achieve what was possible and to omit what was impossible. By the time he had gotten to the fifty-thousandth word, his aims were within reach.

If it was to exonerate the author, the book had to be well written. That was a matter of time, nothing else.

It had to be simple, so that as many people as possible could understand how good it was.

It had to be more than three hundred pages long, so that all who owned it could be proud to be seen with it.

The old woman died. For four days the window was still noticeably cleaner than the others. John was sad, because he would have liked to have given her the finished book as a gift. Dejected, he sat and thought suddenly that his story might bore readers. He decided to visit Eleanor the poet. He wanted to ask how one managed it so that a book didn't bore anybody.

"How much have you written, then?" she asked. "Eighty-two thousand five hundred words," he answered. At that she laughed and hopped. John instinctively encircled her waist with his arm and held her tight. He shouldn't have done that, for she obliged him at the instant to take part in her literary Sunday circle. He tried to get out of it, pointing to his work, even pretending religious reasons that strictly forbade attendance at literary events on Sundays. Nothing helped; she didn't believe a word.

Eleanor's circle was called Attic Chest. Its atmosphere was very Greek. The tapestry on the wall featured temple ruins, an amphitheater, and olive trees. Meander patterns twirled around the cushions, and the chessboard reposed on a Corinthian column. There was also no lack of marble heads with laurel wreaths. Several members of the assembly had thoughts of dying in the near future, preferably in Hellas, if necessary in Rome. John understood this at once, because it was repeated to him several times.

Eleanor read a poem; then a man named Elliott, and finally a bald man named Sharp who gave explanations before and after. For this reason they probably called him also Talk Sharp. When the reading was over, somebody said something full of feeling and all the silent listeners appeared to agree with it, or at least to struggle for objections without success. John imitated them and fared well. Poems, like conversation, were after all about feeling and basic elements. They were talking about the electric basis of sympathy and about the particles of fire that inhere in all matter, giving all things their specific temperaments. According to a theory developed in Breslau, a diamond was really a pebble that has found its true identity. One Sunday was not quite enough to absorb these intimations and insights, not to speak of entering into their discussions. John was very glad that nobody asked him anything. He remained silent and watched the others with growing wonderment, because he had not succeeded in discovering the source of their great animation.

Finally he had it: it had to be a game! They all played the same game, each one in his own way. There were people like Eleanor who talked about themselves loudly and enthusiastically. That gave them a momentum which made it difficult for people to interrupt. Others used "and" at the end of every sentence. But they were powerless against those who were able to inject themselves into the slightest pause before the "and" to make their remarks. Obviously, the main rule of the game was to seize the chance to speak and hold on to it as long as possible.

When he listened, Mr. Elliott so tilted his head that he resembled a close-hauled sailing ship in a strong breeze. After a while he would nod his agreement, and continued to do so more and more vigorously until the speaker stopped to obtain his agreement in words. What would follow, however, was criticism. Or Miss Tuttle. She began her listening with her head held high, then gradually lowered her chin until it finally reached her lace collar. At that point at the latest she began to talk, unstoppable now, whether the other person was finished or not. As a result, every speaker found himself in a race with Miss Tuttle's chin, and nervous people tried anxiously to be brief.

Since John didn't want to speak, he remained outside the game and could observe it with detachment. But that was over soon, because Mr. Sharp asked him about the journey—for the second time. Others called this to John's attention as well. All at once everyone stopped talking; they were waiting for John's words. Now he had to stumble into the echoing silence with his poor sentences replete with repetitions. The more embarrassed he became, the more benevolent they all looked. They had, of course, heard of his fiasco in the Arctic but didn't want to show it, and so they acted as if they were very curious and surprised. He made it as brief as possible. Luckily, the conversation soon turned to something else: to the moment and to the capacity of art to freeze it—they were talking about pictures on Greek vases. John found this interesting because he could imagine what could become of it: how movement could be depicted from several frozen moments! He wanted to tell this to the poets, but now he couldn't get to speak. He took a deep breath, trying to find his good phrases, but no one paid any attention. Even when he made himself look as if he were about to burst with knowledge, nobody took pity on him. So he gave it all up again and looked only at Eleanor's beautiful light-brown eyes and at the way the hair on her neck curled gently; that was enough for him. He, too, could freeze moments, perhaps better than those who talked about it.

When the last guests had gone, John stayed behind for a while. "They find you interesting because you can navigate a ship," Eleanor suggested. "Also, all artists take to a man who should by all rights be dead. Just think of a scar in the middle of the forehead. . . ."

"Do you know the painter William Westall?" asked John.

"I've seen one picture by him," answered Eleanor. *"The Coming of the Monsoon.* He's quite gifted."

All at once John knew that she had the same difficulty he had with finding the right word. Only in her something different was at work. "Gifted"—what a dreary word for a man or a picture! They all failed to find the right words, but they were just quick and so handled this defect in ways quite different from himself.

He said good-bye and went back to Frith Street and continued to write day and night. To hold out, he tossed his will a new morsel: the concluding sentence. He had decided how his book would have to end: "And thus terminated our long, fatiguing, and disastrous travels in North America, having journeyed by water and by land five thousand five hundred and fifty miles." This, and no other, had to be his concluding phrase.

When John became tired, he made his will test whether this sentence could already be written. The simple-minded servant could only answer: "Not quite yet."

The rest of the year 1823 brought three events no one had counted on.

In August, John Franklin and Eleanor Porden were married.

In September, the publisher John Murray brought out John's narrative of his travels. It was an expensive book, ten guineas per copy. Within three weeks, Murray couldn't keep up with the printing, because all the world wanted to buy it. With one blow, John Franklin came to be seen as a brave explorer and a great man. He had not even tried to justify himself; he had only described their misfortune exactly, had left out nothing, and had also admitted his own moments of helplessness. Englishmen liked that sort of thing. They agreed that one could shed this kind of helplessness only with one's humanity.

They wanted to see Franklin victorious or succumb just as he was. Any doubt in his wisdom and his ability seemed petty and shortsighted. He was honored by admirals, scientists, and lords, and everyone came to feel within a few days as though he had known him for years. He was invited into the Royal Society that same month, and the Admiralty hurried to make him officially a captain at last.

The third event: Peter Mark Roget came to visit in order to congratulate him. And he informed Franklin on that occasion that he was not slow at all. He had never been slow, but was a totally normal man.

That's how it was. Suddenly he was normal and at the same time the greatest and the best. Now, like Richardson, he feared that the rest of his life would pass by too quickly.

Each day brought fresh congratulations, and what they wrote in the newspapers! Everyone seemed to look him over studiously, to see what manner of man he was and what he was like in real life.

"I'm only good for the long haul," he told Eleanor. "At moments of sudden confusion like this I have to take my time." He retired to Spilsby, in Lincolnshire, to think it over thoroughly.

Eleanor expected a child. At least that was not yet in the papers.

Thinking about fame is not easy for a famous person; he stands in his own light. To be able to think, therefore, Franklin firmly dismissed the idea that fame had any connection with his real qualities. Rather, it was a matter of sensationalism. To Londoners he was "the man who ate his boots," and when they saw him, each of them recalled a good joke about hunger and cold. Yes, that's what it was: they all remembered something in his story. And so he didn't need to talk appreciably more often than before.

Mr. Elliott had said, "A hero, that's an ill-starred fellow with character. We need heroes more than ever to counteract machines." Sharp had seized the paper-thin pause to toss in: "A rather remote explanation. Nearness to death is the point! A hero is a person who either dies young or gets away alive ten times and then risks his life for the eleventh time. And since lately everyone but me worships death—" Miss Tuttle, whose chin had just reached her collar, became impatient. "Good, let's have it remain unclear. People simply love him! If you tell me how love comes about, you know it all!" Franklin was less interested in its origin than in the best way to live happily with his new excessive notoriety.

To Flora Reed he said: "Fame and ludicrousness are closely related. Neither one has anything to do with honor."

Flora replied: "But I don't envy you at all! What are you going to do with the money?"

"I'd most like to give it away," mused John. "Of course, I'm a married man."

"What do you know!" said Flora.

"And besides, if in spite of everything I don't get another command, I'd have to equip my own ship."

Flora excused herself. She had things to do.

The thought that he might not be slow by nature didn't suit John at all: he needed this quality more than ever. Roget had the machine rebuilt with which Dr. Orme had once measured John's speed. "It has one fault," he said. "The result of the measurement depends on the person being measured. If he wants to be slow, he can see a complete picture at the lowest number of rotations. If he wants to be fast, he won't be content with even the highest number. The time he says 'now' is left up to him."

"My slowness has been observed by many people," answered Franklin, "and I couldn't be quick even when I wanted to be. I was never able to catch a ball."

"I have no theory to explain why you couldn't do that, Captain. I won't presume to have one, either. I can only say what it was probably *not*. Do you find that disagreeable?"

"No, it's irrelevant," John replied. "I know I'm slow. Berlengas! The lighthouse in Berlengas furnished proof that I'm always one full turn behind." This piqued Roget's curiosity, but he didn't find out more, for John ponderously changed the subject and simply didn't hear any attempt to return to it.

Even the picture rotor that so preoccupied Roget interested Franklin less than ever. Writing had lent him other points of view, but it took him a long time to deliberate before he could clarify them to Roget. "I'm a discoverer," he said, "and discovering means: observing directly what a thing looks like. I don't want to be given any illusions by the picture rotor."

"Then you also reject painting and literature?" Roget inquired.

Franklin asked him to wait a moment. He paced up and down in his room a few times. "No," he answered when he was done. "Painting and literature do indeed describe what a thing looks like and by what rules it moves, but not *how quickly* it moves. If they somehow manage to do this after all, one may doubt them at once. That's what's important. For people have to see for themselves how long things last and how quickly they change."

"I don't understand," answered Roget. "Isn't this a rather bombastic objection to a harmless machine meant to produce entertaining illusions? I'd say you're right if one's own way of seeing things directly were replaced altogether by such an apparatus, but that will never be."

Franklin stood at the window and struggled for an answer. He blinked, muttered, shook his head, and got ready to speak several times, only to reconsider once more. It seemed unfortunate that Roget was so tactful. "How long something lasts and how suddenly it can change," said Franklin, "these are never fixed but rather depend on each person. I had a great deal of trouble accepting this: my own speed and the way the world moves *for me*. Even one single illusion can be dangerous. For example—"

"Yes, an example!" Roget exclaimed.

"—the way a man is attacked and fights. How fast he's hit by a saber and whether he has any chance at all to see and act in time! No mere statement about optics can be made that even pretends to be the truth. If my visual perception of movements is wrong, so will be my perception of myself, of everything."

Now it was Roget who changed the subject. These arguments and musings were too abstruse for him. And they surprised him above all in John Franklin, who was usually no friend of hyperbole.

* * *

Father Franklin lay mortally ill and spoke of dying. Still, he took in that his son had made something of himself. "As I've always said," he whispered, "a man is intelligent when he's made something of himself. But both are unimportant. We start as rich folk and end as beggars."

Eleanor arrived from London. She alighted from the coach, wrapped in voluminous garments and looking ill and pale. Franklin drove with her at once to Old Bolingbroke, to Father. "A shame I can't see your wife anymore," his father said. "Main thing is she's healthy."

John was in love with Eleanor, and since that only increased his patience, he had won her heart for a time. She had reveled in his tenderness. He had decided he could endure her talk for days, happy to listen to her as long as he could always simply watch her face and movements. The wedding had been a little painful. Franklin had tried to learn how to dance a quadrille. He liked to memorize everything except dance steps and degrees of relations—both were unavoidable at weddings. And what was actually played at his own wedding were mostly Viennese waltzes, a world inaccessible to him. But he tried it anyway out of love.

Then the new topic: children. She wanted to bear many children; she found this wonderfully archaic, and the helpless state in which every new life began so creative and somehow "religious." John saw this more simply, but he wanted children too.

As Franklin's general popularity grew, Eleanor's affection began to cool. She had published a somewhat dull epic on Richard the Lionhearted in several volumes, which sold only moderately, although the booksellers always added that the author was the "wife of the man who ate his boots." In the long run, that was not good for the love of a poet. Eleanor began to be sickly, and to nag. She hopped no longer, and she didn't laugh.

But now they were not in London. Franklin had hoped to win her here forever—for himself, for this quiet land, for the eccentric country folk of Spilsby and Horncastle. He wanted her to live with him here in Old Bolingbroke and to raise their many children here. But Eleanor found Lincolnshire too provincial, the dialect too broad, the landscape either too flat or too hilly, and the climate harmful. She liked only old Franklin: "What an adorable little old man!" But to live here was out of the question. She coughed until John Franklin agreed.

One time they quarreled about love. When Franklin admitted that he was perhaps more interested in discoveries than in love, and in love mostly for the act of discovery, she became theatrical and personal at the same time, an unfortunate mixture. "I shouldn't have gotten so close to the great conquerer of hunger and ice! What looks like strength from a distance turns out to be logic and pedantry from close by!"

Franklin considered this. He didn't want to put any obstacles in her way, not in her talk or in her rage. But what if she wanted him to be very different from what he was? "I've got to be this way! Without preparation and firm rules there's chaos in my head—more than in yours."

"That's not the point," replied Eleanor. This sentence worried John, for since the time with Flora Reed he knew only too well: a quarrel in which one person told the other what it was all about left no room for a solution.

During the days before her return to London, Eleanor's cough became more severe; she read Mary Shelley's *Frankenstein* and, worse still, spoke very little.

Hardly was she gone when the father died. It seemed as though he had been waiting for the air to clear.

Life passed very quickly now. John Franklin suffered from this. "It deeply offends my sense of honor," he wrote to Sir John Barrow, "that I should harvest fame for an enterprise that was neither successful nor brought to a conclusion. My profession is to produce good sea charts for the particular benefit of every person. But now no one has any benefit from me. I sit in London, grant newspaper interviews, and generally talk only to people with whom I have nothing in common except dates of appointments. I beg you in all humility, sir, give me a new command. I believe that I can find the Northwest Passage."

Eleanor got her child and John his command on the same day. This time a new overland journey was to take him down the Great River in northern Canada, to be continued in suitable boats from the estuary both in a western and eastern direction. Franklin met immediately with Dr. Richardson to discuss crew and equipment. George Back had gotten wind of it and wanted to be included. The two men conferred and decided they owed Back a thing or two and didn't want to stand in the way of his career. "That he loves men has nothing to do with it; he must come along." Richardson then asked Franklin whether he could leave his ailing wife and his child at this time.

Franklin answered simply, "It can be done." He thought it superfluous to tell Richardson his story or even complain. Friendship consisted of plans and actions; everything else only falsified it.

The child was a girl, christened Eleanor Anne. Friends came to visit. Franklin said, "This is Ella." The baby kicked her legs and cried murderously. She clearly didn't want to be judged. Hepburn looked at the cradle and finally dared to comment after all: "She looks like the Captain when observed from the wrong end of the telescope." Franklin found this not very flattering to his daughter, but he kept silent. Soon thereafter they were busy with preparations for the journey.

Eleanor was gravely ill. The doctors came and went; the diagnoses contradicted each other; the cough remained. The illness didn't bring their love back, but it made John charitable toward Eleanor's little tricks, which were now of little use. Her efforts to dominate John by feeling wounded and reproaching him did not work out. He sat at her bedside listening to her, kindly and guiltily, and thought intensely about pemmican, snowshoes, waterfalls, and supplies of tea.

Shortly before his departure, Eleanor discovered herself as the devoted wife of a famous explorer who, through the intensity of her devotion, rose to be his equal. In no case, she said, must he stay behind on her account; under no circumstances must he sacrifice the Northwest Passage on the altar of his marriage. With painstaking labor, lying flat in her sickbed, she sewed and embroidered a huge British flag, her hands raised high over the covers. Again and again the needle dropped in her face; it was not easy work. When she was done she enclosed John's hand in hers and said, "Ride on, Lionhearted! Unfurl this flag at the proudest point of the journey." "Gladly," he murmured. "Very gladly." And suddenly he thought he knew for sure that he would never understand either love or women. Women wanted something different in this world; one could only respect that.

Eleanor died a few days after John Franklin and his companions had boarded the ship in Liverpool. He heard the news months later in Canada, after he had written her several comforting and cheering letters. He was hardly surprised by the sad news.

"She died for the cause of Arctic exploration," wrote the newspaper. "Of course she died," Elliott commented. "But she lived for literature." Mr. Sharp was annoyed about this. "She has proved her greatness. It matters little whether one sacrifices oneself for the Arctic, for Greek freedom, or for literature." Miss Tuttle could listen no longer: "She loved him. That's all that matters." Quickly they found themselves embroiled in a quarrel in which each was sure what it was all about. They missed Eleanor—the old, laughing Eleanor who at once dispelled each disagreement by talking loudly and enthusiastically about herself. Oh, how quickly everything turns into the past!

The second land journey, from 1825 to 1827, was as easy and happy as a child's dream during school holidays.

Now they knew how to do everything and learned to do more. Franklin had good boats specially built for the river journey and the coastal exploration. Supplies were plentiful, connections with the fur-trading posts uninterrupted. The only danger could come from hostile Eskimos. But it was the greatest good fortune of this expedition that they came only upon tribes responding in kind to their offerings: fearlessness and good will. Franklin recorded and learned whatever he was able to see and to hear, for one thing was sure: the Eskimos could live here, and if one lived as they did, one could, too. Augustus joined them again and translated everything—important as well as seemingly unimportant matters. Franklin converted his new way of looking at things into a new way of questioning the Eskimos. He discovered that it made no sense to ask "leading questions" that had to be answered with yes or no: out of a sense of misguided and misleading courtesy, they always answered them with yes. Franklin's most important word therefore became "how."

His notebook filled up: *"Erneik* is the harpoon with the seal bladder, *angovak* the big spear, *kapot* the little spear, *nuguit* the slingshot used to shoot birds." Each implement had its purpose, and if one wanted to use it, one had to learn still another thing: the concentration without which one could neither see nor hunt anything in this terrain. And failure in hunting was equivalent to death.

It was their further good fortune that Back finally understood what was important. Perhaps he had grown up; perhaps he had simply learned that discovery and slow observation belonged together, and even more: "If we have the advantage of intelligence and rifles over the Eskimos, then intelligence consists in getting along without rifles"—a sentence written by George Back, Lieutenant, Royal Navy, if you please.

Eskimo dress: drawers made of the padding of little auks' feathers, trousers of fox or bear fur, stockings of rabbit fur, beds made of the coats of musk oxen—nothing froze on them!

Although they brought their boats along, the whites learned how to make good boats of split walrus skin and bones. They also noted how to make a sled by packing furs and meat supplies into bundles and letting them freeze hard. The weight saved made it easier for the dogs. With wooden knives they carved bricks out of the snow and built igloos, which conserved warmth better than any Army tent. Much of the stuff Europeans drag along on their travels soon appeared to them only as life-threatening ballast.

At one point Franklin noted in his diary: "Actually we couldn't be happier."

Learning increased in a geometrical progression, and they felt an overwhelming enthusiasm for seeing and knowing that worked on them like an intoxicant. When, after waiting for hours, Back harpooned his first seal, which had stuck out its nose through the ice hole from below for only a moment, he danced with joy on the ice; he slipped, landed on his back, and called out, beaming, "I can do it!" He had tried it so often, but until now without success. How was it possible that he had been able to learn it? Could one become faster than one was by nature after all? Franklin had his fixed look for emergencies, but that look conferred speed through the selection of the object, not through a faster reaction. "How did you do it, Mr. Back?" he asked. "Very simple, sir. You just mustn't think of anything except that one thing." "I can do that," said Franklin, "but if I concentrate on one thing, it just goes round and round in my thoughts until my head knows it precisely." "But that's just what this is not," Back countered. "Only a small part of the brain must be affected, just the one that has to do with punching the seal. Try it sometime." Franklin hesitated. "I first have to think through precisely whether it works. Then I'll try it," he answered. He knew he would never be able to bag a seal. But what he had just heard preyed on his mind.

Back carried his seal to the igloos. They ate the raw liver and learned still more: the hunter gets no part of his quarry; he hunts for the others. That fitted into Franklin's System: at least it was worth some thought.

Although the Northwest Passage was not found, the journey was a success nonetheless: a considerable stretch of the coastline was explored and mapped, and their ethnographic notes were numerous and of good quality. From the mouth of the Coppermine River to the Bering Strait, the course of the Northwest Passage was now clearly discernible. There remained only the segment from Hudson's Bay to Point Turnagain.

Where was "the proudest point of the journey"? Franklin

unfolded Eleanor's flag at the estuary of the Great River, which he named after its discoverer: Mackenzie's River.

Franklin wanted to call the report on the second journey into the Canadian north *The Benign Arctic.* His publisher was dead set against it. "Nobody wants to hear about a benign Arctic, Mr. Franklin! It must be desolate and terrible, so that the discoverers will seem even more heroic!" "But that's just what a discoverer is supposed to do," responded Franklin. "To explore something long enough until he discovers its benign aspects." "Yes, but that should remain between ourselves," the publisher answered. The book was given the neutral title *Narrative of a Second Journey to the Polar Sea,* and it sold well. But John Franklin remained famous for the earlier journey. Mr. Murray had been right. The readers understood only what they already thought they knew from the first book, and it was not a good thing to persuade them otherwise. Time was short, opinions firm, and new ideas remained in hiding.

London was steaming. The accretion in implements, machines, and iron constructions grew daily. This was called progress. Many worked at it, and few reaped its benefits. Most of them stared at it with glassy eyes and said admiringly, "Madness." Progress was madness, but it served England's glory, and even those who didn't make a profit loved their country.

A man named Brunel—John had already heard of him in Portsmouth—had wallowed in the mud with big machines since 1825 in order to dig a tunnel under the Thames. And there were "locomotives" now. Although they ran on smooth iron rails, they attained the speed of a good horse and were able to pull as many as three cars. Charles Babbage explained to John about his plan to build an enormous calculator, as big as a house, composed of a calculating and a printing part. Working ceaselessly without interruption, it would supply the entire world with logarithmic and nautical tables. The human brain would no longer be burdened with anything that needed to be calculated! Gifted people would again be able to think instead of scribbling

257

numbers. Franklin liked that. Babbage caught fire. He explained the details of how the machine would calculate, how its function would be quite different from that of the human mind, much faster and more reliable! It could produce the most incredible new insights, far beyond the kind of mathematics presently in use, and perhaps, drawing on statistics, could even design poor laws and tax laws.

The conversation was not exactly fluent. Franklin had to put on the brakes time and time again in order to be able to understand him. Babbage was impatient, irascible, and massive. He loved neither women nor children nor anything else in the world; only his ideas. Franklin thought about all this, staring at the mathematician's antiquated breeches in order to keep steady in the face of so much progress. As for himself, he had already begun to wear the new trousers consisting of two long pipes, and was putting on his two-cornered hat not crosswise but lengthwise in a forward direction, as was now the fashion.

When Franklin managed to understand something, he made it work for him as he saw fit. No, the machine has its limitations, he said, to the inventor's annoyance. It could always calculate only what can be found out in response to "leading questions"—to questions, in other words, that could be answered only by yes or no. He told Babbage of the Eskimos and of the impossibility of getting anything new out of them by asking them questions that set up alternatives. "Your machine can't be amazed and can't be confused; so it can't discover anything alien to itself. Do you know the painter Westall?"

Babbage passed over the question. "For a sailor you think pretty fast," he said in a subdued voice.

"No, I think with an effort," Franklin replied, "but I never stop. You know too few sailors."

They remained friends. It was true that Babbage loved only his ideas, but now and then he found some interest in people, at least insofar as they had the courage to contradict his ideas.

Franklin became engaged to Jane Griffin: first of all because for once she happened not to be abroad, and also because she had already announced her next departure. No one knew travel as she did! She knew all the Channel boats by name, converted European currencies into pounds and shillings at lightning speed, procured special passes that made officials bow in reverence from Calais to Petersburg, and knew how to make goods that were subject to duty completely invisible by covering them with a few silver coins. "You'd be a fine first lieutenant," Franklin told her.

Jane dominated everything: parties, lovers, her household, all fashionable topics, and changes in facial expression. She was quick, yet retained her sense of loyalty. Franklin's friends said: "Now his career can't be stopped."

When she talked, Jane's eyelids fluttered and she always kept the left eye closed a little more than the right one, which injected a roguish note into everything she said, even condolences. But Franklin was intrigued most by her manner of seeing. She could absorb an astonishing number of simultaneous experiences, for she entered none of them very deeply and so was quickly free for the next impression. But she forgot none of these details! It seemed as though she retained everything just for the sake of retaining it, as though she were constructing inside her head, on a smaller scale, a panorama true to nature made up of the thousand details her eye had registered. She liked most to sit in a fast-moving coach, looking out and consuming the landscape with inexhaustible perseverence. John, too, liked riding in coaches, and though his way of seeing was somewhat different, they enjoyed traveling together.

His fame grew and grew. The populace read the narratives of his expeditions and continued to be thrilled by the intrepid hero of the glacial desert. The dockworkers found him all right, too. "He risks his bones and others benefit: he's like us." Even the gentry praised Franklin: "Old English stock. Even if it's rotten, it can't be destroyed. People like that can be sent anywhere," Thus Lord Rottenborough in an after-dinner speech.

Franklin knew where he wanted to be sent and said so. But prospects for yet another expedition command were slim. Interest in the Northwest Passage had decreased noticeably, since it was obviously not very useful for trade. "What do you still want in that ice?" the First Lord of the Admiralty asked paternally. "We need you for more important tasks." What could be so important? But for the time being, these tasks were hard in coming.

Franklin tried to enter foreign services on his own in order to be charged with an Arctic expedition—science was international, there was nothing against it. But success eluded him. In Paris he had to stand through endless receptions, listening to long conversations in French, and even make a speech, because they had given him the gold medal of the Geographical Society. He breakfasted with Baron Rothschild, dined with Louis Philippe of Orléans. A great deal of interest in his person, but little in further explorations of the Arctic! Indulgent smiles about his experiences with the Eskimos. His hardest task was tea with Madame la Dauphine, whose choice pastry he would have exchanged for *tripes de roche* had he not had to answer her chatty questions.

Jane spurred him on. "Too slow? Not anymore! Look around: you move at exactly the same speed as all important people when they move among more or less unimportant ones! The King does, too; Wellington and Peel also make pauses after each word. And if you haven't understood this or that word and have ignored it for that reason, it will only strengthen the impression of majestic dignity." Still, Franklin didn't enjoy public appearances. He was glad to meet a young geographer from the Kingdom of Poland, a Dr. Keglewicz, who wanted to be nothing but an explorer and therefore knew the meaning of discovery. He was tightlipped and surly, yet also eager to learn and ambitious to the point of bursting. In spite of his scrawniness, he reminded John of a powerful and relentless Babbage. John could talk to him for hours without even mentioning humanity, heroism, or character, let alone education. That had become rare. In St. Petersburg the Tsarina received him and asked what was in his books. And they already existed in Russian! They made him an honorary doctor of jurisprudence at Oxford; in London, the King dubbed him a knight, thus adding a handle to his name: "Sir" John Franklin.

Now he was the greatest and the best, no longer the youngest. Perhaps they honored him only to get rid of him? From all these many honors came not one single serious offer. A gin manufacturer named Felix Booth was prepared to buy and equip a ship for the Northwest Passage provided Sir John would be so kind as to stress this high-minded gesture in his travel report.

Finally an offer from the highest quarters! Sir John dropped the letter sadly: he was to sail to East Asia as the captain of a warship and threaten the Chinese so that they would again have respect for the British Crown. But if the threats are not immediately believed, thought John, they must be carried out. He politely requested permission to decline the offer. He was not particularly suited to be a combat commander. Besides, he was just about to be married.

His friends said: "Now his career is over. Anyone who is against war gets nothing. Very clumsy! Why didn't somebody advise him?" Only Richardson shook his hand and said, "It might be of some advantage. Perhaps now the British Crown holds you in greater esteem."

Sir John walked with his wife—Lady Franklin now—along the sea on the dyke of Ingoldmells. No, he did not love her as he had loved Eleanor. But he liked her. She was an honest person with a clear head, a reliable companion, and he needed her as a surrogate mother for little Ella. It was not more but also not less. They talked about it often. "We're both curious about the world," Lady Franklin said firmly, "and usually the same people get on our nerves. True, that's not exactly love . . ."

". . . but perhaps something even better," Sir John answered.

They looked at the mud flats to the left of them, then to the right at the marshy meadows, and talked about the way their life would continue. Life passed by only too quickly. Their circle of friends was enormous and brought them more obligations than pleasure. Their fortune was considerable, but it was not enough to finance an Arctic expedition of their own.

Sir John panted. Walking was good for him. "Unless you take some vigorous exercise," Richardson had told him, "I won't remain the only doctor in your life. Don't eat so much." John's reply: "Never go hungry again!" But he had promised nonetheless to consider the medical advice.

Ten years! They had gone by so quickly, as though he had driven through them in a coach. Now he was in his mid-forties. His hopes were numerous enough to last for a long life, but his damned body weight tipped the scale on the other side. "You must have some exercise," said Lady Franklin.

"Good," he said. "I shall go to Mr. Booth and report for his expedition. That's the only exercise that helps me. However, I'll demand that he not insist on my naming the Northwest Passage Gin Lane."

But a few days later a dispatch arrived in Bolingbroke from the secretary of state for the Colonies, Lord Glenelg. He was pleased to be able to offer John, upon the expressed and personal wish of the King, the post of governor of Van Diemen's Land.

"That's south of Australia! A long voyage," said Lady Franklin, musing, "and a great deal of money, twelve hundred pounds a year."

"It's a penal colony," answered Sir John.

"Then one must change that," spoke the Lady.

A little later John met the indefatigable Flora Reed and asked confidentially for her view.

"You must try it," she said. "What's the Northwest Passage worth? It serves only fame and greed for geographical information. What's that against the building of a young society where justice still has a chance? And if anybody can manage that, it's you."

"Nonsense," Sir John contradicted her. "I'm a navigator. I don't want to change people or compel them to do anything. If I can prevent worse things here or there, it's already a great deal."

"And worth the effort," added Flora.

When he got home, Lady Franklin had thought of a new argument: "From down there it isn't too far to the South Pole."

"I'll think about it."

In the church in Spilsby now hung a stone tablet: "In Memory of Lieutenant Sherard Philip Lound, Missing at Sea Since Anno 1812."

"Nonsense; he lives," John said, snarling. "Somewhere in Australia. Perhaps even in Van Diemen's Land."

Captains John and James Ross, uncle and nephew, had quickly decided to take up the gin manufacturer's offer. When Franklin inquired once more, he was too late. For the last time he turned to the Admiralty. "Unfortunately not," Barrow answered him. "And even if we were planning a polar expedition, the admirals would rather—forgive me!—choose a slightly younger commander. Of course, everybody knows you're not only the most famous but also the most capable—"

"Never mind," Franklin interrupted him. "Others have to have a chance, too. Take George Back. He's young, and when he is a little older he'll be better than I am."

Then he walked home through fast-moving London and thought some more about the governor's post. I can command a crew, but I have difficulty moving in crowds. Whether I can succeed in governing a colony is a question . . . Another image intermingled with that of the penal colony: the landscape of the South Pole! Eternal glaciers and, in their light, warm lakes with fish and penguins, perhaps even land with tribes of men who did not know how to hurry.

No, stop this! He could not agree to govern a colony only because he wanted to travel to the South Pole! Van Diemen's Land was a matter that had to be considered on its own merits. Perhaps he would die of the first attempt to prevent only the slightest evil. It was that serious.

"Good," said John Franklin. "Van Diemen's Land. But, then, seriously."

[16]

◆◆

THE PENAL COLONY

"You'll be a little surprised about Sir John," Dr. Richardson wrote to Alexander Maconochie. "Sometimes he doesn't seem to notice everything. He laughs or hums to himself and gives evasive answers if he wants to turn something over in his mind. But he is a man with a heart. You can find a friend in him if you . . ."

Richardson erased the last two words. He continued in a different vein: ". . . After all, I have recommended you to him as a fellow combatant." He wasn't completely satisfied with this sentence either, but at least it covered up what he had suppressed.

"Don't expect quick actions from Sir John. Help him to avert evil with your presence of mind." Richardson hesitated. Why did he write this at all? Doubts in Maconochie? He crossed out the sentence again. Later he would rewrite it all in clean copy.

"He is never lost, even in extremely doubtful situations. Even in politics . . ." No, that's not right! "This is undoubtedly true of . . ." That's two 'doubt's. Delete.

If Franklin found no support in Maconochie, if he didn't comprehend the political situation, if he was blind to relations of power? Then this missive wouldn't help either! Richardson tore it up, tossed it away, and folded his hands. If a letter did not achieve its end, it could usually be replaced by a prayer.

264

The barque *Fairlie* was overcrowded. Emigrants, adventurers, churchmen, careerists, reformers—and in the midst of them all, the new governor of Van Diemen's Land with his wife, his little daughter, Ella, and his niece Sophia Cracroft. Also aboard was his private secretary, Maconochie, with his numerous family. And Hepburn had come along, the loyal and helpful companion of the Arctic. He had grown slightly fatter—that, too, was comforting.

All day long, Sir John heard himself continually addressed as "Your Excellency" here and "Your Excellency" there. It seemed as though they had all taken this ship only to say a word to him sometime. "A foretaste," said Jane. Good practice, thought John.

Van Diemen's Land, discovered in 1642 by the Dutchman Abel Tasman, had been thought part of Terra Australis until the end of the eighteenth century. Matthew Flinders and his friend Bass had circled the island and mapped it. From 1803 on, it had been a penal camp; since 1825, a colony independent of Sydney, where free settlers who had not originally arrived as convicts also lived.

John had hardly any questions about its history. The geographical details, too, were known to him, including the locations and names of the most important settlements, capes, mountains, and rivers discovered to date. One of the rich investors traveling with them on the *Fairlie* said, "A new era rides with us to Van Diemen's Land. With us and Sir John." The island would have to become the granary of the south and one of the most beautiful places in the world, and Hobart Town the most beautiful city. . . . And why not? John did not intend to serve out his regular term of six years there as a glorified prison warden. Where there were settlers, an open, practical sense prevailed; something could be done with that. And the convicts? It depended on the crime. If a person stole a loaf of bread or poached in the forest of some lord or other because he was hungry, he showed no more than sound common sense.

John's predecessor, George Arthur, who had ruled the colony for twelve years, had viewed it only as a penal institution and had done little more for the settlers than send them convicts as workers. This probation and exploitation system was called "assignment." Other than that, he had increased his own property and left the island an extremely rich man. How had he managed that?

The original inhabitants of the island, a brown, woolly-haired people, had been nearly exterminated by Arthur, who had not been ashamed to call this misdeed a war.

Not another word about Arthur! If only for the sake of discipline, John decided to act at first as though he would continue his predecessor's work. As governor, he had to take matters of state to an executive and a legislative council, but if he made a decision contrary to their votes, no one could object. He was subordinate only to the Secretary of State for the Colonies in London, but to him without ifs, ands, or buts.

In the mornings, that bothersome crick in his neck again. He had perspired and tossed back and forth. But that was part of any important task: fear and panic had to be suffered through in turn. Once he heard a voice: "If there is one thing you can't do, John Franklin, it's politics."

He was now over fifty. Along with experience, his death had grown, too; it took shape slowly: perhaps another ten more years, perhaps twenty. But the house was solid. John would have no further alterations to make until the beams began to rot.

A colony of forty-two thousand people. Good. After all, "governor" meant the same as "helmsman." John said, "It's a matter of navigation." He read publications about administrative and criminal justice, memorized social classes and their possible interests. He put himself in the place of the landowner who wanted to have cheap labor, of the merchant who needed well-paid customers, and of the government official who longed simultaneously for praise and land ownership. And in his intense brooding he also discerned what the convict desired: justice, equal treatment, and above all a chance.

John stood on deck for hours, examining the braces, stays, shrouds, backstays up to the *Fairlie*'s three mastheads, and wondered about the running and standing rigging of government, from finance to class mobility. Only a person who was well prepared could recognize the danger signals. Politics could hardly be that different from navigation. Hepburn saw it that way, too.

Dr. Richardson had written that Alexander Maconochie was possessed by the fire of love for mankind; at the same time, he was quick-witted and determined, the best ally for any reformer. Although a Scotsman, Maconochie was in no way churchy or dull. He looked, indeed, like a reformer—more than that, like a Jacobin. His scrawny, sharp-eyed face, his pointed nose, the wide mouth that he kept constantly in a state of sensually bold and somehow heroic tension—all that reminded John of his teacher Burnaby. Maconochie embraced new theories with zeal—for example, the idea that whites had descended from blacks, that it was intelligence that had made their skin white.

It was not a very good start: Sophia soon noted that the secretary had a conspicuously dark skin. Lady Franklin, on the other hand, liked him because he was entertaining. When he talked about the inhumanity of the criminal law, he could use illuminating phrases that stuck in the memory: "It does man no good if nothing good is expected of him." He did not believe in penitence or deterrence. "Punishment springs from bourgeois fear and love of comfort. Only education can be effective." One day John responded to one of his maxims by saying, "It depends on each individual case." He knew that a philosophical radical didn't like such statements. But even here Maconochie retained his optimism as a pedagogue: Sir John did not yet possess—and no wonder!—ultimate insights into all these matters, but he was on the right track. John thought to himself, Maconochie is a bit presumptuous, but he will improve when we actually work together.

When the dark, steep shores and rugged mountains of Van Diemen's Land emerged, Lady Franklin was almost sad. For her, the great traveler, the voyage could have gone on for months, even in this overcrowded ship. John saw it differently. He wanted to get to work, and he looked forward to it.

A pretty harbor town with white houses lay before them, and above it Mount Wellington, a dark gentleman commanding respect, with a slanted parting on its rocky top. When the *Fairlie* anchored, a launch came toward them from the shore bearing a reception committee. First, a little man in a black frock coat stepped toward Sir John. When he wasn't bowing, he stood as straight as a soldier, his glance tranquil but a bit watery. His mouth looked as though it had already spoken everything important and was now closed until further notice. Hands and arms were engaged in elaborate movements, not insecure or nervous but with theatrical deliberation. He was John Montagu, colonial secretary, and after the governor the most important man here. For ten years he had been Arthur's closest confidant; he was his son-in-law and continued to be the administrator of his property. John greeted the other officials who had lined up. He purposely spent much time fixing names and faces firmly in his mind. He wanted his subordinates to get accustomed to slowness as soon as possible.

As the launch approached the pier, a breeze came up. The lines of the cutters and whalers lying at anchor began to whir and beat against the spars; it sounded like a joyous applause. On shore, settlers, military men, and officials stood waiting, a hundred on horseback alone, and behind them thirty carriages with waving ladies. John did not trust his ears: they were shouting with joy all along the beach, yes, shouting with joy. Suddenly it occurred to him: Perhaps I'm not supposed to walk to Government House but must ride on horseback! And what kind of a speech shall I make, of all things from on top of a horse?

The sun was shining. They had set up a little stage on the quay, and next to it stood waiting what John had feared: the horse. A sturdy fellow held the reins.

Montagu opened the proceedings. He welcomed, expressed hopes, was delighted in all their names, greeted once more, was moved in closing. John looked cautiously at the horse. It snorted, tossed its head, and almost pulled the reins out of the fellow's hand. Now John realized that it was his turn.

He spoke the single sentence he had formulated aboard ship: "I want everyone to have a chance."

The horse squinted, snorted, and kicked.

"I won't be firm in the saddle at once," John announced. "I first want to look at everything carefully on foot." Approving laughter. Someone shouted: "Hear! Hear!" Sir John stood still, like a memorial, and waited until they were quiet again. Then, with a quick decision, he ordered the young fellow to take the horse away. "This way I get more out of it," he added under his breath. Then he started to move and the others strode behind him, solemnly and a little surprised.

John studied reports, files, administrative directives, land registers, verdicts of the courts. He constantly met up with new technical terms—"land grants," for example: allotments of land with which until a few years ago the governor could make grateful and compliant friends wherever he needed them. By several circuitous routes, Arthur's own fortune had come from land grants. At the same time, John searched in vain for Sherard Philip Lound among lists of titles. Neither here nor in New South Wales was there a settler by that name.

Newspapers made somewhat odd reading. In the *Van Diemen's Land Chronicle* one could read about the new governor: "He is one of the toughest fellows in the world, at the same time an impeccable gentleman. We now have a governor as we have wanted him. If Sir John does not take too much advice from Mr. Montagu, Arthur's ghost will haunt us only at night in our dreams and no longer, as until now, in police uniforms and judges' robes in the bright light of day." John could not really be pleased about that. It seemed they loved to exaggerate here. He turned back to the files.

The third day in office. The first session of the legislative council. Dignified gentlemen in black frock coats; solemn speeches. Too little money in the government till. Direct taxation of the settlers: not possible by law! What to do? Before that question had been fully deliberated, a new one: "Can a governor give orders to the Tasmanian Land Regiment if he is only a navy captain?" Without transition they went on to talk of possible measures to be taken against escaped convicts ravaging settlers' homes. From there the debate leapt to the last seventy aborigines who had been resettled by Arthur on Flinders Island, north of Van Diemen's Land, and were not exactly flourishing. What did that have to do with bush pirates, regiments, or taxes? While John pondered the question, they moved on to the state's responsibility in case of postal theft, then to the distribution of convict labor among landowners, and, before John knew it, to a few minor revisions of regulations for procedures in the execution of . . . of . . .

The word still resisted his tongue. Why could he enunciate the more difficult phrase "revisions of regulations for procedures" without a flaw but not "execution of punishments"? John wiped the sweat off his forehead. The whole thing reminded him of a chicken yard: if he looked closely at a problem and shut his eyes to think about it, instantly it became a different one, and when he opened them again, the old one still fluttered about unsettled and wouldn't let itself be caught, while the new problem stood in its place and glared menacingly.

He had to arrange quickly for slower agendas. This was most effectively accomplished by holding the sessions in public: then the old hands were no longer just among themselves and had to explain what they meant. Too many different points one after the other destroyed concentration, especially for a man who carried a chaos of individual pictures in his head. He alone was the governor. Only he had to decide how much time had to be allotted to giving hope or disapprobation in each individual case! From this day on, sessions of the legislative council of Van Diemen's Land were public.

Fourth day in office. Only two days before the first detailed inspection of the penal institutions and prison settlements. Everything depended on what they would allow him to see. He knew that under the files and reports, worse truths were buried.

He therefore read them with heightened zeal, for as a first step he wanted to make sure that files and actual events agreed with each other. During the inspection trip he wouldn't be able to manage without the fixed look: he was determined not to be moved or depressed by what he saw. He was governor; he had to gain an overall perspective so as to see what he might do. Action! No tears, no hate, no trembling.

Maconochie believed he already understood what had to be changed in the colony. He gave John advice. John told him of Matthew Flinders's rescue voyage after the shipwrecks. "In navigation one must fix one's starting position as precisely as one's objective." But the secretary knew only land war.

The inspection tour: the prison of Port Arthur; the last original inhabitants on Flinders Island; the coal mines, where the most serious offenders were working. Together with Lady Franklin— and against the advice of the official who guided them—he crawled through the darkest tunnels bathed in sweat and stopped everywhere until he had understood each operation. He controlled himself, concealed his terror, asked questions about procedures, glanced at Jane now and then, looked away quickly.

Life expectancy in the coal mines: four to five years on the average. Fifteen to sixteen hours a day at hard labor. Lashes with the whip for anything and everything. Coal dust in the wounds. In Port Arthur his first question concerned horizontal stripes scooped out of the backs of a column of prisoners. Answer: "Oh, they're Barclay's Tigers!" Lieutenant Barclay himself had cheerfully announced that he was keeping those tiger stripes open with regular whipping.

What kind of a governor had Barclay expected? He was dismissed immediately, and the prosecutor was requested to issue a complaint against him and against a man named Slade. George Augustus Slade of Point Puer Prison had boasted that twenty-five whip lashes by his hand achieved a greater effect than one hundred lashes administered by anyone else. That was now over!

By the way, caution: the prosecutor was a man of Arthur's clique. Re-examine his past actions! Take notes.

Onward! Point Puer, the prison for boys on top of the steep, rocky shore. Every month several youthful inmates hurled themselves over the edge of the cliff—most recently, two nine-year-olds. He saw them alive, with Lady Franklin and his niece Sophia. Emaciated bodies, scars. Strange large eyes, perhaps in contrast with their small faces. Such faces need weep no longer to convey their misery. Sophia was so touched that she simply embraced the two and kissed their foreheads, to the visible chagrin of the warden. The boys whispered to her that they would be very severely beaten, then fell silent. When John inquired about them a day later he found out about the suicides. The warden delivered a well-concocted story: the sinful boys had taken Sophia for an angel because of her long blond hair and had killed themselves in the presumptuous hope of meeting her in heaven. John recalled the warden's face at the time and composed a different verse. Order: disciplinary transfer for neglect and improper supervision. More he could not do without witnesses and evidence.

What kind of a doctor did they have in Port Arthur? What kind of a clergyman? These were not meaningful reflections. Forward! John heard the order as clearly as at that time on the *Investigator*. He didn't want revulsion and rage to work on him too much, for he wanted to act. Here it was more complicated. It was not enough to hoist a flag. He couldn't dismiss or incarcerate all the wardens in one day. Above all, he couldn't dismiss his own minister without a good, well-documented cause.

Then Flinders Island. He looked forward to this, probably because it bore Matthew's good name. And the rest of the original inhabitants of Van Diemen's Land were reputedly receiving the best of care.

Sixty-seven emaciated, miserable creatures with matted hair, listless expressions, dirty skin, and bent backs were the remaining survivors. They squatted apathetically on a desolate, nasty piece of land and waited for death. Children were no longer born, and that made sense: what should children do in a world where there was nothing but Flinders Island? The sad pictures penetrated John's eyes; he tried energetically to stop them inside his head, but they found their way into his bones. There they sat, and asked, What are you going to do, John Franklin? He answered, Not allow myself to be paralyzed.

How different they looked now—the pretty white houses, the purple-dark mountains, the blue river, the wide-sleeved ladies and the gentlemen with buttoned overcoats and stern faces beneath respectfully doffed felt hats! Behind the high-sounding phrases different truths emerged.

The police were no longer the protectors of civil order. The sumptuous villas at Battery Point no longer allowed admiration for progress and constructive development, and the streets, the Cathedral of St. David, the houses—they were all built by convicts.

Now Franklin knew not only what the convicts wanted but also what they lived through. The newly built ship dock with the sweet smell of wood from half-finished hulls became repellent once one knew that the shipbuilders were walking in chains! Even the smell of fish on drying nets on Salamanca Place had nothing comforting about it anymore. How often did these nets hold one of the dead who had plunged down the steep shore!

Sir John Franklin barricaded himself behind his desk. His office became his main headquarters. He didn't want simply to oversee, punish, make war, but also to win over people who had the same feelings in their bones as he did. And they must multiply!

He had to find a better place to live for the original inhabitants! He discussed this with Montagu in a friendly but cautious way. The latter did not agree and raised several objections. But the next day John's plans for the establishment of a large reservation were on their way to London.

Jane played her role as the governor's wife to perfection. When John had to appear in public she was a watchful ally. She concerned herself with the women's prison and corresponded with someone named Elizabeth Fry in London about matters of prison discipline. She invited wives and daughters of officials and settlers to hear string quartets and scientific lectures. She ran the entire complicated household and cooked cheerfully, though with moderate success, for twenty people when the cook was ill or had escaped. She spoke her opinion about everything frankly and without shyness; it never occurred to her to be an immaculate, stupid first lady on the model of Mrs. Arthur. She had traveled too widely for that, had read too many books, and had observed too many different people on three continents. She concealed her high spirits as little as her beauty. Jane's enterprise became nearly infamous: a fortnight after their arrival she became the first woman to climb Mount Wellington—4,165 feet high; that was no mere stroll. John was independent of Jane's judgment but listened to it with respect. He loved her without passion but confided in her more than he had ever confided in Eleanor. He did not need her around him all the time, but she was also never in his way. Happily, it was the same for her. If this was not love, well, then it was mutual understanding.

"Don't expect anything from Montagu," warned Jane. "He's Arthur's man. He wants to make you dependent on him and paralyze you."

"I know," answered John.

"He thinks governors come and go, but Montagu remains."

"That may be," answered John, "but I still need a first officer who's quick, knows the ropes, and is part of the government. Without such a person I wouldn't have a free hand for the real work. Hepburn can't do it. Maconochie has too little insight. And, foolish as it is, it can't be a woman."

Jane knew that. "I can't take government business off your shoulders. But I can warn you, and I'm now warning you of Montagu."

"Good," said John. "And I'm warning you of Maconochie. He's an idealist. We mustn't betray our politics with sentimentality."

Jane looked at him intently: "Nor the other way round!"

At night she put her head in the hollow between his shoulder and neck. This way she could even fall asleep while he lay awake and watched that her head rested comfortably. Now and then she read an adventure novel and put out the light long after John had begun to snore. One morning she said, "You've been grinding your teeth at night; you're worried!" He confirmed this.

John Montagu declined to speak more slowly to a slow Excellency. In this the colonial secretary reminded Sir John of officers Walker and Pasley on the *Bedford*. He was well informed and could present his information to others clearly and rapidly; he was circumspect in his actions and forgot nothing—no name, no appointment, not the merest slight. Sir John treated him benevolently but, after careful consideration, no more so than anyone else.

Ambition kept the colonial secretary in a state of tension; he acted like a cat before jumping. He concealed this tension behind a seemingly relaxed and open manner, making himself accessible to everyone and laughing jovially, his watch chain clinking over his bulging waistcoat, never taking his watery eyes off the other person for even a second.

When Sir John made the legislative council into an open forum, Montagu was already "worried": a meeting had just taken place of three hundred thirty-six settlers demanding representative government. To him that was a danger signal. When John became interested in excesses in the punishment of prisoners and dismissed a few officials, he did so against Montagu's advice. Montagu also opposed the resettling of the aborigines on better land. And when Sir John made it a regular practice to go on board the arriving prisoner ships to tell the convicts not only about their duties but also about their rights, Montagu began to rally Arthur's old allies around him. Still, he also sought to persuade Sir John to change his ways by reciting to him with emphasis the two "iron principles of a penal colony":

"First: Any deviation from a principle once acknowledged as being correct is treason.

"Second: Any deviation from current accepted practice is a weakness and encourages the miscreants."

John looked at these practices thoroughly from all sides. Then he suggested Montagu consider that a combination of these two maxims would exclude any change. For him, however, a person was also a traitor who had discovered a *new* principle as being correct and was too cowardly to act on it.

It appeared that Montagu took this reply as a personal affront. In circles of the Arthur party he said with a bittersweet smile, "For Sir John I've recently become a coward and a traitor. He's simply always a discoverer; nothing remains hidden from him."

Maconochie heard about this by way of a servant and conveyed it to the governor. He did not believe it. In other words, he decided to ignore the hint.

Ella was Eleanor's daughter through and through. When Jane told her not to impale a piece of meat on a fork and point at the guests with it, she specifically asked for an explanation. Sir John told her about Trim the tomcat, who wouldn't have let such a chance slip by. "That's the one the city's named after!" Ella exclaimed. "Was supposed to be named after," John corrected her. "They later thought Lord Melbourne was more important." Jane glanced over to the guests and suggested it might be better to change the subject. Sophia laughed.

Early in the morning John walked with his daughter under the eucalyptus trees in the garden of Government House. Everything seemed so clear and simple. This colony would someday be a land where children could grow up without one half of everything having to be concealed from them all the time. As it was, Ella had asked about convicts and prisons long ago. "How does one become a miscreant?" she once asked. She was used to the fact that Papa always had to think for several minutes before giving an answer. She preferred that to explanations which merely repeated in different words what she already knew. "A miscreant," said her father, "doesn't know his own correct speed. He's too slow on the wrong occasions and too fast on the wrong occasions as well." Ella wanted a more exact explanation. He went on, "He does too slowly what others want him to do, for example, obeying and helping. But he tries much too fast to get what he wants from others, for example, money or—" "But you're slow, too!" Ella declared. "A governor is allowed that," answered John, biting his lip.

John Franklin's system matured; it took on contours appropriate to a colony. He believed that he had found, theoretically, at least, the correct method for life, discovery, and government.

"There have to be two persons at the top. Not one and not three. Two. One of them must conduct the day-to-day business and keep up with the impatient daily inquiries, requests, and threats of the governed. He must give the impression of vigor and still concern himself only with cheap, unimportant, and urgent matters. The other maintains calm and distance; he can say no at crucial moments. For he does not worry about immediate urgencies but looks at specific individual details for a long time. He acknowledges the duration and speed of all events, allowing himself no respite. He makes things hard for himself. Listening to his own inner voice, he can say no even to his best friends, above all, to his first officer. His own rhythm, his own well-preserved long breath, is his refuge from all apparent urgencies, from all supposed emergencies, from short-lived solutions. If he has said no, he is obligated to give reasons. But with that, too, there need not be too much of a hurry." This is how Franklin formulated it and wrote it down.

"That's the monarchy!" exclaimed Maconochie. "King and Prime Minister—you have invented the monarchy! That's how far we've come."

"No," said John. "It's the art of governing in general. The monarchy is only most easily recognized in it."

"And where's the people?" asked Maconochie.

"It can take the place of the King," answered John. "Without slowness nothing can be done, not even a revolution."

The secretary was not satisfied. "That only means waiting!

Whom do you seriously want to recommend this to? At sixty-five I won't make a revolution anymore."

"I, I," John repeated involuntarily.

The government in London sent their convicts: workers who had destroyed machines in Devonshire, rebels fighting for Canadian independence, supporters of general suffrage who refused to be intimidated by the police. For Maconochie they were heroes; for Franklin, "political gentlemen." Montagu spoke of them as miscreants against God and Crown. He recommended that they be confined in Port Arthur, the prison for the most serious offenders, for this had been the custom until then. Under no circumstances were political prisoners to be sent to settlers as workers: "The spark can easily leap from one to the other!" John decided otherwise, although he knew that any decision taken against Montagu's vote took a toll in nerves and paperwork. Montagu understood like nobody else how to sabotage decisions already made.

And Maconochie said: "Office work does not suit me too well. I don't see my mission realized in the misery of day-to-day administration. I want to help this land call up a brighter spirit, to lend my sword to justice."

John replied, "You can do that only within the administrative routine. It's particularly favorable for you because you're my secretary here."

Maconochie felt misunderstood, as always when a polished speech had left no impression.

Especially dedicated was his fight against assignment. He favored closed penal institutions and the scientifically founded rehabilitation of prisoners with appropriate personnel. Justice, he said, was the basis of education. But a criminal could find justice only in a prison, not with private masters, whom no warden could supervise effectively.

John was of a different opinion: "It follows by simple logic that in prison nobody has a chance. The error of too many felons can be found only in their confused sense of timing. They've got the wrong speed, sometimes too fast, sometimes too slow. How could they possibly learn the right speed behind high walls? In prison, time is perceived differently from the outside world."

Maconochie did not understand this because John had spoken much too haltingly for any impatient listener to be able to follow. But Maconochie knew what his objections to assignment had to be: "The settler is a poor helper on the way to virtue. He doesn't improve the convict; the convict corrupts the settler! Assignment is a temptation to commit injustice and cruelty. The settlers don't spare the whip, either, and they drag female convicts into their beds."

John feared that the discussion would degenerate into a mobilization of arguments in which details were forcibly recruited for a general war of conflicting opinions. He wanted to change the subject, but Lady Jane listened to them and said, "No prison administration is the least bit interested in treating prisoners justly, and that has had its effect, as we can see! The settlers are different: they need the convict for good work for their own profit."

"And exploit him!" exclaimed the secretary.

"But in the long run nobody can treat another person badly in his own home," Jane replied. "People of good will have a chance on assignment; in prison even the most harmless person becomes a relentless foe of mankind. You yourself are saying that one should trust men to be good! But you're too much of an educator; you trust freedom only when it's developed from your pedagogy! Why can't you bet on the good sense of the settlers? After all, they alone represent the future of this island."

Again Maconochie felt himself misunderstood. Closing his lips tightly in a heroic gesture, he bowed and retired. John did not find any of this amusing, but Jane laughed. She loved combat of any kind.

John Franklin placed his bets on the free settlers. He consulted with Alfred Stephen, one of their most independent political leaders, and invited not only government officials but also cattlemen and merchants to his receptions. He wanted not only to acknowledge their existence but even to talk with them. Iron-mongers, linen weavers, greengrocers, cobblers felt they were noticed officially for the first time. They praised the new governor.

Politically, the free settlers still had little more say than the convicts, and that rankled with them. True, there were some slight beginnings of popular representation—three settlers sat in the legislative council, but they were reliably outvoted by six government representatives. The executive council, on the other hand, was composed only of officials, and of them the majority belonged to Arthur's party. John bet on the settlers, but he knew only too well that he had taken by far the most insecure and inconvenient way—the political way.

The settlers had earned good money during the decades of high grain and wool prices. They were independent, well established, and aggressive. They had no safety valve for their over-sensitivity and self-importance, and no worthy opponents except for the governor's officials. Petty jealousies among individual families were a mere pastime. Even the different newspapers printed in Hobart and Launceston, which sparred regularly, suffered from political ineffectuality. As a result, they shifted even further toward a journalism of pinpricks, especially against the colonial administration: its personalities, personal offenses, suspicions.

John looked at the homes of the wealthy landowners and their expensively decked-out daughters. He listened to the moralizing speeches, observed the well-groomed gardens. Behind all this something else seemed to be concealed. John thought he sensed a false bottom in the settlers' speech, an appetite for conflict hidden behind reasonableness, particularly among the big cattlemen at the border of the wilderness. This depressed him, especially since he did not immediately understand malicious innuendoes and had to ask for them to be repeated. He longed for more businessmen, for shopkeepers with flexible, calculating minds, with friendly ways and the patience of merchants. But in Van Diemen's Land these were in the minority, and of booted gentlemen talking alternately of eternal principles and of making short shrift of anything, there were far too many.

The first annoyance came soon enough: John's desire to return a small area of land to the original inhabitants seemed to these booted folk like an attack on their very life and property. They had money and connections, and lo and behold, soon a dispatch from the government in London instructed Sir John to leave the Tasmanians where they were. Maconochie suspected that Montagu was behind this. John said, "Nonsense! True, we're adversaries, but he is a man of honor."

Their difference in point of view about penal sentences weighed more heavily between them. The landowners' newspapers, *The True Colonist* and *Murray's Review,* raised outcries over the "new fashion of granting rights to prisoners and prosecuting supposed abuses of corporeal punishment." And a landowner with whom John talked privately said it even more succinctly: "If Port Arthur is no longer a place of terror, how can we intimidate the working convicts who are assigned to us? If prison becomes a paradise of fair treatment, our own workers will bash our heads in so as to get there."

Oddly, of all people, Maconochie appeared to the newspapers as the proponent of strict prison discipline, perhaps a misunderstanding. And it was just as odd that the secretary accepted this impression and did nothing to correct it. Obviously he enjoyed the praise. He thought it was useful for a good cause, whether or not it happened in error.

The system was good, but John lacked a business manager he could depend on. In practice, therefore, it looked different. He had a premonition of evil. If he had to supervise everything, his sense of duty commanded him not to waste time and to use every minute for the good of the colony. But the more he did this, the more he limped behind, until he lost the present altogether. The multiplicity of things made him nervous. He caught himself making quick, improvised decisions only to get some burden temporarily off his back.

One late evening he left Jane to her adventure novel and walked out of the house. At first he thought of visiting Hepburn, for whom he had procured a position as a tutor. However, he decided not to seek comfort but to think.

Drinking from a bottle of rum, he walked barefoot in the governor's garden in order to keep himself open to a few useful and promising ideas. If natural slowness proved inadequate to protect peace and concentration, he simply wanted to help it along a little. So he decided he would dispose of only part of the governor's business quickly and get the other part done with deliberate slowness: more pauses in sentences, more partial deafness when others reported to him. And as for demands made upon him, only those who refrained from making them for a long time would receive positive replies. He needed to create reserved space for himself in which he could protect his time.

The rum went to his legs.

John had wanted to start with tea. Whatever the pressures, tea time needed to be kept. And so gradually he wanted to lift the cup to his lips so that others thought him dead, yessir. He wanted to stir in it so that nobody could tell whether he stirred left or right. In the *Van Diemen's Land Chronicle,* one could read: "Proof delivered! The governor doesn't move at all anymore."

His Excellency Sir John Franklin giggled and sat on the wall. He swung his legs and looked out on the sea, glittering in the moonlight. Before him he saw the distraught faces of Montagu and Maconochie at tea. He burst out laughing and slapped his thighs. He was governor; he was allowed everything! What was needed were calm, clarity, and durable projects. He wanted to put that together while there was time.

He noticed that his laughter had become tired. The sea seemed as distant as a star yet also deep down below him like an abyss. That's how it looked from the top of the cliff at Point Puer. But he didn't think at all of flinging himself off. That's the advantage of growing old, he thought, without having ever been confronted with the law. I was lucky.

He no longer needed a water column rising out of the sea

against the force of gravity to devour his enemies or to show him the way. He no longer missed the white-clad Sagals, who turned a friendly face to him and rocked him in safety. None of all this! He was fifty-two years old now. He looked out for himself and for others.

Sixty years was nothing, Sophia had said. Sensitive! But how did she get to sixty? I should have met her when I came back from the war. At that time she hadn't even been born. . . .

He went back into the house, a little drunk, only slightly invigorated.

The system? It didn't work. Besides, he didn't like the word anymore, because his opponents were using it. In some strange way the concept permitted them to succumb to all their pitilessness and blindness. No more system! No pose of a wider perspective, but a real perspective gleaned from the observation of details, navigation.

What remained was the habit of taking everything to its proper conclusion. On firm land this was hard. "What does that mean?" he grumbled. "It's never been easy."

[17]

◆◆

THE MAN
BY THE SEA

There is a lawyer in Hobart Town who employs a convict cook on assignment as a domestic servant. The lawyer is known as a champion of leniency in criminal justice, the cook as a master of his craft whose sauces taste three times as good as those of his colleague in Government House. The lawyer goes on a trip and leaves the management of his house to the cook. When he returns he finds that some of his furniture has been sold, coins are missing from his strongbox, and files are gone whose contents might have been very interesting to some people. The cook maintains he knows nothing. The lawyer reports him to the authorities for punishment. The cook is convicted and sentenced. He is glad that he is not sent to Port Arthur.

Now enters a further figure: the colonial secretary, an adherent of law and order, a fighter for loyalty to principle, and, moreover, a man who values good food. He has often been able to convince himself of the cook's excellence. He therefore persuades a judicial figure loyal to him to make an exception and assign the cook to a new employer: himself.

The lawyer is not pleased. He complains to the governor. After a fresh examination of the case and careful deliberation, the governor orders the cook transferred to road construction in accordance with the sentence. The colonial secretary feels deeply humiliated by the decision: true, principles have to be upheld as a basic policy, but a good cook is not just any convict; he is of interest to the state; and the colonial secretary is not just any subject.

Then there is the governor's private secretary, who sees himself as the unyielding fighter against slavery. In line with his readings of scientific tracts, he believes in the natural superiority of the white race, so he finds the enslavement of white-skinned people the worst of all evils. This slavery he believes is realized in the system of assignment that the governor supports. This he calls slavery, whereas he designates as criminal justice all the cruelties of bored wardens in state prisons. Although he is only a private secretary, he believes he can put his position to good use for his cause: when a committee of jurists in England, with the noblest intentions, wants to know further details about penal sentences in Van Diemen's Land, he composes a lengthy, sharply worded report in which he attributes all the evils in the colony to assignment, including even alcoholism and venereal disease, converting a few exceptions into regular occurrences to support his thesis. Resolutely he slips the manuscript into a cache of papers sent home by the governor so that it reaches London as an official document under his seal. A few months later the governor finds out from *The Times* that his private secretary, purportedly in agreement with him, has called the settlers "incapable of the humane treatment of convicts." The settlers are horrified and feel betrayed by the governor. He dismisses the secretary, without, however, exposing him publicly. At the urging of his wife, the governor even allows the secretary to stay for a limited time in his house. The big landowners and the colonial secretary see this as a sign that the governor has merely sacrificed his secretary to whitewash himself, that in reality they are in cahoots. The "sacrificial lamb" does nothing to correct this impression; rather, he makes remarks like "I could say a good deal more about this." He interprets his dismissal as an act against progress and humanity and thinks of himself as a saint more than ever. "This governor," he said, "does not deserve my services."

Meanwhile, in London the Home and Colonial Offices are debating the recommendations of the committee of jurists. Should "assignment" be abolished? The former governor of Van Diemen's Land, the very man who had initiated "assignment" and practiced it inhumanely, now solemnly speaks against it and calls it perfect slavery. Sir George Arthur knows when and how to gain approval.

The present governor knows less about that and doesn't care. He conceives of humanizing the assignment system as the best way of giving convicts a chance to prove themselves outside the prison walls. At the same time, he continues, not without success, to fight against corruption and cruelty in the penal institutions. He tried to base his policy on the support of city people—merchants, craftsmen, shipbuilders—who agree with his objectives, and he applies to London for permission to change the legislative council into a chamber to be picked in general elections.

At this point, the colonial secretary asks for an extended furlough, supposedly for personal reasons, and leaves for England.

John preferred saying "the colonial secretary" to saying Montagu, and "the private secretary" to saying Maconochie. But that helped very little. The terms had become dusky vocables just as much as the names. Even by rearranging language, the tormented, sullen head would not be relieved of its bitterness.

Maconochie, Montagu. Why was he chagrined by two individual gentlemen of questionable character? There were hundreds or thousands of their ilk in the world. But the bird's-eye view didn't help anymore. If one wanted to purge oneself of bitterness and regain the ability to have a careful view of things, one could not of all things take refuge in the fixed look.

London turned down the request to convert the legislative council into a parliament—that was Montagu's work. The consequences were embarrassing, for the tradesmen and craftsmen were disappointed and felt they had been dallied with.

They believed that Sir John had taken the first step only to withhold the second. "In his reports to London," the word went, "he talks quite differently from the way he talks to us."

Finally, the Coverdale case.

An old man lies dying after a bad fall from a horse. His family sends for Dr. Coverdale, a convict physician in the government health service assigned to the district. The messenger does not wait for the return of the absent doctor but leaves a message. This the doctor doesn't see—perhaps the wind blew the note away. The patient gets no treatment and dies. The family points to the messenger's statement that he had informed the doctor personally; they demand the doctor's punishment and dismissal from the health service. Montagu supports this claim; the governor decides accordingly. But soon doubts arise concerning the messenger's credibility. Settlers support the doctor, who had done nothing wrong until now. The governor talks with him, then with the settlers, and also wants to hear the messenger. Montagu advises strongly against revoking the earlier decision. Lady Franklin, however, believes the doctor is innocent and refuses to keep this opinion to herself. The governor finds contradictions in the messenger's statements. He rehabilitates the doctor and restores him to his position.

From this day on, reading the *Van Diemen's Land Chronicle* gives Sir John Franklin no more pleasure. He is called incompetent and vacillating. He is charged with being but the pitiful shadow of the erstwhile polar hero, now under the thumb of his wife, doing whatever she prescribes. She alone is the governor. One word he had to look up in the dictionary. It was "imbecile": "weak, especially feeble-minded, idiotic."

He suspects that the colonial secretary makes common cause with the editor of the newspaper. Montagu denies this. A little later, however, the lie is exposed because the editor himself brags about his prominent support. Now Montagu switches arguments and talks about misunderstandings. He had been co-editor of the paper for years and had mentioned this to Sir John long ago. Moreover, he had hardly any influence on editorial policy. Sir John has a different picture in mind. He knows Montagu now. He dismisses him from his post.

Caught in an open lie, Montagu loses any sense of guilt, any remnant of self-doubt for just that reason. He is permeated by solemn feelings; lies become truths. Everyone now hears from his lips that Lady Franklin exercises a witchlike influence upon the governor. At the same time, he applies to her personally in the name of friendship and begs her to intercede with Sir John in his behalf. He acts so contrite that she finally does so out of pity, for she believes in the reconciliation of all men of good will. With Sir John she is unsuccessful. Montagu has to be content to represent her intervention—against all logic—as one more proof that she meddles with politics. Then he leaves Van Diemen's Land, returns to England, and does everything possible there to effect John Franklin's dismissal from his government post. In London a new secretary of state for the Colonies has been installed, Lord Stanley, with whom Montagu has some connections.

"Details," John told Sophia. "They're time-consuming even to enumerate, and the sum total can be bitter. But it's not the fault of politics. I did something wrong myself. Why didn't I dismiss those two in time?"

Tasman Day, 1841, the day of the Grand Regatta.

John had been in office for five years. He knew that there were better governors, for he knew the work intimately. Navigation was important here, but it was not enough.

Blue flags with silver acacia blossoms were flying everywhere in the harbor. Lady Jane had designed the emblem herself before leaving for New Zealand. In place of the first lady, Sophia Cracroft was permitted to accompany the governor as he strode down to the shore to open the festival.

He wore his blue captain's uniform, all buttoned. The two-cornered hat covered his baldness as well as the old scar on his forehead—lately the head wound was used in the colony to explain John's slowness. He held a bouquet of red roses, the

"English roses." Symbols alone were enough to keep a governor busy.

Sophia had said something. Uncertain, he looked into her eyes. "Beg pardon?" John always heard less well with his right ear. Deafness, the legacy of Trafalgar, which he had so often feigned to gain time for a reply, had now become real. Unfortunately, it was customary for the gentleman to walk on the left side of the lady because of the sword. He couldn't even move closer to Sophia because crinolines had come into fashion: with those bell-shaped wire frames, the ladies had become even more full-bottomed.

Sophia repeated her sentence: "Are you sad?"

"Not sad, but hard of hearing," he answered, "and a bit blinder than in the past. I see more things at once, even more quickly, but with individual things my eyesight is worse. I also forget a good deal." He became conscious of the fact that he would have never complained about his condition to Jane.

Jane believed in goodness, trusting everybody gladly, fighting cheerfully. But when she encountered chronic pettiness and hurt, she turned cold and bitter. Eyebrows raised contemptuously, she withdrew and looked for life elsewhere. Now she was in New Zealand, officially because of her nerves. In truth, she had had enough of Tasmanian narrow-mindedness for a while. Should he have kept her away altogether from the irritations of governing? Or should he have let her collaborate more fully?

They heard the regimental band tuning their instruments. Sophia addressed him once more. John stood still and turned his good ear toward her. "I want to fight for something," she said, "but I don't yet know what for." John contemplated her furious, pretty nose. Sophia was a quiet young lady tending more toward deep thoughts than wild flare-ups. Just for that reason she looked a little droll and touching with the wings of her nose distended in her anger. John turned his eyes away and smiled at a child. The child beamed back. They walked on. Again I can't get rid of that smile, he thought. Imbecile, feeble-minded.

"He is an unerring temporizer and a well-meaning colossus.

Unfortunately, he has the disastrous tendency to make honest speeches. But at least he is no windy character." So much for the prose of Lyndon S. Neat, one of the "interpreters of personality" in the editorial offices of *The True Colonist*. A few lines farther on: "Sir John moves at a reception like a sea lion on land." At least Neat was not a creature of the cattlemen; that was a gain. But why couldn't he do better than alternately admiring and ridiculing a hard-pressed governor? Couldn't he fight on the right side rather than only write about everything? Good. He probably didn't want it any different.

"The things you'll fight for," John told his niece, "you've been carrying around inside you for a long time."

Did Sophia understand such phrases at all? It was his experience that hardly any person understood what he was told. Yet everyone wanted to understand: they were all angry when success was withheld from them. Even Lady Franklin.

But Sophia wanted to learn from him. After Dr. Orme, she was the second person in John's life who seriously wanted to learn from him. Lately she had put it in her head to learn about slowness. She even moved slowly, and on her that even looked beautiful.

Now the time had come. John stepped up to the balustrade and surveyed the waiting crowd. "In the name of Her Majesty the Queen"—pause for "Queen"—"I herewith open the regatta in honor of the one hundred and ninety-ninth anniversary of the discovery of Tasmania."

Hurrahs, cannon salvos, the blaring regimental band. John returned to the grandstand and sat down with Sophia, raised the telescope, and waited for the four-oared gigs to start their race. The glass was excellent. John viewed the beer tents, the cheese stands, the stalls for showmen, the shooting galleries, children, flowers. At the slightest movement of the glass, his sight raced across hundreds of faces turned to the starting line with craned necks. People were standing all along the entire quay; the crowd thinned out only at the farthest point. Back there someone was sitting a little higher on a wall of the pier. He was the only person who did not look toward the starting line but out to sea.

Clearly, those goings-on did not concern him; he was waiting for something more important—perhaps he saw it coming. It was a good glass, but the man was too far away, his face barely recognizable. Probably a hooked nose and a strong forehead. An old man. He watched—not "like a hawk" but "like hawk." John felt the glass trembling in his eye.

"Mr. Forster."

"Your Excellency?" The police chief bent toward him.

"Take my glass. Do you see the old man at the point?"

It seemed as if Mr. Forster had never held a telescope in his hand. Endlessly he adjusted distance and sharpness and scanned the horizon. Then he had the man in focus. "That's a recently released convict."

"His name?"

"It's probably false. Beg pardon, Your Excellency, but he called himself John Franklin."

"What do you mean, 'called himself'?" asked John. But he did not wait for an answer. Indistinctly he heard questioning and welcoming voices, realized suddenly that he had risen long ago and was now walking toward the point, past the beer tent, past the cheese stand.

Ten steps before the old man he stopped.

"Sherard Lound?"

The man did not react, looked far into the distance, and ate. He broke off morsel upon morsel from a roll he held in his left hand and put it—odd, where? John still saw only the profile of the left part of his face. It seemed as if the man put the morsels of bread into his right ear. Behind him, he heard Mr. Forster's voice: "Don't be shocked. Because he has—"

Now John remembered the name and called, "John Franklin?"

The man turned his head but briefly, then looked out to sea again. John walked up to him, behind his back. He now stood on the man's right side, took off the hat. And as the hat was lowered there emerged behind it Sherard's face inch by inch: the white hair was matted, the sallow brown forehead was deeply wrinkled, then below the temple the skin became strangely white—a scar—and now the picture remained as if printed inside the eye, superimposed on everything else. This does exist, John thought again and again. This does exist. Sherard's face reminded him of the nightmare in which the symmetrical figure was suddenly torn asunder into spikes and rags. For there was no face anymore.

The flesh of Sherard's right cheek was gone, perhaps cut by the blow of a saber, perhaps burned. The cheek was not there, and the teeth with their many gaps were exposed deep into the back of his mouth.

"Presumably he was a sailor during the Napoleonic Wars," Mr. Forster muttered. "Now he is—excuse me—imbecile. He speaks with no one. Fifteen years he spent in Port Arthur."

"What for?" John sat down beside Sherard, laid down his hat, and also looked out to sea.

"Piracy," answered Mr. Forster. "When our frigates caught him, he was in possession of a British brig on course to the South Atlantic."

"Leave me alone," said John. "Send them all away from here. I'll follow later."

They sat silently. Sherard continued to break off morsel upon morsel of bread and to put them into his face from the side. He pushed the bites deep down, chewed them, and held up his hand so they wouldn't fall out again. He seemed to have found his peace. There was something he was still waiting for, but entirely without impatience. His eye remained riveted on the horizon, but not as if he expected the decisive event to happen there at the next moment.

John recalled the island of Saxemberg that had never been found. Sherard had said then: "If nobody finds it, it will be mine."

"Where were you going, Sherard? To Saxemberg?"

No reaction. John looked again at the destroyed side of the face and wondered what actually was so horrible about it. Everyone wanted a face to look at him in an agreeable and friendly way. Everyone wanted to find himself pleasantly mirrored and was horrified when it grinned at him or threatened him with a sneer, when it seemed to grind and curse with teeth of a death's head. That alone was the reason! With that knowledge, Sherard's face became bearable.

Still, John could not control his feelings. They were connected with the face only on the outside. He felt like a man without footing, not knowing whether he was sad or glad, whether moved by pity or thirst for knowledge. What went on in his head did not torment him, because it was strange to him. It was no battle; rather, it was like a surface of water moved by the wind, and his thoughts swirled up like silt from the bottom of the sea near the shore.

They're all gone, he thought. Mary Rose, Simmonds, Mockridge, Matthew. Even Eleanor left me. I only anticipated her. And Sherard comes back, dreadfully beaten, a convict bearing my name, administered by me, punished by me.

Suddenly John asked himself if he was a good man. That was only one of many unanswered questions that drifted along and beat against the shore with the surf; it was like the sea working on the sand. John wanted to admit every question and suffer with confidence what it wrought. I have never been good, he thought; even slowness does not produce good. And often I should have had more malice.

Then Sherard, without turning his eyes away, passed him the bread to break off a bite for himself. Lound's store to prevent famine, "Franklin Harbour," the cold store the Feeding of the Five Thousand. It was all again present in John's mind. He took a piece and chewed it, in tears. Like a crocodile, he thought. To top it off, he even had to laugh. Maconochie, Montagu, and Tasmanian politics were far away.

Sherard Lound sat peacefully and guarded the horizon. A rock on the shore, not to be shaken again. He has reached my goal, thought John.

John shielded his eyes with his hands and peered attentively into the dark. When he looked around again he did not know how much time had passed. Everything was so clear now: children, boats, show booths. The faces that looked over to him seemed friendly. Wide awake he felt, alive, thankful for his life, strong in head and limbs. Strangely young.

Forster reported.

"Your Excellency. The awards ceremony! The victors are already—" John only laughed. The victors can wait.

Sherard now lived in Government House. Nobody knew whether and with how much comprehension he still perceived things. During the day he still sat at the shore on the very same spot, with strangely wakeful eyes. "He won't live more than six weeks," surmised Dr. Coverdale, who examined him on orders of the governor. "This disease is incurable. But he seems to be more content than we are."

"Perhaps he has found the present," John murmured. "At any rate, he'll die a discoverer."

Dr. Coverdale scrutinized him, astonished.

That John had fallen in love with Sophia he admitted only to himself, not to her. He walked through the park on her right side, without a sword, and watched her movements from his window when she walked alone. He drank tea with her, stirred his cup endlessly, and told her of William Westall and the coastlines in the Arctic. He did not permit himself more. If he found love again, he also put it where it belonged. The moral quality of all his acts lay in the length of time they had endured or in their intended duration. He did not believe that exceptions to this rule could bring him luck. When one evening Sophia stood alone with him in the drawing room and suddenly embraced him, he stroked her hair and hurriedly recapitulated the entire agenda of the legislative council in order to remain completely calm. The end of each paragraph read, "Your wife is called Jane." Then he kissed the top of her head. But that was all.

"I will certainly be dismissed soon, so I can forget about tactics." John Franklin no longer had to be careful about the opinions of the men in big riding boots and their newspapers. He wanted to use his remaining time to leave lasting traces behind. The entire coastline of the island was mapped anew; the sea charts were corrected. Whalers and local trading vessels were freed of harbor fees, whereupon the number of ships increased rapidly. "A few more sailors will do this land a lot of good!" John said in public. Over the furious protest of several big landowners he did everything he could to relieve the island of the character of a penal colony. He applied to London for a change of name: instead of Van Diemen's Land it should be called Tasmania in the future, for the merchants, craftsmen, and townspeople called themselves proudly Tasmanians and hated the old name—John didn't worry about the resistance to the change he encountered in both councils. He founded a Tasmanian Museum of Natural History, and with meager funds completed Parliament House and supported the theater. He bought land on the river Huon, leased it to former convicts under liberal conditions and for little money. Week after week he spoke every evening with scholars, churchmen, and settlers about problems of education. He wanted to found a school.

When Lady Franklin returned from New Zealand he ostentatiously solicited her advice in all government affairs. Although she had no right to participate in discussions of the councils, she was present at every session. Her unofficial role was accepted as a matter of course. The malicious voices and nasty rumors ebbed away. People could see that it was not weakness but a sense of sovereignty that led a governor to choose the advisers he found most suitable for him.

Dropping grain and wool prices led to a shortage of money in the colony. Times were bad. On top of it, London now sent more convicts than ever before and at the same time discontinued "assignment" altogether. New prisons therefore had to be built and more money found to support the convicts. Franklin made as much use as possible of his right to pardon minor offenders and kept his eye on his supervisory personnel with unwavering distrust. Only big landowners, remnants of the Arthur party, and prison officials were against him. "But that'll be enough to topple me," he said to Jane with equanimity.

295

"First we'll travel across the unexplored part of the island," she demanded.

"And while we're at it, we'll discuss the new school."

Sherard brought good luck, or, more probably, kept bad luck and those who might perpetrate it away. He said nothing, perhaps also understood nothing, but anyone who didn't avoid Government House altogether sensed an effect: shock, mourning, thoughtfulness, serene calm, joy in activity. John considered having Sherard take part in the council session but abandoned the idea as too crazy. Also out of respect for Sherard's love of the sea: for him a session would have been a waste of time.

Despite the physician's definite verdict, Sherard was not yet ready to die. He took evident pleasure in every ship that anchored at the mouth of the Derwent. They were not only prison ships. The old *Fairlie* brought a number of scientists, including the Polish geologist Strzelecki, as well as Keglewicz, that always dissatisfied land surveyor with his mad drive for precision and his suffering soul. A few weeks later the ships *Erebus* and *Terror* arrived, commanded by John's friend James Ross, with the mission to explore the Antarctic. John set up a navigational observation station for him at his own expense.

It seemed as though Sherard's eyes pulled in people of good will from beyond the horizon while keeping the others out of range.

"The new school must teach lasting values without being dull," Lady Franklin mused. "That's just what schools can't do."

It rained fiercely. One could barely light a fire. But Gavigan, one of the convict crew, tried his best. And the travelers were as happy as children. "Once again the governor does as he pleases," the chronicler of the *Chronicle* had written. "Instead of preparing himself for a presumably early departure, he goes on an adventure trip into the bush with his wife and a band of convicts." Now the fire at least started to smoke. "The pupils must learn how to discover things. Above all, their own way of seeing and their speed, each for himself," said John. Jane was silent, because she knew that when John's eyes were still fixed on a specific point, he hadn't finished yet. "Bad schools," John continued, "keep everyone from seeing more than the teacher—"

"On the other hand, one can't force the teachers to say more."

"They must be respectful enough," John countered, "not to push anyone to hurry. And they must be able to observe."

"Will you order that?"

"Demonstrate it! Respect comes from seeing. The teachers must be not only teachers but also discoverers. I had one of those."

"As founders we can't prescribe more than the usual school subjects," Jane declared.

"Not even those, if the Church holds a different view. The Church wants Latin."

"What do you want?"

"Anything that gives the pupil a chance. Mathematics, drawing, above all, observation of nature."

The cloudburst gained momentum; the fire went out. John shut the tentflap. Jane put her head in the hollow between his neck and shoulder. "You should write all this to Dr. Arnold in Rugby. Perhaps he knows a good headmaster for your school."

The convicts proved their mettle, above all Gavigan, a strong, heavy-set man with eyes that were red with watchfulness and presence of mind. Also circumspect and dependable was French, who looked as if two medium-sized men had been put on top of each other: he was exactly seven foot, two inches tall. At river crossings he relied on his height and therefore got himself too easily into deep water. Still, he never lost his footing. The other ten were as eager as only convicts can be who hope to preserve their dignity for a few months.

Lady Franklin sprained her ankle in a thicket and had to be carried for a while in a wooden contraption. It went on raining; the rivers became swollen. Time was short. A schooner had been waiting for them in the Gordon estuary for weeks. They were late. Finally, one river—the Franklin—could not be crossed without a boat. If the ship left them stranded they would be lost, for in the meantime even the streams they had managed to cross had turned into wild torrents. There was no way back. "Somebody must get across and let them know," said John.

"I'll carry Gavigan across the river," said French, after long deliberation. "I can touch bottom, and his weight gives me enough firmness to stand." He hoisted the heavy man on his shoulders and started wading. Although they were overturned and momentarily disappeared in the rapids, they got across alive, shouting *"Cooee!"*—native Tasmanian for "Hurrah!"—through the hollows of their hands. They covered the remaining fifteen miles to the Gordon in less than four hours, found the bend of the river where the schooner was just about to weigh anchor. They stopped it in time, asked for some food, and five hours later were again at the Franklin shouting "Cooee!"

After two days a good outrigger had been finished. The party got across the river without getting wet. The trip ended happily. John relieved the two rescuers of the remainder of their sentences. No sooner were they free men when they married. This, too, was something that distinguished convicts from free citizens: convicts were not permitted to marry.

Sherard could no longer go down to the shore to keep the dangers away. He had to accustom himself to the sickbed and did so without resistance. The year 1843 was irrevocably the year of Sherard's death. More and more he looked like a hawk, and pale like yellowed paper.

A ship landed at the pier of Hobart Town and discharged a man who was constantly surprised at everything. He asked to be shown the way to Government House, and each time he received directions he muttered: "Odd, odd!" When he got there he asked to speak to Sir John, was finally admitted, and gave his own name. "Eardley Eardley," he said, evidently seeming to expect a reaction. John only nodded politely and kept on looking at him. "Eardley Eardley," the other man murmured once again. John thanked him for these kind repetitions but asked him to refrain from continuing them. "But that's my full name," responded the new arrival. "I'm your successor as governor of Van Diemen's Land. Here is the written confirmation from Lord Stanley." He probably imagined that now Sir John would introduce him to all the officials with pomp and circumstance, but the governor only laughed uproariously and could not stop himself. Finally he shrugged his shoulders. "Mr. Montagu must have succeeded in placing all the blame at my door. How does he do it?"

Then he turned to packing.

Sherard remained in Tasmania to die.

Hepburn took the post of assistant master in the new school. Little Ella cried because she had to leave her pony behind. Sophia wept because she knew that the man she loved had been unjustly treated and hurt. "If only I were the Queen!" she exclaimed, sobbing. Lady Franklin laughed, cursed, and organized the entire move from her bird's-eye perspective.

On the day of departure, beach and harbor were crowded as otherwise only at the Grand Regatta. John counted three hundred riders on horseback and far more than a hundred carriages. Settlers and their families came from far distances to wave their farewells. An extraordinary number of women and men pressed his hand, many in tears. Former convicts, sailors, small farmers, tailor's apprentices, trappers from the bush, and, in the midst of them all, Dr. Coverdale and massive Mr. Neat of the *True Colonist,* who rushed up to him, grasped his hand, and declared, "If this land ever finds the way to dignity and good neighborliness, it will be in the footsteps that the noble, patient spirit of Your Excellency has left behind."

Neat had sweaty hands, but they took none of the comforting effect away from his words. John put the moistened hand to his heart and said, "I only wanted to give everyone a chance."

[18]

◆◆

EREBUS AND
TERROR

Unwavering, John Franklin glanced at the arrogant features of the Foreign Secretary and Secretary of State for the Colonies, Lord Stanley, and demanded an explanation. "Why, Milord, did you believe in Mr. Montagu's unproven stories and act upon them without giving me a hearing?"

Lord Stanley, fourteenth Earl of Derby, administrator of the British colonies and hence de facto one of the most powerful rulers on earth, beautifully raised his right eyebrow. He managed that convincingly: he could raise each eyebrow independently of the other. "I shall give you no explanations. At any rate, I owe those only to the Queen and the Prime Minister." He considered it beneath his dignity to revise an opinion once he had formed it.

Stanley reminded John of his father in the early days when he had caught up with him in Skegness and shut him up in a small room. Meanwhile, he had come to see himself as the father of that father, and the lord could have been his son, a stupid, pitiless son. It was one of those encounters in which both sides believed that each person could preserve his dignity only at the expense of the other.

Addressing the minister's glassy eyes, John now spoke the

words he had prepared for this occasion: "It is not my place to criticize the procedure you have elected to follow. I would only like to remark that it has no parallel to date in the annals of the Colonial Office." He rose, bowed, and asked for permission to take his leave. He thought, I know you, but you don't know me. Perhaps I can make it happen that the Queen and the Prime Minister will ask you exactly the same questions.

Following this conference, John wandered about London for hours. He felt no inclination to accept his defeat and armed himself with a number of well-aimed arguments. Now and then he stumbled over a curbstone or collided with someone just leaving a shop. For the sake of some well-chosen phrases, he collected scratches and bruises, but only in order to pass them on to Lord Stanley in some other form.

By and by he became calmer. His anger now seemed petty. It was difficult in any case to focus on oneself when there was so much to read and to see. The streets were bedecked with a clamor of alphabet letters: here they exulted in praise of low-priced coachmen for hire, there they formed a parade of signs offering pure gin or venerable tobacco; letters billowed on cotton sheets swaying on wooden poles where proponents of general suffrage were demonstrating. John found it difficult to see and to read at the same time, especially since new, complicated words were flashed everywhere. One of them was "daguerreotype." John stepped closer and saw smaller writing: "Allow yourself to be drawn by the stylus of nature." A little farther on, at the lens grinder's, another sign: "Eyeglasses, the gift for the advanced years." The advertisement seemed to be having success: thick glasses, once the symbol of a lack of perspective, now embellished many faces, even younger ones.

John watched two splendid funeral processions and noted that nowadays not only frock coats but also coffins had been shaped to show waistlines. It looked as though violincellos were being taken to their graves.

He spent an hour in a bookshop. There were two novels by Benjamin Disraeli whom Franklin had known when he was a small boy, and Alfred Tennyson, one of John's relatives in Lincolnshire, wrote passable poems that now sold as far away as in London.

He walked through the harbor, enveloped by the coal fumes of the steamboats. The view was still clear enough for one of the dockworkers to exclaim: "Look, there's Franklin! The man who ate his boots!"

John plodded on as far as Bethnal Green and smelled the moldy odors from the cellar dwellings. Patiently he listened to a thin thirteen-year-old girl who wanted to invite him into one of the flats. Two of her brothers had just been deported because they had stolen a half-cooked cow's foot from one of the shops and had eaten it. She would be happy to undress for the gentleman, very slowly, and sing a song, all for a penny. John felt touched and sick at heart, gave her a shilling, and fled in confusion.

There was hardly any glass in the windows here, and doors were unnecessary because there was nothing for thieves to find. The police seemed to have been reinforced: watchful men in uniform were lurking everywhere, sensibly unarmed.

At King's Cross Station John heard the locomotive hissing and read a newspaper standing up. Three million inhabitants now. They're using two hundred cartloads of wheat and are butchering thousands of steers daily, and that was still not enough!

The beggars, by the way, spoke too quickly—they didn't want to bother people for too long. If they spoke more slowly, thought John, it would not be a bother but the beginning of a conversation. But perhaps that's just what they wanted to avoid.

During the following weeks, John visited his friends—those who were still alive.

Dr. Richardson said, "Now we're sixty, dear Franklin. We'll have to be taken out of service like old ships of the line. Fame changes nothing in that."

John replied, "I'm fifty-eight and a half."

Dr. Brown received him among books and plant specimens in

the British Museum. While they were talking, he providently kept his thumb in a folio. When John told him what Stanley had done to him, Brown moved it by mistake and was annoyed about both, the presumptuous lord and the lost place. He said: "I'll talk to Ashley! He's a man with a heart. He'll tell Peel, and then we'll see. That'll be a laugh!"

At young Disraeli's, John ran into the painter William Westall. His eyebrows were now tangled gray shrubbery almost obstructing his vision. He spoke in chopped phrases, often only in single words, and he was visibly pleased to see Franklin again. They were almost immediately back on the question of whether the good and the beautiful had to be created or had existed since the beginning of the world. As a discoverer, John believed in the latter. The best phrases were coined by Disraeli. John did not succeed in recalling even one.

A few days later he visited Barrow, who looked healthy and was of lively speech but understood only the answers "yes" and "no." He did not like to accept "no." "Of course you'll lead the expedition, Franklin! *Erebus* and *Terror* are ready, the money is available, the Northwest Passage must finally be found! It would be a disgrace otherwise! What important business will keep you from it?" John explained. "That's Stanley!" scolded Barrow. "He does everything with his left hand and still wants to be correct. I'll talk with Wellington, who'll say a word to Peel, and Peel will take Stanley in hand."

Charles Babbage, too, was complaining but, as usual, in his own behalf. "The calculator? I wasn't allowed to finish building it! Too expensive. But there's always money for the Northwest Passage. Every child knows it's useless—" He stopped, looked John uncertainly in the eye, and continued in a softer voice: "I won't begrudge you this, of course."

"I'm not going," said John. "James Ross will go."

Peter Mark Roget had founded a Society for the Promulgation of Useful Knowledge, presided over its sessions, and conducted linguistic research on the side. He still hadn't quite lost sight of the picture rotor: "Except for the production of pictures, all problems have been solved. A man named Voigtlander on the Continent has tried it with daguerreotypes, but that's not worth anything. For every individual picture, the performers have to freeze and be exposed in each phase of their movement. And one needs at least eighteen pictures for a single second. The process is too complicated and too slow."

Roget had visited the Franklins mostly because he was curious to see how Jane looked now. He was without doubt the most beautiful and elegant old gentleman in London.

Finally John met Captain Beaufort, the hydrographer of the Admiralty. Beaufort explained his scale of wind velocities, which was now prescribed for all logbooks of the navy. It took him a long time to explain, because with every wind velocity they remembered stories. As he departed, Beaufort said, "I'll tell Baring about the Stanley matter and he'll talk about it to Peel. That would be a laugh! By the way, don't you really want to go to the Arctic anymore?"

John answered, "James Ross is going."

Yes, he had friends who did things for him. And for all that, he could hardly remember having done anything for them. That was friendship!

In January 1845, John Franklin received a letter from the Prime Minister. Would he come by for a little chat? 10, Downing Street?

Jane said wryly, "Well, in any case, I don't think he wants to invest in Tasmania."

"In my entire career," said Sir Robert Peel, "I've met no one with such active friends. I know your story in five versions—all of them more complimentary to you than to Lord Stanley." He laughed and rocked onto the balls of his feet. "But I already know a few things about you, and perhaps something that's more important. Dr. Arnold at Rugby is an acquaintance of mine." John bowed his head and thought it best to remain silent in agreement. He still didn't know what Sir Robert would ask him once he finished rocking.

"To say it at once, I don't wish to comment on the way Lord Stanley conducts his business," said Peel. "I wouldn't even be able to do that, because his ways of doing things have been so different from mine. From childhood on."

John lowered his glance to keep from staring the other in the eye for too long, but only down to the bright bow that held together Sir Robert's stiff collar, which was so tight that its corners constantly poked the Prime Minister's cheeks. The sight heightened the self-tortured, correct impression he gave, as did the long trousers, much too tight. It was a garment that might make a beautiful figure more beautiful, but it made Peel's short legs appear even shorter. John began to like him somehow. "It has been suggested to me to propose you to the Queen for an elevation"—he raised himself on the balls of his feet—"to baronet. But that would be an affront to Stanley and is out of the question for other reasons as well. I foresee a better possibility. Let's sit down."

We are not dissimilar, thought John. Order is not self-evident to him. There is chaos in his head and he has to undergo terrible strain. A bourgeois. He must struggle painfully to achieve his own rhythm. All my life I've looked for a brother—perhaps he is at least a cousin.

"I've read your brief about the founding of the school," said Peel. "Dr. Arnold gave it to me at Oxford. Slow look, fixed look, panoramic look—excellent! The idea of tolerance based on differences among individual rates or phases of speed is very illuminating. We're in agreement about the school. Learning and seeing are more important than education. I'm constantly involved with educators conscious of missions these days: with Anglicans, Methodists, Catholics, Presbyterians. One thing is common to them all: seeing plays no part in it; developing a character pleasing to God is all they care about."

John felt warmed by so many assenting words. Still, he remained watchful. Being praised as a theoretician is not all a practitioner wishes for.

"There must be more of our navigators' spirit in the school," said Peel, "and less of our preachers'." He pulled his watch out of his waistcoat pocket and placed it on his right knee to read the time. Far-sighted, then; John had already heard about it. "To make it short, my dear Franklin, I want to create a new Institute headed by a Royal Commissioner for Education. With such a post I can meet many pedagogical demands and also keep them under control. Among other things, the new position should also involve responsibility for the protection of children and observance of children's work-time regulations. The appointee in this Institute should keep an eye on unification plans and present a comprehensive annual report on all matters relating to schools and the position of youth. For that I need someone who is not precipitate, who has no personal stake, who represents no religious or other reformist interests, and who shows himself to be undaunted by screams of protest. He must be someone with a reputation for integrity, and one whose nomination cannot be perceived as a provocation by any of the religious groups. All that applies to you, my dear Franklin."

John sensed that he blushed and made an effort not to give in completely to his pleasure. Like himself, this Peel seemed to have discovered slowness out of an inner necessity and was clearly ready to acknowledge it. John felt as though he were stepping through a wall out into the open. The utopian visions of his life were present to him again: the battle against unnecessary acceleration; the gradual, gentle discovery of world and men. A speaking pillar seemed to rise from the midst of the sea; before him he saw machines and equipment designed to serve not the exploitation but the protection of individual time, territories reserved for care, tenderness, and quiet reflection. Schools also seemed possible in which learning was no longer suppressed and the suppression taught. There was hardly a more powerful empire than the British empire, hardly a more powerful man than its Prime Minister and a more respected man than Sir Robert Peel. If he were a brother . . .

"Take your time with your answer," said Peel and once more placed his watch on his knee. "And let us still keep this between ourselves. If Ashley got wind of the matter . . ."

John became watchful again. Lord Ashley, Earl of Shaftesbury? That was the man who fought for the abolition of child labor. John gathered up his courage and asked, "I'm not supposed to be too enterprising, I presume?"

"We understand each other perfectly," the Prime Minister answered. "The point is to stay in place with great dignity. Sudden changes in this area would call up many dangers—but whom am I telling this to?"

"You need someone who is responsible for everything but who doesn't do much," John mused, and rose. Should he close his eyes and accept this questionable offer? It would certainly pay well. He stepped to the window. In spite of Peel's noticeable impatience, John thought it through thoroughly. Then he turned. "You have offered me the right thing, Sir Robert, but for the wrong reasons and the wrong purpose. Indeed, we'll be quiet about this to everyone." With that he bowed and went.

For the first time in his life John did not need to brood over something for any length of time. He went directly to the Admiralty and told an astonished Barrow that he was available for a command immediately after all.

As if a password had been spoken, all doors opened at once. Within two days John took over the ships *Erebus* and *Terror*—a helpful James Ross had notified them speedily that for reasons of health he had to give up the command of the expedition. Nobody doubted that John Franklin was most suitable, and indeed was called, to find the Northwest Passage. The same was true of the vessels. *Erebus* and *Terror* were solidly built former mortar carriers, a little clumsy but firm and roomy. The rigging was that of three-mast barques. The admirals met every wish in providing equipment, even some Sir John didn't think of. When Jane asked him about his talk with Peel he answered only, "Nothing special. He has discovered slowness."

On the afternoon of May 9, in a concert hall in Queen Square, Sir John and Lady Franklin were listening to three piano sonatas by one Ludwig van Beethoven, played by a vigorous old man named Moscheles. John didn't like the very high notes; he also would have liked to dwell longer on the lower notes. But he enjoyed the repetition of easily recognizable figures. He had not expected much. His deafness was becoming troublesome. He knew as good as nothing about music and believed he could not follow the fast passages. For this reason, he thought about the supply of fresh meat for the expedition: quality and disposition, salt content, the selection of live food animals—he wanted to leave nothing to chance. Two or three winters—one couldn't get through those with luck anymore, only with thorough preparation.

At the final sonata—it was numbered Opus 111—something strange happened. His thoughts soared high above beef carcasses and supply barrels; his eyes left the old man and his grand piano without changing direction. The music was at once sad and playful, bright and clear. The second movement was like a walk along the shore with waves, footprints, and fine-ribbed sand. At the same time it was like looking out the window of a coach with the observer always free to see distant objects passing by and nearby objects shimmering with illumination. John felt he was actually meeting up with the fine skeleton of all thought, the elements, and the ephemeral nature of all structures, the duration and slippage of all ideas. He was imbued with insight and optimism. A few moments after the final note sounded he suddenly knew, There is no victory and no defeat. These are arbitrary notions that float about in concepts of time invented by man.

He went up to Moscheles and said, "The second movement was like the sea. I know my way around there."

Moscheles beamed at him. How this old man could beam! "Indeed, sir, the sea, *molto semplice e cantabile,* like a fond farewell."

When they were driving home, John said to Jane, "There's still so much. When this passage is behind me, I'll learn a little music."

In an atelier, they made one daguerreotype for every officer and petty officer in the expedition as a souvenir. One after the other they took their seats before a draped velvet curtain, looking straight and noble. It smelled like a battle because the necessary light was provided by powder burns. Sir John kept his hat on to conceal his baldness. And so all of them kept their hats on, too, for his sake—down to the youngest midshipman. "They're all excellent people in every respect. The crew is worth its weight in gold," declared Captain Crozier, second in command. "That it is," John said, and nodded. "Just a moment, please." He made a note of something to keep from forgetting it. Shortly thereafter he wrote a letter to Peter Mark Roget: "If one needs to use daguerreotypes for the picture rotor, one must decrease the intervals between individual picture takes so that the performers need not always relax and then reassume their positions. Perhaps one could have so many takes per second that they can retain their natural movement. By the way, my reservations about the picture rotor still stand. It's just a matter of using it for the right reasons and the right purpose. After I get back, I'll have some technical suggestions about that."

When on the morning of May 19 the two vessels moved away from the pier, Sophia turned and wept. John saw it from the quarter-deck. Jane seemed to want to cheer her up with a joke. John knew that Jane's cheerful lack of understanding would be a better consolation than the profound pity of others. Ella didn't allow herself to be diverted. She kept on waving and hopped about laughing, as her mother had once done. They all figured the voyage would last no longer than a year. Even Crozier had said, "If everything goes smoothly, we'll get through this summer."

Two hours later, the pier of Greenhithe had disappeared beyond the great river bend. The *Erebus* was towed down the Thames by a small paddle-steamer called *Rattler*, the *Terror* by the still smaller *Blazer*. For decades, the wisdom of all navigation had been for John that a ship had to reach its destination by itself if nothing is put in its way. He never said "Let's go there!" but always "Let the ship go there!" He still had to make his peace with being towed, especially since the high bow of the *Erebus* couldn't keep the heavy smoke away. John coughed and growled, but deep down he was as happy as he had been as a child in Skegness. He grabbed Fitzjames, commander of the *Erebus,* and shook him. "We're afloat," he said. "Our flight's successful!" Fitzjames laughed politely. "Forgive me," John said quietly. He remembered that Fitzjames was violently in love with Sophia. "One, two years are a long time," answered the lieutenant. "I think so, too," murmured John. He rather counted on three years. Amused, he thought of all the believers in progress who moved their fingers along a line on the map north of Canada through the profusion of islands and assumed that the ships would follow them, only more slowly. Sailing a thousand miles, then waiting eight months in ice, then sailing a few hundred miles, then waiting again—every concept of slowness would soon take leave of these people. After three months of waiting they would no longer believe in movement and would lose their minds.

Next postal station: Stromness, in the Orkneys, to send letters; Petropavlovsk, on the Kamchatka Peninsula, or Hong Kong to receive them. They had seven carrier pigeons on board, two thousand books, and two barrel organs that could play almost thirty different tunes but not Opus 111. Food supplies were sufficient for four winters. Messrs *Rattler* and *Blazer*—Franklin had been unable to allow them the female gender—took their farewell near the island of Rona. Soon they were recognizable only as two dirty little clouds in front of the coastline.

For a good month the heavily laden, copper-armored ships were en route across the Atlantic. During this time, John Franklin himself conducted twelve religious services, and though the crew noticed that the sermons did not come from the books designated for this purpose, they were content. The sail master said, "Our Franklin is a bishop disguised as a captain, and therefore much holier."

At the end of July they sighted a whaler named *Enterprise* in Baffin Bay. The skipper came on board and conferred with Franklin. The ice was heavier this year than it had been the year before. "I trust we'll get through all right," Franklin said in a serious tone, "and the crew has confidence in me."

The captain of the whaler was a man of logic. "And if you die, sir?"

John bent over the railing and looked down at the water. "What remains of me need not always be my personal self." That was a sentence from one of his strange sermons.

Since the wind was favorable, they soon separated again. The *Enterprise* remained in its position because a whale had been sighted. *Erebus* and *Terror* sailed northwest, into the Arctic. Even before they were out of sight, it began to snow.

Sturdy vessels abundantly equipped, vibrant sailors, respectable officers, all fearless and in high spirits under the command of a patient and steadfast old gentleman—this was the picture of the expedition that remained before the eyes of the world.

[19]

♦♦♦

THE GREAT PASSAGE

Until the beginning of the winter of 1845 Franklin kept looking for a passage northward from Lancaster Sound rather than to the southwest, as he had been ordered by the Admiralty. He still hoped for an open polar sea. However, the ships only rounded a big island, Cornwallis, without finding anything except increasingly massive ice. Franklin wintered here until the spring of 1846 in a protected bay of Beechey Island, named after his former first officer on the *Trent*. Three men died here, two of illness, one by drowning. They erected carefully chiseled tombstones for them, as if it were an English village churchyard. Then the *Erebus* and the *Terror* put out to sea once more, this time in a southwesterly direction. But this year, too, did not turn out well. The stream of ice became thicker and thicker. Laboriously the ships fought their way through towering ice floes with wretched slowness. Franklin was unperturbed.

A dangerous narrows in which several fields of drift ice were jostling one another Franklin called Peel Sound. Without question he meant it as a compliment to Sir Robert.

The crew worked well and depended on Franklin. Their tendency to crack jokes had increased slightly, but so far it was not worrisome. Franklin knew what it sounds like when a crew is no longer intact. He had many little worries but no big ones.

* * *

Jane Franklin spent the winter in Madeira with Ella and Sophia Cracroft. In the spring they visited the West Indies. Jane found Sophia's worries about the expedition slightly exaggerated and felt that a little change would do her good. Ella returned to England; Jane and Sophia went to New York.

They saw an advertisement in the *Herald:* "Madame Leander Lent transmits information concerning love, marriage, and absent friends. Prophesies all events in life. 169 Mulberry Street, first floor, rear. Ladies 25¢, Gentlemen 50¢. Promotes marriage quickly for extra charge." Jane, who would never have ventured to a fortune teller in London, decided that this milieu ought to be studied as well. They went. Madame Lent was about twenty-five years old, terribly filthy, and almost bald. In the light of a candle stuck in a beer bottle she laid out the cards for John Franklin and declared that he was in excellent condition. He was about to reach the goal of his life. He would, however, reach it not all at once but piecemeal. When she noticed that no marriage was desired she disappointedly pocketed her twenty-five cents and declared that eleven more people seeking her help were waiting outside.

No more progress with mere sail power! The drift ice had thickened into a closed surface. The men spent half their time on watch pulling the cable at the bow or chopping and sawing their way out. Despite a violent cough, Franklin was on his feet for days on end, hardly allowing himself any sleep and only now and then a game of backgammon with Fitzjames, which he won regularly.

On July 15, Franklin was on deck with his sextant taking a bearing in relation to a star when he thought he heard a scream coming from the ice fields behind the stern of the *Erebus* louder than any human cry. Surprised, he lowered the instrument and stared aft. Nothing unusual in sight. Behind the *Terror* the gigantic egg of the sun slunk along the horizon toward the east. Thousands of ice floes reared up like a city of red glass, but a movable city, gnawing its way south along with the ships and

313

never stopping. John looked at the glaring egg on the horizon and thought, Why sun, really? What does sun mean? His legs gave way. Careful, it's all nonsense, he thought. In falling he held on tight to the sextant, trying to protect it. The first thing he had learned from Matthew about sextants had been that they must never be dropped. He lost consciousness.

When he came to, he was lying in his cabin on a blanket spread out on the floor; he looked up at the faces of Fitzjames and Lieutenant Gore, who were bending over him. They were joined by the face of Goodsir, the medical assistant. But he recognized those faces only when he put his head in a certain position. The optical axis of his face, to which he had so long been accustomed, had now to lead past the object so he could grasp it. Like a chicken, he thought, dumbfounded, or rather, that's what he wanted to think, for he couldn't assemble the words. He also wanted to say something to relieve the three men of their worries. What came out of his mouth was not especially clear, it seemed, because their expressions became even more anxious. But he could laugh and get up, couldn't he? He tried it. Nothing doing with his right leg! Time and again he continued to see that red thing in the sky and the city of glass. Had that gotten mixed into every picture before? And what was this thing, this bright thing, called? Now he knew: something had happened.

Something should have happened long ago. If it hit anyone, it had best be himself.

London in the summer of 1846 churned up so many new events that news from the Arctic would have hardly made an impression. In Parliament the debate about the corn laws went back and forth, a debate that had in fact been obsolete for a long time. Since there was famine in Ireland and a catastrophe at the door, a decision against protectionism became more and more urgent. The price of bread had to be reduced even if a handful of influential landowners cried murder. Robert Peel, who had long been a defender of the corn laws, as befitted a leader of the Conservative Party, changed his position publicly, showing both independence and courage. He abolished the laws and earned the fury of his aristocratic colleagues. Although he lost his office, he gained the gratitude of the hungry.

On July 15, 1846, Lady Jane and Sophia were on their way home from New York to London in a beautiful clipper. They rounded the Irish coast in bright sunshine hoping for the first news from the *Erebus* and the *Terror* when they returned to London.

On the same day a terrible storm raged over Spilsby. Many old trees were uprooted, two people were struck by lightning on the open road, and a few cottages in the settlement of the poor were blown down. The grain lay in the fields flattened by the rain. If anyone had told the people of Spilsby what had happened that same day in the polar sea, they would have stopped to listen. But only a few minutes later they would have turned back to their own fate—rightly so.

On September 12 off the coast of King William Land the ships were utterly locked and enmeshed in ice. Several currents of pack ice moving south had conflated and pushed on top of each other as they squeezed between two coasts that acted like a funnel. Gigantic ice floes tilted and for one or two days reared up high like a lateen sail, brightly lit by the sun, until they collapsed toward the other side. Towers and cones grew high, then sank again; the massive ice was caught in a rotating motion as though being plowed. Day after day the sailors fought for the life of their ships, sawing, detonating, and dragging ice floes unceasingly. The risk increased that the hulls would be squeezed to pieces by the uncertain movements of the ice field, until the ships were lifted up through mere pressure and finally rested on top of the ice as if it were a pedestal. Now care had to be taken that this support did not give way. Drawings were made with architectural precision; statistical calculations were attempted; anchors were dropped. Franklin knew the ships were drifting south, although of course extremely slowly; they would reach the coast of the continent only in many years. But he still wanted to sluice his men and ships through this mill.

Franklin sat on deck and glanced into the sun whose name he no longer knew, and appeared in high spirits and full of hope. He could neither speak nor write, and he needed help every time he stirred. The cook fed him; sometimes Fitzjames did. But he could still read sea charts and calculations with some effort and give orders by shaking his head, nodding, and pointing. He even continued to play backgammon, won, and laughed a crooked, happy laugh. No one doubted his mental soundness. Nothing was lost so long as he was alive. It had always been the dying for whose sake everything occurred: Simmonds, 1805; Lieutenant Hood, 1821; in her way, Eleanor, 1825; Sherard Lound, 1843. Now it would be his turn: John Franklin, 1846 or 1847.

Half the supplies were still there; one or two winters could still be afforded if they kept their nerve, and that was, after all, John Franklin's strength.

As late as the spring of 1847 the ships could not break free. Scurvy demanded its first victims. Franklin watched his crew closely, and his narrowed field of vision helped more than it hindered. Their morale did not drop; it rose. And as Franklin knew from all catastrophes that came on slowly, when the first few perished, the insouciance of the survivors was greater than their understanding. But long before the majority were endangered, knowledge would come to them. Only toward the very end would it be lost again. They hadn't reached that point yet. Franklin lived. He was slower than death; that could be their salvation.

On a reconnaissance march in May 1847, a group of officers and sailors of the *Erebus* pushed through King William's Land to the estuary of the Great Fish River. From that point on, the course of the coast westward was known. George Back had drawn the map several years ago. When the group returned to the ship and reported the results, he laughed with one half of his face and wept with the other. The Northwest Passage had been found, but it was completely useless because of the ice, something everyone had suspected. Franklin signified that he wanted a celebration, and so it happened. It was a great feast, though three men died on that day alone.

Franklin pointed at the maps and with great effort lolled a few single words he had painfully relearned. His neck stretched forward, those wide-open eyes—he looked like the child trying to climb into the carriage that was about to take off. But no one giving the right answer had to look good; he was simply allowed to take his time.

It took hours before Crozier and Fitzjames understood what the old man wanted to say. In exactly six weeks the strongest and healthiest among them were to start a southward trek to try to reach fur-trading posts or Eskimos or Indians to get help. Not immediately, not in the winter, above all, not as late as next spring! Franklin knew that the reindeer would not get to the Barren Grounds before late summer, and the men needed strength to hunt them. The two officers exchanged brief glances and understood each other. Under no circumstances would they leave the sick.

On June 11, 1847, Sir John Franklin, Rear Admiral of the Royal Navy, died, in his sixty-second year, of another stroke.

The ice master detonated an opening for his grave in the pack ice. The crew assembled and drew their hats. Crozier said a prayer. A rifle salvo crackled under the clear, frosty sky; then they slowly lowered the coffin, weighted with an anchor. The vault filled up with water. Within a few hours it froze into a tomb plate of dark glass. "Happy voyage!" Fitzjames spoke into the silence.

That was no empty phrase. For with the drifting ice masses the old commandant had surely been on his way for some time.

In 1848, the Admiralty sent out three search expeditions, one of them under James Ross, who had recovered conspicuously fast. All three searched much too far north—Ross knew well that

Franklin had believed all his life in an open polar sea. They wintered in ice and returned the next year without success.

Until 1850 a large number of ships were dispatched, which searched back and forth across the Arctic Archipelago and carefully mapped every island. They discovered only that Franklin had spent the first winter on Beechey Island. Now the admirals were going to call off the search. They would have done so already in 1849 had it not been for Lady Franklin.

Supported by the acclaim of the entire public, Jane insisted on a further search for her husband with everything at her disposal: her own fortune as well as John's, slyness, power of conviction, rage and derision, genuine and even artificial tears whenever necessary. She rented a room in a hotel across from the Admiralty in order to be as close to her adversaries as possible. Her scenes were dreaded. In vain the bureaucrats tried to pretend they were not in. Jane became an expert in arctic navigation because she carefully studied all the reports and had an excellent memory. She corresponded with the President of the United States, with the Tsar, with a spendthrift New York millionaire, and with several hundred other influential and knowledgeable persons throughout the world. She went to Lerwick, in the Shetlands, to challenge the whalers to voluntary searches in the high north. Her speeches to sailors were as successful as those to ladies of the Horticultural Society. No one could resist her. The newspapers sang hymns to the heroic wife of the explorer. She bought several ships with her own money and chose the crews herself from legions of volunteers. Shortly before his death John Barrow said, "Jane is my successor."

Jane was allowed what was not permitted a woman, not even a queen, by written and unwritten law: to show energy and to prevail over men. But even the men agreed. After all, the action concerned a husband, and, in addition, one hundred and thirty men lost in the ice of the Arctic.

She found devoted friends, heroic servants! Old Dr. Richardson went to the high north once more to search for his friend. John Hepburn traveled all the way from Tasmania and went along. During this time, Sophia remained with Lady Franklin.

Often she seemed to be even more passionately involved in the search than Lady Franklin herself, but no one had any cause for surprise. She was her secretary, messenger, friend, straw man, spokeswoman, comforter. She did not marry, although she could have chosen among the volunteers as freely as John's widow in naming her ships. Until 1852 these two women prevented Franklin and his crew from being declared officially dead, and when it finally happened, they managed to stir up such a storm of public indignation that the lords of the Admiralty did not leave Whitehall without drawing the curtains in their carriages.

Of course, their fortune melted quickly, much to the chagrin of John's daughter, who had not married a wealthy man and was fearful about her inheritance. But no one could prevail against the imperious posture of a hero's wife—not even Ella, who had much of her father's persistence.

But "Jane and Sophy" became a symbol of friendship and loyalty between women. That they also exchanged tenderness fortunately escaped the notice of the zealously virtuous. Those who suspected it nonetheless were not quite so virtuous and found it simply irrelevant.

The most important task, however, remained unfulfilled: the fate of Franklin and his sailors still remained shrouded in darkness. Since, as before, a high reward was offered for clarifying his fate, voluntary search missions by whalers and rich friends continued even after 1852. Above all, there were Jane and Sophia, determined to sacrifice their last penny for this goal.

In 1857 Jane Franklin purchased her irrevocably last vessel. Named *Fox*, it was a small steamer equipped with a modern propeller. She entrusted it to a young captain who had already been on the Franklin search as a helmsman: Leopold McClintock, a man whom she loved like a son and who honored her like a mother. He was among those who were interested not only in the solution of the riddle and the financial reward but also in John Franklin himself. He had heard much about him from Dr. Richardson and Hepburn, Lady Jane and Sophia; he had read both his books, and had even been allowed to see the "Logbook of Punishments" from the *Trent,* in which John had jotted down his ideas. "I simply want to get to know him," said McClintock, "and to that end I shall find him. It may well be that he is alive, perhaps among the Eskimos. He never lived quickly, so he won't have stopped living quickly either."

That was McClintock, a short, wiry man with black sideburns. He left Aberdeen harbor on June 30, 1857, with a Scottish crew and a Danish interpreter.

On May 6, 1859, McClintock's people found a note under a rock pyramid. It was signed by Crozier and Fitzjames and told of the fate of the expedition and of Franklin's death. It was dated in the spring of 1848. The ships did not get free. The crew had given them up. The message closed with the words: "And start on tomorrow the 26th to the mouth of Backs fish river."

They continued their search in that direction. It soon became evident that it was no longer necessary.

One hundred and five men had set out from the *Erebus* and the *Terror* in the spring of 1848, evidently already in a state of deep physical and mental exhaustion. Soon the caravan of the dying had split into several groups, one of them trying to return to the ships. Many men dragged table silver with them, perhaps to exchange it for food with the Eskimos. Others had pulled heavy boats across the ice, which they had to abandon on the way, most of them with part of their food supply. McClintock found several skeletons next to the boats, along with forty pounds of still edible chocolate. In the bay at the mouth of the Great Fish River they found more skeletons, most of them dressed in faded but fully preserved uniforms.

McClintock called the bay Starvation Cove. He met a few Eskimos who recalled the ships in the ice or had heard that they had sunk in the fall of 1848. An old woman had, in fact, observed the march of the whites from afar. "They died while walking. They fell down as they stood or walked and were dead." Why hadn't the Eskimos helped the whites? "There were so many of them, and we were hungry ourselves—worse than ever before."

The captain obtained by barter a number of things the Eskimos had found: silver buttons, a set of table silver, a pocket watch, even one of Franklin's decorations. He asked for books, notebooks. Yes, they had found bundles of paper and had given them to their children to play with. Now nothing was left of them. Disappointed, McClintock left the Eskimo huts and returned to Starvation Cove.

Since they kept on finding food, they could not believe that the catastrophe was caused solely by hunger. The next obvious answer was scurvy. Examination of the skeletons showed that in many of them the teeth had fallen out. It also revealed something else: that the remnants of the crew fighting for their life had seized upon the final desperate means of survival in this place. McClintock found bones neatly separated, with smoothly cut surfaces that could have been made with a saw. The ship's doctor crouched across from him. Their eyes met. The doctor whispered: "From my point of view . . . scurvy is a deficiency disease. The flesh of a man who dies of it lacks exactly the same ingredients that the sick require for their survival. It therefore didn't even—!"

"Please go on," said McClintock.

"It did them no good," said the doctor.

When they had collected the bones in order to bury them, McClintock said: "It was a worthy and brave crew. The passage of time was too slow for them. Whoever does not know what time is cannot understand a picture, not even this one."

The only person who didn't listen was the photographer of the *Illustrated London News*. He had quickly placed his camera, Talbot System, in position to capture the skeletons' condition in a picture.

◆◆

AUTHOR'S NOTE

John Franklin existed in real life. His true story has contributed countless details to this novel that could never have occurred to me on my own. This obligates me to name at least a few titles from the literature on the historical Franklin, in many ways undoubtedly different from the fictional Franklin of my novel.

On Franklin's family and the stages of his career, more exact information can be found in:
    Roderick Owen. *The Fate of Franklin.* London, 1978.
    Henry D. Traill. *The Life of Sir John Franklin, R.N.* London, 1896 (before Owen's book, the classical Franklin biography).
The above authors give no details about what happened on the voyage to Lisbon and in the Battle of Copenhagen. More is known about the Australian voyage:
    Matthew Flinders. *A Voyage to Terra Australis, Undertaken for the Purpose of Completing the Discovery of That Vast Country and Prosecuted in the Years 1801, 1802, and 1803 in His Majesty's Ship "The Investigator."* 2 vols. and atlas. London, 1814 (official travel report).
On the great navigator Matthew Flinders, see above all:
    James D. Mack. *Matthew Flinders, 1774–1814.* Melbourne, 1966.
The expedition report on the first Arctic voyage is:

Frederick W. Beechey. *A Voyage of Discovery Towards the North Pole, Performed in His Majesty's Ships "Dorothea" and "Trent."* London, 1843.

The following reports on the two land expeditions are Franklin's own:

John Franklin, *Narrative of a Journey to the Shores of the Polar Sea in the Years 1819, 20, 21, and 22.* London, 1823; Philadelphia, 1824 (translated into German and published in Weimar, 1823).

————, *Narrative of a Second Journey to the Polar Sea in the Years 1825, 26, 27.* London, 1828; Philadelphia, 1829 (translated into German and published in Weimar, 1828).

From the hunger expedition on, the novel does not follow the exact chronology outlined in the first narrative. In the encounter with the Indian Michel Teroaoteh, the roles of Franklin and Dr. Richardson have been reversed.

Franklin was not asked to direct military operations against China. However, from 1830 to 1833 he was commander of naval forces in Greek waters, where he succeeded in preventing armed conflict.

On the Tasmanian period, the following title will give the best information:

Kathleen Fitzpatrick. *Sir John Franklin in Tasmania, 1837–43.* Melbourne, 1949.

The elaborate defense by Franklin himself, justifying his tenure as governor, may be of additional interest to readers:

John Franklin. *Narrative of Some Passages in the History of Van Diemen's Land During the Last Three Years of Sir John Franklin's Administration of Its Government.* (Reprint facsimile ed). Hobart: State Library of Tasmania, 1967.

Many ingenious theories have been advanced concerning Franklin's last voyage. The best-known books are:

Richard J. Cyriax. *Sir John Franklin's Last Arctic Expedition.* London, 1939.

Leopold McClintock. *The Voyage of the "Fox" in the Arctic Sea: A Narrative of the Discovery of the Fate of Franklin and His Companions.* London, 1859.

Vilhjalmur Stefansson. *Unsolved Mysteries of the Arctic.* London, 1921 ("The Lost Franklin Expedition").

Noel Wright. *The Quest for Franklin.* London, 1959.

The best information on Franklin's first wife can be gained from their published correspondence:

Edith Mary Gell. *John Franklin's Bride: Eleanor Anne Porden.* London, 1930.

On Jane Franklin, see:

Frances Joyce Woodward. *Portrait of Jane: A Life of Lady Franklin.* London, 1951.

Lasting traces of Franklin's accomplishment can be found above all in Hobart, Tasmania.

In Spilsby, the house where Franklin was born still stands. Statues of him can be found in Spilsby and London. In Westminster Abbey a memorial plaque for him bears an inscription with the following lines by Alfred, Lord Tennyson:

Not here! The white North has thy bones, and thou
Heroic Sailor-Soul,
Art passing on thine happier voyage now
Towards no earthly pole.

The archipelago north of the Canadian mainland is called "District of Franklin" to this day.

Printed in the USA
CPSIA information can be obtained
at www.ICGtesting.com
JSHW082355070224
56925JS00001B/1

9 781589 880245